The New Men

Jon Enfield

The New Men

Text by Jon Enfield.
Edited by Dorothy E. Zemach.
Cover design by DJ Rogers. Author photo by David Coughlan.
Published in the United States by Wayzgoose Press

ISBN-10: 1938757122
ISBN-13: 978-1-938757-12-9

Table of Contents

Part Three: Bravely and Instantly

Acknowledgments

Jay and Candace helped me to realize that the Five Dollar Day deserved proper attention, and the experts at the Benson Ford Research Center and the Cranbrook Archives helped me to provide that attention. Terri, Ben, Matt, and especially Emily read more drafts than I care to admit or they to remember. Jessica helped me discover the best version of the novel and then fought for it against the barbarian hordes, and my parents offered to murder the barbarian hordes in their sleep. Mike found the book a home, and Dorothy made that home sturdy and elegant.

—J.E.

A Note on Style, Spelling, and Diction

In writing this novel, I not only wanted to get the historical facts and cultural perspectives right but also to capture how different people in Detroit spoke and wrote in the 1910s.

To learn how they used language, I supplemented my academic training in the period by immersing myself in historical archives, period publications, and wide-ranging secondary sources. To convey how they used language, I let my characters—particularly my narrator—do what would have seemed right to them, even though some of their choices might strike contemporary American readers as odd or even wrong. Probably the most obvious examples of that are the spellings such as "employe" and "sceptical" and the omission of the period at the end of some abbreviations (e.g., "Mr Ford" and "Dr Marquis"). The novel includes words that were commonly in use at the time that are no longer used, at least in the same way. That includes words like "Negro" that were not (deliberately) offensive at the time but would be out of place in any halfway respectful conversation today.

There are subtler differences as well; for example, grammatically attuned readers will note the frequent use of "which" as a restrictive relative pronoun. (And, of course, there are also spots where the characters simply make mistakes with language, as people do in every time and place.)

In short, the editors and I promise you that if a particular character writes or says something a certain way, we went to great lengths to verify that a similar, actual person in that time and place might well have written or spelled it that way.

—Jon Enfield
Somerville, MA
May 2014

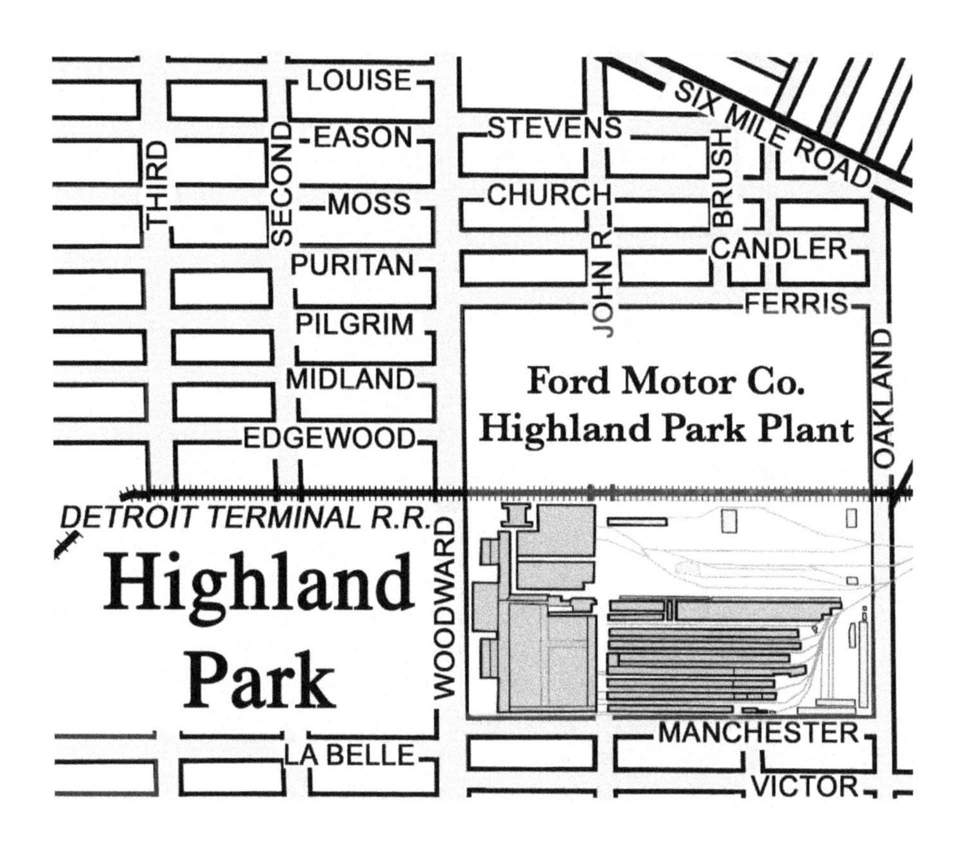

The Ford Motor Company Highland Park Plant and environs, Detroit, Michigan, 1910s

The profit-sharing plan of the Ford Motor Company is after all but a development in harmony with the march of education; a practical expression of a correct conception of the truest Christianity. It is the fruit from the efforts of the ages; a result absolutely certain to follow the broader development of the human intellect, and consequent larger human sympathetic appreciation of justice.

The plan is sweeping away the turbulent strife between labor and capital with the convincing evidence of accomplished fact, that they who share in the toil of brain and sweat of brawn shall share in the profits of this union of efforts for the universal benefit of humanity.

– *Ford Times* editorial (1915)

Let us every one "sit still and not rock the boat"! The relations between labor and capital, between employe and employer, are strung out to the extreme tension. The condition is not local but universal... Henry Ford has never failed, and he is helping to bring about the new dispensation. Great changes cannot be made in a day.

– *Ford Times* editorial (1920)

PART ONE

The Grace of Mr Ford

Chapter 1

I AM STARING AT A FALSE HORIZON. HOVERING BEFORE IT, A GREAT OCEAN liner churns a cerulean sea. The spray and the wake stand out vividly against the calmer surrounding waters, and the indistinct flags of sixty nations flutter from the ship's smokestacks as though from the proud masts of clipper ships.

I am standing beside a stage. At its front edge, stubs of rope-wrapped telegraph poles have been placed on end to suggest a pier. The ship and its flags have been painted upon a false wall at the back of the stage.

This is a graduation ceremony for the English School of the Ford Motor Company. It's being held in a cavernous hall in downtown Detroit so as not to disturb work at the company's Highland Park plant. Five hundred Ford workers, immigrants all, have come to receive their diplomas from the school, and I have come to watch. The men, waiting backstage, are in a celebratory mood, and so am I. I've just been promoted, from clerk for Employment to investigator for Sociological. Also, I know many of today's graduates. Like many white-collar Ford employes, I donate a few hours each week to the English School, where I distill America into short phrases and corresponding pantomime. "I brush my teeth," I say while miming the act. "He laughs"; "We hold the tea-cups"; "She rinses the child's hair"; "They buy the tickets."

Half the ship's hull swings to one side as a door opens, and now the graduates begin to appear. They step through the just-opened door and, as if disembarking, walk down a wide gangplank toward the front of the stage. They are all wearing cleaner, better-stitched versions of the clothes they wore in the old country. As they reach the bottom of the gangplank, they step as pairs into a huge mock cauldron. Once they have all crowded in, Mr Conway, the head of the English School, appears at the rim of the cauldron and pulls forth a great *papier mâché* ladle, with which he begins to stir the pot.

So that's how Noah and his wife kept the ark clean, I think. They rendered all the unwanted pairs for tallow. All the unicorns, the wyrms, the nameless piles of fur and fang, they made soap of them and later scrubbed the decks until a rainbow stretched across the newly benevolent sky.

(Well, I *should* think that. It would be a useful premonition.)

Eventually the melting pot begins to bubble over as the men reëmerge, now wearing their American best and waving American flags. I feel glad for them all, proud of them all, especially the ones to whom I taught tea-cups and tickets, hygiene and hilarity.

I'm not wholly wrong to feel so pleased. This graduation will help them in many ways. If nothing else, graduating from the English School will make it easier for many of the men to receive their first papers from immigration officials. For all the men, it means automatic enrollment in Ford's American Club.

(One of many American clubs. Others are swung freely by Irish patrolmen. Most are closed to Jews, Negroes, and other undesirables.)

Not one of those graduates came to America half so easily as the ceremony suggested, but now the mock cauldron will simmer in their minds, in my mind. Over time, what actually happened and what we remember happening will cook together. It is all happening in memory now, all at the same time, bits and scraps bubbling to the surface and sinking back down.

And indeed it *is* all happening in memory now. I'm not staring at that false horizon and haven't been for many years. That horizon, that painted ship, that graduation, they're all memories now—at once distant and intrusive.

What I am actually doing, at this very instant, is trying to figure out where it all began. It's tempting to say that everything began with that graduation, and in many ways it did. But to speak with scrupulous precision, that graduation came both a little too early and a little too late to be this story's starting point.

The graduation occurred late in the summer of 1915, but the relevant events started as early as November 1913, when I secured a position in Ford's Employment Department. Previously, I had been a very junior manager at Godfrey's department store, but I had left there for the same motive which two years earlier had forced me to abandon my studies at the University of Michigan: my family needed more money.

I left the university after Father died of a stroke, making it my duty to provide for Mother and for my teenaged brother and sister, Carl and Kitty. Two years later, I still had to provide for them, and Ford offered higher wages and better prospects for advancement than Godfrey's.

I arrived at Ford just in time to witness the start of a grand experiment. In those days, the company's Highland Park plant was growing at a rate astonishing by any measure—the production of cars, the number of buildings, the complexity of physical organization, all of it. This required ever more laborers, but, though tens of thousands signed on each year, tens of thousands left too, often the same men. Ford's executives were forever grousing about the turnover, and with good reason. In 1913, it was 380%. The damage to efficiency is easy to imagine. And so, with Mr Lee from the main office leading the charge, in February 1914 Ford famously raised its lowest rate of pay from $2.34 per day to an astonishing $5.

As you may remember from the 'papers, when the Ford profit-sharing plan was first announced, ten thousand men queued along Woodward Avenue for weeks to get a chance at one of the miracle jobs—at the "Five Dollar Day," as some inside and outside the plant soon informally came to call it. The company had to erect a fence to keep them in place. A few times Ford men turned fire hoses on the job-seekers to stop them from charging the offices.

(Fire hoses in February should have meant something to me.)

Until April, I didn't go home for lunch because going home would have meant going outside, and outside waited the applicants. Often burbling in languages I couldn't identify, they would clutch at me—at any man with a clean collar and a tie)—entreat me, offer me money or strange foods. Sometimes I would stand, sandwich in hand, at the front window of the administration building, looking down on the queue and pretending to myself that I wasn't remembering my childhood.

That's what happened *before* the graduation ceremony. Something started during that time, as I watched the applicants shiver and beg, strive and hope. As I ignored my childhood memories. But the story which I want to tell here begins truly and fully mere moments *after* the graduation ceremony. It begins when I saw an Italian graduate, aged about forty, a Neapolitan by the look of him. He was walking out of the hall with his family, his old-country shirt slung over his shoulder.

It began with that shirt, I think. I have just said that the melting pot and the painted ship will forever shape my memories of coming to

America. The melting pot is a good story, and a good story will wipe a real experience from memory and replace it with a new one, usually a stronger, simpler one. But even the best stories never wipe the slate completely clean. Memory isn't a slate, really. It's more a Victor record into which one can carve new and smoother grooves. But each new groove crowds the disc a bit more, comes closer to the scratchy, forgotten grooves, as in those trenches and tunnels of northern France in which opposing armies hunched within a spade thrust of one another and didn't know it. (Or told themselves that they didn't know it.) Sometimes the new and old grooves crowd so closely that they meet and collapse into one another. And then you once again hear the voices of ghosts, of exiled complexities and disowned selves.

And that's what happened to me after the graduation ceremony when I saw that Neapolitan with his old-country shirt. The shirt was slung over his shoulder just as Father's had been the morning on which, at long last, he had been released from prison.

Of course, by the time I witnessed that English School graduation, by the time I saw that Neapolitan, it had been nearly two decades since Father had left prison. And for me, the phonograph needle had long since settled into happier grooves, from which singers crooned of suffering redeemed. Even so, when I saw that shirt on the Neapolitan's shoulder, I was a small boy again. I remembered that in prison Father had been so long without a proper shirt he'd refused to wear the one which Mother brought him, that he'd draped it over his shoulder as he'd taken Mother's hand and begun to walk cautiously homeward. I remembered Mother, her voice heavy with tears and laughter, scolding and kissing Father before plucking the shirt from his shoulder and forcing him to don it. I remembered Father's funeral, four years before the English School graduation. I remembered all the funerals, and the ghosts spoke louder for a while.

Here's what some of the ghosts said:

My mother, Maria Teresa Ranieri, was the daughter of a tax collector in the flea-bitten, dust-stricken town of Ghilarza, Sardinia. My father was Gianluca Gramazio, a Neapolitan, the son of a colonel of the Carabinieri. Father came to Ghilarza as a municipal registrar in 1880 or so. Unlike nine of ten Sardinians in those days, Mother could read. And her father's Salernitan family spoke mainland Italian at home rather than Ghilarzese. That probably was enough to make Father fall in love with her (or in whatever people used for love those days in Ghilarza). He courted her, and they married a year later.

Mother was a strong woman—broad-faced, broad-shouldered. She was never beautiful, I suppose, but then and in my early memories she was vibrant, like a plow horse loosed from harness. Father was tall and thin, his bearing stiff. When I was a young boy, Mother had luxuriant dark hair which fell to her waist, and Father had a receding hairline and a struggling mustache. Somehow they complemented one another as they walked down the street.

Father and Mother's first three children—Gennaro, Ilaria, and Angela—were all healthy, likely tots. Mother says that at the time I was born, eight-year-old Gennaro was already showing signs of becoming a hearty, handsome young man and Ilaria and Angela were charming little girls aged six and five. Then I came along, with my twisted spine and knotted innards. The superstitious Ghilarzans (all the Ghilarzans) muttered that I was a bad omen. When Kitty was born three years later with a weak leg, the townspeople began to mutter about God's judgment and Jews in the well. It didn't seem to matter to anyone that a year after Kitty's birth Carl came into the world perfectly healthy or that Elisabetta did too just a year after that. Until the day we left town, Vedova Caffarelli held up her gnarled fingers in the sign of the cross whenever I passed her shack.

In 1896, when I was five years old, Father went out while Mother wept bleak and silent tears. He didn't come back that night. Or the next. Father and Mother for months had been holding quiet, bitter discussions when they thought we weren't listening, and I feared that Father had fled to the mainland, as men sometimes did. When I asked Angela where Father had gone, she said that he'd been convicted of sin and sentenced to six years' imprisonment. I rushed to our little village church and begged Father Tacchi to intercede with the Pope, whom I imagined to have personally pronounced Father's sentence. Father Tacchi explained that the local magistrate had actually convicted Father for *peculato* (embezzlement) rather than for *peccato* (sin).

By the time Father went to prison, I have since learned, he had been suspended without pay for three months, so the family's savings vanished soon after he did. Mother tried to support her seven children by working fitfully as a seamstress and by coaxing eggplant and fennel from the small, *stanco* plot on which our home stood. We kept chickens, but they seldom laid eggs, and their gamey meat was as much a reproach as a meal.

When Father went to prison, Ilaria was eleven or so, and Angela a year younger, so they were old enough to help Mother. Gennaro was almost fourteen, big and strong enough to do real work about the village, sometimes for pay but usually for food or barter. Elisabetta, Carl, Kitty, and I were too young to do much except wish that we had more to eat. During those years, Ilaria remained level-headed and even sometimes cheerful. Angela managed to hold herself together by converting her fiery rebelliousness to a fiery piety much like Mother's. (Both of them spent hours each day discovering how every new portion of misery was secretly a blessing from our beneficent Lord.) But Gennaro was constantly angry, mostly with Father. I now realize that in those days Mother must have feared that Gennaro would run away to try his luck in a larger town—Oristano, Sassari, Cagliari, or even one of the great mainland cities. That fear (along with her pride in raising educated children) was, I believe, why she tried so hard to keep Gennaro and the older children in school, if only part time.

I attended school full time because I was good there and useless everywhere else. Too young, too sickly. We were too poor for candles or lamp oil, so I had to do all my school-work during the day. Ilaria helped me whenever she could, both because she was kind and because she couldn't attend school nearly so often as she wished. I enjoyed learning, enjoyed my time with Ilaria. And, though it was hard to study with an empty stomach, studying was easier than almost everything else. With an empty stomach, one is best at dreaming, hating, and stealing. The first two I did quite well, but there wasn't much in Ghilarza to steal.

If one sleeps long enough with an empty stomach, one will sleep forever. That happened to my sister Elisabetta, who died of some sort of fever before reaching her third birthday. Mother blamed poverty. Gennaro blamed Father.

Elisabetta's death came about two years after the magistrate sent Father to prison. A few months after that, a new regime took over Ghilarza, and the new magistrate pardoned and released Father. Whether Father truly had been guilty of peculation or merely of supporting the new regime before it had enough power to protect him, I will never know. He refused to speak of it, even to Mother.

When Father returned home from prison, he was thinner than he had been, but so were we all. I was thrilled that he was free and even more thrilled when he moved us from Sardinia to the mainland, to

Naples. Ghilarza was a bone-yard to me.

Father's parents were dead, and he was estranged from his brothers, so in Naples we were alone and adrift. But I didn't care about that. Father was back, and our bellies were full. That was more than enough to compensate for living in a dirty, crowded quarter of Naples, for enduring taunts and half-hearted beatings from local boys nearly as ragged and skinny as I. It was enough to compensate for having a father who spent most of the day oblivious and silent as he stared out the window at a small patch of distant sea. At night, he sometimes screamed in his sleep.

Gennaro was less accepting. In the dark as we lay in bed, he would point out that Father wasn't working and would speculate bitterly about how we could afford food and lodging. Even Ilaria and Angela would whisper about it as they kneaded bread dough or scrubbed the kitchen floor.

After two months or so, Father announced one evening over ravioli that he had bought steerage tickets to America for the entire family. We would sail in a week. Two days later Gennaro came home wearing the uniform of a cadet of the Carabinieri. "I am Italian," he declared. "I will remain here to fight for Italy's glory and honor."

Gennaro had learned to say "honor" in a way which made Father turn purple with ire. Father bellowed. Mother cried quietly. Angela cried too, having already learned to see tears as tokens of piety.

Ilaria nudged Angela, Carl, and Kitty into the parlor. I followed them there, responding as I always did to such scenes: by climbing onto the arm of a chair in order to hang from an exposed beam. Long before, the doctors had said that such hanging might straighten my corkscrewed spine. It hadn't, but I'd kept faith, even when the Ghilarzan children—and my own siblings—had started to call me Scimmia (Monkey). Besides, hanging had given me strong arms and shoulders, no minor improvement for a runty boy already showing signs of a hunch. Mostly, however, hanging was fantastic for hunger, especially in the dark hours when there was nothing to do but dream, hate, and feel my stomach gnaw itself. Hanging from a beam in the moonlight until my shoulders burned would quiet the hunger and intensify the dreams, the hate.

That evening, I had been hanging only a few moments, staring through the window at the sun setting into the sea, when Gennaro stomped through the parlor and flung open the front door. He didn't even close it behind himself.

I ignored Ilaria's call and chased after my brother. He was striding fast, almost trotting, so he was a good distance down the street before I caught him.

"Go home, Tonio," he said without looking down.

"But Gennaro—"

"Go home."

"If you stay and we go..."

He stopped then and stared down at me. My tall, broad-shouldered brother in his uniform, the gloaming gentle on his strong face. He would be a hero, I knew, and I was overcome with pride for him—for his uniform, his terrible defiance.

"I know, Tonio," he said.

"No one will call me Tonio." My parents called me Antonio, and my brothers and sisters called me Scimmia.

"They say everyone in America gets a new name. You will become..." He thought it over. "Edison. Or Rockefeller. McKinley."

"McKinley Gramazio," I said. "It sounds wrong." I began to sniffle a little and looked away in shame.

"Any name worn with honor sounds right," Gennaro said. "Remember that." He took my hand. "This is important, Tonio. Ilaria is sensible, but you will be the eldest manchild. You will have to lead them when Father fails us again."

"Come to Am—"

"I will come to say good-bye at the ship."

But he didn't. Mother waited and wept, and I waited with her. Father had to shoo us up the gangway. In the end, Ilaria carried me, the tearful, fragile monkey child. Mother and I stood at the ship's railing, searching the crowd, pointing whenever anyone in any uniform neared the dock. But Gennaro never came.

Later, in a crumpled and much forwarded letter, he apologized. It truly hadn't been his fault. A cadet of the Carabinieri has little say in his comings and goings. But at the time, I didn't know that. At the time, I pictured him shipped to North Africa and killed. I pictured him lounging in the barracks, glad to be free of his dangling brother and peculating father. During the cramped, stifling weeks of the voyage, I pictured all manner of things. Except for the rare hours when we were permitted on deck, I clutched a metal beam which smeared my hands with dirt and rust, and I swayed like a plumb bob over an ominously shifting floor. The whole time I saw Gennaro living a thousand lives, but I never pictured the one he actually lived. Of course, it is too much to expect an eight-year-old boy to imagine how stupid our lives can be.

Colossus.

Mother of Exiles, her mild eyes commanding, her torch imprisoned lightning. The wretched refuse of our teeming shore washed homeless at her feet.

Anthony? Anthony?

A nurse in a floor-length skirt and a white cap and bib. She wears a navy blue blouse beneath. Doctor will see you now, Anthony.

I step forward with my familiar clumsiness.

Antonio?

The official, the gatekeeper, shakes his head slightly. Anthony? *he asks himself before nodding slightly.* Anthony. A minor change, a major improvement, *he says in native Italian. The phrase is worn at the edges with use.* Easier for them, so easier for you. No, it is not required, of course. Personally, I recommend it. But recommend only.

Father so tired, so Italian. Maybe the two feel like the same thing. A change of name isn't required, but some change is. He nods to the official, and I become Anthony. They say everyone in America gets a new name, but Anthony sounds wrong.

Gennaro, the hero of Italy, always to be Gennaro. Suddenly I miss him more than ever. Suddenly even Ghilarza seems sensible and beautiful.

Father's Gianluca becomes John Lucas, and Katerina becomes Katherine (and eventually Kitty). Carlo becomes Carl. In officialdom only, Ilaria becomes Hilary, and Mother's Maria Teresa becomes Maria Theresa. Angela escapes unchanged, and Elisabetta will always be Elisabetta.

Those of us still together are recommended into Grams.

Dr Blodgett has a kindly face and very large eyebrows for a young man. He talks politely to me, interested that I will be attending the University of Michigan in the fall. He too studied there, he says, before medical school.

A minor change, but it will help quite a lot. What's that? No, no more hanging like a monkey. Unless you wish to, naturally.

Grams. We are in America more than a month before we learn the meaning of our new name: an inconsequential unit of weight, 15.4 grains. Specks of sand in a city of millions piled into lonely buildings, in a colossal nation stretching west into darkness.

We settle in Manhattan, in a cramped apartment off Ludlow Street one story beneath Mother's cousin Claudia and her husband Alfonso. Our block is a tiny pocket of island Italians, Sardinians and Sicilians, surrounded by a sea of central European Jews and the general slums of Push-cart Street.

Grams—American for inconsequential. Gramo—Italian for wretched. Gramazio—Sardinian for both. These things, these connections, one wants them to mean something. When you're too poor for meat, you feed on connections.

After the spinal surgery, I spend two weeks locked in metal braces, staring at the hospital ceiling. Mother digs out the battered copy of Gildersleeve's Latin Grammar *which I won at St Xavier's in Chicago. Latin comes easily for an Italian with a parochial school education, even a muzzy-headed Italian who keeps imagining omens in the ceiling plaster, so I don't really need the review. But I need the company, as does Mother.*

The Gramses are safer by then. Ilaria and Angela are married and living in Chicago, though Angela married a lout. The rest of us are in Detroit, where we have reason for hope. Father has a respectable position with a cigar manufacturer. I will soon be moving to Ann Arbor to matriculate at the University of Michigan. Carl and Kitty are robust (save Kitty's occasional limp), and they speak and live American without accents.

Still, the fear remains for those of us old enough to remember the poverty and shame of Ghilarza, the hunger and confusion of Ludlow Street, the nerves and the stink of Chicago's meat-packing district. My helplessness in the hospital reminds us of our fragility. Father works late and never visits me, and I stare at the ceiling like a soothsayer while Mother intones conjugations from Gildersleeve's *like a liturgy, like a spell of protection:* Timeo, times, timet... Amo, amas, amat... Gramo, gramas, Gramazio...

Chapter 2

"AND SO, WITH EYES AGLOW WITH HAPPINESS, THE HONEST, HARD-WORKING Polish peasant and his doe-eyed wife stepped across the threshold of their modern and sanitary home and expressed their gratitude and thanks to Henry Ford, the Ford Motor Company, and all those who had been instrumental in bringing about this marvelous change in their lives."

Wiping away a tear, an investigator whose name I hadn't caught collected his speech and relinquished the podium. As the next speaker made his way to the front, I clapped along with the other hundred or more Sociological investigators who had gathered in the Ponchatrain Hotel ballroom to share Human Interest Stories and bask in the warm glow of brotherly love and the bright light of the chandeliers.

At my particular table, no man clapped more loudly for the Pole's marvelous change than Caleb Smythe. Smythe was a natty little man with a motion-picture sheen to his thinning hair and a rodent's twitch to his long, narrow mustache. I was just beginning in Sociological, and he was to be my new supervisor. We were both developing the suspicion that this would pose difficulties.

Smythe pointed to me with his wineglass. "Gentlemen," he told the others at the table, "we have an addition to our ranks. Welcome to the foundry of men, Mr Grams." His mustache twitched at us as his smile tried and failed to convey goodwill.

The investigators at our table raised their glasses. They seemed good, hearty men, as did nearly all the investigators. In those days, investigators were almost always men of bustle, good cheer, and missionary zeal. The hope of the Five Dollar Day was simple: pay the laborers better, and they'll stay longer. But the fear was simple too: pay the laborers better, and they'll go to pieces. After all, having more money would bring drink, women, and gambling easier to hand. Perversions might corrupt the swarthy, the Slavic, even the ruddy-cheeked Anglo-Saxon. So the extra money came not as a wage, but as a "share of the profits." A profit-sharer had to be at least twenty-two years of age, or married, or the sole support of a close relative. He had to be sober, saving, clean-living, and decently housed. And he had to let Sociological investigators confirm his being all those things.

In the twenty or so months since Sociological's inception, investigators had been visiting the men's houses. (A select set of them had been visiting the women employes' too.) The investigators had done what I would soon be doing: checking bank books, rent slips, the quality of the men's furniture, the cleanliness of their children. They had filled out Forms 928 about men who saved and spent wisely, about men who beat their wives, men who left their wives, men whose wives lavished eighty cents a day on bread or an hour a day on some other fellow who *wasn't* working long hours at the plant. They had filled out 928s about men who didn't get along with their mothers-in-law, about men who snuck across the Canadian border to buy heroin, men who sent money to the old country, men who bought cars they couldn't afford, men who sold their co-workers imaginary oil wells in Honduras, men who worked in the tubercular building and hacked blood onto the parts they machined.

By the night of that banquet, Sociological was a victim of its own success. Ford men had come to believe that savings accounts and shower-baths weren't only for the rich. More importantly, Ford had reduced its annual turnover of employes from 380% to 16%. Accordingly, having rendered themselves redundant, about half of those pioneering investigators had been shuffled out of the department in the preceding months. And we all knew that many more at that banquet would soon be treated likewise. For men with a suspicious turn of mind, my very presence as a new investigator was a puzzle, especially since investigators tended to be at least ten years older than I.

Smythe's puzzlement was verging on open hostility, checked only by his worry that I might have powerful allies. He was just beginning to test that possibility when our table was visited by the Reverend Samuel S. "Mark" Marquis, who would soon be taking charge of Sociological. The Reverend Marquis, whom I quickly came to think of simply as "The Boss," stood over us and patted me on the back. The Boss was then about fifty, with thick, dark gray hair, gray eyes, a round chin, a large, square forehead, and what in this country is called a Roman nose. "A pleasure to see you again, Mr Grams. Making everyone's acquaintance?"

"Yes, sir."

Smythe had already popped out his chair, and he eagerly extended his hand. "Dr Marquis, Caleb Smythe at your service, sir. I'm a senior investigator with the department, sir."

The Boss shook hands cheerfully.

"Dr Marquis will soon be replacing Mr Lee as head of the department," Smythe told the rest of us unnecessarily.

The others greeted The Boss with good humor, and he smiled generally at the table before rejoining Mr Lee and a few other Ford big men at the head table.

Smythe resumed interrogating me, this time about my connection to The Boss. It was nerve-wracking, but it gave me a useful map of Smythe's mind, as well as some hints about the flow of power at Ford's Highland Park plant and the possibility of a rival to our plant emerging from Ford's Fordson tractor factory on the Rouge River. Smythe seemed to suspect that I might be spying for unspecified eminences from that plant, but the truth was far more pedestrian. Though The Boss had arranged for my transfer to Sociological, he and I moved in very different circles. He was a friend to the Fords and had, until a few days before the banquet, been Dean of St Paul's Episcopal Cathedral. In contrast, my family's eminent social connections included our next-door neighbors, the Daszkowskis, proud proprietors of the corner store that bore their name. So my first meeting with The Boss, but a month or so previous, had been entirely coincidental.

The Boss was a thoroughgoing social gospeler who often gave public lectures on civic uplift, and Mother dragged me along to such lectures whenever I couldn't produce an excuse. At the reception following The Boss' talk on "The Citizen and the Future," he and I had reached for the punch ladle at the same time and fallen to chatting. I'd happened to mention that Kitty's leg had been troubling her, as it had intermittently since infancy. He'd said that his daughter had suffered a similar bout of infantile paralysis but in the end had been restored to full health by a skillful physician. We'd both gotten a little teary. Two weeks later, Mr Henkel had summoned me into his office to tell me that I was to be transferred to Sociological.

I told Smythe none of this as he questioned me. I wanted to have a chance to establish myself in the department before he felt safe in disliking me openly. Besides, it amused me to keep him fearful that I was The Boss' confidant, a Fordson spy, or even Henry Ford's love child.

Eventually, Smythe shrugged without relaxing his eyes and turned to one of the other investigators. Seizing this opportunity, the investigator beside me struck up a conversation. His name was Torassian, and he was a solid man of middle age with luxuriant black hair and a prodigious mustache apparently held in place by the individual hairs' pride in their accomplishment. He smiled readily, his crooked white teeth a contrast to his olive skin. He was a Turk or a Kurd, but I missed the exact details because he explained them through a buttered supper roll. Soon he was eating peas and having an easier time talking.

"Were you perhaps in attendance on Americanization Day this summer, Mr Grams?" he asked in his lightly accented voice.

I had been. Early on July 5th, Mother, Kitty, and I had gone to Campus Martius, the center of Detroit's coordinate system, and had taken up a position across from the fountain, at the seam of the Opera House and the Wonderland building. Six thousand neatly shaved and crisply dressed Ford employes, fully one percent of Detroit's population, had formed ranks in the park, filling it and radiating outward in preparation for their march to Belle Isle, where they would mass in the sun and intone in one great, accented voice the citizenship oath that I had helped many of them to understand. It was an impressive spectacle, and Mother and Kitty had enjoyed themselves. But, though I would have been ashamed to admit it, I'd been uneasy. I'd thought of a *festa del lavoro* a half-dozen years earlier, when the mounted police had ridden into a crowd of Italian workingmen only a few blocks from our home. Father had closed the shutters, but the clatter of hoofbeats and the cries of rage and fear had come through clearly. At the time, I'd thought mostly of Gennaro and had felt ashamed to be inside, to be so *grateful* to be inside.

"And you?" I asked Torassian. "You were there?"

"But of course, yes. It was my work—our work—on the march. A splendid group of American gentlemen. That day we made more new men than Mr Ford makes cars in a week."

He clearly wanted me to ask, so I did: "New men?"

"For us, the new man, he is one of two things," Torassian said eagerly. "First, he is the new worker, a man we instruct and investigate until his probation is complete. But also he is an idea. In the foundry, they make parts. On the line, they make autos. But in Sociological, we make men. We say, okay, ten hours each day is too long. It breaks a man down. So, nine hours. We say, okay, no man can feed a family on twenty-four cents an hour. So we give him double that, more. But we want the wage to make him stand on his own feet. So he must give the company fair return. He must do his job right, stay alert. He can't be in debt all the time, worried and distracted. He can't be tired from chasing women or beer."

"Hard to keep a man from his beer," I said. Torassian and I were the only ones at the table not into our second or third glasses of wine.

He caught my tone and smiled. "Beer alone is not a problem. Not if a man learns to be moderate. For the foreigners especially. Were you born in America, Mr Grams?"

"Italy."

He nodded vigorously. "Then you will understand, perhaps, what I wish to say. In Turkey, in Italy,"—he waved a hand vaguely—"in all the Old World is 'great tradition.' And is—it *is* a great tradition. But when fancy people in old countries say 'great tradition,' they mean really they are proud to have all these people, to *be* all these people, who do nothing."

I half expected him to quote Lazarus about ancient lands, storied pomp, and huddled masses, but he simply attended to the last of his peas.

After a while, he added, "When I came to America, I was sixteen years of age. Nobody taught me how to read when it is easy, when it is just Jane and Dick running after a dog. Common people like me, to read? Never. But in this country, I learn to read. You have read the Russians, perhaps, Mr Grams? *Anna Karenina?*"

I shook my head.

"A great book full of stupid people. The peasants are all one person, and the fine people are useless. In one city, five hundred princes, a thousand countesses. Ticks on a dog. But in America even a man in an expensive suit must work. The old men in the old countries, they see America getting rich, and they want such riches. But they are wanting to be ticks yet also to have a dog that does not scratch. And it is one or the other, Mr Grams. The businessman or the tick. The new man or the dog."

I remembered Ghilarza, where many of the peasants did not own the land on which they lived but rather paid rents to the fine people of the towns and cities. Even in that ballroom, such thoughts made my shoulders tired, my back sore.

A tall, greasily handsome Minnesota Swede named Jaspersson

leaned in, leering with agreement. His cheeks were so flushed that they each looked to have directly absorbed a glass of red wine. "That's the biznai, Merry." He stuck out an emphatic finger. "Tell Mr Grams here about the fellah with the baggy trousers."

"Katcheli?" Torassian asked with a hint of annoyance.

"The one with the pagan plus-fours," Jaspersson said.

Torassian sighed. "Katcheli. An investigation from the very first day." He paused uncertainly. Jaspersson made impatient noises, and Torassian waved a hand at him.

"Mustafa Katcheli is a Turk," Torassian said at last. "In the old country, we would have been enemies because the old men want us to be enemies. 'Hate the men of the next village and love the dirt in this one,' they say. He came here from Elaziz—Harpoot—by himself. Alone. First, he went to Canada, to Windsor, and was very unhappy there. Freezing in the winter. Now America, Detroit, and still unhappy. Freezing in the winter. He is living in a slum downtown, knowing nothing of English, knowing only other sad men from Harpoot who also miss their wives and their dirt. But then he gets a job at Ford. So I say, 'Mustafa, I'm telling you what I tell Mr Gemijian, an Armenian sent by the Turkish government to Tripoli after the killings. I tell you we Ottomans are no longer old enemies. We are new men. New friends. Americans. Is that not wonderful?'"

He seemed to be asking me also, so I nodded.

"And now he speaks English," Torassian continued. "He has his first papers and has saved almost six hundred dollars. His little wife has come over from Harpoot also, with the babe in her arms he saw only in her belly, and they live in a very nice four-room cottage in the Yemens subdivision. All through the grace of Mr Ford."

"And no more pagan pantaloons," Jaspersson said. "Proper pants and a proper God to boot."

Torassian looked expressionlessly at Jaspersson. I slowly chewed a bit of roast.

"You know this, though, Mr Grams," Torassian said. "You are Italian. Your country is fighting against Austria-Hungary for same reason the Ottomans are fighting beside it, which is no reason."

"I'm American," I said, more emphatically than I'd intended.

Torassian smiled placatingly. "As am I. You are not Italian, I am not Ottoman. And here we are, friendly over our fine supper."

As a child I hadn't considered myself Italian either. I'd been Sardinian. To the extent that I'd had any political creed, it would have been "Throw the mainlanders into the sea!" (Which, of course, I would have said in mainland Italian—and that only until the Sardinians threw my mainlander father in jail.)

To prevent Jaspersson's speaking again, I asked Torassian, "So he was a Mohammedan, then? Katcheli?"

"Yes. As was I. But now he is a proper American gentleman."

"All through the grace of Mr Ford," I said. Missionary zeal and the Primum Automobile.

"The real biznai," Jaspersson declared.

Waiters brought around the apple cobbler, then brandy and cigars. The room filled with smoke and chatter about chorus girls.

Eventually Mr Lee rose and tapped a spoon against his glass for silence. "Now, gentlemen," he began, "you will perhaps remember a little number we sang at the anniversary supper."

Soon enough we were all standing, and I held a rectigraph of the lyrics in front of me so that Jaspersson and Torassian could see it.

"The tune is 'Mister Dooley,'" Mr Lee told us. "Follow Mr Jenkins on the piano. I expect the true Sociological spirit. Show the Reverend Marquis what a splendid group of fellows he will be inheriting."

The piano began, and all the men sang:

Who is the guy
That asks you why
Your money is all spent,
And quiz-es you
And wif-ey too
About e-nor-mous rent?
Who counts the kids
And lifts the lids
To see that things are clean?
And sure he'll say
Most an-y day
Your bank book must be seen.

In-ves-ti-gator
In-ves-ti-gator
The greatest man you really ever knew.
In-ves-ti-gator
In-ves-ti-gator
He starts the rocks a-piling up for you.

Pretending to be dissatisfied with our spirit, Mr Lee obliged us to sing again, even louder. All the in-ves-ti-gators seemed very happy by the end. They had me wanting very much to meet—to make—all the new men.

4 January 1900
Turin

Dearest Tonio,

I am pleased that you all have left New York after the family's troubles there, but I am sorry to hear that Chicago is just as cold as New York.

It is good that already you are thinking of attending university. It is good to plan and not act always on impulse. Whatever you do, don't join the American Carabinieri. A common soldier doesn't earn enough to send his excellent brother a real birthday present. And whatever they say, there is little glory to be had in an army. Mostly we patrol the streets and dodge the rocks thrown at us. Often by children, some younger than you. Sometimes we put down strikes. There are always strikes in Turin. I think that is why none of the soldiers with me are Turinese. We are mostly Neapolitans with a few Sardinians. Sometimes we are supposed to attack strikers and throwers of rocks, but it is harder to beat or shoot a man you know, even if you know he deserves it. The sergeants speak of glory and combat, but those are words learnt by heart.

Do not mention these things to Mother or the others (except of course Ilaria). And do not mention them in your letters to me. I am posting this letter from town, not the camp, but the censor can read all mail that arrives here, if he wishes.

But do write and tell the others to write too. I long to hear about the family.

Your loving brother,
Gennaro

Chapter 3

Sociological was housed in the administration building. The department's main doors opened onto a wide, deep common room. Arranged in a tight grid near those doors were the clerks, stenographers, and typists, perhaps three dozen in all. Beyond them, the majority of the room was dominated by another, somewhat larger grid of investigators' desks.

I arrived early, while the department was largely empty. Taking directions from an ink-spattered clerk, I followed the narrow aisle bisecting the desks all the way to the back, where there were several private offices around the perimeter of the common room. I knocked on Mr Smythe's door and entered at his command.

He squinted his eyes and twitched his mustache before telling me that I would be spending two weeks with an investigator to learn the job. "You seemed pleased to know Mr Torassian, so I've assigned you to him. Good man, our Merry. Has a way with the turbanites."

Smythe's smile had nothing to do with admiring Torassian. He'd just put me at the bottom of the pecking order—subordinated me, egads, to an Oriental. No doubt he imagined that in so doing he'd cannily denied me potential allies in my villainous quest to destroy Smythe, Sociological, and Ford.

"He'll be delighted to show you the ropes," Smythe continued. "And if he isn't, I'll be delighted to know about it."

I returned to the main room to wait for Torassian, who moments later entered the department singing the real lyrics to "Mister Dooley." He saw me and smiled. "Mr Grams. A certifiable pleasure, sir."

After I'd shaken his extended hand, he beckoned me to follow him to a desk near the middle of the grid, from which he extracted an attaché case. "Do you know, Mr Grams," he said while adding and removing files, "I have been singing 'Mister Dooley' since the banquet. Many years ago, when my Gulsa and I were living in New York, I took her to *The Wizard of Oz*, on Broadway. 'Mister Dooley' was in the show, and Gulsa liked it very much. She was humming it when I proposed marriage to her."

"Call me Tony. Also, I should tell you that I am supposed to accompany you on your rounds for two weeks."

He grinned. "Excellent. And, Tony, you must call me Merry. Merwan, then Merwin, and so Merry. America has made me Merry." He checked his watch. "Well, it is time to go to the garage."

As he led me out of the department, he added, "Do you know, that after my Gulsa accepted my proposal, she said Dorothy was a stupid girl. 'I am in Oz,' she said. We were still walking down Broadway under those great white lights, you see. 'I am in Oz. Why should I want to go back to Kirkuk?' I think she was unjust to Kirkuk. Kansas is just a long train ride with corn. But, yes, Oz—to walk Broadway at night. Or here in this plant, in this Crystal Palace at any time..."

Once we reached the garage, he signed out our Model T and we got underway. He drove, which was just as well. When I had first gotten my position at Employment, I'd decided that a Ford employe ought to be capable of driving an automobile. I'd borrowed a friend's runabout and practiced steering it around Palmer Park, striking terror in nearby pedestrians and trees. My driving had hardly improved since.

It was an Indian summer day, so the breeze was welcome as we pulled out of the drive and turned onto Woodward, then Manchester, then south on Oakland. Men were still traveling to work, so we progressed no faster than did the Fourteenth (Through) trolley beside us.

"You replace Mr Vismara, who went to Chicago," Merry said. "So I suspect you will get the Italians. You know Little Italy?"

I nodded.

"Good, good. My usual people are the Orientals—Ottomans, Greeks, Syrians. Especially Syrians. But first, this morning, we go among the Russian Jews. I am visiting a new man on behalf of Mr Trebakoff, who is ill."

Merry continued to chat of his Gulsa (pretty and delicate as the day they met), of his two sons (fine young fellows certain to become fine American gentlemen), and of his plans for retirement. Having started at Ford at the old Piquette plant as a tool-and-die man eight years earlier, he wanted to finish his career with Ford, but he hoped to take "his old bones" somewhere warmer after doing so.

"I am thinking Miami or Los Angeles," he said. "Especially Los Angeles. They say it looks much like Kirkuk. Clean air and fruit trees. Alligator pears, oranges, lemons. Men on horseback still—cowboys. And of course there is the ocean. That is better than Kirkuk, the ocean. It would be good to be an old man beside an ocean, I think. Or a young man, but it is good to be a young man anywhere. If I were a young man—I tell my sons and I tell you now—I would sell electric cars. Mr Ford has announced he and Mr Edison will offer an electric car soon. Think of that—a car powered by lightning. And when I was a boy I admired tradesmen with mule carts. This century," he said, shaking his head in grateful wonderment.

I spent the next half-dozen miles in a haze of dreams and sunshine, imagining myself made a millionaire by selling lightning-powered automobiles. Then Merry put an end to my daydreams by halting the runabout on a muddy section of Rivard Street near the docks. The neighborhood reminded me of slums I'd known as a child, and the particular house in question was a small, squat frame cottage, the front porch of which had sagged nearly to collapse. Someone had propped it up with a pair of ash barrels which themselves needed propping up. The siding hung in great strips because the nails had rusted and snapped. Only the occasional hostile shard of glass remained in the windows, whose panes had been individually mended with scraps of rag and waxed paper.

Merry shook his head slightly before opening his door. He stepped ahead delicately, avoiding the muddier patches of the front walk. I did the same. We navigated the porch, which looked every bit as bad up close, and Merry rapped at the front door. A moment later, a sharp, birdlike face poked through the slight gap which appeared between the door and the frame.

"Tatyana Abramoff?" Merry inquired politely.

"Who asks?"

Merry introduced us as Sociological investigators come in place of Mr Trebakoff, and the woman opened the door wide enough to spit on the porch. She hadn't aimed at Merry, but she hadn't aimed away from him either. Through the crack, I could see that she was a gaunt woman.

"Sociological," she said with some difficulty and clear resentment. "Maybe, maybe not."

Merry pointed to the Ford star badges pinned to his lapel and mine. "These are star badges, Mrs Abramoff. You know they signify we are salaried employes of the Ford Motor Company. Your husband must have told you we would be coming by."

"Many peoples knocking at the door saying Ford. Henry Ford says buy silver mine, buy lottery ticket. All not real."

"But Mr Grams and I wish to sell you nothing, madam," Merry said. "We are here because it is five months your husband works at Highland Park. This interview will let him become a profit-sharer."

I could see it. The brief flicker of hope at the mention of profit-sharing, the way she opened the door a little wider. And then the suspicion—eyes tightening, door closing even more.

Merry spotted it too. "Mrs Abramoff, Ford will be *giving* your family more money. For lottery tickets, you must talk to someone else."

She stared at Merry for a moment and then glanced at me. I did my best to look honest without looking as though I wanted to look honest. I have never mastered the skill.

She said something angry in Russian and then opened the door to admit us into the dimly lit parlor. Its scant furniture had seen better days, and whatever eyes it had used for seeing them had long since been gouged out.

"There is no tea," she said. "I can make."

"Only if you planned to make it already, Mrs Abramoff," Merry said, "only if."

She paused for a moment, turning the back of her patched calico dress to us, as if pondering whether she had been planning to make tea. "Come to kitchen," she said, stepping a few paces through an open door.

The kitchen smelled of cabbage and grease. The walls' bare, cracked plaster was adorned with only few dented tin pots and pans hanging from nails and a few thumb-tacked illustrations cut from the 'paper. Both the kitchen chairs had broken backs neatly repaired with lengths of wire coat hangers, and the table scarcely looked sturdier. Still, it was a shockingly clean kitchen.

"Sit," she instructed. We complied.

I had expected a samovar, but there was only a dented kettle, which she put on the stove before bustling from the room. Merry and I had scarcely enough time to raise our eyebrows at one another before she returned and thumped a battered wooden box onto the table in front of Merry.

"Papers," she said defiantly.

Merry opened the box and pulled out bank books, insurance records, bills. As he pored over them, I watched Mrs Abramoff, who stood at the stove, her back resolutely toward us until the kettle boiled. After some complications with the tea strainer, she began to pour out three cups.

"Milk and sugar?" she asked.

Merry and I both declined. She shrugged and brought the tea. She stared into my eyes briefly as she handed me the cup. It was a fierce look, accusatory. I knew it: *You have made me see my poverty through another's eyes, but I refuse to show my shame.*

I thanked her for the tea. She nodded curtly and placed a cup at Merry's elbow. Then she moved toward the window, her back toward us as she looked out at the junk-choked back yard.

After a few minutes of scrutiny, Merry made a worried sound.

"What?" she asked without turning.

Merry took and released a slow, silent breath. "I am surprised to find you here still," he said. "In April, your husband told Mr Trebakoff you would take more suitable lodging."

Mrs Abramoff's shoulder blades drew together slightly at the same time as mine.

"Suitable?" she asked.

"Appropriate, Mrs Abramoff," he said. "Proper. Good."

She turned to face us. "I know what is suitable. Is not enough money for suitable."

"Your husband earns enough to pay for better," Merry said gently. "For this house he pays two dollars forty a week, not nearly enough for suitable housing. I cannot see as he is saving much, either. He had no savings until May 7, when he deposited twelve dollars. His balance now stands at fourteen dollars."

"Is not enough money for saving."

"But yes, there is, Mrs Abramoff. Unless there perhaps are expenses we do not know about?"

"Life is expenses."

"Mrs Abramoff—"

She turned suddenly, her face white with anger. "Aaron is good man. No vodka, no cards, no *bludnitsa.* I am good wife. I cook good. I buy careful. You come here, in my home, drink my tea, and you say 'suitable' and 'savings.' You are wrong." She turned her gaze to me briefly. "Even tax men in Russia not come to my house and say 'suitable.'"

"I am glad to hear," Merry said soothingly, "that your husband does not drink or gamble, and I will suppose *bludnissa* have something to do with women."

"*Bludnitsa.*"

"*Bludnitsa.* Good. Aaron's foreman says he is a steady worker. But a profit-sharer must live in a healthy, decent home."

She was shivering with anger now. "Home is decent."

"It's very clean inside, yes," Merry said. "Mr Grams and I are both impressed with that. Yes, Mr Grams?"

I nodded.

"But the building itself is unsound—no good," Merry said. "It's dangerous, insanitary. You could work all day, every day, even the Sabbath, and it would remain so."

The shivering subsided. "Is no money," she said simply. "Aaron, he says Mr Ford give us more money so we move in a good home. Now you say no money because no good home."

The shivering was gone, but not the anger. That was restored to its proper pitch, and it went beyond people, beyond Merry and me in her forlornly tidy kitchen.

"But you have had money, Mrs Abramoff. Enough for better, and I'm afraid I must know where it has gone. Mr Ford wishes everyone to share in the profits, but he will not give profits where they will disappear into nothing." He held his hands up to forestall protest. "Now, if you have a sick mother in Vladivostok, or a starving nephew in St Petersburg, or a drunken brother-in-law in Hamtramck who needs care in a sanatorium..."

Just a fraction, her head turned to look directly into his face. I could see the mutual understanding flicker between them. There was a long pause.

"Aaron sees house in Joseph Campau development. Five rooms," she said. "He says there, after profits."

"A very nice development that one," Merry told me. "Modern. Clean. Gas stoves."

Gas stoves—for an unguarded instant, Mrs Abramoff's face resembled that of a Madonna with child at breast.

"Very well, Mrs Abramoff," Merry said. "Your husband's profits will begin in one month. But two months from now, if we find that you haven't suitable lodging, the profits will stop."

She looked at him warily. He winked at me before carefully repeating himself. She grinned and offered to make us several pots of tea. We all smiled at one another for a while, nodding foolishly, until Merry led us out the front door and off the slowly collapsing stoop.

Hoping that a little conversation would dissipate my uneasy, nervous mood, I asked, "Was it a drunken brother-in-law?"

Merry shrugged as we picked our way across the muddy walk. "A family without a drunken brother-in-law is a family with few brothers-in-law. But perhaps some other relation."

"There are no children," he added as he bent to crank the starter, "and that is always sad to me. They will have to be very saving for their old age, I suppose."

The engine chortled to life, and Merry settled into the driver's seat. "Or die young. They could always get lucky." He laughed cheerfully, amused by his ability to imagine cynical notions.

8 December 1905
Cagliari

Dearest Tonio,

I have left the Carabinieri, and I am glad. But the penalties for desertion are terrible, so we have come to Cagliari, where nobody knows us. I am now Giovanni, my wife is now Cassandra, and we are both Granatos. (Please remind the others to use those names in their letters.)

I do not think anyone will actually try to find me. I am not important. But if I am found, then I am found. I couldn't oppress my own people any longer. And all people who sweat for their daily bread and whose daily bread is never quite enough, those are my own.

Cassandra feels the same way. And more scientifically. She puts me to shame, and once I helped her learn to read! Our little home is full of pamphlets. If we could eat pamphlets, we would be the fattest and happiest Socialists the world has ever known. Even as it is, we are happy. Cassandra tries not to be, the world being what it is, but I am not so noble.

We have many times discussed going to America as you wish. I would so much love to see the family again. Even Father. I was foolish to hate him, as if men ate honor and built houses with bricks made of glory. But Cassandra is with child, and we will not travel for a while. It is at once an optimistic and a fearful thing to become a father. All the more reason to forgive ours, probably.

All my love,

Giovanni

Chapter 4

During my two weeks' apprenticeship with Merry, we spread optimism and other American ideals to dozens upon dozens of new men, Orientals mostly. (Though none of Ford's executives was keen to admit it, more than half the men at the plant were foreign.) We went into home after home of Avakians, of Hosseins, of Mitropolouses. We went into dozens of clean little homes shining with thrift and brimming with newfound comforts. We went into dozens more Abramoff homes, sagging, moldering wrecks. Wherever we went, Merry was the soul of precision.

"Scrupulous," he said when I complimented his precision. "I have just discovered that the scruple is also a measurement. A very small one, which is good. The new man is more precise than the old one, and I should be precise about him."

While I admired Merry's precision, I admired his flexibility even more. He spoke several languages at least a little and was a mosaic artist of broken English. He assembled his interviewees' fragments and his own carefully small phrases into careful interviews which resembled nothing so much as confession administered by a respected priest. Grown men and women who might have brained us with a flatiron for meddling instead offered us nothing stronger than Turkish coffee, nothing more awkward than shamefaced justifications of poor thrift and questionable cleanliness.

Naturally, there were quite a few soreheads. Most of them were drunk, hung-over, or twitching toward the nearest saloon. A few of them were sober but loyal to their homelands, or simply cantankerous and unwilling to learn English even at cost of their jobs. Still others were politically motivated—several Socialists accused us of paternalism.

(Because he reminded me of Gennaro and Alessandra, I nearly hugged one Swabian youth as he turned pink-faced with indignation.)

And there were the schemers and the penny-ante con artists. To qualify for profit-sharing, a man had to be married, the sole support of close relatives, or older than twenty-one. A woman had to be the sole support of close relatives. Some nineteen-year-old men married simply to qualify for the profit-sharing (giddy at the first interview, sullen at the fifth-month interview), but many Get-Rich-Quick Wallingfords borrowed wedding bands and paid girls $3 per interview to masquerade as their wives. And that was the *least* brazen fraud. Never before had the laws of biology been so routinely and utterly broken. Twenty-pound infants were born mere hours after conception. Dependent grandmothers rose from the grave. Plump-cheeked malarial uncles returned suddenly from the jungles of Brazil to cough studiously into their sleeves. A parade of the peg-legged, the neurasthenic, the dropsical, and the gently fainting marched in showy affliction through the bedrooms and parlors of Mr Ford's Detroit.

Still, soreheads and schemers were surprisingly rare. In general, the men and their wives willingly, often proudly, displayed their bank books and receipts. Doubled wages doubtless put them on their best behavior, as did Merry's bluff cheer. But there was something beyond that, some seduction of self-improvement. Especially by the fifth month, they were grateful for our interest and proud to display the improvements in their manner of living. Wives showed us shiny tots, tidy radish patches, new backyard coops bursting with indignant broiler chickens. Men who labored more to sign their names than to stamp a dozen fenders would proudly show us their newly purchased copies of the great books (including quite a few whose authors held laborers in profound contempt).

I often wished that Merry had been awaiting the Gramses when we'd arrived in America. At first, we'd been nearly as hungry in New York as in Ghilarza, and not entirely for want of money. Within an hour of arriving in Manhattan from Ellis Island, Father had twice been shortchanged by men who'd spotted him as a foreigner, so for weeks afterward (to Mother's growing exasperation), he wouldn't let any of us—including Mother—spend money. And he wouldn't purchase so much as an apple without first going to every shop and stall south of Central Park to compare prices, muttering "*truffatore*" (bunkum artist) as he went.

After those weeks with Merry, I began my solo rounds. We had not yet changed the name of our department from Sociological to Educational, but it was an educational time for me as well as the men. I learned about Poles, Roumanians, Canadians, Germans, and, of course, Italians, my specialty. Of Detroit's 12,000 Italians, 1,500 worked at Ford, and nearly a third of those made their homes in my district, which included Little Italy, where my family had lived until moving to Highland Park. And so, perched on an attaché case full of blank 928s, I drove erratically along Gratiot Avenue and the side streets of Little Italy, struggling with but usually overcoming the challenges posed by unfamiliar local dialects and customs. I rode the Springwells line and bounced off the shoulders of Lombard factory workers in overalls. I wore shoe leather thin stepping past Genovese and Sicilian fruit sellers. I confirmed marriage certificates at San Francisco and Holy Family. I viewed corpses prepared for funerals at Calcaterra's, at Bagnasco's.

Even the corpses couldn't keep me from enjoying my work. And I was happy outside of work too. I whistled popular tunes and sang the chorus of the investigator song. Twice each week I took my break at lunch counters (on Fridays, Merry joined me). I always ordered a slice of pie because I liked the idea of pie, even though the actual pie did my oft-delicate digestion no favors. I began to follow the Ford strictures on saving and even to imagine what sort of gown a hypothetical lady friend might wear when I escorted her to an evening of the theater. If I'd been just a bit taller and straighter, I might have done more than imagine. I might have courted and married one of the dark-haired young girls in neat ribbons whom mothers occasionally nudged in front of me when I came to investigate. My good spirits bubbled over, fresh and clean as new men from a cauldron.

I still didn't understand how such men were cleaned.

Chapter 5

KING
by Edgar Guest

Giuseppe Tomassi ees stylisha chap,
He wear da white collar an' cuff,
He says: "For expanse I no giva da rap,
Da basta ees not good enough."
When out weeth hees Rosa he wear da silk hat,
An' carry da cane lik' da lord;
He spenda hees money lik' dees, an' lik' dat,
For Giuseppe, he work at da Ford.

BEFORE I'D FINISHED REMOVING MY SUIT COAT, KITTY MET ME AT THE front door. She was moving well, no limp to speak of, and she was all smiles and ribbons. The ribbons were genuine.

"What now?" I asked. Then I answered my own question: "Angela?"

She nodded.

A test of my good cheer: our sister Angela and her youngest, Crocifissa. All of us, of course, wanted Angela away from her drunk and belligerent husband Stefano, but her visits were difficult. Angela was an unhappy woman, and she seemed to regard misery as a blessing that ought to be shared. Only Mother truly enjoyed Angela's visits, and that was largely because Angela was the most Italian of Mother's children—the most Catholic, the most tied to the old ways. After a decade and a half in America, Angela spoke English with scarcely more mastery than my English School graduates. Much the same was true with Mother, of course, but if one is scolded as a child, baptized, confirmed, married, made a mother, made to mourn the death of a child in a language, that is one's true tongue.

"Speak of the devil. Hiya, Sis," I said as Angela stepped from the kitchen.

She looked wan and faintly forlorn in her shapeless gray woollen dress. She was still as slender as Kitty, but not nearly so light in her movements.

"Don't mention that one," Angela told me in Italian, crossing herself irritably.

"What the devil do you mean?" I asked in English.

Kitty flickered a grin at me before turning around. "He's dreadful, isn't he, dear?" she asked, also in English.

"Devilish," I said.

At the sound of voices, Carl appeared at the top of the stairs, fixing his cufflinks. As always, he looked like a better-wrought version of me—medium height, olive-skinned, an intense mop of black hair which flopped over much of his broad forehead. He wore a suit finer than any I owned. While I'd been with Employment, I'd helped Carl to secure a well-paying tool-making job at the Highland Park plant, and wearing overalls all day seemed to goad him to look like a fashion plate at night. *Carl Grams ees stylisha chap.*

"You're going out?" Angela asked in Italian.

Carl had reached the bottom of the stairs. "Sorry, Sis. Plans." He gave his familiar lopsided grin, kissed Angela and Kitty on the cheek, and slapped me on the shoulder. Then he donned his silk hat and glided out the front door. He'd gone through us every bit as gracefully as he went through defenses for his Sunday soccer team.

Angela frowned and then pretended she hadn't. Then she padded back to the kitchen.

Kitty and I sighed, knowing that Mother and Angela would be cross with us because Carl had gone out. "He has a sweetheart, I think," Kitty said. "He's always on the 'phone with her at Daszkowski's. I suppose she's not Italian, or we'd know more about her."

"He should bring her by this evening," I said. "Angela could lecture him on the dangers of courting undesirables."

We both managed to laugh.

Her long, just-graying hair pulled into a bun large and sturdy enough to serve as a trench helmet, Mother covered the dining room table in an Everest of spaghetti, fennel sausage, and pecorino.

In the dining room, we were supervised from all sides. A photograph of Father, stiff and stern before he went to prison, hung over the doorway to the kitchen. Father was staring directly across the room toward an oil painting depicting Elisabetta seated in a gooey green meadow and surrounded by a urinous wash of yellow intended to represent heavenly light. On the wall facing me were the Popes. A faded Pius X in a vast Fabergé egg of a hat looked disapprovingly at the modern world, and beside him hung Benedict XV, a gnome in crisp white robes. Directly behind me, Christ dangled from the cross. Carl and I always sat with our backs to Our Savior because the blood dripping vividly from His wounds inspired the sensation that someone had splattered Our Lord with marinara.

Angela was seated directly beneath Father's photo, her gaze wandering back and forth between crucifix and Crocifissa, who was napping on a blanket folded in the corner. I looked at Angela beneath Father and noticed for the first time that if only she'd been taller and more misfortunately mustachioed, she could have passed for him.

Meanwhile, Mother was interrogating Kitty about some young man she'd met at Mass. In the main, Mother spoke Italian, Kitty English. "And this Andrea—"

"Andrew, Mother."

"This Andrea, he has a good job?"

"I've told you he works at the bank."

"Does he earn enough to support a family?"

"Honestly. We scarcely got past the weather and his people. The Lagorios, before you ask, from right there on Grove, near the park."

"What kind of a man invites himself to a woman's home for such reasons? Living near a park? Antonio makes a living good enough to marry on, and he doesn't invite himself to strange girls' homes. Although possibly if he did—"

That's when I stopped paying attention. After eating, we moved into the parlor, where we were again supervised, this time from above the fireplace by a portrait of Gennaro in his Carabinieri uniform. I suppose in some metaphorical way, one is always under the eyes of the distant and dead, but I have never enjoyed the more literal fashion.

Kitty asked Angela careful questions about Chicago until Mother insisted that Kitty read to us from *La Tribuna*. This was a typical after-dinner entertainment. As soon as Italy had declared war on Austria-Hungary in May, Mother had started buying any newspaper with a story about the war. She read in order to fret. She fretted over our unthreatened relations in Salerno and Sardinia—who certainly hadn't fretted over us during Father's imprisonment—and she especially fretted over her grand-daughter Elisabetta (and vaguely about Alessandra). I didn't worry about the war's harming Alessandra and Elisabetta, who were still in Turin, far from Austria's reach. If my niece and sister-in-law were in any danger, it was from the Italian government, which might easily have considered Alessandra's fiery brand of Socialism treasonous.

That risk further strengthened my indifference to Italy's fate. That nation's endless squabbles and squalid backwardness had condemned Father to prison, my spine to crookedness, my infant sister to starvation, and all the rest. Not long after Father's death, Alessandra had sent me the findings of a parliamentary inquiry which showed that in Abruzzo and the Basilicata (where the country's most deranged religious fanaticism still prevails), nearly one-third of families engaged in incest. This was the glory and honor of Italy which Gennaro had rejected, the glory and honor for which millions of Italian soldiers were killing and dying. I didn't imagine that the Austrians and Germans were any better, but they were unlikely to be worse. At the very least, the parts of Italy which the Austrians occupied until 1848 were far less prone to cousin-humping. As Kitty read to us that night, I yet again half hoped that the European war would take *more* lives, that it would bore into Europe's diseased brain like a great auger and either kill the continent's masters or open a hole through which its medieval demons could escape.

I looked across the room at Angela, who had Crocifissa in her lap. The child had woken and was pulling her feet to her face, one after the other. Possibly she wanted to suck her toes, but her tiny shoes prevented it. Whatever her reasons, she seemed resolute and undismayed.

Only a few months after my transfer to Sociological and not long after Angela had swaddled Crocifissa back to Chicago, my aching back pushed me out of bed early, and I stepped into the dark, chill morning before even Mother had risen. We lived close by the office (near Pilgrim and Third), so despite walking the long way I found the office nearly empty. It had an eerie feel somehow, and I stood there for a moment gaping.

"Ah, young Mr Grams."

I turned to see The Boss emerging from a file room, a sheaf of papers in hand. At that point, he had but recently taken over from Mr Lee, so I had little sense of him as a supervisor. Still, I was encouraged by his strongly stated belief that our department's treatment of laborers should be fraternal rather than paternalistic. Along those lines, a week or so earlier he had changed our name from Sociological to Educational and our title from Investigator to Advisor.

He smiled slightly at me as he riffled through the papers. "You're in early this morning, Tony. A man after Benjamin Franklin's heart," he said, still riffling. "A terrible immoralist in many ways, Franklin. Still, he had the wit to pick his sins and the resolve to pursue them with method. Doing so is very nearly as good as behaving properly, and every bit as demanding. Ah!" he said triumphantly, extracting a memorandum from the sheaf.

He traced his finger over the text. "Tomorrow and tomorrow."

"Someone made a memo of *Macbeth*?" I asked.

"What? Ah, very good. No, I was simply verifying certain dates." He shifted, indecisive about something. "Settling in well, are you, Tony? Quite comfortable going about your rounds?"

"Yes, Dr Marquis."

This seemed to help him decide. "I fear, Tony, that soon I shall be manacled to my desk like a galley slave to his oar. Before then, I should like to see some of my men on their rounds. Would my presence today make your rounds difficult in any way?"

Naturally, I said he was welcome to join me, and fortunately I was in fine form that day. In the interviews, I reasoned, cajoled, praised, and remonstrated as appropriate, all according to Educational's "fine democratic spirit of helping the other fellow." The Boss seemed impressed. I was still nervous about my driving, of course, but I managed not to run anybody down.

My last interviewee of the day was Mrs Martelli, the materfamilias of a Sicilian family living on Napoleon near Riopelle. Mrs Martelli was a scrawny woman who looked incapable of having birthed six strapping sons and daughters, most of whom were galumphing about the small home until she shooed them away. I knew some of them by sight from having lived in Little Italy.

The interview had scarcely begun before there was a knocking at the door. The Boss and I read documents while Mrs Martelli rose to answer it. Over her diffident protests, a stranger entered her parlor. He paused upon seeing The Boss and me seated at the dining table but quickly smiled and removed his hat in greeting.

"Signora," he said, "gentlemen."

His face suggested southern Italy, and his accent suggested south Chicago. He wore a twenty-dollar suit with twenty cents left in it, and his hair looked like he'd combed it with dirt. He was probably younger than I by a few years.

"I'm sorry," Mrs Martelli said to The Boss and me.

"No, no, I'm the sorry one," the interloper said, tilting his hat and rubbing the stained underside of its brim across his forehead. "I'm barging in, making a mess of things. I'm just too tired out to think straight is all, and I'm a blamed fool anyway."

"What is your business here, young man?" The Boss asked.

The stranger let out a brief, bitter laugh. "I intend no disrespect by laughing, sir. Only I find any connection between myself and business a bit ironical, is all."

"I'm afraid I still don't understand, young man," The Boss said.

"Aw, hell—heck, I mean, Father," he said. "I only halfways understand it myself. See, it's like this: I used to live a pretty rough-and-tumble kind of life, me and my buddy Roberto Esposito. My name's Gino, by the by. Gino Rossi. We're both Chicago boys, me and Roberto. Grew up there between the nigs and the micks, and didn't we use to fight 'em plenty, ever since we was ankle-biters. Give us a dust-up and we was hogs in wallow. Well, the day comes when we was about seventeen, when fellahs start to move from fists to knives and it's not kids' scrapes no more. Hey," he said, with pleased surprise, "that's going from scrapes to cuts. I'd surely like to tell Mr B that one."

"Mr B?" asked The Boss.

"Mr Fred Banville. He's the gentleman I want to speak on, only I'm making a mess of things as usual."

Gino had been standing awkwardly to the side of a chair at the far end of the dining table from The Boss and me. Now he pulled out the chair and settled into it, looking footsore and exhausted. Mrs Martelli continued to hover uncertainly at the threshold.

"Mr B, anyway, me and Roberto met him at a lunch counter. We was embarrassing ourselves—talking real loud, making love to the counter girl, that sort of thing. Mr B's been watching the whole thing, and after a while, he says, 'And how's this working out for you?'

"I said the sorta thing that usually leads to a fight, but Mr B he just looked at me and asked, 'And how's *that* working out for you?' He knew I wanted a fight, see? Well, I called him all kinds of names even though there was ladies present. Roberto did too. But Mr B, he just waited, sorta shaking his head and smiling.

"And when we got tired of cussing at him, he said, 'I know why you're angry, boys. You're unhappy. Ten or fifteen years ago I was just like you.' Now, we didn't believe that. He wasn't even Italian or nothing. But he said some things that showed he understood pretty good after all, and before we could get our guards up, he offered us jobs at his printer's shop sweeping up the place and such. Me and Roberto, we both left school when we was eleven, so we didn't read too good, but Mr B helped us learn our letters. Pretty soon every day we was working and thinking, and we gave up real quick on the pool halls and the brawling. Our own mothers were glad to see us for a change. We even learned to read and write pretty good. We ain't no Shakespeares, mind you, but we can set type reliable."

Mrs Martelli was smiling faintly in approval. The Boss was too, though he tried to keep his face stern. "Your Mr B," he said, "sounds like a fine gentleman, but I don't understand why you've come here in this—"

Gino shook his head. "Sorry, Father. I know I ain't telling this right. I ain't really a telling kinda guy. The point is after a few years Mr B got sick. The kind of sick you don't get better from."

His voice caught, and he stared at the wall for a while before continuing.

"Mr B, he said he didn't mind going to meet his Maker, but he sorta felt like he had more on earth to do 'fore he did. So he come up with the idea to write a book where he put down his ideas so's lots of boys could learn about a better way of doing things, just like me and Roberto. And that's just what he did. He sold the press but made sure me and Roberto and some others like us got to stay on there. And then he spent his last two months on earth burning the candle at both ends to finish his book. And it's a cracker.

"Now, he took a heap from the Good Book, and he says that right up front. But Mr B, he laid out all the hard stuff so even a thickhead like me could understand. And then he had it printed up at the same shop he used to own, three thousand clothbound copies on quality stock and everything, only then he died before he paid the second half of the printer's bill. Then there was some hold-up with his estate that I ain't never gonna understand, and now the new printer—

"The new printer," I interrupted, "isn't going to release any of those books, and so the only way you can get them out of hock with him is to raise money by selling subscriptions."

Gino turned wary eyes upon me.

"Only," I continued, "you and your pal, the two of you are pretty nearly the worst salesmen in the world, so you're starting to lie awake at night, feeling like every gust of wind brings the lamenting voice of the late Mr B, and wouldn't it be a fine thing if some mother of six, say, could find it in her heart to pay a mere two dollars fifty for one book. Or six dollars for three. And what fine and improving gifts they would make for any young men—or even young women—headed down the garden path, and if we'll just write our names and addresses here you'll be sure to personally hand-deliver each and every copy and in no wise do you intend to just pocket the cash and be on your way back to Chicago to put the pomade back in your hair and buy drinks for chorus girls."

Gino shrugged and smiled wryly before showing himself out the door. I admired him for not blustering, and I admired myself for achieving the calm irony which had always eluded Father in dealing with *truffatore,* especially with the young man in Chicago who had run the same con on him and Mother. The young man had painfully resembled Gennaro, and Mother and Father had spent five dollars on the nonexistent books and three months blaming one another for losing something so important.

8 August 1906
Cagliari

Dearest Tonio,

Gennaro always ~~speaks spoke~~ speaks of you with such fondness and respect, so I address this to you.

You probably think of me as Cassandra Granato, but I say proudly my name is Alessandra Gramazio. I am your brother's wife and mother of your niece Elisabetta, who was born just weeks ago and who is a comfort and a joy to me.

Tonio, I have terrible news. Gennaro is dead, killed by the Carabinieri a few days ago. I am so heartbroken for you and your family, especially your mother. And I am so heartbroken for myself and our daughter. Gennaro was so noble and brave.

For so long we feared that the Carabinieri might find Gennaro and put him in prison, but we never thought that they would kill him. The worst is they didn't even *know* they killed him. He was in a group of Socialist protesters, and a group of Turinese Carabinieri fired without knowing or caring who they hit. Gennaro deserted because he loved the Turinese and didn't want to point a gun and order them about. And now the sons of those people have killed him because the King or the Prime Minister or the Pope or whoever it was who really puts soldiers in the streets is afraid of people looking at the world around them and saying, "In this life we can do so much better."

Maybe you or your family will blame me for his death, but I did not ask him to protest. I was not there at all, and he was there only because he was returning with the day's bread, which he always bought when there was no ship to unload. He was still holding tight to the bread when I found him in the street.

Most call deserters cowards, but it takes courage to remove a uniform when everybody marching and some fat sergeant with a mustache is bellowing "Fire!" More courage than it takes to fire. He wanted to be their brother. And they would have wanted to be his brothers if they had known him. He *was* your brother, and he loved you very much, Tonio. And I loved him very much, so I will write you again and always because such love is sacred, more than what they call sacred, more sacred than anything but justice, and there is no justice without love.

In love and sorrow,
Your sister,
Alessandra Gramazio

Chapter 6

There is such a thing as a man being too proud to fight. There is such a thing as a nation being so right that it does not need to convince others by force that it is right...

– President Woodrow Wilson (1915)

It is only through misapprehension that we fight each other... Take away the capitalists and you will sweep war from the earth... I would spend half my fortune to shorten the war by one day.

– Henry Ford (1915)

For years, Mr Ford had been watching with bafflement as the European war killed millions and disrupted commerce. Eventually, he decided that Europeans urgently needed a robust dose of old-fashioned American horse sense. (I wouldn't be surprised to find that Mr Ford thought the war could have been averted if only Franz Ferdinand and Gavrilo Princip had gone to the Ford English School long enough to learn how to talk to one another in a rational tongue.) And so he suggested the Peace Ship and its Committee on Continuous Mediation. President Wilson declined to endorse the plan, but Mr Ford figured that politicians were half the problem anyway. So he chartered an ocean liner and set to work filling it with peacemakers. Immediately after the time of my triumph over Gino and his imaginary Mr B, The Boss informed me that he would be joining Mr Ford aboard the Peace Ship.

The Boss was deeply (though discreetly) sceptical of the Peace Ship. We now know that he was right, that the mission was a fool's unarmed charge into the teeth of steel gears big as countries, heavy as history. But it didn't seem that way at the time to those among America's starched and sequined classes, who believed fiercely in the power of hygiene and educational lectures. For them, the European war confirmed that the Old World was steeped in barbarism and that peaceful, civilized America must save her cousins from their lamentable foreignness. They believed that war, all war, was a dried-up mummy that must crumble into dust when given a firm, no-nonsense American handshake. And so the decades of Europe's cutthroat competition for African and Oriental colonies, the centuries of its rulers' indifference to the fate of the vast majority of the people of their nations or of any nation, the erotically charged apocalyptic fantasies, and the sheer blind stupidity did not deter the peacemakers, many of whom knew nothing of those realities.

At the time, I wondered whether those Progressives had forgotten America's past or simply shoved it on a letter spike and imagined that they'd killed it. Did they not remember the Alamo, the Bull Runs, the *Maine*? For that matter, had they forgotten how the *Maine* had led directly to fifteen years of guerrilla war in the Philippines—which, for reasons unclear, America *still* occupied?

But I didn't wonder too much or too long. After all, I wasn't to be aboard the Peace Ship. Though dubious about the Peace Ship's chances of success, The Boss nonetheless had Progressive faith in the bully power of clean hands and firm handshakes, and he had resolved to do more to protect Ford families against predation by Gino and his ilk. Having impressed The Boss, I found myself involved with Educational's efforts to protect Ford laborers against flim-flam artists. This put me at odds with forces perhaps as obstinate as those confronting the Peace Ship. And, naturally, it put me at odds with Caleb Smythe.

"I agree with the principle, Dr Marquis, of course," Smythe was saying, "protecting the men and the like. But surely we already do a great deal to protect the men against sharpers?"

A day or two before The Boss was to leave for the Peace Ship, there were four of us gathered in his office to discuss the matter: The Boss, Smythe, Fred O'Hara, and I. Like Smythe, O'Hara was a senior advisor. He was a few inches taller and perhaps ten years older than I and looked like a sharp-eyed, ruddy-cheeked cherub in a rumpled vest. I knew him well enough to exchange greetings, but this was the longest I'd spent in his presence. In the abstract, I trusted him no more than I did Smythe, but he exuded none of the personal antipathy toward me that Smythe did.

"We do a lot, Caleb, sure," O'Hara said breezily. "But we don't tie it all together like we oughta. If the Dean wants Grams here to give it a whirl, I'm not opposed. In fact, I'd be willing to look in on him, help him along. If you need help, of course, Tony."

I nodded with proper deference.

Noticing The Boss nodding in agreement with O'Hara, Smythe moved smoothly to his next objection. "Not to cast aspersions on Tony's work, which, in the main, has been satisfactory for a man so new to the department—"

"Highly satisfactory," The Boss said, almost as if he weren't correcting Smythe.

"Of course, of course. Still, Fred does raise a point. This sort of work, if we're to do it, would demand a great deal of experience with laborers *and* advisors, so a senior man might be preferable. Especially with all those Eye-ties already keeping Tony busy."

The Boss nodded thoughtfully and, with consummate politeness, overruled Smythe and made clear that he expected me to get to work on a fraud-prevention scheme while he was with the Peace Ship and that he expected Smythe and O'Hara to support my efforts.

Smythe flashed me an adder's grin as we filed from The Boss' office. Hours later, just as I was headed home for the evening, he summoned me into his small office and, on the pretext of some bit of business elsewhere, left me waiting at its threshold for a full fifteen minutes, long enough, I suppose, for me to remember that he had an office, while I did not.

"So the good Dr Marquis has conceived a project, Tony. Maybe with your assistance?"

He looked at me with feigned good humor, and I tried to look the affable rube. Neither of us fooled the other. Smythe snorted faintly and added, "I owe Dr Marquis my support, Tony. As his subordinate. But remember that you are *my* subordinate, and I expect your support. You have duties still, and you oughtn't forget them."

"I won't forget, Mr Smythe."

"No," he agreed. "You won't."

This was clearly a threat—though of what, I was uncertain. Probably he was too, at least so long as I had The Boss' backing. I walked home in the dark winter night, wondering what Smythe would do to undermine or circumvent that backing.

For fear that I would direct Smythe's antipathy toward Merry, I hesitated to involve him in the task which The Boss had given me. But Merry would have none of my circumspection.

"We are friends, yes?" he asked me at the lunch counter to which we went on Friday afternoons.

"Yes." I supposed we were, even after only a few months. I certainly could see no reason we wouldn't be, and it was in my nature to search carefully for a reason.

"Then it is settled," Merry said.

"That's noble, Merry, but Smythe—"

"It is the opposite very of noble," he said with a chortle. "We are friends, and so Mr Smythe will take his little vengeance upon me for helping you even if I do not actually. So I might as well do something to deserve it. As with my father and his whippings."

I accepted Merry's assistance on the condition that he not provide it when Smythe was within earshot, and he began to help me then and there by suggesting that I consult Sergeant Aidan Regan, a police officer who had coöperated with him on various Educational matters.

With Merry's introduction, I arranged to meet the Sergeant the next day. Police Headquarters were so close to my portion of Little Italy that I simply finished my last home visit of the day and walked over. Once inside the building, I walked another several blocks in search of Regan, first to find his modest, paper-flooded office and then to find him. At last, I ran him to ground in an office much larger and more tastefully furnished than his own.

The door was open, so I stood and watched the sergeant shaking hands with three fashionable young ladies. Regan was a tall, heavy-featured Irishman of about fifty whose ginger hair was giving way to gray and whose broad shoulders and chest had begun to answer the call of gravity. One of the ladies was a neat, sharp-featured brunette with the uneasy appeal of a straight razor. The lady beside her was statuesque beauty with curly raven hair, pale skin, and piercing gray eyes. She wore a quietly fashionable navy dress sheer enough to whisper fascinating suggestions. The cheeks of her otherwise pale face were slightly flushed, perhaps from the cheery laughter she was sharing with the third lady, who looked very much like a slightly trimmed and muted variation of her and might easily have been her sister.

Aware that I must have seemed gauche or outright rude, I found myself staring at the woman in the navy dress. This was unusual with me. Poor boys on the rise are expected to long after high-class women, but after my time with Godfrey's and Educational, the mere sight of a standard American luxury mammal automatically irritated me into tabulating the cost of every furbelow, flounce, and second-hand notion about The Opera. Still, there was something about this one which made me forget that. It sounds vapid, I know. Probably it was. But I couldn't shake the feeling of difference and destiny, and I managed to break my gaze only once Sergeant Regan at last noticed me.

"And how may I help you, my lad?" he asked in hearty tones lightly tinged with brogue.

I hesitated for an instant, painfully aware that the object of my interest had turned her gaze upon me. "My name is Tony Grams, Sergeant. From the Ford Educational Department. We have—"

"Mr Grams! I apologize. If I hadn't been captivated by the charms of these lovely lasses, I'd be waiting for you in my office already. A hundred thousand pardons."

I wanted to say something debonair about the charms of the lovely lasses, but I've never had much flair for the blarney. "No need to apologize, Sergeant. I'm in no rush."

"Don't let us detain you, Sergeant," said the "sister" of the woman in the navy dress. "You've already been so generous with your time."

"It isn't being generous if you receive more than you give, m'dear," he said with a roguish grin.

The sharp-featured brunette moved slightly to stand directly in front of him. "And you will let us know about the girl, won't you, Aidan? She *can* be salvaged."

"You've my oath on it, Mrs Richardson," he assured her solemnly.

I stepped aside to make way for soft fabric and expensive *eau de parfum* as the ladies smiled politely by. Involuntarily, I turned to watch them depart.

Regan dispersed my cloud of ill-formed fantasies by calling me in and shaking my hand firmly. "Being gone to the country, the Captain lent me his office to meet the fine ladies from the Girls' Protective."

I nodded and settled into the indicated chair. "Girls' Protective?"

"The Girls' Protective League. Feminine uplifters. Trying to get to girls before they go bad. A bit like you fellahs, but prettier to look at." He smiled and sat in the high-backed chair behind the heavy desk. "Merry gave me the low-down, so we might as well get direct to business."

And we did just that. Sergeant Regan turned out to be an intelligent and utterly practical man with an encyclopedic knowledge of confidence games and those in Detroit likely to play them. He handed me a crudely typed but thoroughly helpful list of his own creation which indicated the names and schemes of fraudsters who knew their way around the County Jail and the Recorder's Court. He further promised to grant me access to any files—"even the ones only in this thick skull of mine."

When we had concluded the main business, I thanked him profusely.

"No need for thanks. I'm a real admirer of this profits plan of yours," he said. "The fewer barrelhouse bums and wife-beating cowards we have to drag in here of a Saturday night, the better. And Commissioner Gillespie feels the same, so you might want to meet with him in person. Good man to have on your side."

I got the impression that Merry had told the Sergeant about Smythe. "The Boss—Dr Marquis—suggested the same," I said. "I wanted to be prepared first."

"Wise man," he said, standing up and ushering me toward the door.

As we opened the door into the outer office, two yards of rumpled seersucker, red hair, and ostrich neck rose from a chair and doffed its hat with mock courtliness. I recognized Ross Robertson, a reporter for the *Detroit Free Press* who had written a few stories about Educational when The Boss had first taken over. I'd always enjoyed Ross' cheerful cynicism and forthright reprobacy, and he seemed to enjoy my earnest commitment to the forging of new men.

"Hey, Tony," he said, scarcely flicking his eyes toward me as he closed the distance to Sergeant Regan. "Evenin', Sarge."

The Sergeant sighed slightly and gave a half-smile. "I got nothing for the *Free Press.*" He kept moving, so Ross and I followed him into the hallway. Ross moved with his customary long but uneven stride, a souvenir of a childhood fight with a milkman's horse.

"Aw, c'mon Sarge, it's me here."

"I got even less for you, Ross," the Sarge said, smiling a bit more.

"Breaking my heart, Sarge. He goes to trial in three days, and I keep hearing how he didn't do it."

"That's 'cause you're listening to him, Ross. This ain't the meller-dramas. Not too many guilty men actually well up with tears of remorse and apologize to the saints, the Virgin, and their poor old mothers. Sometimes they even claim to be innocent."

Ross tapped his pencil to his cheek and feigned astonishment. "That's some philosophical thinking, Sarge, that is. Phil-o-sophical. Too lofty for a humble newspaperman like myself, but—"

"I got nothing for you, Ross. On the level, I don't. He's guilty, far as I know, and anyways the Captain don't want us talking about it to the 'papers. It ain't much of a job, but I aim to keep it." He turned back to me and shook my hand. "Pleasure to meet you, Tony."

With that, he stepped nimbly around Ross and trotted down a staircase.

Ross turned speculative eyes on me. "Don't suppose I can juice any ink out of you on Samuel Billings, can I?"

Billings was on trial for allegedly killing his brother and his brother's wife. "Only what I read in the *Free Press.*"

He waved his hand in disgust. "We're printing nothing but 'Authorities say.' And they don't say shit." He paused. "Don't suppose you'd consider going on the record confirming that the Reverend Marquis thinks the whole Peace Ship—from which I'd be reporting if there were any justice in this sinful vale of tears—is a waste of coal, time, and money?"

Those were, in fact, The Boss' private sentiments, and I was impressed that Ross knew them. But I was hardly going to embarrass The Boss—or lose my position—by criticizing Henry Ford in the press. "Dr Marquis believes that the peacemakers will be blessed."

He guffawed. "Me and some other ink-stained wretches are going to a red-ink joint to complain about being stuck in this one-automobile town while a bunch of bug-eyed spongers are taking a cruise on Ford's dime and Europe is setting itself on fire. And maybe meet a bit of skirt. You want to come along? Only don't get too optimistic on the skirt front."

The invitation was unexpected, but I accepted because my social calendar consisted of hands of gin rummy with Mother and Kitty. "I won't tell you anything juicy about the Peace Ship. Or Educational," I warned him.

"Only because you don't know anything juicy."

I'd imagined "red-ink joints" to refer somehow to the ink-stained wretches of the press, but they were restaurants. I soon discovered that the term came from the color and taste of the table wine.

Ross showed me to a booth crowded by a half-dozen reporters whom I didn't know. Almost all of them were from the *Detroit Free Press,* though there was a woman from the Associated Press who wore jodhpurs and a man's riding coat. After they discovered that I was useless to them in a professional capacity, their conversation became a series of giddy slanders against Ed Ivy, a former *Free Press* reporter who had in recent months become Mr Ford's "peace secretary" and mouthpiece.

"Ed only got the goddamned job because he looked at an Italian clock from thirty feet and could say who made it. Henry Ford thought that was swell," Ross grumbled. "What's an Eye-tie clock got to do with a cushy job and a fat salary?"

"At least he throws us dogs some red meat," said the lady from the Associated Press. "'Millions Murdered by Military Parasites.' Good one, that."

"'Out of the Trenches by Christmas,'" added a young reporter.

Meanwhile, a reporter with a thick English accent—Wilkes—was pounding and propounding, slapping the table as he insisted that there were no German atrocities in Belgium, that it was all propaganda. Ross stage-whispered to me that Wilkes had been a correspondent for a London 'paper until they'd sacked him for uncoöperative dispatches.

"A German magazine," Wilkes said, "ran a little cartoon with a group of Frenchmen standing around the Venus de Milo trying to figure out a way to blame the Germans for hacking off her arms. That's about right."

The others weren't having it. "Hell, you said it yourself," the woman said, "it's a Boche rag. What else would it say?"

"What else would any of us say?" Wilkes said. "It's—what do you Yanks call it—'bunkum'? Bunkum on all sides. Manure sweetened with fairy tales. Corpses in ditches covered in lime and bunkum."

"What about those Belgian babies?" the young reporter asked. "The ones with their arms hacked off? You're saying the Boche didn't do that?"

"Aw, calm down, Bernie," Ross told him. "Those babies are safe now. Even the Boche don't attack unarmed civilians."

That sent everybody into gales of laughter.

Everybody but me, that is. Because just at that moment, two elegant women entered the restaurant, the same women I'd seen scarcely an hour earlier with Sergeant Regan. The handsome Veronese waiter ushered them to a neighboring table, and the raven-haired beauty asked him a few questions in passable Italian. (Naturally, I'd made sure to address him only in my most refined English.) Meanwhile, her friend stared long and hard at the AP reporter, leaning slightly forward as if to ask a question until my bride-to-be recaptured her attention by tapping the back of her hand.

This was a reminder for me to turn my eyes back to my own table, and in general I did. But for the next half-hour I spoke little and found my gaze drifting constantly back to the woman in the navy dress. She and her friend were drinking a much better vintage than ours but hadn't ordered food, so they soon would finish and walk out of the restaurant. I was already feeling like a fool for not contriving to strike up a conversation.

Ross leaned over to me and whispered, "Bet you can't fight at that weight."

That tipped the balance.

"Pardon me," I said to the ladies.

They turned to look at me. Though her friend's expression hinted at cynical amusement, the beauty's expression was polite enough. I managed to proceed without stammering. "I'm sorry to intrude, but I believe we passed one another this afternoon at Police Headquarters. You were speaking with Sergeant Regan."

They both nodded.

Ross leaned in. "I don't care what they say about this man. Those cops shouldn't have dragged him in. He's innocent through and through. Those orphans probably just stumbled into his meat-grinder. Powerful clumsy creatures, orphans."

"Anthony Grams," I said to the ladies. "I was consulting with the Sergeant for professional reasons. I'm in the employ of Ford's Educational Department."

"Dot Richardson," the sharp-featured brunette said, shaking my hand with a surprisingly firm grip.

"Cynthia Mueller," said the object of my obsession. She pressed her fingers lightly into my hand by way of a shake. "Thia to my friends."

"I suppose it's nice to have friends who can keep sin from attaching to one's name," I said, surprising myself more than a little.

Thia and Ross laughed, and even Dot chuckled. "You may," Thia said, "be a little bit clever, Mr Grams. But you're terribly ill-mannered not to introduce your friend."

"Oh, I'm not his friend," Ross said. "It's only that I'm deeply undiscriminating in the company I keep. But it's a forgivable eccentricity for a man of my lofty station. Ross Robertson, *Detroit Free Press.*"

Dot's eyes narrowed slightly. "I recognize the name. You're not always hopeless with the facts, I suppose."

Ross turned to his companions. "Hear that, gang? I'm not always hopeless with the facts."

"Just with femmes and spelling," the AP reporter said. Everyone chortled before returning to the conversation.

"You should report more about the Girls' Protective League," Dot told Ross. "It's important material." She smiled wryly. "And you can always play up the white slavery bits to keep your editor happy."

Ross tilted his long neck and stared appraisingly at her. "Well, Mrs Richardson, I'll report on anything that looks like a story if you squint at it right. What would I be squinting at?"

Dot sighed and looked at Thia. "I'm afraid you'll have to talk to Thia about that. It takes a little time to explain properly, and I board a train for New York tomorrow morning, to join the Peace Ship. Thia, dear, you know which topics I mean."

As Thia nodded, Dot extracted from her purse a card for Ross. "This has the 'phone number for the GPL. You can reach Thia there. Or me, if you don't plan to do any work until the New Year."

"I'll have you know my work ethic is so robust that it finds stories all on its own," Ross said, taking the card. "Which is hunka because that lets me snooze at my desk."

"You and the police both," Dot said.

We chatted a short while longer, and I believe I avoided staring like a lunatic. Then the ladies finished their wine and departed, and I allowed myself to stare like a lunatic as Thia moved toward the door like a sonata in surah.

"Most slick, Mr Grams," Ross said. "But I still bet you can't fight at that weight."

Chapter 7

After impressively detailed dreams and nightmares involving Thia Mueller, I dragged myself out of bed early and met with Merry in the hallway outside the department. He urged me to accompany him on an excursion that evening after work, though he played coy about the excursion's purpose and destination.

Even that evening, as we bounced behind his Model T's headlights through a light snow and heavy cold, he kept mum about our excursion until he parked before a home in a recently completed development on Joseph Campau. Our fellow advisor Leo Trebakoff was standing in the front yard with Tatyana Abramoff and two other men. Leo was talking to one of the men, a fellow in laborer's clothes, and he waved to us quickly before finishing his conversation. As we approached Leo and the others, the laborer nodded, took some money, and walked over to a pair of sturdy horses hitched to an unladen dray.

"I thought you would wish to be present," Merry told me with a grin.

I nodded my thanks as Leo called to us in his lightly accented, cultured tones. "Merry, Tony, glad you could join us. Aaron Abramoff, allow me to present Merry Torassian and Tony Grams, both advisors in my department. Merry, Tony, this is Aaron Abramoff, one of my men. His wife, Tatyana, you know already, yes?"

We shook hands and exchanged smiles as Leo explained that the Abramoffs—"a little later than we'd like, but sooner than they could have imagined in Russia"—had just taken possession of the snug new home attached to the yard in which we stood. Without going to a Rockefeller mansion, one couldn't have devised a more marked contrast between this tidy house and the dirty jumble of shards and sags in which I'd last seen Tatyana Abramoff. Well-fitted, darkly stained shingles and pristine white trim covered the outside, and—we learned as the Abramoffs led us inside with schoolgirl giddiness—the rooms had polished wood floors covered with neatly patterned rugs. The lights were electric, the shower-bath was modern, and the stove was gas-burning. The furniture was mostly oak, and the bedstead was enameled. The bed wore a blanket whiter than any of the snow falling outside.

"Is ours," Tatyana Abramoff said with a smile that could have powered the lights. "Mortgage, not rent."

"Mortgage," her husband said with several nods of his ruddy, bald head.

There was now a samovar, and it had been readied. We had only to sit in the sturdy oak chairs at the large oak dining table to enjoy the tea that Mrs Abramoff proudly poured into new porcelain cups. Before drinking, I caught Abramoff's eye. "We hold the tea-cups," I said.

He chuckled at this reminder of the English School.

After a cup of the surprisingly bitter tea, Leo said, "And now we reach, I think, the main event. To the backyard!"

In the backyard, it became obvious that what had come to this new house upon the removal man's dray was the rickety furniture from the Abramoff's old lodgings. It had been nudged into kindling and piled on a patch of dirt, the reason for which became clear as Leo struck a match and applied it to a torch. He passed the torch to Abramoff and gestured at the pile of broken furniture. Smiling and encouraged in Russian by his wife, Abramoff stepped forward a few paces and touched the torch to a former chair at the bottom of the pile. In scant moments, the whole pile was ablaze, and not too much later, it was a sullen mess of ash and ember sizzling faintly under the snow, which had become fatter and faster-falling flakes.

Their eyes moist from smoke and gratitude, their tumbling words moving back and forth between Russian and English, the Abramoffs thanked us, Henry Ford, and the entire Ford Motor Company for everything we had done.

"Is better than lottery," Tatyana Abramoff said, staring at the embers with an expression of utter release.

Merry and Leo were beaming, and I must have been as well.

That Saturday after work, Merry and I met for supper at Eloy's, a workingman's restaurant near his home (a snug Victorian off Michigan not far from the river). Just as we were scraping our bread across the last patches of gravy, Ross appeared as promised. He'd taken a lively interest in me that I would have attributed to my scintillating personality if I'd had one. Still, I'd gone from years of hard-working loneliness to having two plausible friends, so I was happy to inspect that particular horse's dental hygiene less rigorously than I did my men's.

I introduced Merry and Ross to one another and was relieved that they fell easily into friendly chatter. Merry was even enjoying himself enough to indulge in a small glass of beer. But once he'd finished that, he took his leave.

"Nice bird," Ross said. "Did I offend him by suggesting a night on the town?"

I shook my head. "But he enjoys going home to his wife and 'the little gentlemen.'"

"Funny, he didn't *seem* off his nut. So, Mr Grams—wine, women, and song?"

"Sounds a bit highfalutin for us."

"Beer, broads, and warbling?"

"That's the proper Sociological spirit," I told him.

The evening actually began as a high-toned undertaking. We went first to the bar in the Imperial Hotel, where we were soon joined by most of the same reporters whose acquaintance I'd made in the red-ink joint.

"Occasionally," Ross explained, "it's nicer to drink away your wages where people call you 'sir.'"

"I could do without that, actually," said the AP lady reporter.

"You could always wear a dress, Doreen," Wilkes reminded her.

"I'll wear a dress when you learn to pronounce the American language, you limey cocksucker."

Having given up serious drinking when I'd stopped visiting cathouses after Father's death, I knew better than to try to hold my own with that crowd. Ignoring their mocking hoots, I stuck with simple tonic water and therefore found myself drifting further and further from the center of the evening. Eventually, I began looking around at the calmly expensive furnishings and the people calmly at home among them, longing with helpless fervor to be one of that fortunate set. I thought guiltily of Alessandra, who continued to send me lovely letters and Socialist tracts (usually illogical), which I dutifully skimmed in order to keep in her good graces. After all, she was the only person I knew who had loved Gennaro as an adult, the only person who could tell me about the daughter who carried his blood and bore the name of our dead sister.

Truth to tell, however, Alessandra almost certainly would have forgiven me had I utterly ignored her propaganda. After Gennaro's death, she had returned to Turin and eventually taken a job in the Fiat factory there. So, as a Socialist and as a laborer, she was fascinated by the Five Dollar Day and what it suggested about the difference in conditions between Detroit and Turin. For example, Turin's factories were full of women, even more so once the war had begun, but most of the women on Ford's payroll were wives of Ford men who had died or fallen ill. As I watched Detroit's shimmering quality drain their glasses, I tried to imagine what would happen if America were drawn into sending its men to the trenches. The Highland Park plant might well fill with women. Certainly other Detroit factories (including Regal Cigars, where my father had worked during most of our time in Detroit) already had women and girls on their pay rolls because they had nimble fingers and commanded lower wages. I was resolved that Kitty would never have to endure such labor, and had Alessandra been willing to join us in Detroit I would have done everything possible to spare her —

A crash from behind us jolted me out of my reverie. A fat man in evening dress lay splayed on the floor beside his overturned chair. Another fat man stood over him. The other men in their company moved to separate them as nearby ladies raised conventionally horrified hands to their mouths. Impeccably dressed men with barrel chests materialized from the wainscoting and ushered the belligerents outside. Scenting a story or at least a free show, the reporters at our table hastily followed the men outside.

By the time I caught up to the reporters, the fat men had squared off on the sidewalk, and a small crowd of spectators was gathering 'round. Once it became clear that the men were more likely to injure one another with a paunch than a punch, Ross began to amuse the crowd with a breathless blow-by-blow that pretended to be chronicling that year's championship bout between Jack Johnson and Jess Willard.

Our laughter eventually penetrated the fighters' awareness. The shorter and more aggressive fighter, whom Ross had dubbed "Johnson," turned on Ross. His hair dripped with sweat, and his face burned red. "Johnson's a nigger," he said angrily.

Turning toward Ross meant turning away from "Willard," who punched him in a kidney. Johnson staggered forward slightly, and the onlookers came between the two, muttering censoriously.

Johnson struggled with those restraining at him and yelled at Ross, "You'd better not be calling me a nigger!"

"Is it so shameful to be a Negro?" demanded a large man holding one of Willard's arms. "Aren't all men brothers?"

Johnson twisted inside the arms restraining him to glare at the speaker. "I've no niggers in my family, sir."

"Exactly so," said the man holding Willard's other arm. "I don't mind if a man's a nigger-lover, but he ought to keep his foolishness to himself."

The egalitarian released his hold on Willard's arm. "I hardly think the proposition that all men are created equal is 'foolishness.'"

His debating partner released Willard's other arm. "And *I* hardly think the Declaration of Independence applies to orang-outangs and mongrels."

"You ought to have stopped after 'think,' really."

"Oh, you *think* so, do you?"

All eyes were now upon them. Both were broad-chested exemplars of Mr Grant's great and doomed Nordic race, and they looked likely to further reduce that race by one. The crowd pulled away slightly. Willard promptly took the chance to punch Johnson in the throat and then crash a fist into his temple. Johnson's knees thudded on the pavement, and a scrum of onlookers surged forward again, this time permanently separating Willard from his victim.

After the fracas had subsided, Ross' colleagues went back inside, but Ross and I remained outside. He grinned at me. "Did you catch what that was about, or were you too busy wool-gathering?"

"Wool-gathering."

"They're both pacifists, is the beauty of it. Arguing over whether it's unpatriotic to oppose Wilson's preparedness declaration." He laughed for a while, then raised a furry red eyebrow at me. "And now I think we should go to the burlesque."

En route to the show, tugged and electrified as any trolley, Ross and I wandered Woodward Avenue toward a theater he knew. Even with a slivered moon, Woodward was incandescent with electric light and the headlamps of Model Ts, a faerie kingdom made from electrons and aspiration. It put me in mind of Merry's account of proposing to Gulsa, how it made perfect sense that Broadway would have struck them as Oz.

The sidewalks were crowded with people and their overlapping intensities. Memories of Thia Mueller blended with the faces of the women we passed, conjuring up a dull ache of love respectable and otherwise—flashes of curls and gloves, of calves and cleavage, of taut garters and torn garters, of teeth glinting through reddened lips. Sometimes a beautiful or a forgiving face would hone the ache to a stabbing. I hardly heard Ross' ceaseless monologue as we walked.

At the burlesque, brass blew raunchy notes along sleek and sinuous lines of legs. Afterward, Ross wanted to find some whores. But his empty wallet and my strained resolutions nixed that plan. We parted company there with a great deal of hairy-chested back-slapping, but rather than board my tram, I wandered alone until the crowds turned to strands of stragglers staggering along the noisy borderline between hilarity and battery.

Hilarity and battery alike seeped away as I slept fitfully and then drowsed through the next morning's lengthy Mass, during which Carl and I had to poke one another to avoid snoring, shocking behavior which made Mother frosty toward us the rest of the day. But by Monday morning I was safely distanced from such villainy and once again ready to pass my stern moral judgment on Ford men.

However, in those days stern judgment was seldom required. The men were still eager to please, so my initial home visits generally went smoothly, and my six-month follow-up usually ended with my granting the men a share of the profits. That morning's visits were typically cheerful, and the one directly before lunch break went especially well. That visit, a six-month one, began when neatly dressed Salvatore and Anna Messi greeting me at the door of their spotlessly clean apartment in Little Italy. They were both Romans, arrived separately in the country a few years earlier and married for scarcely a year. He was a handsome man of twenty-two who looked even younger, and she was three years his junior and appeared to be constructed from luminous skin and flinching modesty. Since my initial visit, they had moved from less attractive quarters a few blocks away, so I praised Mrs Messi's housekeeping and pointed out that their new lodgings compared favorably to those my family had taken when we'd first arrived in Little Italy. Sal beamed, and Anna blushed so powerfully that I almost felt guilty for offering the compliment.

The Messis had cleared every hurdle of hygiene, morals, *et al* without difficulty, save that of thrift. But it would have been churlish of me to object to their spending, since the money had gone into precisely those expenses which Educational advocated—higher rent and respectable furnishings. "I took a risk, Mr Grams, that you say I'm ready for profits," Sal said. "I hope that's okay. That is okay, yes?"

On another day, I would have made him squirm a moment or two before saying it was okay and telling him he was approved for profits. A man must be sober about risk, after all. But they were both so endearing that I nodded.

Besides, Sal's gamble had inspired me to take a risk of my own. Specifically, it made me think of Thia Mueller and even generated a workable plan. Over luncheon, I 'phoned Ross and explained it. He agreed without hesitation to play his part.

I can hardly describe my notion as a strategy worthy of Alexander, but it was direct and promising. Even Merry approved it, and Merry didn't much hold with stratagems when it came to matters of the heart. Ross would ring my inamorata at the Girls' Protective League and persuade her to meet him in the Imperial's barroom to conduct the interview. And I would lurk there out of sight, waiting for my opportunity to step forward and say, "Goodness me. Ross, Miss Mueller, please accept my apologies for interrupting. I could have sworn that Ross and I were to meet at this hour." Whereupon Ross would say, "On the contrary, Tony, it is I who am at fault, for indeed I did mistakenly appoint this time for our meeting, and thus I must apologize to you and Miss Mueller." Then, dazzled by my punctuality, the lady in question would melt into my arms.

Minus the melting, the plan went more or less as devised. Thia appeared at the appointed hour, disturbingly beautiful in a cream-colored, densely sequined evening gown with more harmony in its movements than most symphonies. Of course, in the real world, a respectable lady would take the sensible precaution of bringing a friend when meeting a stranger in a bar, and so Ross ended up interviewing not only Thia but also the woman from the police station who might have been her sister.

"My friend and colleague, Emmeline Ward," Thia said by way of introduction after I had made my dashingly punctual appearance.

"Delighted, Miss Ward," I said, hoping Miss Ward would suddenly remember a prior engagement.

"Likewise, Mr Grams. Please call me Leen."

Thia was eyeing me amusedly, and I suspected that my crafty plan hadn't fooled her in the slightest. I flushed faintly but told myself that, so long as she didn't fling her gin and tonic in my face for being brazen, her wisdom wasn't fatal to my cause.

"If I recall correctly, Tony," Thia said as I took a seat beside Ross and across the table from the ladies, "you work for Ford's Sociological Department. Making you, I believe, a lieutenant of the Reverend Marquis?" She gave the question an ironic tinge by saying "leftenant."

I nodded.

"I read in Ross' 'paper this morning that, from the Peace Ship, the Reverend has called upon men of all faiths to seek a way toward peace. I must say it's pleasant to hear a man of the cloth calling on people to look beyond their own countries. Of course, if my rabbi were to call for international harmony, people would brandish *The Protocols of the Elders of Zion.*"

She looked at me with an innocent face, but she was waiting for my reaction.

"Regrettably, I left my copy at home," I said. "I'll have to borrow Miss Ward's."

"You're quite confident for a short man, Tony," she said.

Ross guffawed, and I managed not to flinch.

"Thia," Miss Ward said reprovingly.

"Don't be a scold, Leen. It's an observation, not an insult. I don't care about a man's height. I concern myself only with the size of his cock. Another gin and tonic with lemon, please. Beefeater," she instructed the just-materialized waiter. "Will you take anything, Tony?"

I spluttered for a moment before being able to say "tonic." It was some little consolation that Ross was just as disconcerted as I. Miss Ward simply rolled her eyes and sipped her champagne.

Once the waiter had disappeared, Thia said, "I do apologize once again, Tony. That was a shocking thing to say."

"You got that right, sister," Ross said. "I think I swallowed a molar."

"No, no, that's quite—quite all right," I managed.

Thia lifted her silver cigarette case from the table and then a matching lighter, which she applied expertly to the cigarette. No wonder all the editors were up in arms about the perils of the New Woman.

"No," she said earnestly, "it's quite rude to say something like that to a man without knowing whether he has a large penis. Have you a large penis? Either of you?"

The air in my lungs turned into a painful mix of laughter and splutter. Something worse happened to Ross.

"Oh, *Thia*," Miss Ward said. "Honestly."

"But I'm being perfectly honest, Leen. You know that's a great virtue of mine."

Miss Ward sighed again.

Eventually, the waiter brought our drinks. As Thia squeezed the lemon slice into hers, I wondered how many she'd already had.

I looked carefully at my tonic water. "Do you promise not to shock me while I drink this?" I asked her.

"Shock you?" she asked, the picture of innocence.

I risked a sip.

She smiled more genuinely. "I do apologize if I've offended you, gentlemen. Truly. Leen says I ought to introduce my true self to people in small, careful doses, and I daresay she's right, even if she does make me sound like arsenic."

"But scarcely three-quarters so dangerous," Miss Ward said with a faint grin that her friend returned. After a moment, Miss Ward looked up and said, "Ah, the boys are here."

Two gentlemen in faultlessly tailored dinner jackets appeared smoothly at our table, and tolerated introductions before whisking the ladies away. Emmeline left on the arm of St John, a reedy man whose scarf looked to cost more than my monthly mortgage payment, and Thia left on the arm of Bertie, every inch the Anglo Saxon football hero. Shoulder to shoulder, the latter two strode away in a way suggestive of both the virtues of vigorous physical culture and the vices it made possible.

Gape-mouthed and foolish, I watched until they turned from sight.

More intensely than I had since being a monkey child with a sinful father, I felt twisted and tiny. I wanted to kill the man for being what he was, to kill the woman to prevent her from ever comparing me to him, to kill myself for being myself, for my spiteful urge to obliterate from the planet everything healthier and straighter than I was. I wanted to embrace them in congratulation. To embrace him as savages wrap themselves in the bloody pelts of animals whose strength they wish magically to absorb. To embrace her until she could feel my heart beating as hard and purposeful as any within a sturdier chest.

"What do you reckon about the size of *his* cock?" Ross asked.

I glared sidewise at him. "I'd punch your skinny Scot face if I could reach it."

"You're just surly because you've been in this overdressed room too much. Spend too much time among the swells and you get seasick."

The next day at work, I silently agreed again and again with Ross' remark about seasickness. My colleagues were honorable men (excepting Smythe the toad and Jaspersson the sex fiend). My men were the salt of the earth. The rich were the rich and nothing to do with me, unless Alessandra was right and they were my enemy. Whatever they were, they certainly didn't merit bubbling in my skull like greasy chunks of rage and desire in a noxious stew. Certainly not.

As Merry and I ate sandwiches together in a nook overlooking the intricate mechanical ballet of auto assembly taking place in Craneway C, I explained this to him at least three separate times. He had the good grace to nod and mutter as if hearing the wisdom of Solomon.

Then, late that afternoon, Alice Andrews, one of the older girls from the steno pool, handed me an envelope bearing the crest of the Girls' Protective League. "That wasn't me that broke the seal," she whispered. "It was Mr Smythe. He told me not to tell you it was him that peeked, but he's a crape-hanger and a snoop."

"Thanks, dear," I told her, too afire with hope to summon even ceremonial indignation at Smythe's meddling.

It was a note on GPL stationery. From Thia! In a calm, forceful hand, she told me that her intended escort to a League charitable function to be held the following night would be unable to attend and that she hoped I might take his place.

The affair would be black-tie only, and I didn't own a proper dinner jacket. Smythe's jealous eye be damned, I scuttled out of work a full half-hour early to find one. A new soup-and-fish was out of the question, of course, but with mere moments to spare before the close of business, I managed to find a respectable second-hand jacket in a Hamtramck store. It was slightly too large, of course, and wouldn't fit properly even with the urgent alterations I negotiated with the proprietor. But it was of good material and something like a fashionable cut. It would have to do.

Because the dinner jacket had been an extravagant purchase, I walked home to save on tram fare. It was less than a month until Christmas and must have been a biting cold evening, but I was too embarrassed, elated, and gut-churningly fearful to feel it.

When I went after home after work the next evening to don my newly altered finery, Mother and Kitty interrogated me like a pair of pushy Pinkertons, but I didn't want to tell them anything about Thia, even her name. I couldn't believe that anything would truly come of the evening, so explaining Thia (and her religion) to my family would have been a waste of time and hope. When I could no longer dodge their questions, I simply skedaddled an hour early.

The charity dinner was being held in the Imperial Hotel's main ballroom, so I had plenty of time to sit in the lobby, getting ever more seasick. I remembered with searing shame that as a sixteen-year-old I had come to the Imperial to apply for employment as a bell-boy, only to find that the bell-boys were intimidatingly fine and easeful, and the customers a dozen times more so. I'd fled then, and several times that night I nearly fled again. What if Thia had intended the invitation for someone else? Or worse—what if it was some sort of cruel hoax, some jibe about my thin wallet, my crooked back, or my unimpressive penis? What if even at that moment Thia and her football hero were peeping from behind some corner, snickering up their silk sleeves at the under-sized interloper squirming in his too-elegant surroundings?

But at last Thia entered the lobby. She was unaccompanied and wore a blue and subtly iridescent gown which caused my heart to bumble about my chest. Forcing myself not to sprint, I walked toward her.

"Thank you so much, Mr Grams—"

"Tony."

"Thank you so much, Tony, for being my knight protector on such scant notice."

"I hope nothing is wrong with—I believe his name was Bertie?" Nothing worse than, say, a mild case of being eaten by bottom-feeding fish in the river.

"No, no," she said, taking my arm and leading me toward the ballroom. "Mr Lescott is simply otherwise occupied. So, it develops, is Leen."

"Oh," I said. "*Oh.*"

She caught my tone and laughed. "Oh, nothing like that. Leen is far too upright for such behavior. And Bertie—no, that wouldn't be Bertie at all."

With Thia taking the lead, we passed inspection at the threshold to the ballroom and soon found our table. There were a half-dozen other people at the table, all to my eye more at ease in their fancy duds. At first, I feared they would spot me as an intruder. But beyond polite greetings, pleasantries about the weather, and the occasional request for the salt, they largely ignored me. Even better, Thia seemed to take some pleasure in my conversation. I certainly took pleasure in hers. On subjects ranging from the gold standard to gun emplacement, she was better informed than virtually all the men I knew. So I wasn't especially surprised to learn that she and Dot had both graduated from the University of Wisconsin with degrees in economics.

"Mother and Father approved of my desire for an education," Thia said. "Especially Father. But Dot's mother was a holy terror. It wasn't until a month before graduation that Dot dared to tell her that she wasn't taking her degree in *home* economics. But by that time she was preparing to take her MRS, and all was forgiven."

"I don't suppose you've had any news from Dot," I said, "not with her aboard the Peace Ship."

"*Au contraire.* She just sent me a wireless telegram from the Atlantic. 'SENDING WIRELESS TELEGRAM FROM ATLANTIC. AM QUITE IMPORTANT.'"

I grinned back. "I suppose Mr Richardson doesn't object to the expense."

"Howie isn't on the Peace Ship to object. He and Dot find that they get along together best when they're not actually together."

Howie Richardson, I gathered from Thia's next few stories, was a financier by trade and a twit by training. And that was how most of the evening passed, with Thia telling stories. Some of them she shared with the company, but most of them—including several that nearly made me choke on my wine—she shared only with me. The whole room was full of money, of music from half an orchestra, of light broken by chandeliers and refashioned on polished surfaces. The whole room was full of Thia. I was giddy with it, with her.

Somehow (my wine helped) dessert ended with laughter, and by then I'd stopped imagining disaster and shame. Somehow (her wine helped) Thia decided that she wanted me to join her at the Wiana Club, which I knew only by reputation. Ford muck-a-mucks and the rest of Grosse Pointe's most elegant society had famously been rendering themselves cross-eyed there for years. After we slid from the taxi and stepped inside, I found it full of men upholstered in thick wool suits and prosperous fat. Here and there, more intriguingly upholstered ladies sparkled in the dim lighting, each sequined dress itself a sequin on a dark, room-sized gown.

Sitting across the small table in her own shimmering dress, Thia seemed to glow and spark like arcing electricity. I could almost smell the ozone, the impossibility. Deep down, I knew that I was the undistinguished son of a peculating cigar-counter and that she was the daughter of an eminent physician. I knew that in real life she walked on the stronger arms of wealthier men, that any interest in me must be fleeting, capricious. I knew some great clock of the Real was fast approaching midnight and I'd soon find myself knee-deep in pumpkin muck. But I refused to leave until the carriage stopped rolling and the mice slipped their outsized reins. So I asked hungry questions about her.

I had learned some of her story over dinner, and as we drank I urged her slowly to fill in the rest. She did, though she spoke in fits and starts and coated everything in layers of irony and self-mockery. She had been born in Detroit a couple years before I'd spun from the womb. Her parents were Austrian Jews who had immigrated to America after deciding that no Jew, whatever his promise and his training with the great physicians of Paris, would ever rise in Viennese society.

(*Alessandra and Karl Marx were right,* I decided. *The downtrodden will make common cause and lose nothing but their chains and impeding undergarments.*)

Once in Detroit, her parents settled in the German Jewish quarter, where her father established his medical practice and where Thia began to attend a secular Jewish school near Brush and Willis, not far from Shaarey Zedek. Eventually, her father's reputation and income flourished enough to move the family to a finer neighborhood. After that, she was schooled among Anglo-Saxons and secular Jews. Then came the Grand Tour and the economics degree, which turned out to also have been followed by an MRS degree conferred by Mr Benjamin Mueller, a German Jew from a prominent Detroit family whom she had met in Madison.

(*Curse you, Karl Marx,* snarled my detumescing cock.)

She caught me staring at her bare ring finger. "Widowed," she said.

"I'm sorry." My excitable organs once again began to stir hopefully.

"Oh, don't apologize. Unless you're a member of the *Luftstreitkräfte?*" Her tone wasn't as gay as intended.

Her husband, she told me, had woken one morning that February at the usual hour. But rather than go as always to the successful law firm at which he would soon have become a junior partner, he had instead taken the Windsor ferry. Two days later, he wrote Thia a short letter informing her that he'd joined the Royal Air Force and that she was not to visit him in Canada. Within months, he finished his training and was shipped to England, only to be shot down during one of his first missions.

"These things cannot continue," she said.

"I'm sorry."

"No, that's what he wrote me. 'These things cannot continue. I am sure that you will understand.'" She snorted. "I don't even know what things he meant. I told him he was a goddamned fool, wrote it out, g-o-d. I still don't know why he enlisted. He'd never shown any real interest in the war."

She paused for a long time before resuming. "Dot says he was a dope, that dopes are always crossing to Windsor to buy laudanum and morphine and the like."

She found the wall behind me very interesting and might not have known she was crying.

"Sometimes I like to think that he *was*," she said eventually. "A dope. That he took the ferry across and found himself standing in front of the druggist's, shivering or twitching, and he saw a recruiting poster saying, 'Why Don't I Go?' And so he went. Because it was better than going into the druggist's. I like to think that because if that's..."

(*If I cannot choose how to live, he vowed, then I will choose how to die.*)

"Yes," I said, into the silence.

We sat unspeaking until a clock, real or otherwise, sounded a late hour. We took a cab to Thia's house, and I escorted her up the walk and stood by awkwardly as she unlocked her door and kissed my cheek in farewell. I then took the taxi back home and paid the driver more than I could afford. I undressed reluctantly and lay a while in my bed, imagining her in hers, wondering what she might be thinking, feeling. Eventually, I grew angry with myself for believing it could ever truly matter to me.

Chapter 8

I MANAGED NOT TO OVERSLEEP THE NEXT MORNING ONLY BECAUSE MY BACK objected to something in one of my dreams and decided I needed an interlude of searing pain to distract me. As I stepped gingerly to work, muttering curses with every slip on the ill-shoveled sidewalk (Carl had again failed to clean our own walk), I indulged in any number of vivid fantasies about Thia. She was even fully clad in some of them, I believe.

At work, I realized that I had relatively few office consultations and home visits scheduled for that day. Normally, this would have meant remaining in the office to catch up on a good deal of dreary clerical work, but with Smythe noting my every action and trying to peer into my skull like Prof. Roentgen, I decided to escape the office by taking Sergeant Regan's suggestion that I meet with the Commissioner of Police. Using The Boss' approval as a shield against Smythe and as a sword against interfering secretaries, I managed to secure an appointment that very afternoon.

The Commissioner's secretary had no sooner deigned to permit me into the inner sanctum when the Commissioner, a bluff man of less than forty with an Eastern accent and a businessman's manner, exited said sanctum. "Mr Grams? John Gillespie, a pleasure, sir. Would you mind walking with me, Mr Grams? George, I've been called to an urgent meeting, and I'll not be back this evening."

Without waiting for a reply from me or his secretary, the Commissioner stepped lively through the office and down the corridor. I scurried after him.

After a dozen paces, he slowed his rate of progress. "My apologies," he said with a smile. "Mayor Marx just called to invite me for a round at Red Run. I don't know as that qualifies as 'urgent,' but George tends to tut-tut when golf is involved. I believe it's because he can't swing a pitching wedge to save his life. And, truth to tell, it might actually be urgent. When Hizzoner invites me to play golf, he generally has some wild scheme in mind. Probably wants to sell the municipal water system to the Canucks or somesuch."

"Not a problem, sir." My back had only partially relented in its assault upon my nerves, so even the Commissioner's reduced pace presented a challenge. But a Ford man never says die, so I bustled along beside him as we descended to the ground floor.

"So how can I help Dean Marquis keep Henry Ford's men off the liquor and out of my jail? It's a very fine job you people are doing on that score. Very fine."

"Well, sir, Dr Marquis actually wants me to figure out a way to make sure they keep all that money they're not spending on liquor. To avoid phony silver mines and the like."

"Aidan Regan's your man for bunkum. First-rate on it. Tell him I said he should pitch in."

At this point we'd left the building and were standing in front of the Commissioner's auto, a shining touring car with a shining uniformed officer at the wheel.

"Well, sir, I've spoken with Sergeant Regan already. He's been very cooperative, but he thought I might wish to speak with you directly."

"And here you are. Initiative. Well done, and a pleasure to meet you. But it's my considered opinion that if Aidan Regan don't know about it, it isn't fraud. If you need some weight thrown around or somebody blustered at, then tell George that he's not to give you any guff getting through to me. But until then, Aidan's your man. And now I'm off to convince the mayor not to replace all my policemen with automatons."

With that he let himself into the auto's rear seat, and the big machine rolled away.

"Jilted?" a voice behind me asked.

I turned to see Ross standing behind me. "Do you live here?" I asked.

"Might as well. It's the Billings case. Been trying to find something. Trial's getting closer to a guilty verdict, but I don't see it that way."

"That's a shame," I said.

"That's Detroit. Or the world. I dunno. Anyway, this was my last bit of sleuthing on it. My dowsing stick says there's water, but the well's dry, and dry don't sell 'papers. The boss says if I want a hobby, I can race pigeons. Guess he's right. You get just as much shit with pigeons, but at least there's fresh air."

We'd started walking, drifting down Grafton toward Woodward. Ross paused to smack a lamppost and stare back at Police Headquarters. Eventually, we started walking again.

"Speaking of which, how did it go with the upper crust last night?" Ross asked. "You notice they never say upper crust of *what.*"

"How'd you know about that?"

"Emmeline Ward's father is Maxwell Ward," Ross said. "A big man in real estate. The boss said I should do a Girls' Protective story or two and find a way to work the lady's name into it. Make a friend, sell some ads. So I rang Miss Ward up this morning, and she mentioned that you had escorted milady to a ball. I assume you'll escort her to your other one at your leisure."

"You missed your calling as an instructor of etiquette."

"Actually, I'm supposed to tell you that milady apparently enjoyed herself, which the other milady says she doesn't do much these days. I guess you're expected to get on the buzzer and give her a 'Watson, I need you.'"

I suspect that he said this mock-casually to see how I'd respond. I reacted by not noticing him, or my feet, or downtown Detroit. We must have said our good-byes, but the next thing I remember clearly is trembling in a druggist's, urging the 'phone operator to connect me to milady.

To my significant surprise, it turned out that Ross hadn't been spoofing about Thia's desire to hear from me. When I reached her, she was still at the Girls' Protective League, which was close by. Surly back and all, I dog-trotted there, doubtless kicking countless little old ladies and perambulators into traffic as I went.

I found Thia waiting in the lobby. Soon, we were taking a taxicab to the Wiana Club, and soon after that we were drinking to each other's health while a pianist filled the air with Culture in an attempt to sublimate the fog of cigar smoke and cologne.

At great cost to my manhood, I didn't try to match Thia drink for drink as she labored to drain Detroit's supply of Porto Rican rum. I suppose drinking slowly was unsporting of me. On the other hand, my mind was playing on continuous projection a motion picture of Thia stepping from the frothy sea naked as Aphrodite, and surely it was unsporting of her to have taken that rôle.

I looked away from the film long enough to notice that she was staring at me oddly. I realized that her amusing anecdote had trailed off into something else.

"Is something the matter?" I asked.

She shook her head. "No, not at all."

And suddenly I noticed that her hands were wrong. Not trembling or clumsy like a drunk's. The opposite, really. They were locked in place, the thumbs beneath the tabletop as if she were hoping to tip over its considerable weight.

"Actually, truth to tell," she said in a judicious tone, "I'm having a perfectly dreadful evening."

"I'm sorry to hear it."

She tilted her head slightly, like a quizzical spaniel. "Yes, I think that you really are." She smiled lopsidedly. "I'm not sleeping at home this evening. Dot gave me the keys to her house before she left. To spy on her servants, she said. Since Howie is also out of town."

"Ah."

"I've already told Mother that I'll be sleeping there."

"Ah," I repeated.

She raised her eyebrows at me. "Only it's a little frightening there because the servants aren't actually there to be spied upon. They're a lovely married couple, and they've gone to visit their daughter in Grand Rapids."

"*Ah*," I said. Aphrodite froze midway from the surf, bathed in light like a holy icon. Then I realized that I'd perhaps assumed too much. "Ah?"

She unlocked a hand from the table and placed it atop mine. Her skin was moist and slightly cool from the marble tabletop. "Ah," she said.

I could spend pages on the agony of every stage of the journey to Dot's large and stately home—"mansion" might be the proper word. I don't mean my excruciating priapism throughout, though that was part of it. I mean I became painfully conscious how complicated it was to move from one place to another in a city. The technology of cars and streetlamps. The exquisite blend of casualness and pretence required to convey respectability or at least respectable degeneracy to a world of doormen, cab drivers, invisible neighbors, and unsympathetic angels. All of it, I knew, any of it might induce Thia to undo her decision.

If she'd even *made* a decision, of course. Well before we left the Wiana, she'd removed her hand from mine, and not even after we stepped inside the Richardsons' ornate front door did I dare try to resume that intimacy. Walking two paces ahead, like a bodyguard or perhaps the guard of a condemned prisoner, she led me up the long, curving stairway to a woman's room with a bed larger than my childhood home in Ghilarza, and she never once looked at me, not until she fell languidly onto the bed and rolled onto her back, letting her shoes drop daintily to the floor.

"I believe I shall just lie here for a moment," she said.

I made a noise inarticulate by Cro Magnon standards. All sorts of interesting things happened in my veins and trousers.

Looking at Thia was complicated, so I examined the room's furnishings, which looked to have been polished with fifty-dollar bills soaked in ambrosia. This was just as intimidating as Thia, so I compromised by looking at the nightstand. That helped not at all—my first sexual dalliance had begun with my placing three dollars on the nightstand and had ended after about fourteen cents' worth of friction. That encounter had led to a burning sensation of guilt, a burning sensation in my urethra, and several rote phrases from my confessor about burning in hell. The urinary discomfort cleared up after I summoned the courage to visit a doctor, and the other discomforts faded with it. The next time I had three dollars, I returned to the same whorehouse armed with prophylactics. Minus the tubal burning, I completed the cycle of longing, orgasm, and guilt a few more times until Father died. Soon after that, even my best rationalizations of the expense failed. In the intervening five years, I had occasionally opened my own throttle or enjoyed particularly vivid, sheet-assaulting dreams, but I had not once been meaningfully near a woman.

After a long silence, Thia asked, "Do you know what a hysterectomy is?"

I gargled affirmatively, still not daring to look at her.

"Good." She paused. "I've had one. About three months ago."

"Ah."

She laughed. "Yes, 'ah.' Well, that's polite, certainly. You're polite, Tony. A less cultivated man would already be trying to ravish me—"

Ilaria and Angela have taken me to the lakefront point past the end of Garfield Avenue. It's summer, and we have escaped the humid stink of Chicago's stockyards. My teenaged sisters are talking about foolishness—beauty, marriage, living in a mansion in Kenwood—so I escape them too, into the lake's chilly waters. When I emerge, Ilaria and Angela are both tittering, though Angela is trying not to. After a moment I realize that they're watching two dogs play, a St Bernard and something that's more miniature schnauzer than anything else. But, no, the dogs aren't playing. The St Bernard bitch is in heat and doing her best to accommodate the schnauzer as he labors to mount her. She stands patiently, her tail raised and her head cocked to look along her flank as he scuttles away and whirls to approach at a run. This happens several times, and each time his run-up ends with a leap, which turns into a frantic scrabbling as he tries to sink his paws deep enough into her coat to hold himself in place. However, neither paws nor penis are proving sufficient anchor, and every time the poor fellow thrusts in earnest, the shift in balance pulls him inexorably onto the ground. Eventually the St Bernard loses interest and trots away.

Woof, I thought.

She was looking at me quizzically, her head turned toward me. I realized I'd been chuckling mordantly. "Sorry."

She grinned fleetingly. "I mention the hysterectomy for two reasons. First, it's helped make me such a shambles lately. It's not an easy thing. Ironic, of course, to be hysterical *after* a hysterectomy."

I provided the expected smile.

"I tell a lie," she said. "I'm mentioning it for three reasons. The second is that the scar is one of the modern ones, but it's still unsightly and I wouldn't want you to be surprised. The third is that you shouldn't, obviously, worry yourself about me as a mother."

She sat up and looked unblinkingly into my eyes.

So it really was in the offing, or at least in the offering. But clearly I had to say no. Clearly, a good man would have sat beside her lush body laid across the lush bedclothes, kissed her cheek, and whispered that, while he had naturally wished very much to ravish her, he suspected that in her deepest heart she didn't wish to be ravished that night. A good man would have taken a rain check and offered to listen to her talk about her dead husband and her excised womb, about the desperation which had stranded her half dressed and half drunk in her friend's elegant boudoir with an inelegant stranger.

I removed my trousers and began struggling with my long underwear.

She began to help, and as she unbuttoned my fly and lowered my underwear, the casual brushing of the back of her hand detonated a month of semen, which soaked her face and hair, leaving her purblind and convulsed with laughter.

I was beyond apology. I shoved the offender back in my underwear as if to undo everything.

When she had mostly controlled her laugher, she asked for a handkerchief, with which she wiped her face. She handed it back to me with the daintiness of a debutante. She rose and padded to the wash basin, wetting her hands and rubbing her face.

My face was making noises without assistance from my brain, and she interrupted to ask, "Do you want to make amends?"

I nodded, which led to some complicated undressing on her part. Her hysterectomy scar wasn't so much unsightly as unnerving. It ran along the lower edge of her belly, shadowing the curve of her pelvis, and strongly suggested a cynical grin that, off-puttingly, put me in mind of Dot Richardson. But I had little chance to contemplate it, as I spent the next ten or fifteen minutes with my head vised by her thighs. I developed a sharp pain in my back and a dull ache in my jaw long before her belly shuddered gratifyingly, but the pain seemed suitable.

By this time, my own excitable bits had rallied, which led to some interestingly salty kissing and some genuinely tender and successful lovemaking where all the parts fit in their intended ways. She came a second time, which set me off too.

Afterward, she laughed a little, and we lay back, companionably close. With the lamp turned off, the room was dark and cold. We could have been under water. As always after intercourse, I was at first troubled by half suppressed depression and panic. I felt trapped. I wanted one of us to apologize. Eventually that faded into a more complicated and diffuse yearning for vague and beautiful things—bright shapes and destinies, undoings of the ugly memories schooling like fish just beneath the surface of the moment.

"If I may, I'd like to tell you about the hysterectomy," she said. She laughed. "I feel like one of Father's neurotics."

"Pardon?"

"My father. He's an alienist."

"A nut doctor? You said he was a physician."

"He was. Is. He trained as a neuroanatomist."

Upon settling in Detroit, she explained, her father had quickly developed a reputation for dealing effectively with neurasthenics, particularly well-educated, well-to-do Jewesses and other German-speaking women who suffered from diseases with no known physical cause.

"Other physicians found them bothersome," she said. "Most dismissed them as hysterical without ever wondering what it *meant* to be hysterical."

"What does it mean?" I asked.

"Do you truly care? Father's work is really quite fascinating, but it strikes many as unscientific. He had awful rows with Dr Beard's crowd when he first began to publish."

"Fascinate away," I said.

"Well. Let me give you an example. A woman develops a sort of painful heaviness in her lower back, let's say. It isn't constant, but when it strikes, it leaves her quite unable to do many of her usual household tasks. She can't even supervise the servants. Now, the condition first affects her after a fifth-month miscarriage. Your diagnosis, Dr Grams?"

My first reaction was that she was lucky to have only intermittent back pain. I had spasms old enough to go on profit-sharing.

"Maybe the pregnancy damaged something in her back," I suggested. "A nerve?"

"Possibly. Indeed, let's say that the pregnancy often pained her back. But the pain after the miscarriage doesn't correspond to the anatomical arrangement of the muscles, skeleton, or nerves. It's more a pain in the area one loosely thinks of as one's lower back."

"Like having a pain in your chest shaped like a Valentine's heart?" I was starting to be genuinely interested.

"Well done, Dr Grams."

"And she isn't hoaxing me?"

"One can't be sure. But she seems sincere, and her husband has offered to hire additional servants. So she isn't avoiding drudgery or seeking attention which she otherwise wouldn't receive."

I suspected this quite possibly wasn't a typical post-coital topic of discussion. Then again, I was hardly an authority. My only previous post-coital discussions had involved reminders that if I wanted to stay longer, I'd have to pay more.

"It's a stumper," I said.

"Hardly surprising. I've left out a few crucial details. Father is always complaining that it takes him ages to get the right details out of his patients. So let us add that the woman, prior to the miscarriage, had already given birth to a girl who two years later died of pneumonia."

I detected the slightest catch in her voice. She was describing herself, of course.

"She and her husband had doted on the child, and the loss struck them hard, the husband particularly. He'd been looking forward to the new baby—a fresh start. But the mother, she was, well, exhausted by it all. By the pregnancy, by her misery over her daughter's death, by the strain at home. Anna was the daughter's name, and when the doctor told her that she had miscarried, her first thought was 'At least I won't always be comparing another child to my Anna.' That's when the problems with her back began. The area was already achy, but the pain began in earnest then."

I muttered my failsafe "ah."

"Don't you see? What sort of mother experiences relief at a miscarriage?"

For as long as I could remember, Mother and then Angela had muttered darkly about neighbors who stopped having children at early ages, women whom they suspected of jumping off furniture and drinking gin in warm baths. I felt morally certain I had met many such women on my rounds for Educational. I'd definitely encountered women—and men—who considered miscarriages belated blessings.

"We all of us think awful thoughts," Thia continued. "Usually they're censored, but when our censors are distracted and tired, it all bobs to the surface. And then we have to acknowledge them—or find a way to un-think them entirely."

On a sunlit day, a flat ocean liner sinks soggily at a high angle, dissolving into a floating swirl of oil paints and jetsam. Stray hats and mismatched boots, old clothes and new clothes submerge and emerge, bob and duck. There are perhaps people in them. Beneath the water, the people may have faces, fat and rotten with saltwater. They bump against one another above and below. They may be dead or battling one another. As the Germans had learned when bits of their stealthy sinkings drifted to the surface, there's no such thing as spurlos versenkt, *no traceless sinking. Everything is* schrecklichkeit, *even if the atrocity re-appears slowly.*

"The back pain," I said.

"The back pain," she said. "It distracted her from her thoughts about the miscarriage. If left unchecked, that pain might have distracted her from many other unpleasant thoughts."

She sighed.

"Fortunately, I knew how miserable people will make themselves in order to avoid suffering. So I answered the question. What kind of a mother experiences relief at a miscarriage? One on the verge of exhaustion, consumed with grief. One who has let herself become dangerously weak and must change."

We lay silently for a while. I admired her then as I have admired few others.

"Benjy never took Father's work very seriously. It's harder for men to listen to themselves in that way, I think. Which means it's easier to listen to others—why don't I go?"

Dot's mattress would have concealed a cantaloupe from even the most particular princess, so I fell asleep quite easily. But I awoke well before dawn in a panic, realizing that my family had expected me home hours earlier. I'd told Mother not to expect me at dinner, but I hadn't warned her that I wouldn't be home at all.

If I'd thought ahead, Carl would likely have helped me craft a suitable alibi. He certainly owed me for all the alibis I'd provided him over the past year or so. Even Kitty might have gone along. But fantasy had become reality far too fast for any clever planning. So Mother must have been worrying, and when Mother worried, she lost sleep. And even on her calmest day she preferred to rise before the sun. There was no possibility whatsoever of my claiming simply to have come in after she went to sleep and then gone to work early.

I lay there in the darkness, listening to the radiators gurgle and Thia breathe soft and slow a few feet away. I had never fallen asleep beside a woman before. To wake beside one was at once unsettling and calming. I wanted to touch her skin but didn't, for fear of waking her. I remembered it, though, the smoothness of it, of even her scars. I thought of her miscarriage, her lost daughter, her dead husband. I thought of Mother muttering about women who drowned their unborn babies in gin. Obviously, Thia had been trying to drown her ghosts in gin. For some time now. What had just happened between us was part of that, I knew, and that knowledge was a knife of many points.

I shifted slightly and found that my back hurt less than usual after long hours lying down. Was it simply the fine mattress, or had falling asleep beside someone soothed some psychic portion of my pain, as Thia's father would no doubt have suggested? I remembered then The Boss speaking glowingly of the Emmanuel movement, a Christian belief which seemed to say similar things about the body and the mind, the body and the soul. Thinking of The Boss while in that bed, with Thia beside me, made me more than a little uneasy. I heard him expounding upon one of his favorite metaphors, that of the human being as a three-cylinder engine: *All three cylinders, Tony, body, mind, and soul, are connected up to one shaft, and all must be in perfect condition in order to obtain the best results.*

Best results. I wasn't sure what those might be in that bedroom, in that mess of longing, fear, and tenderness. I was relieved that The Boss was still on the Peace Ship and wouldn't be there to look me in the eye, relieved that there would be no advisor sent to ask Mother and Kitty about the regularity of *my* conduct. Still, I knew that I would rather be ashamed beside Thia than unimpeachable alone.

A few hours later, I was waiting for Carl at the John R gate. I had showered, shaved, and used some of Howie Richardson's expensive cologne, so I probably looked presentable, but I felt furtive and vaguely defiant as laborers filed past me to begin the day shift. My discomfort doubled whenever the occasional advisor greeted me, and I responded with smiles as phony as Washington's teeth.

When Carl at last sauntered into view (it takes a graceful man to saunter through four inches of grimy December slush), his grin for me was broad and gleaming. "Aw, shucks, does this mean Ma'll have to put you back in the will?"

"She knows I didn't come home last night?" I swore and tried to think.

"Meet a femme?" Carl asked. "Or did you spend the night making sure that the men were clean and thrifty when they bedded their femmes?"

"You suggested to Mother that I was with a girl?"

"Course not. I suggested you were cracking safes and turning Lutheran. Well, whaddya want? I didn't suggest anything. I didn't know nothing to say nothing. I just played dumb and went upstairs early to get away from Ma and Kitty gossiping and worrying."

"You're a source of support and comfort, brother mine."

One advantage of being an Educational advisor is that one learns quickly which lies get easily caught out. So I kept mine simple. A couple of hours later, between home visits, I stopped at a corner store to ring Ross at the *Free Press*. He agreed to send a box of cigars to my home that afternoon with a note reading, "Thanks for standing watch over an ailing pal." He agreed to take repayment in beer and details. Next, I called the Daszkowskis' store, just down the street from home, and asked Mrs Daszkowski to send a boy to Mother with a note saying that I was well and apologizing for my overnight absence, which I would of course explain when I came home for supper.

On my luncheon break, I stopped at a stationer's to find something sufficiently impressive on which to write Thia a note. I mentally composed a dozen different epistles ranging from the cringingly grateful to the winkingly knowing. In the end, I simply thanked her for "a wonderful evening" and suggested that we meet up again soon if it suited.

Chapter 9

I MADE A GREAT POINT OF CASUALLY SPENDING THE NEXT EVENINGS AT HOME, and Mother and Kitty made a great point of not at all scrutinizing my every gesture and intonation. We were all a calm and cheerful family sitting in the parlor and entertaining one another by reading newspaper accounts of slaughter in the European trenches and Kraut *schrecklichkeit* on the high seas. And gradually the reality began to match the pretence. The cigars from Ross and my own cheerfully innocent manner had partially allayed their suspicions, at least to the point of forestalling outright accusations.

I'm sure it also helped that Kitty didn't particularly care what I'd done. Unlike Angela, Kitty didn't take pleasure in sniffing disapprovingly. Besides, she was distracted by a courtship of her own, albeit one far more wholesome and aboveboard than mine. Andrew Lagorio, who had begun his suit around the time that Angela had last visited us, had become a more frequent presence in the house. For weeks, I'd tried to dislike him because he was tall, brown-haired, and blessed with the square-jawed handsomeness of an Arrow Collar man. But he'd proven too friendly to resent satisfactorily. And he suited Kitty. He was bright and ambitious, and his gallant tenderness strengthened my gracile sister. Mother's initial resistance had vanished quickly, especially because having Andrew about the place gave her another man to fuss over and scold, no small blessing given Carl's increasingly frequent absences.

Indeed, the following night was a Friday, which meant that Andrew visited after supper and that our parlor veritably glowed with the ennobling influence of Good Home Conditions as Andrew read us stories from *The Saturday Evening Post* about other families with similarly glowing parlors.

Throughout, my longing to see Thia again intensified. I thought of her when dispensing homilies at work. I thought of her at night with my hand inside and outside my underwear, with my mind in and out of sleep. So when I came home from work Saturday afternoon to have Kitty hold up an unsealed envelope from Thia, my heart hammered like a piston-punch. Kitty kept it back a long moment, staring at me apprais-ingly. For a moment I feared discovery, but when I was finally permitted to read the note, I found it a model of discretion: "I so enjoyed our eve-ning at the GPL fundraiser that I'm being dreadfully forward by suggest-ing that we attend a lecture this evening at the Civic Uplift League. If convenient, would you mind terribly collecting me at the Richardsons'?"

Shellacked with pomade, I knocked at the Richardsons' door a few hours later. Thia answered the door herself, drink in hand. She seemed almost entirely sober, however, and was severely beautiful in a conservative woollen dress.

"No servants this evening, either," she said with a wryly mischie-vous smile. "I hope I wasn't too unladylike in inviting you here. I've been told that I ought to let men do all the pursuing because 'men prefer the hunt to the meat.'"

"What a disgusting phrase," I said as she closed the door behind me. "Is it Austrian?"

"Dot's," she replied as she ushered me down a long hallway to a smallish den toward the rear of the house, where a large fire began to melt the frost from my marrow. "Of course, I can't really claim that I was hunted. In truth, I threw myself on the spear." She smiled. "Yes, that's revolting too."

She pointed to a stuffed armchair and mixed me a stiff gin and tonic before lounging into a nearby seat, her elbow resting above her body on the chair's arm, her glass dangling insouciantly from her fingertips. We were close enough to touch, but we didn't, though my fingers twitched and trembled toward her.

"And here we are, Mr Grams."

There was an unsettling breeziness to her tone and posture. I won-dered at its source. Embarrassment? Regret? She wasn't taking herself seriously, but I took her seriously, and I was desperate for some excuse to take us seriously together. I had begun to understand much more fully Gennaro's love for Alessandra, for a beautiful and ferocious woman who cared about all the things which no one wanted her to touch and to know.

Once this thought occurred to me, I couldn't force Gennaro from my mind. Eventually, Thia asked me what was the matter. I started to shake my head, to dismiss it. But then I remembered everything she had told me during our last night together. I knew she had dared to do so only because I hadn't truly mattered, because I was a stranger, an amateur alienist also willing to fiddle with her groin. Even so, she had told me, and we were connected. So I told her about Gennaro. About his meeting Alessandra and deserting from the Carabinieri, about bread and blood on the cobblestones of Cagliari.

When I'd finished, she asked, "Do you remember the kosher riots? About five years ago?"

I'd heard something of them, though I'd been in Ann Arbor at the time.

"I was with Mother," Thia said, "in the immigrant Jewish quarter of the east side. Sometimes Mother enjoys going there. She finds the Russians, and the Poles, and even the Yiddishers truly Jewish, if that makes sense. We're reform, and Father isn't even Jewish enough for temple. 'Only for pogroms,'" she said, imitating him. "But then I don't think it's truly religion that Mother's after. It's intensity, or..."

She shook her head before resuming. "At any rate, we were in a bookseller's, and we heard shouting from outside. It was hard to understand at first, but we finally worked out that people—women—were shouting *'treyf.'* 'Unclean.' Or 'not kosher,' really."

She spotted my incomprehension. "That means the meat hasn't been butchered properly. According to custom, I mean. The women were shouting so loudly, and they weren't stopping. Mother and I went to the window to look out. All of these women in head shawls and calico dresses, they had surrounded some butchers' wagons. They started dragging the drivers from the wagons. One man was badly trampled by the women—and not just young women. Little old ladies who looked scarcely strong enough to carry their hunches."

She paused, realizing, then concealing her realization. I pretended not to notice.

"Soon the women were throwing the meat off the wagons. Then they started raiding the butchers' shops. There was a shop beside us, and I could see them pouring in, in a frenzy. *'Treyf, treyf.'* I could hear them. There was so much banging. Clattering, thuds. The butcher and his assistants were nearly killed." She shook her head. "A brick comes through the window of the bookshop, simply explodes through it like a gunshot. It nearly kills Mother. The glass cuts her face, her neck. It's a little ferret-faced girl of fourteen or fifteen who throws it. Heaves it like Harry Coveleski."

Not a lot of ladies know the Tigers' pitching rotation.

"The clerk locks the doors and closes the blinds. We all move into the back room. The clamor from next door, it's as though they'll push through the wall."

She paused.

"Eventually, the police stepped in. Rows of men in uniforms swinging truncheons at Jewish ladies."

"All this over how to cut up a cow?"

"More about high prices. People were hungry. Very hungry. Still," she added angrily, "Mother very easily could have been killed that day. The 'papers all said that 'order was restored.' Restored? I wonder."

"Why tell me this?" The comparison seemed disrespectful to Gennaro somehow. He'd been gunned down by soldiers, not annoyed by meat critics. "It's hardly comforting. It's not even amusing."

She raised her eyebrows. "Those are hardly the only choices."

"No," I said.

"No." She rose and poured us fresh drinks, sipping some of hers with ritual slowness before returning to her chair. She was leaning forward now, her fingertips on the inside of my thigh. "I'll confess that don't feel very much like an Uplift lecture tonight, Mr Grams."

The fucking was vigorous, angry, and excruciatingly good. Afterward, it took an act of heroic will to rise from Dot's disheveled bed. Thia allowed me to kiss her forehead farewell, and I showed myself out the door. I walked home numb with something deeper than winter.

At about this time, mid-December, dispatches from the Peace Ship began to make clear how divided its delegates were, how forlorn the mission's hopes. I empathized. Thia and I met a few more times, as before, hiding from families and servants. She pretended not to see her ghosts as they crowded the bed. I pretended not to indulge hopes that something worthwhile might come of our dalliance. And then, a week before Christmas, she put an end to it by leaving Detroit. I learned this two or three days after the fact by a letter dispatched from Royal Oak, where she had gone to stay with Emmeline Ward's family for Christmas. She thanked me for my kindness and hoped that "we might see one another again at some future time."

I spent days tending to my anger as though it were a hothouse flower. At bottom, of course, I was less angry than heartbroken. And ashamed. I was too ashamed to tell Ross how the affair had ended, and I'd been too embarrassed to admit to Merry that it had begun. So there was nobody to talk me out of my conviction that Thia had left me because I wasn't good enough for her. I wouldn't have faulted her for that (hated her, perhaps), but she owed me the courtesy of discarding me in person. And make no mistake, soon I would collect. I would be dignified but warm, stern but understanding. And she would see me, would see how I dealt with the situation, and she would realize the error of her ways and repent. We would part amicably, Thia chastened and fruitlessly longing. Or possibly we would end up lounging in bed, naked except for my silk top hat and her white veil, and we would revel in sunlight and sensuality whilst approving priests and rabbis pronounced us man and wife.

Or something in that vein.

At home I paced my room, hatching and discarding schemes to find Thia and claim my apology, her love. Like a simian Scrooge determined to ruin Christmas, I dangled from a doorjamb, glaring at Carl whenever he passed, daring him or the others to ask me questions which I wouldn't answer.

I'd refused to tell Ross the truth about Thia's casting me aside, but he wasn't a fool. He guessed what had happened long before either of us spoke the truth aloud. Once I had, he dragged me to a fancy downtown restaurant, where he had arranged for us to meet with Merry.

"Good grub," Ross said during a brief pause in his methodical absorption of a rare steak. "In the war countries, they're drinking coal-tar coffee and eating rotten mashed potatoes sculpted to look like lamb chops."

Merry sighed and shook his head. "So much death over foolishness."

I thought of Alessandra's impassioned letters against the needless death and destruction. She was angry with Italy, with the whole world, and never finished a letter without writing, "War is an engine, the blood of workers its gasoline." I worried sometimes what would happen to my niece if the authorities jailed her mother for treason. It was one thing for Henry Ford to say such things, another for a Fiat employe.

"Hear, hear," Ross said, agreeing with Merry. "That Princip nut did 'em all a favor. Too many archdukes as it is."

"Fleas on a dog," I said, smiling at Merry.

He smiled back faintly. We both sighed.

"At least have some proportion, Tony," Ross said. "You're sighing over a broad. Merry's sighing over the millions of deaths."

"A woman?" Merry asked me.

"She wasn't here long enough to be a woman," I said. "She remains an idea." That was equal parts lie and truth, and thinking about it confused me. I tried to tell myself that Ross was right, that a war gutting a continent deserved my sighs more than a stillborn love affair. I tried very hard.

"Good grub," Ross repeated.

A memory floated unexpectedly to the surface of my thoughts: young Scimmia Gramazio, the angry, half starved child of a jailbird. Always dirty, his upper lip moustached with snot. Always running awkwardly from Ghilarzan children determined to toss him into a tree. What would he have become if Father had meekly accepted our lot there? Who would the twenty-five-year-old Antonio Gramazio have been? Odd though it sounds, it comforted me to imagine my starveling, even more lopsided Sardinian self as he hopped up and down in faint hopes of finding food or fainter hopes of holding some Ghilarza girl's attention. At least Tony Grams got good grub.

PART TWO

Scraps

Chapter 10

At about the same time I was eating steak and thinking about Alessandra's letters about the blood of the workers, her own blood was pouring from her slit throat and puddling in an alley not far from the Fiat plant. The logical suspects in her murder were Fiat goons or their allies among the Carabinieri. But it could also have been a rival Socialist or simply some thieving lump of proletariat. In any case, Alessandra's friends decided that Elisabetta might also be in danger (or simply too expensive to feed and clothe). So, in an exchange of transatlantic telegrams, they arranged with us to ship her to Hoboken in the charge a comrade who had business in New York. Either Carl or I would have to meet Elisabetta there a week into the new year, and the task fell to me because, as a star man, it would be easier for me to secure leave from Ford. Easier, but hardly easy. The Boss had only just returned with Mr Ford after the Peace Ship had foundered on the shoals of reality, and with his return, Smythe had resumed his campaign against me.

Frustrated in love, I'd thrown myself into succeeding in fraud. I had devised a set of sensible proposals to make Educational more effective in protecting the men against swindles: compiling descriptions of the most common bunkum schemes to be distributed and explained to the men, arranging weekly meetings with Sergeant Regan to exchange useful information, encouraging the men to report to their advisors any suspected instances of fraud, and so forth. The Boss had approved them all. Given The Boss' approval, Smythe also endorsed my suggestions, but he wanted to be the one implementing them. Moreover, he wanted funds to place operatives in the plant to actively ferret out any dishonest conduct among the men. The Boss (and I) viewed such a measure as likely to erode the men's trust in Educational, so Smythe was treading delicately on that point. But he did manage to successfully invent an epidemic of fraud throughout the plant, which lent urgency to enacting the new measures. *And given Tony's regrettable absence at this critical juncture...*

Triumphant, Smythe smirked at me so serenely for the rest of the day that it was a positive pleasure to board a train for Hoboken that evening. The trip itself was far less pleasant. I had brought along a copy of *The Wealth of Nations,* but, interesting though it was at other times, for those seven hundred miles it was merely a weight on my lap. The whole trip, my mind was a greasy stewpot of images and ideas bubbling individually and jointly to the surface before sinking back. Thia, naked and clothed. Thia, seeing me as I raised my niece more successfully than she had raised her dead daughter. Gennaro in his uniform. Gennaro on the cobblestones. My niece Elisabetta, whom I had last seen in a photograph which Alessandra had sent three or four years earlier. My niece's face fused with the face of my sister Elisabetta, dead almost two decades. Alessandra bleeding from her throat as a murderer dug in the knife. Smythe bleeding from the nose after I punched him in the face.

I arrived in Hoboken the evening before Elisabetta's ship would dock, so I spent a night on a lumpy mattress in a drab hotel, nightmares about murder or Thia's cruel laughter more than once waking me from sleep. During my waking moments, the radiator would thud violently in its cage a few times, clatter nervously, and then subside into a gentle hissing while my heart did much the same. I was at the center of a dark universe.

In the sullen inkling of dawn, I sat naked in the lukewarm bathtub and told myself that I couldn't go to pieces simply because I was lovelorn, not even because I was shocked by the senseless snuffing of yet another bright soul. My family, now including my little niece, needed me to persevere.

It was a cold, grim day at the Hoboken port. At first, there were only several dozen sleepy people from the north shores of the Mediterranean waiting for the *Diogenes,* Elisabetta's ship. Gradually, though, the ranks of those waiting grew, and a few men came to sell hot dogs and pretzels. As morning neared noon and the ship grew tardy in arriving, the crowd began to mutter angrily about the Huns and their U-boats. A pair of heavily whiskered men of rotund middle age indignantly explained to a group of suspicious Roman grandmothers that the Dutch were nothing like the Deutsch. *Nederland,* they insisted, *Nederland.* But the grandmothers continued to grumble and glare.

At last the *Diogenes* hove into sight and made port with two tugs nipping at it like collies. It settled against the pier, its smokestacks jutting above the customs building between the crowd and the dock. I tried to press to the front because my niece and her escort were travelling second class and so would glide through customs rather than endure the medical inspection and twenty-nine questions at Ellis Island that awaited steerage passengers. But I was among skilled jostlers. The customs house door appeared through hats and shoulders only in flashes, and soon I was too short to see anything except shoulder blades and handbags. The man behind me kept jabbing me with—I hoped—his walking stick.

After a half-hour the crowd had thinned enough for me to watch the remaining passengers come into view. Some strolled out confidently, while others milled about uncertainly as sharpers tried shopworn cons which Sergeant Regan would've considered beneath contempt. Each girl between the ages of four and fourteen looked like my niece. But none was, and the crowd thinned further.

I should have known—a Socialist would pay to be in second class only in order to avoid scrutiny by the Bureau of Immigration, and he would do that only to accomplish some criminal mission. If he hadn't thrown Elisabetta to the sharks en route, he had abandoned her and already was planting bombs at the Stock Exchange. My niece would be easy prey for the sharpers and mashers circling the pier like seagulls. Already I had failed her. Gennaro and Alessandra would haunt me forever.

I was no more than ten yards from the customs exit, hopping in place on a rickety crate when someone poked my arm. The finger belonged to a woman in a long dark coat, who asked in Italian, "Pardon me. Are you Mr Antonio Grams?"

"Anthony Grams, yes," I said, also in Italian. "Is anything wrong?"

She shook her head briefly and turned to look back. I followed her eyes to an eight- or ten-year-old girl with neatly combed hair and a deeply tired face.

Elisabetta. *Thank God.*

The woman introduced herself and Elisabetta before shaking my hand and handing me a canvas bag containing all the child's possessions. Saying that the ship's tardiness obliged her to go immediately to New York, the woman took her leave of us and was gone before I could reproach her for leaving a child with such an obvious incompetent.

Wide-eyed and grave, Elisabetta stared up at me. She was a mildly pretty girl with intelligent, careful brown eyes. I had resolved to speak with her as with my pupils at the English School. *I brush my teeth. He combs his hair. We hold the tea-cups.* I remembered my embarrassing English during my first months in America. I remembered Father's impotent sense of always being cheated. The sooner Elisabetta learned English, I had decided, the sooner such unpleasantness would pass for her.

"Would you like something to eat?" I asked in English, putting invisible food to my mouth.

When she tilted her head quizzically, I remembered New York as I'd first seen it, a great threat of cold bricks, ramshackle boards, and oddly dressed men and women impatient with anyone who slowed their pace. "Are you hungry?" I asked in Italian.

She nodded slightly and put her hand in mine. It was small and bare, a sacred trust.

Lisa—for so she wished to be called—ate ravenously but spoke little. She showed little sign of interest or concern, even as we boarded the train for Detroit. Then, after an hour's travel, she asked how much longer our journey would last.

"Two days," I said. "*Due giorni.*"

"*Due giorni?*" she asked. "*Veramente?*"

"*Veramente.*"

She nodded thoughtfully and then returned her attention to the darkness outside the window. A lonely house flashed by, lit from within. I realized that her shoulders were shaking with sobs. Something had just sunk in.

Chapter 11

Mother, Carl, Kitty, and even Andrew greeted Lisa and me upon our arrival at Union Depot. To my surprise, they were joined by Angela. I didn't like to think why she had come to Detroit.

Mother stood in the vanguard, looking at Lisa much as Roosevelt had looked at San Juan Hill. Lisa ducked behind me.

"Lisa," I requested in Italian, "please come out and meet your American family." I gestured first to Mother. "This is Nonna Maria Teresa, your father's mother."

Mother had clearly planned a speech, but her throat caught and she could only mumble some greeting. I introduced the others in turn, and Lisa nodded seriously and repeated each name. When I'd finished, she looked at me and asked, "Zio Tonio, why do some of you have Italian names and others not?"

As I wondered how to explain recommendations and everybody's different idea of how to be American, Mother swooped in and lifted the girl to her breast. "Elisabetta," she said. "My Gennaro's daughter. Elisabetta."

Eventually, Kitty managed to prise the girl from Mother's arms and return her to the ground.

Andrew's town car was big enough to hold most but not all of us, so we decided to let Andrew drive Mother, Lisa, and the luggage home. The rest of us would take the Woodward House to its terminus and walk the last few blocks. Mother made a fuss about Kitty's leg, but Kitty ignored it.

Flattering myself that Lisa might care about her separation from me, I explained our plan carefully.

"Model T?" she asked delightedly. "Model T? *Veramente?*"

Kitty grinned at me over the girl's head.

Upon walking home from the trolley, we had scarcely stepped into the foyer before Mother descended upon us. Lisa, she whispered sternly, was sleeping upstairs and we were not to "stomp our heavy feet about the house like circus elephants."

Out of Mother's sight on the sofa, Andrew caught my eye and made an elaborate production of silently lowering his tea-cup to its saucer.

After donning house shoes, we tiptoed into the living room while Angela and Mother returned to the kitchen, which was already filling the house with savory odors.

"We positively staggered back from Gratiot Avenue under the food," Kitty said, crossing to the sofa to sit beside Andrew. "I was plucking and chopping all morning." She turned to Andrew with a great fluttering of eyelashes. "You wouldn't expect your wittle Kitty Kat to cook for you, would you, darling? Only consider my cuticles."

Interestingly, Andrew flinched at neither the hint of marriage nor the suggestion of Kitty's helplessness in the kitchen. Of course, he'd already sampled Kitty's cooking and knew that she was perfectly competent in that wifely duty. But she viewed cooking as a necessary task, whereas Mother and Angela worked with food the way hoodoo witches worked with potions. When there was enough in the pantry and the icebox to permit free choice, Mother's every emotion, every fear, every hope, had a proper pot and a precise spicing.

Did Thia cook? I couldn't picture it.

"They already give you the third degree about the girl?" Andrew asked me.

I nodded.

"Then I'll get the scoop from my dish later."

"English, dear," Kitty said, swatting him on the shoulder.

I asked him how Lisa had liked the Model T.

"Saucer eyes." He paused. "She cried toward the end, but I don't think that was the car, poor kid."

After a sad silence, Kitty said, "Carl, tell Tony your good news."

Carl mustered a grin. "I got a raise. To seven bucks a day, almost."

That wasn't too far off what I was making. Of course, a good toolmaker was hard to find. If Carl continued to improve, he could make ten dollars a day.

"And Andrew has been appointed secretary to Mr Venture," Kitty said proudly.

"I don't get a raise, of course," Andrew said, trying to sound cynical.

"Not really. Just a bigger desk for all the new paperwork."

"The bank has already put Andrew on salary," Kitty told us. "He'll get a raise by May."

"When dames start worrying a fellah about raises," Carl told Andrew, "he needs to go on the bum for a while, maybe see California."

Andrew chuckled, and Kitty pretended to take offense.

I excused myself and went upstairs. Lisa was sleeping in Mother's room, where she would stay while Angela was sharing Kitty's room. I cracked the door. Lisa's body was an indistinct mound of dark blankets, but her face glowed faintly in the light from the doorway. I realized that I'd been expecting something dreadful to happen to her—a strange accident, a kidnapping, an assassination by members of the Serbian Black Hand. But there she was, safely swaddled.

My whole body unclenched, save the eternal near-spasm between my shoulder blades. With the calm came exhaustion, and I scarcely had the strength to walk down the hall and remove my shoes before collapsing into sleep.

Conscious of owing The Boss some extra hard work and wanting to get to Educational before Smythe could put mousetraps in my attaché case, the next morning I rose before everyone except Mother. Still, I hesitated at the front door, feeling that I should stay home, to protect Lisa in some way. But when Mother shooed me out, I realized that she could have protected Lisa against a legion of Hearst's horrible Huns.

I reached Educational a half-hour before the other advisors started to trickle in. Smythe was among the first. "Delighted to see your family difficulty is resolved enough to permit you to join us, Tony," he said before continuing to his office.

"Thank you for your kind wishes, Mr Smythe," I told his back.

"What family difficulty?"

I turned to see Jaspersson's cold-pinked face set in its habitual leer. Jaspersson leered even while sleeping off a hangover at the back of the file room.

"What family difficulty?" he repeated as he tugged off his overcoat.

Merry arrived at that moment and pumped my hand in enthusiastic welcome. Then he repeated Jaspersson's question. I turned it back on him by asking after the little gentlemen, whom Merry could never resist discussing. After offering the latest on their progress, he once again described his notion to move to Los Angeles and sell the Ford-

Edison electric car once it was ready for market. At first, such talk had been merely a spill valve for his overflowing enthusiasm, but by then he seemed at least half serious. He even showed us a brochure from the Los Angeles Chamber of Commerce.

"Land and sunshine. A cornucopia. And a whole river piped two hundred miles across a desert to water lemon trees and fill bathtubs, all built in five years. Imagine it—a pipe big enough for a locomotive. Go west, young men, I say to the little gentlemen. Go west. It has always worked for me. But you," he said to me, "you have gone east and added to your family, I hear."

"So that's it," Jaspersson said. "You dog, Grams." Even louder, he said, "Grams knocked a baby out of some New York *kvinne* with k-nockers so big they clattered him about the room." The sally pleased him so much that he repeated it twice more.

A few half interested advisors turned their eyes toward us. "I'm an uncle," I told them. "To an orphaned niece."

Jaspersson stopped chortling and looked down. But a moment later he was mumbling to himself about *kvinne* and k-nockers.

Just as I was preparing to set out on my rounds, The Boss came by. He shook my hand warmly and asked briefly about my niece. He didn't linger overlong, but I spotted Mr Smythe watching us from across the room.

> To grant a share of profits to a confirmed drunkard, gambler, or to one addicted to any other evil habit, would be largely instrumental in promoting his degradation. As one of the principles of the Ford Plan is to elevate mankind, every conceivable effort should be made to reform an unfortunate of this type and instill him with new ambition, which will enable him to have higher and better ideals.

That day I went to a dozen houses to approve new men for profit-sharing, but I didn't enjoy it as much as usual. I was unsettled, conflicted. I counselled purity while feeling Thia's warmth beside me. I encouraged men above all else to save for the future and for their families, encouraged young wives to leave employment to their husbands and to focus on filling their homes with children and warmth. But all the while I was thinking that Gennaro and Alessandra were heroes because they had aspired to leave their daughter a new world rather than lace curtains and a tidy bank book. And yet, at the same time the realization percolated into my marrow that my dangerous—and risible—fling with Thia could easily have cost me the very position which now allowed me to keep Lisa decently clad, housed, and fed.

After all the new men, I had time for a few withheld men, those either denied profits or temporarily taken off them. The last of those was young Sal Messi, whom I hadn't visited since approving him for profits months earlier. He'd recently come to work wearing clothes with more patches than the eyes of the pirate fleet and had confessed to his straw boss that he'd lost his presentable clothes along with his pay packet while gambling in a back-room joint off St Aubin. Smythe had taken him off the profits and sent me a sternly worded memorandum about selecting "only those men likely to benefit from a scheme that depends upon the sober judgment of each advisor." Naturally, he had sent a carbon copy to The Boss.

Before rapping the knocker (*k-nockers, k-nockers*), I tried to set aside my resentment at Smythe's deviousness and Thia's betrayal by mentally rehearsing homilies about the correlation between Good Habits and Good Home Conditions.

Messi answered the door wearing a ragged shirt, even more ragged trousers, and a rueful smile. He led me into a parlor emptied of some of the furniture so prominent during my last visit.

"Almost I break my wife's heart, selling the sideboard," Messi said.

Hovering at the parlor's far threshold, Mrs Messi made a discreet noise which might have signified heartbreak.

"Mrs Messi," I said politely. She smiled nervously in reply.

"A fine Messi I've made of things," her husband said with a complicated smile. "Please sit, Mr Grams."

As I did so, a girl of Mrs Messi's age or slightly younger appeared at her side only to disappear an instant later, leaving a vague impression of nervous muslin. The girl's quick footsteps sounded from a hidden hallway but stopped after only a few strides. I pictured her skulking behind a doorway like a child listening to quarrelling parents.

"My wife's sister, Sofia," Messi said. "She came to live with us, if you need that for the report. She's a bit strange," he added, as he handed over the documents needed for my evaluation.

I opened the bank book. Current balance $7.09. Two months previous, the balance had been $187.82.

"The first bad month, that's me losing the money at the gambling," Messi said. "Last month, that's me getting so sore at my foreman and Henry Ford for taking me off profits I go lose more money. I'm in debt if I didn't sell the furniture. But since I teach everybody a lesson by giving all my money to that damn *fiorentino* and sell my wife's furniture to learn her good for marrying me, ever since then no gambling."

I looked up at his wife, who was nodding faintly, a serious look on her face. When she caught me looking, she stopped and turned her head, a young girl's gesture.

"So you're reformed?" I asked sceptically.

He shrugged his shoulders. "That *fiorentino* and me, we're great adventurers together when I gamble. To the North Pole, *contro il destino*. Then I come to tell him I got no money, and all of sudden I'm selling my wife's sideboard. I don't want no new back room, no phony adventure. We lived with the profits and without them, and it's better with them. Especially with Sofia here now."

I nodded with slow sternness so that I could pick the most suitable gambit. I decided to go with an old standard, a variation on the Drunkard's Reformation.

"You're not a father, Sal."

"No, Mr Grams."

"But you intend to be? One day?"

"Yes, sir."

In the background, I saw Mrs Messi's hand go anxiously to her belly.

> When a woman's condition has to be stated on the investigation report, the following "Code" must be used: "This woman visiting friends in the country." However, unless this information is positively necessary to complete the investigation report, no mention shall be made of this condition.

"Maybe," I said, "you should think again."

"What?"

"A father has to teach his children. What lesson can you teach a child when you gamble away all your family's money?"

"I wouldn't—"

"How to wear shabby hand-me-downs that let the cold right through? How to go hungry?"

"But, Mr Grams, I wouldn't do—"

That was as far as the gambit should have gone. But somehow I couldn't prevent myself pushing onward. "How to get feverish and sickly? How to be buried in tiny coffins?"

"No!"

"You don't trust yourself with the money, do you, Sal? Not yet."

His silence spoke for him.

"Do you trust your wife?"

After some hesitation, he nodded.

"Even to tell you, 'No, you can't have the money' when you bluster at her and insist"—I stared at Mrs Messi and let myself get loud, as Merry had taught me—"that you're a hardworking man who should be allowed some of the money you break your back all day to bring home?"

Mrs Messi straightened a little and let her hands fall to her thighs. Eventually, her husband nodded.

"Then," I told him, "your wife will open a savings account in her name only. Once you give me proof of that, I will instruct Employment to put your pay in her name and restore your profits. Mrs Messi, can you come to the factory each week at the proper time?"

She said something inaudible.

"Mrs Messi?"

"Yes, sir," she said, a look of nervous wonder on her face.

Obligations at the bank had forced Andrew to cancel his supper visit, so we were all speaking Italian, allegedly for the sake of the *bambina,* who was ignoring us in favor of the large hunk of freshly baked *civraxiu* in front of her. Rather than dipping it into her beef stew, she was using it to further mash her potatoes.

I told my family about my visit to the Messis (omitting names, naturally). I was hoping for praise, and Kitty obliged. Carl asked only how much the unnamed family paid in rent and whether it wasn't the case that smaller but respectable quarters might be had for half that. In response, Mother pointed out to everyone but Carl the expense and disadvantages suffered by a man living without wife or family.

Angela, of course, signalled her disapproval of my story with myriad *hmms, tsks,* and sighs.

"And so," I asked Angela, "when Kitty executes her grand plan for Andrew—"

"Honestly, Tony," Kitty protested.

"Well, let's say that in five years Andrew were to become a degenerate of some kind. A drunkard. Even a drug addict." (*Why Don't I Go?*) "Do you really think she shouldn't be able to hold on to his money so that her children eat enough and sleep warmly?"

Kitty began, "Andrew would never be such a beast—"

"I'd kill him first," Carl said in English.

"No, you wouldn't," I said, also in English. "We wouldn't."

It took everyone, myself included, a moment to realize what I'd meant. Nobody said anything. I didn't have the heart look at Angela. I knew how hard she was working to decide that none of us was thinking about her worthless husband.

Lisa had finished mashing her potatoes and was now glopping bits into her stew before spooning them out with a triumphant smile on her face. Somehow, that was what made me sad.

Chapter 12

A FEW WEEKS LATER, I WAS WITH KITTY AND ANDREW IN A GRATIOT Street market. Which is to say I was alone.

"It's Swiss, not Italian," he said about a bar of chocolate. *I love you more, you goose.*

"It's the kind you find in Italy, so to Mother it's Italian," she said. *No, I love you more, you Christmas goose.*

I walked away from them. Turning the corner, I found myself the recipient of a pleasant smile from a girl of about Kitty's age. She was Italian, of course, possibly Roman. She was unremarkable but properly shaped. Though she was even shorter than I, her flimsy coat didn't quite reach to the hem of her muslin dress.

"Hello, Mr Grams! It *is* Mr Grams, isn't it?" She looked at my face long enough to see me nod hesitantly, then turned her eyes demurely downward. "Don't you know me? Sofia Ragnelli? Anna Messi's sister? Anna is Salvatore's wife. You came to the house."

I remembered—the girl who'd snuck off to eavesdrop.

I took her proffered hand. She squeezed lightly with her thumb and first two fingers. There was something at once shy and appraising in how her fingers lingered on mine. She raised her eyes briefly, and I noticed she was slightly cross-eyed, or possibly wall-eyed.

"And how is Sal, Miss Ragnelli?"

"Very well, Mr Grams. He ain't— there's no more of the other."

I nodded sagely. *Unpleasant business, of course, but these young scamps must be set straight, my dear.*

"And your sister? She's well, I hope." I asked.

Several complicated things happened to her expression and then abruptly stopped happening when she smiled broadly. "Oh, yes. I'm doing her marketing now." She raised her half full wicker basket.

She paused and again looked demurely at the floor before looking back up. Cross-eyed, I decided.

"I wonder, Mr Grams," she began before falling mute.

"Yes, Miss Ragnelli?"

"Well, I wonder if you might join us for dinner some night soon? Sal says you treated him swell. So did Anna. They were saying as we ought to invite you to dine, you know, to thank you, and, well, here you are, so..."

The Boss loved this sort of thing. *Fraternal, not paternalistic.* Even so, I was crafting a polite refusal when Kitty popped out from behind the Kelloggs. "He'd be delighted."

"Oh, good," Sofia said. "Next Saturday at six o'clock? You know the address, of course."

"I'd be delighted," I said, glancing at my sister, who pretended not to notice.

I doffed my hat at Sofia as she went to finish her shopping. Kitty poked my chest playfully. "What kind of a man invites himself to dinner for such reasons?"

It's a generous lover who wants the whole world to be in love, I suppose.

Dinner with the Messis consisted of lasagna and cautious conversation in English about the winter weather and poor, brave Belgium. There were also a number of uneasy looks between husband and wife. I hoped that Messi hadn't gambled away dessert.

Sofia's fingers had lingered on my elbow when I met her at the door, and her eyes lingered on me throughout dinner except when she looked down at the table. (What I'd earlier mistaken for demureness was simply a tactic to keep people from looking directly into her crossed eyes.) Eventually, she spun slow spoonfuls of soda-fountain chocolate ice cream in her mouth as her eyes appeared to appraise my ears. I found myself imagining her eyes rolled back in off-kilter sexual transports.

As Sofia (lingeringly) helped me into my coat, she suggested that I escort her on Wednesday to an Uplifters lecture on good soap and good government. "Maybe we could get ice cream after," she said.

The Uplifters lecture was dreary, and The Boss wasn't standing by the punch bowl. Even if it hadn't been bitterly cold, I would still have ignored Sofia's hints about how much she enjoyed long walks in the park. I escorted her home as quickly as civility permitted.

The next day, Ross rang me at work and left a couple messages. Smythe handed me one of the messages himself. "The *Free Press,*" he said. "Not spilling any secrets, are we, Tony?"

"Just warning him how to protect against fraudsters, Mr Smythe."

I guess adders smile while they think about striking. But I still believe that man is the sneakier species.

After work, I used a pay 'phone downstairs to ask Ross what he wanted.

"The scoop of the century and a highland lassie who blows the bagpipes like a gale with lipstick."

"If you'll settle for a scoop of ice cream and a walk in the park, I could introduce you to my charming friend Sofia."

We met a half-hour later in a bar he knew. Two hours after that he was driving us to a cathouse at the far edge of Ferndale. He drove erratically, one hand loosely on the wheel, one hand tightly around a flask of rye, but I was too drunk to care.

The cathouse was a two-story Victorian girded by trees and surrounded by dead cornstalks chittering in the breeze. Ross drove a quarter-mile past it and parked on a rutted lane. "Cops who raid these places sometimes put a car at the top of the drive. Better to leg it through the fields. Even on this wobbly pin."

We walked along the lane, passing the flask back and forth.

"Wilkes," Ross said as we stepped onto the front path. "He has us pegged, and no mistake. Fairy tales we're spinning about the war and the rest, and that's that. Grim fairy tales. Well, tonight I'm gonna dress up a whore like Cinderella and poke her till one of us turns into a pumpkin."

It was a pretty high-class place inside. Ross picked a half convincing redhead and stumbled upstairs after her. I picked a plump, dark-haired woman with gray-blue eyes. I called her Thia and made her call me Scimmia. When she was naked, I used her lipstick to paint a scar-smile beneath her belly, but I was drunk and she was ticklish, so it ended up looking like a rash.

I told her to sit on the edge of the bed and stare up at me. I pointed my manhood at her nose and set to work. It was a raw task, and in the end I mostly missed her face. Seconds after climax, my penis looked forlorn and gonorrheal.

The memory was still there. You can't kill memories on purpose.

Trying to pull a handkerchief out of the pocket of the jacket I'd laid on the vanity table, I tripped and fell, hitting my shoulder on the ornate brass footboard. There's probably some way to apologize to a whore without meaning, "I wish both of us were dead." But I didn't know it, so I just lay on the floor as she started to dress. Eventually, I managed to find my feet and stumble outside. Ross joined me a little while later. We knelt in the snowy field for a while, vomiting what we could.

I must have managed to wind my alarm clock because the next morning it clanged like the Crystal Palace line. My stomach burned, my head throbbed, and someone had coated my throat with dead-fish paste. My aching shoulder bore a bruise the size of a baseball.

After bathing too long and shaving vindictively, I pulled on my last cleanish suit.

I met Carl at the front door. He looked as miserable as I felt. We chuckled quietly at each other. Once we were on the street, he said, "Ma thought—hoped—maybe you were with that Roman skirt."

"Nope. Where are you all the time these days?"

"Why? You gonna put it in my file?"

We walked the rest of the way in silence.

Chapter 13

HALF A PREGNANCY LATER, SMYTHE WORE HIS ADDER'S SMIRK AS HE escorted me into The Boss' office.

The Boss was seated, his elbows on the desk, his face serious. Seated across from him was Sal Messi, shoulders hunched, eyes toward the floor. I wondered if he'd been caught gambling again. If so, at least he still had a tidy suit, innocent of grease and oil.

"Have a seat, please, Mr Grams," The Boss said.

As I did so, Smythe took up a flanking position. He was still smirking.

"Do you care to repeat to Mr Grams what you've just told me?" The Boss asked Messi.

"Why not?" Messi looked up at me. "Sofia is in the family way."

I almost congratulated him before I caught wise. The lingering fingers, the sucked ice cream. The girl had already tried those on somebody else, and they'd worked. But for whatever reason, she'd wanted easier prey.

After a long silence, The Boss began, "Mr Grams, Sal here seems to think—"

"I invite you into my home," Messi said. "I have to let you in, then I *invite* you, and you..."

"The truth is always best, Tony," Smythe said.

"The truth is it's nothing to do with me," I told The Boss flatly.

"That's not how she tells it," Smythe said.

"Has she told it to you, Mr Smythe?" I asked. His rat twitch and knowing smile didn't disguise that he hadn't spoken with the girl.

The Boss asked, "The girl definitely says it was Mr Grams?"

"I say it, too," Messi replied, glaring at me.

"I was never even alone with her," I told The Boss.

"You calling us liars?" Messi asked.

He was angry, yes, but the anger wasn't really for me. "No," I replied. "I'm calling *her* a liar. You're just loyal."

"*Cazzate.*"

But it wasn't bullshit. And, somewhere, he knew it. A fine Messi, indeed.

"When's she saying this happened?" I asked The Boss. "Our torrid affair?"

Smythe crafted some delicate noises which the rest of us dismissed.

"When?" I asked Messi.

He frowned. "After that lecture. And a few times after."

"That was early February," I told The Boss. "But I can guarantee this woman was visiting friends in the country by January."

"Now that's a real lie," Messi said hopefully. "Sofia never left Detroit in January, and—"

"If her baby's born as late as September the first," I told The Boss, "I'll gladly have this talk again. But now I've got work to do."

The Boss believed me about Sofia Ragnelli, which meant Smythe had to conduct his campaign by whispering. Some of the advisors turned cool, others raised their eyebrows in unsavory fraternity. (*Fraternal* and *paternal.*) Jaspersson took a break from finding new ways to use the word "cockwurst" in order to test his alliteration on "*tettas.*" (He favored "tremendous" and "tasty.")

I wanted to wallop someone with a typewriter, but Merry reminded me that a man who couldn't laugh looked like a man with a guilty conscience. Fortunately, my colleagues seemed to forget after a while. Even I did, mostly. For the rest of the summer, I worked to forget Sofia. I worked even harder to forget Thia and romance altogether. I spent wholesome evenings at home. When Andrew and Kitty were too much in love for my moods and purposes, I spent wholesome evenings with Merry, Gulsa, and their little gentlemen (charades were our particular favorite). I treated beautiful ladies on the street like flowers in other people's gardens and ignored the overly attentive girls whose families depended on my 928s. I avoided whores at all costs. For that, Ross denounced me as a crape-hanger and a crummy crony, but he didn't let it interfere with our friendship.

Improbably, my efforts to forget succeeded, at least for a while.

Day after day, the war stacked corpses like wet cordwood in the trenches of the Western Front, and on the Eastern Front it strewed them through forest and field like fruit rinds. Detroiters talked constantly of the war, and the interest was especially keen in the Crystal Palace, where half the laborers were immigrants, many of them mourning for loved ones or fretting about those still within reach of the war. Fights often flared up—Germans with Italians, French with Austrians, German Jews with German Lutherans.

Yet for months I found myself almost appallingly cheerful. It helped that Sofia Ragnelli's daughter Maria came into the world early enough to exonerate me of fatherhood in all eyes but those of her more deluded relatives. More importantly, I found ways to fill the day with bustle that felt much like—and may even have been—usefulness. Five and half days each week, I tooled about Little Italy in runabouts and touring cars, preaching the gospel of thrift, improvement, and shower-baths. Outside of work, I drank in something like moderation, helped the little gentlemen with their sums, and debated Ross about any convenient subject. I discussed baseball with Andrew and chatted occasionally with Mother's matronly friends or with the smiling, beribboned packs of Yeses (Young Suffragettes) whom Kitty often assembled in our parlor. One memorable Sunday, I even gave Andrew permission to marry Kitty, though he insisted the wedding itself would have to wait until his next promotion.

And, of course, I spent time with Lisa. As she grew less likely to hide behind food, furniture, and bangs, I saw flashes of my brother in her. Little twitches of her lips and tilts of her head. The forthrightness, the longing for purpose. Some of that must also have come from her mother, of course. Much of her face did, as best I could judge from the photos Alessandra had sent. Every bit as clever as her parents, the child soaked up English. Within weeks of her arrival she was chattering brokenly, generally about automobiles or the inevitable triumph of the proletariat. She learned not to discuss the latter around Mother or the nuns at the parish school, but she kept faith with the cause. In that, she received some aid from "Angelica" (a friend of Alessandra's named Maria Tomaselli), who once each month sent Lisa a package of socialist propaganda.

At first, we despaired of convincing Mother to call Lisa anything but "Elisabetta," and none of us could explain why Mother always called her "granddaughter" rather than "*nipote,*" especially given Mother's preference for Italian. Even my siblings and I often said "*nipote*" (Italian uses the same word for "niece" and "granddaughter"). But then, at the end of June, I heard Mother cheerfully tell Kitty that she would ask the egg man for an additional half-dozen eggs for little Elisabetta's birthday cake. Lisa's birthday wouldn't be for another month. But Elisabetta's would be in two days. All that time, Mother had actually been saying "(grand)daughter."

The realization left me breathless with pain for Mother—to mourn so long that she no longer noticed the mourning. But it also worried me. Gennaro and Alessandra had died for their daughter's future, and I couldn't permit Mother to curl Lisa's hair in a dead girl's ribbons. I tried to defend Lisa against the ghost of Elisabetta by removing her frequently from Mother's care, so we often went strolling in the evening and on weekends.

For a while, Kitty was my ally. Through that fall, she, the nuns, and *Photoplay* continued to educate Lisa and to defend her against old Ghilarza. But then, in November, Andrew received a promotion and a raise in salary, and Kitty promptly succumbed to an acute bridal mania which ended only after New Years Day, when she and Andrew vanished in a blizzard of rice and snow on their way to Niagara Falls. After that, the house quickly emptied out. Andrew bought a nearby house (on Church, near Six Mile), and Kitty moved there. Then Carl announced that he had taken a room in a boarding house on John R.

Despite frequent nights with his mysterious lady friends, Carl had been dogged in his thrift and could easily afford to lodge at a respectable boarding house. And, indeed, except for paying rent, he remained thrifty, especially when it came to Lisa's expenses. Of course, I had little financial reason to kick as I was no longer responsible for Kitty. Besides, by then I was earning nearly $200 per month. (Imaginary Alessandra: "You were *receiving* nearly $200 per month.") Even so, that was when my unnatural good cheer began to vanish. Kitty and Andrew were planning for children, as was Carl. But what was I planning for? Growing old alone and shrinking enough that I would have to wear schoolboy suits in the last years before my gold-plated watch? After yet another day of helping new men and their new women, after yet more midnight masturbation brought on by yet again watching Theda Bara in *Under Two Flags*, I would often lie back and feel *angry*. I was angry at Carl and Kitty for leaving, at Mother and Angela for believing in God, and at God himself, who, if He did exist, had proven over and over again to be the sort of foreman who punched in forty minutes late, eyes bloodshot and shirttails dangling, only to disappear into a dark closet to sleep until the lunch trolley came. While he slept, the angels on the line had misassembled my body and my life.

At about this time, President Wilson was running for re-election by promising to keep America out of the war. He won just in time to get us into the war.

It was a warm April day in 1917 when America formally declared war, but America and Detroit shivered with suspicion and spiteful ignorance masquerading as patriotism. We had been tense for months. In February, when the street car strike ended and the first car left the yards directly across from the Highland Park plant, the wife of one of my men rang in a panic to say that she'd seen a Gatling gun mounted atop the car. She was terrified that the strike had turned violent or even that the Germans were planning to attack America's street cars. Only days later did I discover that what she had taken to be a Gatling gun in fact had been a motion picture camera put there by the Ford Photography department to chronicle the resolution of the strike.

Once war was declared, every camera looked like a gun, every cloud like a bomb-laden Zeppelin. Detroiters half expected to find U-boats sneaking through the canals into the lake. And the fear only intensified as anti-German stories appeared in every 'paper (many of them, I've since learned, based on propaganda by the federal government's Committee on Public Information). Sometimes Ross complained—quietly—about the stories he had to write.

Given the new climate of suspicion, Merry repeatedly had to protest his loyalty to America. When that didn't work, he had to explain in detail how Kurds felt about the Ottoman Empire and Haji Wilhelm both. On the streets or on a trolley, I occasionally had to remind people that, firstly, I was an *American* dago and, secondly, that the *Italian* dagos had been fighting the Krauts for years before America entered the war. Detroit's Russians had much the same problem, especially after the February revolution overthrew the Tsar and further confused the know-nothings.

Mr Ford's pacifist declarations fell utterly silent once the River Rouge tractor plant began to produce Liberty boats for the war. Both the Rouge and Highland Park were soon producing rumors faster than vehicles: German spies had infiltrated the chemical laboratories;

Pinkertons had shot a would-be assassin at the threshold of Mr Ford's bedroom in his Fair Lane estate; Mr Ford himself had shot the assassin; the assassin had succeeded, and German conspirators had replaced Mr Ford with a Hunnish doppelganger bent on sabotaging production. In Educational, the advisors began to gather in small, muttering groups. Periodically, those small groups would clump into larger ones muttering a little louder that all the smaller groups probably were Kraut espionage cells. The constant formation and dissolution of suspicions and alliances was so absorbing that I found it difficult to concentrate on my work.

I didn't appreciate the full reach of the insanity until late in May, when I found myself standing in the military recruitment office trying to turn my year of college into a second lieutenant's commission. "Okay, okay," I urged the polite lieutenant. "As an infantryman, then."

He looked over my shoulder, where there happened to be a coat-rack. He was simply trying to avoid my eyes while refusing me, but it made me realize that the Army would rather have enlisted the coat-rack. At least the uniform would've hung evenly.

I must have suspected that they wouldn't take me, but I suppose that being chosen would have compensated for being chosen. As it was, I left with a deferment. A deferment and a trembling in my legs that worsened all the way to the tram stop. *Stupid!* To seek glory after Gennaro's warnings, after Gennaro's fate. To condemn Lisa—and Mother—to life on a private's salary. To condemn Lisa to Mother's dangerous love. I was a fool.

"You're a good man and a good advisor, Tony, but that won't be enough."

Merry and I were sitting together in Eloy's, chewing our shepherd's pies without tasting them. Dismissals were in the air at Educational, and Merry felt sure that he would soon be out of a job.

"Fortunately," he said, smiling wanly, "I have followed my own advice. My savings account is fat, and my home is very nearly my own. And you?"

Though not yet fat, my savings account, like its signatory, had begun to go slightly soft around the middle. "I'm okay. But I don't think it will come to that, Merry, and surely not for you. If they can dismiss one of us, it'll be me. You've been with Educational from the start."

Merry smiled a bit more sincerely. "No, if *Smythe* could dismiss one of us, it would be you. But that is because Dr Marquis is fond of you. And since Dr Marquis is fond of you..."

"But I can't see why shouldn't you also rem—"

"We advisors have been too successful for our own good. We are no longer needed." He stared into my eyes and frowned. "Besides, they are cleaning the office, Tony. The big men and Ford, and even Dr Marquis, for all he has a kind word for everyone."

"Cleaning?"

"There is a war. When there is a war, men want to be among men they trust. Americans among Americans. So they will get rid of those who aren't Americans. Or American enough. They can't do that in the factory, of course. They can get rid of the laborers who sing songs for the Kaiser—you notice that they have started to do so already, yes?—but they need men on the line. Especially because the more Americans they send to Europe to fight, the more the big men will need Negroes and men like us on the line."

Us.

"But the offices, Tony, the starched collars, those they can clean." He sighed a laugh. "Like a Chinaman in a laundry."

My throat made noises of protest, but I quickly fell silent as I realized that he was right. With all the stupidity and fear around us, in the nation, the city, and the plant, there was no reason to imagine that Educational would be an island of wisdom and sobriety. After all, we advisors were in charge of making fine American gentlemen. Surely each of us should come as close as possible to embodying that ideal.

Merry chuckled grimly and said, "All afternoon I have been thinking of Los Angeles. But what do I know of Los Angeles but pictures of lemons and alligator pears? Twenty years ago, okay, I moved to New York knowing less. But I was young then, with no wife, no little gentlemen. And yet I am still thinking of Los Angeles."

He locked his eyes with mine. His eyes, like his body, had a strange, almost immobile intensity. Only his wrist moved, making the fork stir the shepherd's pie in small, slow circles. He didn't look like the new man of happier times. He looked, and I felt, like an old man.

Chapter 14

"You're a good advisor and a good Ford man, Tony."

"Yes, Mr O'Hara." I so happy I work at da Ford! Pleasa don'ta fire me!

"And a proud American."

"Yes, Mr O'Hara."

A week or so after my conversation with Merry, with whispers of dismissals becoming ever louder, I was standing in O'Hara's tidy office. He sat behind his desk, leaning back in his chair. There was an empty chair beside me, but he'd given me no invitation to sit.

"Good, good," O'Hara said. "Not longing to go back to Italy? A fine ally in the war against tyranny."

"My home's here, Mr O'Hara. So's my family." It is dispiriting to use the truth in order to avoid unpleasantness. On the other hand, it's usually not as dispiriting as the unpleasantness itself.

He nodded approvingly.

"May I ask what this is about, sir?" Had Merry been right—was I being dismissed for being foreign? Or maybe for being subversive—had someone had learned that Maria Tomaselli was still sending Lisa socialist materials, even through the wartime post? Were the rumors true about Ford operatives' reading our mail? Was Smythe reading my mail?

"You've heard the stories, Tony. Ten thousand Krauts bivouacked in the woods beyond Dearborn. A huge fleet of transatlantic Zeppelins headed to bomb New York and Chicago."

I nodded cautiously.

"Tony, it's crazy. Sure, those goddamned Huns would rape and plunder the country coast to coast just like they did poor, brave Belgium. But they ain't half stupid. They already have two fronts to keep them busy, and they couldn't get the greasers to keep us busy down south. So they're not going to attack us outright, not here. Kaiser Bill won't be sending Zeppelins or U-boats our way."

He looked at me expectantly. I nodded.

"No, it'll be sabotage, espionage." He said the words with gusto and thumped his palm against his desk for emphasis. "So we've gotta be on guard. Against men who talk peace but mean treason. Men who steal blueprints, weaken joints, slow the line."

"Yes, sir."

He paused and scrutinized me for a nerve-scraping moment. "Some of us fellows," he said quietly, "are putting the kybosh on all that. The APL, we're called. The American Protective League. And it ain't just Ford or Detroit, neither. It's tens of thousands of men across America, maybe hundreds of thousands by now. Keeping an eye out."

My scrotal skin crawled. I breathed deeply and told myself I was being squeamish. The Germans clearly were trying to disrupt any plant making war materiel, trying to attack the materiel itself on the lakes or in the canals headed for the Atlantic.

Horrifying or not, the existence of this APL also clarified a few mysteries. After America had entered the war, I'd noticed O'Hara and a man named Spark from Employment closeted together a great deal. Smythe had been drifting near them like a remora. This explained all that. It also explained why Smythe was so eager to worm his way into those conversations—if he played his cards right, the APL would give him a real chance to satisfy his long-thwarted desire to oversee operatives in the plant.

"And we ain't a blamed lynch mob stringing up niggers to pass a summer's night, neither," O'Hara continued. "We're official, pretty much. Working with the Justice Department and the Bureau of Investigation."

He waited.

I waited.

He said, "I'm asking you if you want to join us."

I wondered how this had happened. Had that polite lieutenant at the recruiting office passed along my name and my desperation? "Me, sir?"

He misunderstood my tone. "Sure, the gang is mostly Americans. Born Americans, mean to say."

Born Americans. So had the O'Haras booked cabins in the Irish Catholic section of the *Mayflower*, or had they simply stepped from their wigwams to meet it when it landed?

"Still, it's good to have you fellows aboard. You'll hear talk we can't."

Already I could hear Alessandra and Gennaro offering their opinion of my spying on the workers. But I could also hear the whispers of imminent dismissals, could hear Merry's speculation about the big men cleaning the department of those of us not born Americans. I could hear Gennaro and Alessandra's daughter crying from hunger at night after I was fired for refusing to join the APL and Carl was fired along with me. I could also hear a voice of caution advising me that Smythe would seek to use the APL against me, against anybody else he could, and that I might be able to defend myself better as a member.

And so I mustered a hearty smile and became Operative 3378 in the American Protective League, Eighth Industrial Division. As I left O'Hara's office, I knew something important had happened. It only gradually became clear what.

There were scores of American Protective League operatives scattered about the plant, and every week or so they scrawled or pecked out a report on whatever scraps of paper they found handy. It became my job to digest such scraps because O'Hara refused to allow typists near them. Mata Hari's recent arrest had apparently convinced him that most women were German spies desirous of procuring, above all else, APL operatives' semiliterate slanders against Ford employes who bought too few Liberty Bonds, contributed too little to the YMCA Patriotic Fund, and flew "enemy" flags in their parlors. (The flags generally turned out to be Norwegian or Belgian.) In typing the reports, I eliminated the misspellings and the worst of the solecisms, but I generally left the operatives' indignation intact because Mr O'Hara liked reports "with some darned punch."

In addition to lost time and protests from my conscience, my new job cost me $60 in Liberty Bonds and $185 more for the second-hand 1914 Ford runabout which I purchased after O'Hara hinted several times about showing loyalty to one's employer.

Though I resented being blackmailed into depleting my anti-Gramazio savings, in the end I was grateful for an excuse to buy the runabout. By then I was competent at the wheel and appreciated the freedom of an automobile, though generally I used it only on Sundays after church (which I attended with decreasing regularity), when Kitty, Lisa, Andrew, and I would go motoring through the farmlands surrounding

Dearborn. We soon found a favorite spot, a small meadow at the outer edge of a large farm owned by Janek Sedlacek, a friendly Bohemian with broad shoulders and vigorous eyebrows. Janek permitted us to picnic and lounge there, and sometimes he would even hitch his elderly mare to a nearby post and break bread with us. He always started out cheerfully, but more often than not, his mind would turn to the war, to his nephews in the old country fighting the Germans.

At some point Andrew and Lisa would chase each other about the meadow. Kitty would join them sometimes, depending on her leg. I suppose I could have joined in as well, but I grew very fond of sitting in the sun with a long stem of grass between my teeth and watching. Also, I often napped because working for the APL had already started to disturb my sleep.

One hot July morning I was driving us along the rutted dirt road leading to our meadow. Andrew sat beside me, a jaunty straw boatman's hat on his head. Kitty sat directly behind me, Lisa beside her. I caught glimpses of my niece hanging her head over the side, her unbonneted hair flapping. She looked like a rough collie.

"'It's woman's day,'" Kitty said to Lisa. She was reading from a brochure designed to sell the Model T to lady motorists.

Andrew grunted. "Not this again. Let the girl read it herself, if she's nuts enough to want to."

"'It's woman's day. Her own is coming home to her—her 'ownest own,'" Kitty continued. "'No longer a "shut in," she reaches for an ever-wider sphere of action—that she may be more the woman. And in this happy change the automobile is playing no small part.'"

Andrew groaned comically.

"'It has broadened her horizon—increased her pleasures—given her new vigor to her body—made neighbors of far away friends—and multiplied tremendously her range of activity.'"

"She wants a car?" I asked Andrew.

"Worse," he said.

"'Unlike other cars,'" Kitty continued pointedly, "'the Ford may be started, stopped and reversed without removing the hands from the steering wheel. There is no "hard work" about the operation.' Sounds pretty good, doesn't it, Lisa?"

"Yes, Auntie Kitty."

"And of course there's no 'grease or dirt to soil dainty gowns.' That would be such a comfort to women who are always insisting on having expensive new gowns from Godfrey's or Hudson's. Do you know, Lisa, I've always thought that those women purchase expensive gowns because they lack a more economical diversion."

"You're subtle as mortar fire," Andrew said.

"And do you know," my sister told Lisa, "there are questions of one's health as well."

"Health, Auntie Kitty?" Lisa asked with unconvincing innocence.

"'Out into the country's sweet, pure sunshine—to roam where the heart dictates—in touch with things vital and worthwhile, 'tis health and freedom and joy—'"

"'Tis?" Andrew asked. "What bird wrote that mush?"

"What's worse than her wanting a car?" I asked him quietly as Kitty continued.

"I'd buy her a car in a heartbeat," he said. "We could put it out front and keep it shiny. Plant orchids inside and use it as a hothouse. But she wants me to teach her to drive."

"I like going to the country, Auntie Kitty," Lisa exclaimed. "It's almost as keen as the movies."

"Well, you're not alone, pet," Kitty told her. "'There are women who love the outdoor life, who crave exercise and excitement, who long for relief from the monotony of social and household duties, who have said, "I wish I were a man." Well, the motor car is the end of all their troubles.'"

"And the beginning of all mine," Andrew said.

He'd lost, of course, but the play-acting and the grumbling continued until we reached Janek's meadow. As Andrew and Lisa gamboled about after lunch, I reminded Kitty that I'd already offered to teach her to drive.

"Oh, but I want Andrew to do it."

For some reason it made me think of Thia—which, to my self-contempt, I often found myself doing, even then. Yet again, I had to strain to get her out of my head.

At the first hint of evening, we returned to the motor. Mother was expecting us for supper, and Dearborn was a sundown town. In their crisply laundered clothing, Andrew and Lisa almost certainly counted as white, and, on most days and with most people, Kitty and I did also. But in those days Negroes had just started arriving in Detroit in large numbers, which somehow made me whiter to most Anglo-Saxons but darker to a surly few. And I didn't want the surly ones squinting at me in the twilight.

The drive back was quiet and grateful. Kitty rode beside me silent and faintly smiling, while in the back Andrew and Lisa both dozed in perfectly mixed sunshine and breeze. We couldn't have hoped for a better day.

A few weeks after Merry had predicted it, there was a general winnowing of Educational's staff. Some blamed The Boss, some blamed distant eminences like Assistant Superintendent "Cast-Iron" Charlie Sorensen. A few even blamed Mr Ford. The Boss spent much of one Friday reassigning or discharging the men one by one, and Smythe spent that same time watching, perched like a turkey buzzard sucking carrion jobs down his gullet.

O'Hara assured me that I would survive the purge, so I escaped to my rounds. When I returned that evening, I found a note from Merry saying that he'd been dismissed.

As requested, I met him for supper at Eloy's. I promised him I'd had nothing to do with his dismissal, and he believed me. He even forgave me for joining the APL. But there was little either of us could say, and so after his meal had cooled and his milk had warmed, Merry at last summoned the strength to go home and give the bad news to Gulsa and the little gentlemen.

Like many of the survivors of the purge, I came to the office early on Saturday, starched with zeal and employability. There we found men in denim overalls pushing Educational farther into the common room. By eleven o'clock, one of the accounting departments began to occupy the ceded territory.

It was a large territory. Although more foreign Americans remained than I had anticipated, there weren't many of us. Indeed, there weren't many advisors. Before the day ended, we began to call ourselves "the few men."

Under the new efficiency measures, home visits became far more rare, which kept us in the office more. I soon missed the old rounds, the visits to Little Italy, the cool breeze across a moving Model T. Being in the office also put me even more under Smythe's scrutiny. With the advent of the APL, the man seemed to spend his days lurking in doorways.

Although I stopped teaching for the English School (also much pared down), my duties with the APL kept me busier than ever. As being so constantly in the office began to depress my spirits, I bought a second-hand 12" Underwood so that I might take my APL typing home. I felt better when I could leave Ford while the summer sun stood above the horizon and then eat dinner with Mother and Lisa.

Not that dinner with Mother and Lisa was without difficulties:

Enter the Ghost of Elisabetta, which takes Lisa's seat.
MOTHER: (*Speaking Italian throughout*) Sit down, Elisabetta. Your food is getting cold.
LISA: (*Speaking English throughout*) The table's full.
MOTHER: Don't be silly.
LISA: There's a little girl in my seat. Tell her, Zio Tony.
Tony piles his green beans high and hides behind them.
MOTHER: You heard your uncle. Sit down.
LISA: Not till you make the baby with the pee in her hair get out of my chair.
Tears welling, Mother clasps hand to heart.
TONY: The baby is just a ghost, kitten. She'll go away if you slang at her.

Lisa had grown too old for bedtime stories, but as I typed my APL reports at the small desk in my room I took comfort in knowing that she was in the next room turning the pages of *Photoplay* or *The Saturday Evening Post.* She had recently lost all interest in Maria Tomaselli's socialist tracts.

Still, I kept those tracts handy. I had long since reported them to O'Hara because, although the APL was focused primarily upon Krauts, its members certainly had no love for socialists (or union men). So I hadn't wanted APL operatives somehow sniffing out the propaganda and filing reports on *me.* Especially not the operatives who reported to Smythe. So I'd told O'Hara that I surely hadn't asked for the propaganda, but I did occasionally read it in order to know my enemy. He'd approved of my initiative. In fact, he'd started sending me most of the Communist-themed reports, which multiplied after the Bolshevik Revolution occurred and Russians began to appear in odd places for odd reasons. Fortunately for me, actual expertise was unnecessary. It was actually easier to track Bolo sympathizers than Boche spies because whenever a

Red Russian went wandering (or to the toilet), a White Russian would vindictively urge his straw boss to fire the man on the spot.

After a while, even coming home in daylight stopped feeling like sufficient compensation for compiling the APL reports, which were so often petty and unforgiving, motivated by personal vengeance rather than patriotism. Bringing them home felt like tracking sludge from the factory floor across Mother's carpets.

Still, there *were* Bolos and Boche skulking about the Ford plants, and one of every two or three dozen reports contained vital information. In November, authorities arrested six hundred German saboteurs throughout the Great Lakes area. O'Hara and Clemett had puffy chests and hearty grins for a week. For a while, I returned to my bleary-eyed reading and clumsy typing, proud that I had played some small rôle in preventing very real attacks. Even Mother, who had guessed something of my new task, read the *Free Press* article about the arrests and said it was a good thing for Italy and all the boys in the trenches.

But I've lost the thread.

This needs to be said. The other Americanization. How Ford became more interested in its employes' political convictions than in their thrift and hygiene. Even poor Merry's dismissal. It needs to be said. But not yet, not right here. Right here, I'm using it more as a sign of the cross than anything else, my fingers raised against evil spirits.

A few months after Congress declared war, not long before the reductions at Educational, Andrew's bank reorganized along nativist lines. He was too valuable to dismiss outright, but they cut his pay and reduced his responsibilities. One Sunday afternoon, when the sun had begun to set noticeably sooner on the sundown towns but the air was still warm, Andrew said nothing as Kitty erratically steered us along country roads. I thought he was sulking about her driving, but the next day, despite the irony of such patriotism, he enlisted. (Despite?)

He was erect enough to fill out the uniform satisfactorily, white and educated enough to receive a lieutenant's commission. They attached him to the ambulance corps of the 33rd Infantry (the Rainbows), which was promptly transferred to the 42nd Division and sent to the Camp Mills cantonment on Long Island. After his initial training, Andrew had only a day's leave with Kitty before the train left for New York. He was proud and dashing. She was clear-eyed and composedly tender.

After he left, Kitty broke crockery for a week. For even longer, Andrew's name was an epithet, as were "Army" and "duty."

words learnt by heart

By February, the Rainbows had landed in France and soon saw their first action at the front. Men slow to the gas masks or unlucky in matters of shrapnel began to bleed from horrible places.

little glory to be had in an army

The names of the dead trickled into the 'papers, but we didn't notice. By then, we'd learned already of Andrew's death. Mere days after stepping off the boat in France, he'd fallen beneath the wheels of a Ford ambulance, which fatally crushed his windpipe. The motor car—the beginning and end of all his problems.

Chapter 15

Andrew's death put me in mind of Gennaro's, of Alessandra's, even of Elisabetta's. I think much the same happened with Mother. At any rate, the both of us were furious at the world, and it was far worse for Kitty. For a few weeks afterward, she believed herself with child. When she realized that her body was simply in disarray, she wept for two days before breaking the remainder of her crockery and coming back home to install herself in Carl's old room. Andrew's savings were meeting the demands of Kitty's mortgage, and once his death benefits came through, she would have more than enough to maintain a separate household. But it was to have been *their* home.

There was no actual removal work when she came home. Kitty couldn't bring herself to live in the new house, but she couldn't bring herself to leave it, either.

It was just as well there was no removal work. That winter was bitterly cold, with temperatures several times dropping to fifteen below. Our neighbors' pipes froze and burst. In January, perhaps a thousand men came to the plant with frostbitten ears, and several men froze to death on their way home from work (though the *Ford Times* denied it). Our house was never truly warm because the national conservation and rationing orders made coal hard to come by. (Even Ford itself had to shut down the Highland Park plant for a day.) Whenever possible, Mother kept the oven full and the stove top crowded, both to warm the kitchen and to produce siege walls of pasta intended to safeguard us, especially Lisa, against illness. Pasta and Pape's Cold Compound were our bulwarks against winter.

I bought a fur hat which made me look as if I'd lodged my skull in a badger's anus. But it saved my ears. I tramped to and from work, my absurd hat full of unamusing notions about how hard and sullen the earth must be. The Rouge plant had largely switched production from Fordson tractors to Liberty engines for the war, but I thought perhaps it should continue to manufacture at least some tractors attached to special plows for gravediggers. But maybe the ground was softer along the Western Front.

That winter's brutality only made it worse for Kitty—harder for her to go out, harder for friends to come calling. Even so, the Yeses did come at first, though Kitty generally refused to see them or to answer their notes, and eventually they stopped visiting. Still, our nearer neighbors often dropped in: Mrs McConnell from one side, the Widow Vivani from across the street, Mrs Daszkowski from the other side. These were no-nonsense ladies capable of moral bullying, and Kitty couldn't turn them away because they always claimed to have come for Mother.

Mrs Daszkowski came the most frequently. She was a statuesque Polish woman of hale middle age who helped her husband run the corner market which bore his name. Only a month earlier she had lost a son in the war and still had two other sons in France. She would bring pungent cabbage dishes and pirogis, and she and Kitty would sit in the kitchen weeping quietly. Mother would join them sometimes, speaking of Gennaro and Elisabetta. The conversations always trailed off when I entered the room, so I learned to stay away. There was a frightening possessiveness in their grief, as if they had stuck personal flags in the graves of their dead. But it seemed a solace to them, and I desperately wanted some solace for Kitty. I kept thinking of Thia as she'd sloshed into the chair, into the bed. If staking Andrew's death like a forty-niner's gold claim would keep Kitty's innards from gurgling corrosively, would stop her from limping everywhere as she had begun to do, then I wouldn't interfere.

Lisa was the only one I could help. So when the cold was merely cutting rather than killing, I dragged her out of the house and we tramped about Highland Park and Hamtramck. Often we simply carried her Tuxedo Racer to Palmer Park, where I would let her sled for as long as I could feel my toes, sometimes even for a while longer. Seeing her in her heavy coat and gay red cap and mittens as she flew down a hill with a daring touch on the runners, I felt that sledding was the healthiest and most important thing she could be doing.

Lisa was learning to skate as well, though this made me uneasy.

Sledding was solitary, the work of aviators and racecar drivers. But skating was social, which vaguely involved boys, and Lisa had recently begun to mull over what to do about those creatures. She and the neighborhood girls would cluster together and circle the ice, eyeing the boys with veiled intensity. Sometimes it was simple curiosity; sometimes it was the tense gaze shared by predator and prey, though I couldn't have said which was which.

"Who killed Zio Andrea?" Lisa asked me.

We were stamping homeward, I with the Tuxedo Racer under my arm, she with a snowball in hand. She sighted a tree and threw. It flew well wide.

"Zio Tony?"

"Gavrilo Princip?" I hazarded.

"Grandmother says the Boche killed Zio Andrea. Mrs Daszkowski says so too. But Mama said it was the *capitalisti*."

"I'm sure that she did," I said in my jovial Zio Tony tone.

Lisa had a patient doggedness to her even then, and she wasn't having joviality. "Mama said this was the *capitalisti*'s war. All so Fiat can make cars and capitalists can steal Africa from the coloreds."

In those days it would still occasionally occur to me to marvel that just two years earlier the girl had stepped off the boat with but a few words of English. Now she spoke with the slightest of accents and resorted to Italian strictly for familial endearments and socialist terminology.

"Don't let the secret police hear you talking like that," I said. *Ha ha. Isn't that droll? Secret police in America? And of course because they don't exist, I don't work for them.*

"So you think Mama was wrong?" she demanded.

I should have patted her condescendingly on the head and thought about the warm coffee waiting at home (possibly even with a little rationed sugar). But foolishly I considered the question. Andrew, of course, had been killed by the ambulance driver—in itself, that was an accident. And in the grand scheme, his killers hadn't been the capitalists. Not even J. Pierpont Morgan and Charles Schwab had started the war. They had been smart, ruthless, and lucky enough to make more millions from it, but if it hadn't been their companies, it would have been other companies. Even giants swim in oceans, and whatever was moving whole continents to war, that was sloshing the tides like an elephant in a washtub. *Capitalismo*, perhaps. Or perhaps simply *stupiditá*, which scientists may one day discover to be the fifth fundamental force of nature.

Stupidity certainly shaped my own thoughts, which Alice proved when she tiptoed over to my desk from the clerical desks to let me know that I had an urgent 'phone call from Thia Mueller.

I'll allow that an intelligent fellow might also have answered the call. But he wouldn't have answered it with a hopeful song in his heart. It had been more than a year, nearly two, since Thia had ended our affair, and it had been months since I'd stopped cursing her on a daily basis. It was damfoolishness at its peak to skip behind Alice to the 'phone and to lift the receiver to my ear with sweating fingers.

"Tony? Is that you? Tony Grams?" Even over a scratchy connection, she sounded frantic.

"Yes. Thia. What is it?"

"I need your help, Tony. You'll help me, won't you?"

"Why should I do that, you heartless bitch?" said a smarter version of me in some smarter world.

In this world, I said, "Of course. Of course."

She asked me to come to her house so that she could explain in person. When I finished work a half-hour later, I did just that. Her family lived on Hurlbut near Charlevoix and the Four Mile circle in a stately red-brick home framed by prosperous trees. A Negro servant answered the front door and asked in a Southern accent how he might be of service. If Jefferson Davis had sounded half so refined, Grant would have surrendered out of deference to his betters. The Negro led me along oak floors into a sitting room with tall bay windows and elegant furniture in what I assumed to be the Austrian style.

Thia was at the center of the room, dressed in a simple white house frock, hair hanging loosely. She was facing away from the door, pacing, but she stopped and turned when the Negro cleared his throat discreetly to announce my presence. She looked as beautiful as ever. Striking. Arresting. All the best words for her were taken from accounts of labor battles.

She gestured to a sofa and took a seat in a facing high-backed armchair. Against her dress and the chair's eggshell upholstery, her hair was like a primitive painting of shadows. Seeing her felt like grabbing a frayed lamp cord.

"Thank you so much for coming, Tony."

At the last instant, I managed not to thank her for inviting me. I nodded.

"I'm so sorry to ring you out of the blue, but I didn't know—I wouldn't have if it weren't urgent."

"What's the matter?" I asked.

"It's Father. He hasn't been home for two nights. Mother and I have been beside ourselves, and only just this afternoon we received a telegram from the Department of Justice saying that Father had been detained."

"Detained?"

"Out in Oscoda," Thia said. "The Bureau of Investigation has been gathering up Germans, Austrians, and the like and holding them on farms for questioning. Suspected subversives. And they've taken Father." She waved her hands in exasperation. "For Heaven's sake, he and Mother left Austria because Jews can't get a fair chance there. He has no reason to spy for a country that despised him."

I didn't have the heart to tell her that this sort of thing hardly required reasons, at least not good ones. If I'd been more vindictive—or creative—I could have had her father interned months earlier simply by adding his name to the ever-growing list of potential subversives mentioned in my APL reports, which O'Hara (or perhaps his superiors) forwarded to the Bureau of Investigation. Or I could have simply scrawled an ill-spelled anonymous note and mailed it to any of the quasi-official spy groups—the APL, the National Security League, the American Defenders, the Sedition Slammers, the Terrible Threateners, etc.

So I could understand how her father had been interned. But I couldn't understand why she was talking to me about it. She knew all sorts of fine people with powerful golfing partners. I pointed that out as delicately as possible.

"Oh, I've talked to Commissioner Gillespie and even Clara Ford, whom I know from Girls' Protective," she replied. "And they've promised to help. But you have Dean Marquis' ear, and he has the ear of those same influential men. And sometimes men take requests more seriously when they come from other men."

"Sometimes we take them more seriously when they come from women," I said, not bothering to disguise my sardonic tone.

She blushed. "He's my father."

I thought resentfully that my family would have liked to have influential friends when our father had been imprisoned. But I also thought that no child should have to endure the unjust jailing of a father.

And I also thought that she was still heartbreakingly beautiful, sitting there, her eyes and lips wide and imploring. Of course, she probably knew how she looked. She probably would spend the rest of the evening being beautiful at any man who might help her.

"I'll do what I can," I told her, rising from the sofa.

"Thank you. His name is Sigismund. Glueck, not Mueller. Sigismund Glueck." She stood to shake hands.

"Tony?" she said as I turned to leave.

I stopped and faced her.

"I'm sorry," she said. "For how things ended. For how *I* ended things. I was— Well, a shambles, really. Over Benjy. To be that angry at someone and that desperate for him at the same time... And then you seemed like a human being, and I didn't want human beings."

I didn't know what to say to that. Did I forgive her? Should I? At long last, I said, "Thank you. And I will do what I can."

I left the Gluecks' intending to raise the matter with The Boss first thing in the morning. But as I walked to the Michigan trolley stop, I realized that Scimmia Gramazio would have shoved a rusty knife into the scrotum of a man who would have let somebody's father sit in jail for an extra night simply out of some dim sense of decorum. So I wandered about until I found a 'phone from which to ring The Boss. He was surprised but friendly. I was relieved to learn that I hadn't interrupted his supper.

"And you're certain that the man is innocent, Tony?"

"Well, of course I don't know him personally, sir. But I'm inclined to believe his daughter." I paused and phrased my next remark delicately: "As you know, sir, in times of war, a laudable patriotic vigilance can easily, ah—"

"Become lunatic terror," The Boss said with a chuckle at his own daring. "Yes, I'm painfully aware of that. And, while I have the opportunity, let me say that though I'm not officially enlisted in the APL, my duties do require reading many of its reports, and I've found yours to be refreshingly... judicious. It is no small thing to tar a man as a traitor. Or even as a 'slacker.' And beside the question of justice, an effective undertaking needs accurate information. Crying wolf and so forth."

"Thank you, sir," I said. Interesting. I'd gleaned enough to know that The Boss was aware of O'Hara's involvement in the APL, but I hadn't been sure whether he knew anything more concrete.

"Well, you've done right to bring this matter to my attention, Tony. An innocent man, particularly a solid citizen such as this Dr Glueck seems to be... Well, I'll speak with Mr Cole at the Bureau of Investigation tomorrow and see if we can't unravel the matter."

"Thank you, sir. And I know that Mrs Mueller will be grateful as well."

"Of course she'll be grateful," Ross said. "She'll be grateful to you and grateful to the twenty other dupes she has twisting arms for her. Lot of gratitude that skirt has. Lot of *nerve*. You shoulda kicked her to the curb, what you shoulda done. You want another, I know."

I put my hand over my glass. We were in the same bar to which we'd gone the night of our cathouse triumph, and Ross was drinking a lot faster than I. Like me, he'd been rejected by the army on physical grounds (his bum knee). Unlike me, he'd been rejected twice. He'd tried to enlist a few weeks after the declaration of war and then had tried again just hours previous. I'd been fighting the same urge. *Stupiditá* strikes again.

He stared disapprovingly at the interfering hand on my glass. "Better enjoy it before the prohibition," he explained. "Whole state's going dry."

"Not for a few months yet. Besides, it's not like bears in winter. You can't store liquor."

"Defeatist." After a slug, he added, "Some nerve, sitting in her parlor asking you a favor."

"It would've been jake if she'd been in *my* parlor?"

"So whaddya gonna do about her?"

I shrugged carefully, hoping not to anger the spasm which had settled in since Thia's return to my life. "I asked The Boss to look into it yesterday, and he said he'd talk to Cole over at the Bureau of Investigation."

"Not about her dad. About *her*," he said with a vague and expansive gesture. "You know, now that she's back."

"She's not back. Like you said, she was just asking a favor. I've served my purpose."

Ross gave that a raspberry. "And a tree-sittin' simian is my nephew. She was asking *you* a favor. You, Tony Grams, former beau."

"Get your stories straight. Thirty seconds ago she didn't care about me and was asking every man in Detroit."

"The shameless hoor," Ross said with a cheeky grin.

I laughed. "There's nothing to be done. Her father will go free or he won't, and either way she'll go back to ignoring me."

"Is that what you want?"

I shrugged. It wasn't, but that was just the loneliness and *stupiditá*.

"Well, if she breaks your heart again, you can always get her sent to Oscoda."

"You're a scholar and a gentleman, Ross Robertson."

"No, sir. I'm a fair reporter, a whizbang quaffer of spirituous potables, and a gimpy galoot not fit for this man's army, but I'm no gentleman."

"I withdraw the accusation."

"Durn tootin' you do."

That Friday, I received a note from Thia and felt another surge of idiot optimism. Her father had been released with the apologies of the Bureau of Investigation, and she was sure that I'd had a hand in it. Her father had asked her to invite me to call at my convenience.

And so after Carl and I kept one another awake through yet another Mass, I went to the prosperous trees and sturdy red bricks of the Gluecks' home. It was a cold but bright day at the border of winter and spring, and in the crisp sunshine, it was easy to see how thoroughly the front of the Gluecks' home had been vandalized with red, white, and blue paint.

A serious little man in oversized overalls was leaning from a rickety wooden ladder in order to scrub the highest splashes of paint. We raised our hats slightly to one another as I rang the bell.

The elegant Negro answered the front door and bade me follow him to his mistress. I found her seated in the same room, in the same chair as last time. But her hair was more elegantly arranged, and her smile was more carefree than I'd ever seen it.

She pressed my hand and kissed my cheek in greeting. "Thank you for coming," she said. "Thank you for helping."

"I still say Commissioner Gillespie must have swung things round for you."

"He had a hand, I'm sure, but my friends tell me Dean Marquis was important in the matter as well, and he certainly wouldn't have gotten involved without your help. I truly am grateful, Tony. And so is Father, of course, which he looks forward to saying in person."

"He's not home, then?"

"He's been detained at the office by one of his *problematischen Frauen*."

I raised my hands.

"'Problematical ladies.' That's Mother's term for his patients. She finds them a trifle ludicrous. She'll be joining us shortly as well."

"He sees patients on a Sunday?"

"Well, Sunday isn't the Sabbath for many of Father's patients, you see."

"Right." I'd learned that from my occasional home visits to Jewish workers.

"But today is your day of rest, so I do hope I'm not I'm not disturbing you."

She was keeping me from more APL operatives' reports. Suddenly, I wanted to tell her everything I'd been hiding for so long from my family, my friends. The petty backstabbing, the sullen, know-nothing triumphalism creeping throughout the plant, how making men had turned into making men salute. Of my friends and family, only Merry knew about my work for the APL, and I saw him far too seldom now that he had been dismissed from Ford. I'd gone months talking about my work only to O'Hara and the occasional APL operative who sidled up to me. I needed to talk to somebody better. But I couldn't bring myself to admit it.

I realized that I was staring at her hungrily and turned my attention out the parlor window, through which I could see the lower half of the man on the ladder.

When I looked back, Thia was smiling faintly. No doubt she'd interpreted my hunger as hope that she'd rip her gown open and straddle me, that we could screw on the sofa, ogled by the paint-scrubber's kneecaps. And, once I thought of it, it *did* seem like an excellent idea.

"May I offer you a drink?" she asked. "You probably should have one, to enter into the Glueck family spirit. We're determined to enjoy liquor while we may. Obviously, once the prohibition goes into effect it would be madness for us to break any laws. It's bad enough that Father cannot stop mocking the idea of prohibition. He used to insist that no one is listening to his ranting, but now..."

"Maybe the fellah on the ladder is a spy."

Thia laughed. "Clemenz would never spy on another Austrian. His hatred of his homeland is equalled only by his loyalty to his homeland." She paused. "Of course, Father's right about this prohibition. Michigan is being foolish to think it can stop people from drinking. Criminal syndicates in Illinois and Ohio are already lining up to bring in bootleg liquor once May comes around. This will not be a triumph for the Puritans."

"I wouldn't say they're Puri—"

"Tony, you're a dear, but your job is a Puritan's job as well."

"But it isn't." I was getting excited.

"Oh, I've offended you again. And it's not as though what Dot, Leen, and I do for Girls' Protective is any less—"

"You haven't. Offended me, I mean. But what I do isn't puritanical."

Her eyes flickered to the wall behind me as she searched for a polite way to disagree.

"I'm not defending it, precisely," I said. "And I know that a lot of men at Ford, even in Employment, *do* believe that our mission is religious. Bringing in the new dispensation. I know The Boss sees it that way. But really it's economics. Productivity."

Her eyebrows became curious.

I suppose I really wanted to be talking about the APL, or about my lonely heart, or about how my penis should be slapping various spots on and in her body. But this would have to suffice. "Mr Ford's moral interest in the men's domestic arrangements, maybe it's sincere, maybe it isn't," I explained. "But the real purpose, it's not the new *man.* It's the new *laborer.* Manufacturing requires the assembly line, and the assembly line demands reliable men. Regular men, almost mechanical. But the assembly line can't build them. That's why the company needs us. The foundry of men."

Conscious that I was rushing again, several years of thoughts jumbled up and struggling for escape, I forced myself to pause.

"I see." She was actually thinking it over.

"And, of course," I said, "it's especially about the question of, ah, sexual congress."

I looked at her briefly. She wasn't shocked, of course. With Thia there was always the question of sexual congress.

"For efficiency," I added.

She smiled. "Surely sexual congress would make production *less* efficient?"

"Yes. No. I mean—I mean, it's no coincidence that Educational popped up at Ford. Or that one of the leading prohibitionists is also the President of Reo Cars. You can't have a line worker stupid with hangover or late-night catting around. He'll miss parts, sleep on the job. Stay home altogether. But it's too expensive, too unreliable to force a man to be temperate. Monogamous. You have to convince him to force *himself.* On the line, 'moral' is really just another word for 'efficient.' And the line is what matters."

She thought for a while. I liked that about her, how she would consider things. "There might be something to that, Tony. Mightn't there, Father?"

I turned. Standing in the door-frame behind me was a dignified gentleman in a well-cut tweed suit and polka-dot necktie. He had a neatly trimmed white beard, and his equally white and neat hair was combed backward, away from the large bald patch proceeding from forehead nearly to crown. The thick lenses in his tortoiseshell frames made his eyes look outsized and faintly offended. Or possibly he truly was offended—by the topic of my conversation with his daughter. I felt a slow flush creeping across my face and neck.

Thia rose gracefully. "Father, this is Tony Grams, whom I told you about. Tony, this is my father, Herr Doktor Sigismund Glueck."

I rose to shake his hand. After we'd unclasped, I settled back into the sofa, and he sat in the armchair opposite Thia. I had to turn my head left to see her, right to see him.

"A pleasure, Dr Glueck."

"Sigi will suffice," he said. "And the pleasure is mine, Mr Grams."

"Tony, please."

He inclined his head. "Thia tells me that I owe my liberty to your good offices. I would prefer to owe it to the Constitution, but I am most grateful nonetheless."

"As I've told your daughter, sir, I doubt that I was of consequence. But I'm glad if I did help."

"And I'm grateful that you tried. Many wouldn't have. Including our neighbors, who wish to use our home as their canvas." His tone had turned bitter, even bleak. He smiled carefully and said in a lighter fashion. "But let us not talk further of such matters. I hope that my daughter has invited you already to supper?"

"I was just about to do so," Thia said.

I began, "I wouldn't wish to impose on—"

"There is no imposition. It is the least I can do to thank you. Besides, Martha wishes also to meet you and already has asked Daniel to cook for four."

I tried one last time to defeat my desire to stay by pointing out that I didn't wish to cause Mother worry, but Sigi countered by ringing Western Union and sending a rush telegram to her to explain my absence.

Not long after that genial extravagance, Martha Glueck returned home and joined us in the parlor. Her hair was neither so lustrous nor so dark as her daughter's, as she had made no effort to conceal its graying. Though stouter than her daughter, Martha had clearly bestowed much upon Thia, particularly bearing and taste. She was a tall woman, I realized as she drew near enough to take her husband's arm. After introductions had been effected, the women withdrew in the kitchen to tend to something or other.

While rummaging a tobacco box for pipe and tobacco, Sigi said, "A question for you, Mr Grams, if you don't object. You are Italian, I think?"

I nodded.

"I apologize," he said, beginning to pack the pipe. "That was not the question."

The scent of tobacco reminded me of Father, how he'd smelled coming home from work at the cigar factory.

"My question is this: If you wanted to visit a stranger but feared that he might react unfavorably upon learning your race, would you mention your race in advance in order to avoid an unpleasant scene?"

"I suppose," I said, "it would depend how fearful I was of prejudice—that particular man's, I mean. And how far I would have to travel for the visit."

Dr Glueck nodded and lit his pipe. "Does the question seem queer? I suppose it might. I have asked myself this question many times, but only now do I realize how often." He withdrew a letter from the pocket of his jacket and flicked it with his finger. "From a young surgeon of remarkable accomplishment in neuroanatomy, all the more remarkable because he is a Negro."

The butler had placed two beers in chilled mugs and was stepping softly from the room as Dr Glueck said this. I wondered whether it had been deep tact or simple rudeness on Dr Glueck's part not to ask *him* the question.

Dr Glueck turned to me. "I mean, of course, only that it is very difficult for a Negro to receive first-rate training in anything." He read from the letter: "'I do not know how your opinions on the race question stand, nor your views on social equality, so permit me to say frankly that I am of the Negro race.'"

"I see," I said. "And will you meet with him?"

"Assuredly. But it will be complicated, I realize. To avoid offending this Dr Sucre as well as my patients and neighbors, it will be complicated. Quite a waste of effort, in truth, for a task that should be simple."

"Much of life is," I pointed out.

We had scarcely half drunk our glasses of beer when the ladies called us into the dining room. The table was large enough to force us to speak clearly, but the conversation was lively and genial, and I found Thia's parents every bit as intelligent as their daughter.

And every bit as capable of making me choke on my drink.

"I regret, by the way, Tony," Dr Glueck said partway through the roast beef, "that I interrupted the interesting conversation about intercourse in which you and Thia were engaged when I came home."

I blushed furiously, especially since at that moment Thia's presence had afflicted me with an aggressive erection which I'd concealed beneath my napkin. But I was the only one blushing. Thia was grinning faintly, and her mother simply sighed and turned her attention to her food.

"Tony was making a most interesting proposition," he continued. "About the need to control sexual behavior in a modern factory. Sexuality, I am convinced, Tony, is powerful and complicated in the utmost, yet few give it the consideration it deserves."

"Some," Thia remarked, "would say that most people consider it far more than it deserves."

"I would say so certainly, yes," said Mrs Glueck. Her accent was slightly stronger than her husband's.

"My darling family, really," the good doctor reproved cheerfully. "Hardly considering. Lusting, perhaps. Fantasizing, yes. But considering? That precisely they must not do. Naturalness, Tony, this is the question that haunts us both in our work, I believe."

"It is?" I asked. "How so?"

"I concede," he said, "that there is some fundamental biology of human sexuality that one could fairly call 'natural,' of course."

With all the perversity of its kind, my erection refused to relent. I felt half convinced that Dr Glueck was somehow aware of it and subtly mocking me.

"And yet," he continued intently, "a survey of history will show that what is considered unspeakable perversion in one land has been permitted, even encouraged in some other. It becomes clear, then, that virtually all practices that a civilization considers natural are actually learned, often with great difficulty. Infants, which are very much alive to the world of sensation, are utterly promiscuous in their capacity for pleasure. But by the time they are adults, sexuality has been deadened in all but a very few parts of the body."

Thia cleared her throat noisily.

"My daughter," he told me, "thinks I look at this too much as a man. The important point is that becoming a proper adult, alive in the right places and dead in the others, alive to the right people, dead to the wrong ones, that is hardly natural. It is rather a victory of engineering. A victory every bit as grand and unlikely as the transcontinental railroad, two narrow tracks meeting from opposite sides of a huge continent. Indeed—"

I got lost then in a fantasy in which transcontinental railroad tracks labored over by thousands of sweating eastbound Chinamen and westbound Irishmen were transformed into a conveyor belt carrying along millions of supine men and women, some in evening wear, some shirtless, some in pilgrim's buckles. As the people on the belt progressed from station to station, a Irishman or Chinaman would perform a particular action—lock an eye into a socket with a screwdriver in the shape of a crucifix, tighten a nipple with a socket wrench, shine cheekbones with a garter—

"—whenever I hear the word 'natural,' I become suspicious," he concluded.

"And being suspicious is Sigi's greatest pleasure," Martha said.

"The problem with one's family," he said, "is that they know one too well."

I nodded because it seemed expected. But in a half hour I had just told the Gluecks more about the mess bubbling in my skull than I had told Mother, Kitty, or Carl for months. My life had begun to feel quite messy, indeed. I was thinking on this as Thia showed me out. Even in the street lamp's dim glow, I could see that some vandalism still remained for Clemenz to scrub away in the morning, and I envied him the straightforwardness of his mess. (*Stupiditá,* again and always.)

Chapter 16

AS SPRING CAME, KITTY BEGAN TO MAKE OUTINGS TO THE CHURCH HOUSE, where she would knock down cobwebs, polish furniture, and boil water for tea. In the dead of night, I discovered by accident, she would sometimes limp back and forth between the houses several times. Some mornings, I found her asleep on the sofa, her bad leg resting on an afghan draped across the sofa's arm. I never woke her, and I never asked where or whether she had slept.

Lisa and I accompanied Kitty sometimes on daytime excursions. Kitty was stronger by then and walked almost normally. Still, sometimes in the middle of steeping tea or feather-dusting the mantelpiece, she would begin to sob softly and ask *Why Andrew?* Lisa and I knew better than to answer.

I continued to see Thia now and then. Indeed, Sigi took a liking to me (and I to him), so occasionally I visited the Gluecks on Sunday afternoons when both he and his daughter would be available. That was Martha's day for calling upon friends, so I seldom saw her, though she was always welcoming when I did.

One afternoon, I happened to mention that I wished Kitty would return more fully to society. "I'd even be happy to have the Young Suffragettes cluttering up the place again."

"Your sister is a Yes?" Thia asked.

"She has just risen in my daughter's esteem," Sigi observed.

"She *was*, anyhow," I said. "These days..."

"What was her husband's surname?" Thia asked.

"Lagorio."

"Your sister is Kitty Lagorio?" Thia asked. "I've met Kitty several times. A very sweet girl."

And so, in return for helping her father escape internment (and, I suspect, for some other obscure motives not nearly as romantic as I would have hoped), Thia arranged to pay a call on Kitty the next afternoon.

It's odd. I remember coming home after work that evening and feeling my heart triple its rhythm and my bones change shape simply because Thia was in my front parlor, holding a tea-cup and chatting with my sister as my niece listened. Seeing her in my home, among my loved ones and our familiar furniture, somehow made her more real to me than she had been, even when we were in bed together. It hurt.

"Come *in*, Tony," my sister told me. "I want to introduce you to Mrs Mueller—"

"Call me Thia, dear."

"Thia is here because I've been such a truant from the Yeses. Sit *down*, Tony," Kitty said. "Mother will be out any moment, I'm sure."

"Mrs Mueller," said Lisa from the armchair near the radiator (*my* armchair, the scamp), "is friends with all sorts of famous people. Rosika Schwimmer, Carrie Chapman Catt, and even Jane Addams. But no movie stars."

Thia and Kitty chuckled.

"I've only met those ladies, Lisa," Thia said. "I wouldn't presume to claim friendship."

"Would you claim it with me?" I asked. I'd meant it to sound bantering, but it sounded plaintive and possibly reproachful.

"You know her?" Kitty asked. After silence, she asked, "You know Tony?"

"We're old chums," Thia said. "We met at the police station years ago."

Kitty smiled uncertainly, and Lisa cocked her head.

I couldn't tell whether Kitty remembered Thia's name from that note which she'd teasingly handed me long ago. If not, I didn't wish to remind her. "For Educational," I explained. "Thia was there for the Girls' Protective League."

Soon after that, Mother called us in for supper. The Grams ladies were all quite taken with Thia's beauty and breeding. And her dead husband gave her status, though they didn't much talk about that. Mostly they chattered about suffrage and the broad tides of war.

Since she had borrowed her father's car, Thia declined my offer to escort her home. When she left, the others were cheerful with the pleasures of first friendship, but I felt forlorn somehow, emptied even. The APL reports were even drearier than usual.

The Wiana had re-opened as a blind-pig. The only differences were the extra guard at the door, the lower quality of the liquor, and the higher cost of each drink.

"I thought it was madness for an Austrian to break the law these days," I said to Thia.

She shrugged. "It's madness to follow the law these days, too. It's all madness."

She was tipsy on bathtub gin and drunk on indignation. Her latest suitor, one about whom she'd felt some optimism, had recently reproached her for her family's lack of respectability—by which he meant that her father was a dangerous radical. Somehow, he'd gotten wind of Sigi's misbegotten internment. The young man's mother was a Daughter of the American Revolution, and he hardly felt it appropriate to consort with the daughter of a subversive element.

"He really said 'consort?'" I asked.

Thia grinned sardonically. "I'm sure it's just that his mother didn't approve of his being seen publicly with a Jewess, patriotic or no."

"Mine doesn't either, but she's out of town for another week, so I don't have to cut you until then."

"I'm relieved to hear it," she said, swigging her gin. "Where is Signora Grams?"

"Chicago. She and Kitty and Lisa went to visit my sisters."

"So you and your brother all alone at home? Have you figured out how the ice box works or where the ladies hide the hot meals?"

"Carl has been living in a boarding house for a while now," I said. Then my penis figured out her question. I paused for a moment, letting my brain catch up. "I don't suppose," I ventured, "you'd be willing to break with the sisterhood by coming home and showing me where the good stuff is hidden?"

In the end, we used Kitty's home rather than mine. Kitty's neighbors were less prone to sit on the front stoop, and, unless one was unlucky, it was possible to approach her house from the rear without being observed.

Kitty's guest bed was smaller and its bedclothes less luxurious than Dot's. But I had more pressing worries. "What is this?" I asked Thia as we were beginning to undress. "Nothing glib. Please."

Her fingers stopped on her buttons, and she looked into my eyes. "This is tonight," she said.

"Tonight."

She nodded.

"Not love, then."

She shook her head slowly. "Esteem. Affection."

"Those aren't words for fucking," I said.

"They can be," she said. "But they don't have to be, if you don't wish."

But I did wish. So badly I trembled. She was beautiful. She was willing. That was enough to make any man tremble, especially lonely little Tony Grams. And there was more, of course. As long as there was tonight, I told myself, there was at least a chance of tomorrow.

We were lonely together for a while, and then I escorted her to her auto before midnight. I put fresh linens on the bed and then went home to lie in my own. I was running the same risks as before for the same painful rewards, and I knew how dangerous it was, how stupid. I knew that I shouldn't have done it, that I shouldn't do it again. But I knew that I almost surely would if I got another chance.

Chapter 17

He smoke da seegar wit da beega da band,
Da tree-for-da-quart' ees da kind,
Da diamond dat flash from da back of hees hand
Ees da beegest Giuseppe could find.
He dress up hees Rosa in satin an' lace,
She no longer scrub at da board,
But putta da paint on da leeps an' da face,
For Giuseppe, he work at da Ford.

I FELT MORE THAN A LITTLE GUILTY STEPPING INTO MERRY'S HOME. I HAD been away from it and him for too long.

But if dark-eyed, lively Gulsa felt slighted, she showed no sign of it when greeting me at the door. She smiled broadly at me before returning to the kitchen. Drew and Bradley, the young gentlemen, were as well-scrubbed as the house and bright as newly shone shoes. They kept discreetly away from Merry and me once we went upstairs to the spare bedroom, where he and I stood shoulder to shoulder, looking out the dormer. Through a gap in the buildings beyond, we could see a patch of the river, its currents, sails, and smokestacks glimmering gaily in the summer sunlight.

Once we were alone, disquiet tinged Merry's good cheer, which intensified my guilt at having kept my job at Ford. "How are you finding Cadillac?" He had found a position as a senior clerk at a dealership, but I suspected that his salary was much lower than it had been at Ford.

"It is nice, for there to be more than one model of car," he said with a faint grin. "But after so long with people, to work mostly with numbers—not as pleasant, I don't find. And then it is still Detroit and half the year freezing. Now California..."

He said "California" the way Angela said "*Paradiso.*"

"There are not many Kurds there, of course," he added. "But then there aren't many here, either."

"Of course we're all Americans now," I said dryly.

He chuckled. "But still, that *is* true. What else could we be but Americans? I think to live in Kirkuk again would feel like a dream. Not a good or a bad dream. Simply not real."

I tried to imagine living again in Ghilarza. "Maybe every place feels like a dream until you actually go there."

"Yes. But then," he said thoughtfully, "once you go there and look at it for a very long time, then it is again like a dream. As when you say a word over and over again and it becomes only a sound."

"Like 'cockwurst,'" I suggested, remembering Jaspersson.

Merry roared with delight and slapped my shoulder. "I have missed you, my friend. The Swede, not so much."

We stood silently for a moment. "Speaking of Swedes—or is it Danes?" Merry asked. "Is 'Sorensen' a Swedish or a Danish name?"

I shrugged.

"No matter," he continued. "What I wish to say is that some Ford men I know have gone to work at the Rouge plant now. I have thought of applying there myself. It is certainly a growing concern. Cast-Iron Charlie Sorensen is seeing to that."

I nodded. In the three years since the Rouge's construction, Sorensen had guided it through rapid growth, especially since they'd widened the river and expanded the plant to make Eagle boats for the Navy. With the river enlarged, the Rouge was a perfect destination for barges bearing raw materials, so it was destined to grow. Although at that point the Rouge's operations were still small compared to Highland Park's, there was already talk of installing the world's largest blast furnaces at the Rouge.

"I think you will need to be careful, Tony. In my time with the company, Sorensen was never a friend to Sociological—"

"Educational," I said with false primness.

He chuckled faintly. "Sorensen was never its friend. The men I know at the Rouge say that he makes no secret of trying to keep Educational out of there altogether."

I nodded. It was becoming obvious that Sorensen wanted nothing to interfere with his control over his men and his plant.

"So it is strange, I think, that two of the men I know there also mentioned to me seeing Caleb Smythe there, talking with Mr Sorensen. More than once."

"Smythe?" I asked. "At the Rouge? But why?"

"My friends didn't know. But I think it is a thing to worry about, perhaps, given Mr Smythe's feelings toward you."

The more I thought about it, the less I liked it. Possibly it was just Smythe's remora instinct, his need to swim among the biggest, meanest fish and pick at their scraps. Sorensen certainly had the teeth. But I had a hunch there was more to it than that, and that it wouldn't be good for Educational. Or me.

Dot sounded like I felt. "Granted, Thia's a darling," she said, "an uttermost darling—"

"The cat's pajamas," Peter Everett interjected gaily.

Everett was a tall man of about thirty who clearly held a position which required cashing large pay checks and occasionally signing documents placed in front of him by deferential secretaries. He had pale skin made paler by the intense darkness of both his hair and his uncannily disciplined eyebrows. He was as shapely, as well dressed, and as clever as a tailor's dummy. As the kindlier American gentry often do, he had learned to turn his incomprehension into a source of stubborn good cheer.

I wanted to stab him through the eye with my dessert fork. Him and Thia both.

Thia had told me the truth when she'd said our encounter was only for that night. In the two weeks after it, I had sent her three polite notes (just this *one*, just this *next* one…), which she had ignored. And then, another week or two later, Kitty came home delighted with the news that Thia had invited the two of us to dine with her and some friends. The friends turned out to be Dot, Emmeline Ward, and the tailor's dummy. Was this a gesture of friendship to Kitty? To me? A gesture of mockery? Of careless indifference? Throughout dinner, I'd been staring at Thia beyond the bounds of politeness, but her face gave me little indication.

As she had been for much of the meal, Dot was eying Everett with contempt. Thia in turn was looking at her reproachfully. Across the table from me, Emmeline Ward regarded me with nervous amusement. Kitty looked at all of us, smiling, though at what I couldn't tell.

This round of glances was taking place over half eaten *crème brûlée* served on bone china resting on a linen tablecloth cleaner and better starched than the boiled shirt beneath the dinner jacket I had bought for my first evening with Thia. I was painfully sober and felt as awkward as always in the second-hand jacket. (How many more outings did it have before it turned shabby? *Had* it turned shabby?) Kitty and Emmeline had each been sipping discreetly at a single flute of champagne since the *hors d'oeuvres,* while the others were upending theirs with abandon.

Everett seemed simply to be enjoying himself, but Thia and Dot were proceeding with rictal grins and gladiatorial intensity. All night, Dot had been trying to enlist me on her side in the struggle, whatever it was.

"Dot is a darling, too," Thia said, "even if she can be positively sinister in her compliments."

"*Moi?*" Dot asked, fingers delicately at her collarbone.

Kitty and I looked at one another across the table. She looked entertained. I hadn't seen her looking entertained since Andrew's death. Whatever my own sufferings, I decided, Kitty's enjoyment made the evening a success.

By that point, even Everett had sensed the hostility. "Mrs Lagorio, you know Dot from the League, you said?"

"We actually met actually through the Yeses," Kitty replied cheerfully.

"Those suffrage females?" he asked.

Dot rolled her eyes. "Some of the millions of suffrage *females,* yes."

Everett caught the warning. "Leen, how about you? Are you up to anything hunka at the Board?"

In addition to working for Girls' Protective, Emmeline was an investigator for the Board of Health. We had already established that we spent much of our careers poking about in the same sorts of lives.

"Nothing unusual," Emmeline told Everett, taking a cosmetic sip at her champagne.

"Leen is too modest," Thia protested. "Tell them about the police."

"That's still just vapor," Emmeline protested.

"Girls' Protective," Thia explained to Kitty, and perhaps to me, "has been petitioning Commissioner Couzens for almost a year now to appoint women police officers and assign them to the ladies taken to the jail."

The Ford Motor Company's elite exerted a tidal influence on the city. Mrs Ford, at least in name, ran the Girls' Protective League. And

James Couzens, a former vice president of Ford, had succeeded John Gillespie as Commissioner of Police. He was already running a mayoral campaign for the fall election, and Mr Ford himself was beginning a run for the Senate.

"In the jail?" Everett asked. "Hardly a suitable place for ladies."

"Hence the petitioning, darling," Thia said.

"I meant respectable ladi—"

"A woman is respectable if she defends her sisters," Dot said. "That's what *makes* her respectable."

There was an unfamiliar note in Dot's voice. Sincerity, maybe. Kitty nodded approvingly.

"But surely—" Everett began.

"Call me Dot," she said.

He blinked for a moment. "But—"

Dot turned to face him directly. He flinched. Glancing at Thia before returning her stare to Everett, she said, "When Thia and I were together in Madison we assisted Dr *Helen* Sumner in her research into women in industry. Did you know that in 1900, twenty percent of women were breadwinners for their families? And that over a quarter of them worked in factories?"

"I fail to understand—" Everett began.

"Constitutionally," Dot remarked.

"The point, Peter, which Dot wishes to make," Emmeline said, "is that some women have little choice but to spend their days in 'unsuitable environments.'"

"Including their families," Dot said.

I nodded. So did Kitty. We looked at each other, then looked down, knowing we were thinking of Angela. I considered Thia's champagne flute. Did the very existence of champagne prove that somewhere somebody was suffering?

"—and so," Emmeline continued, "these women and girls confide more willingly in a lady officer. In cases of white slavery alone—"

"There's no need," Everett said firmly, "to talk of white slavery. Or jigaboo slavery. Not over supper."

"Dot," I asked, "do your figures include the economy related to prostitution? I'd wager its economic significance is substantial."

Everett spluttered gratifyingly into his champagne. Thia visibly did sums in her head.

"As the wife of a financier," Dot replied, "I can safely say that all economy is an economy of prostitution."

The party dissolved soon after that. Thia took Everett's arm and led him toward the exit, their every stride a blend of slosh and splendor. Kitty and I followed them out into the moist early summer evening. Emmeline and Dot remained at the table.

Kitty and I didn't want to pay for a cab, but we also didn't want to admit that. So we waited with Thia and Everett.

"Drat," Thia said, rummaging through her reticule. "I can't find my atomizer. I wonder if Leen still has it. Peter, be a dear."

Everett bowed crookedly and swayed gallantly back inside.

Thia looked at me, her face suddenly sad. "Tony, I really was beastly to you, back then. I was beastly to him. And he was kind to me," she told Kitty. "Especially about Father," she told me. "Thank you."

She leaned forward and kissed me on the cheek, a fraction too close to my lips. She clumsily rubbed the corner of my mouth with her gloved thumb. "I wish I'd done better," she added.

I wondered whether I was feeling love or rage.

"Your cab, madam," the doorman told Thia.

Kitty's face had gone tight. She opened the door for herself and tugged me along with her. "Good night, Mrs Mueller," Kitty said as she stepped into the cab. I stepped in behind her and limited myself to a wave. After we'd gone a couple expensive blocks north, Kitty leaned forward and asked the driver to let us out.

"What was that about?" I asked.

"Will you take my arm, please, Tony? My leg."

We walked a ways to the nearest trolley stop. She leaned on me heavily, helping me home.

I'll be more forthcoming here than I was about Andrew: Carl was drafted in June 1918.

Until then, Carl had ignored the reproaches and insinuations, relying upon his excellence as a toolmaker to protect him at Ford and upon Ford's importance to the war effort to protect him beyond that. I never entirely understood Carl's attitude toward the war. He wasn't opposed, exactly. And he wasn't more cowardly than other men. He simply had no interest in fighting. Appeals to patriotism slid off him as easily and entirely as Mother's recriminations for leaving home, and Andrew's death seemed only to have intensified his lack of interest.

Still, he didn't buck when he received his notice. He took his leave at Ford, spent a week eating unhappy dinners at home, and then reported for duty to Camp Custer, where he was mustered into the 339th ("Detroit's Own"). In August, he and the others were dispatched to France.

For whatever reason, unless I remind myself of the unhappy dinners of that last week, I always think that the last time I saw Carl before he left was a chance meeting at the John R gate the day before he received his draft notice. We were both coming off shift. I assumed that he was sneaking off to see his latest girlfriend because he was in such a hurry that he bumped into me and got shirty before realizing who I was. We laughed a little and went our separate ways.

Chapter 18

As soon as Carl was drafted, I started to wish that I'd made more of an effort to see him after he'd moved to the boarding house. That wishing intensified when we received a much-delayed letter from him in which he said that the 339th had been halfway across the Atlantic, zigzagging to avoid U-boats, when they'd been rerouted to Newcastle, where they were being equipped for winter warfare against the Bolsheviks in Russia's Archangel Oblast.

It was around that time I began to mistake my growing scepticism and distrust for patriotic vigilance, and consequently began to wander the plant before and after my work hours. This was foolish, of course. I didn't really understand the plant well enough to patrol it. Too much happened there. During each of the three shifts in Highland Park, fifteen thousand men in overalls transformed rubber, brass, vanadium steel, plate glass, and hair (twelve millions of pounds annually) into one Model T after another, several thousand each day. At the factory's loading docks, those Model Ts were in turn hefted onto freight cars—three hundred or more daily—and trundled away from the plant to the Detroit Terminal, then to the Grand Trunk, then to the whole world. Only a few of the big bosses truly comprehended the weavings of all the lines, the metamorphoses along the way. The rest of us experienced only the same dim intuition of order one has watching a large flock of birds shift its formation.

From the proper vantage point, the sheer physical presence of it all was beautiful. Some of us in white-collar jobs liked to spend a bit of our breaks in some perch from which we could watch a choice portion of the process. I particularly liked the buildings abutting and opening onto the craneways of C Building, where sharp, peculiar shadows would fall from the skylights onto the blue steel warren of machines and stockpiles. In the quiet, early moments just after the night-shift men had shuffled out, it was soothing to watch the day-shift laborers flow toward their various stations, moving in rivulets through the buildings' great, greasy naves.

But, though it remained awe-inspiring, it wasn't so beautiful when you went down into it. The *noise* of the place—it was something felt as much as heard. Even when I tried to master myself, my teeth ground from the strain of hearing. The creak and clatter of the lines, the moan of the hoists, the eruptive hiss of the air hoses, the thunking and grinding of the individual motors powering each machine. In much of the plant, the men shouted to be heard. And the air, despite the great humming ventilation fans, smelled of grease and burning and felt dirty and heavy in the lungs. The air tasted like the floors looked—thick and slick with black ooze from dirty shoes and leaking oil.

The men were more accustomed to the noise and the work, but I don't think they ever became comfortable with it either. Many took breaks simply to crane their heads out a bathroom window for a few minutes, and even in the quiet minutes before a shift there was something tense and insincere in their laughter as they took their positions. Once they had settled into the reality of the day, they hollered at one another in whatever language was handy, usually about the finer points of poon-tang or crapping.

One morning in September, at about the same time (I later learned) Carl was disembarking in Archangel, I found myself again assaulted by the noise of the line, crowded by the open-throttle coarseness of laborers trying to hold on until their lunch break. I'd been summoned to see one of my men, Frankie Farelli. A twenty-year-old returned veteran, Farelli was perfectly sound of body. But the war, in its ruthless medical curiosity, was teaching us that the mind can be wounded without any blow falling.

When Farelli had first begun raving to himself more than the typical line worker, I'd recommended that he be kept away from moving machinery. He'd been put to weighing pistons, which seemed satisfactory until one day he hurled a high-compression piston—one of the old, heavy ones, mind you—at lethal velocity toward the skull of a Negro worker he mistook for a German. Then they assigned him to hang fenders on the conveyor. He'd been there almost three weeks without incident.

But now I found him sitting on an overturned bucket, coughing miserably. He was head to toe with black paint and looked like the most miserable minstrel singer on earth. He looked at the filthy rag clutched in his hand and dropped it to the floor before looking up.

"I done it again, Mr Grams." He pointed over his shoulder a few yards to the ten-foot deep, 500-gallon tank of the black enamel in which the fenders were dipped before being hung to drip and passed through the drying oven. "I went for a swim," he said.

I didn't embarrass him by asking why. He didn't always remember his actions, much less his motivations. I caught the attention of a nearby straw boss, Smolnarek, a short, broad man in his mid thirties. "Somebody should hose him down," I said. "Before the paint dries."

Smolnarek called in a runner, who nudged Frankie off his bucket. They disappeared out of sight behind a screen of unpainted fenders.

"What happened?" I asked.

Smolnarek spat reflectively to one side. "Crazy wop just went into the vat. Yelled something about an ambush. Best we can work out, he thought he was under fire from the Krauts in some river in France. Where he had his war, I guess."

"Had it the first time, anyway."

We stood for a moment silently.

"Can't have booby-hatchers hanging fenders," Smolnarek said. "Give the poor son of bitch his last envelope. Or a suit and a desk."

I nodded. Smolnarek spat again and returned to the line.

I had a pile of APL reports waiting for me in Educational, so I wandered back into Y Building until I found a cranny to lurk in. For a while I watched the men move in rhythm, lifting their arms and bending their backs like soiled and bloated chorus girls. At a distance, the mechanical ballet of so many men was impressive. Up close, it was still impressive but also distressing. Even accounting for Mr Ford's commitment to hiring the crippled, too many men on the line were wrong in large or small ways. There were the mine-lung coughers and, recently, mustard-gas coughers, as well as a large contingent of the unusually pallid and the unnaturally flushed. There were many big men, but, like most line workers everywhere, most of them were bulky without vigor. Other men clenched their tools with gnarled, nervous hands. Quite a few even looked like me—subtly twisted, spasm or bone defect pulling one shoulder lower than another, or one leg further to the side than the other.

After a few minutes, the lunch carts appeared and the foreman hollered break time. A lunch cart had stopped in front of me, maybe ten yards distant. The men were upon it before the cart man could set his brakes. The men in theory had a half hour for lunch, but if there had been any delay on the line—as happened frequently—the straw bosses would be keen to recoup that time from the break. So the men always moved to their food at top speed. Since it was forbidden to run, they adopted a peculiar gait requiring much hip-swiveling and arm-swinging. They looked almost to be skating across the grease.

From various carts issued flurries of pint bottles of milk and hot coffee, of sandwiches, hot Frankfort sandwiches, boxed lunches, big mikes and granny smiths, cuts of pie, and chicken soup steaming inside *papier mâché* cups. Before the carts trundled off to their next spot, I counted at least a hundred men served in three minutes (good cart men could feed double that if needed).

As the nearby men bustled off to eat before the straw bosses yelled for them, one man, an Italian of about thirty or thirty-five, turned toward me. He stared at me briefly, then took a few unfriendly steps forward. A pair of his friends followed suit.

"You're Tony Grams, aintcha?" he demanded. "Proud of yourself, are you?" he asked.

"And who might you be?"

"I ain't nobody, I guess. I guess I ain't even here."

Actually, he was very present. Whether burly or simply bulky, he was big. As were his two friends. All three men stood at arm's length, glaring. I could only imagine that he knew about the APL. Somebody had slipped, and now this big Italian Socialist wanted to bang my head against industrial equipment.

"Well, if you were here," I said, "it would be a pleasure to meet you."

"Adamo Ragnelli, you runty rat. That's who I am."

Sofia's brother. I noticed he was cross-eyed, more so than his sister.

"I hear it was a mighty big baby for seven months," I said. "'Specially with me such a runt and all."

The floor was every bit as slimy as it looked. And he was wearing good solid work boots, my ribs discovered. After some further pain, he was dragged away, and I was sitting in Medical, spitting blood into a tin dish.

Dr Collins, the most junior and—from what I could gather—most competent doctor in Medical—set the dish aside. "The boys in the blacksmith shop thank you," he said.

"Huh?"

He adjusted his spectacles and smiled. "Our little joke around here. Blood has iron in it. In the red cells. We're always saying that Pete Martin and Cast-Iron Charlie Sorensen are working on ways to mine the iron for parts."

"The red cells are forming men, eh? I'll have to stomp that out."

Only after I said it did I realize it was a dangerous joke. But Dr Collins didn't seem to notice.

Smythe was Ragnelli's advisor. When I returned to work, he made me discuss the matter in the main room, where a half-dozen other advisors could hear. "We could of course dismiss the man outright." *If, of course, you're petty and vindictive and have a guilty conscience.* "Or we could make allowances." *If, of course, you're weak and frightened and have a guilty conscience.*

"I leave it in your capable hands, Mr Smythe," I said.

Two days later, Kitty and I were in her parlor, drinking weak tea. My ribs still hurt (Dr Collins had warned that one might be cracked), but my jaw felt better.

Kitty had kept her large, framed portrait of Andrew in his finest suit, but she'd moved it into the kitchen because she found it somehow more pleasant to see him there. The parlor was now decorated in neatly framed pages from the *Saturday Evening Post,* along with a blurry, gay watercolor of Susan B. Anthony, which she'd painted with the aid of a correspondence course.

We had the little house to ourselves. Lisa and her movie-mad schoolmates had giggled off to the pictures, and Mother had stayed at home with Mrs Daszkowski. And, of course, Carl was somewhere far to the east, probably in danger.

"I'd never figured you for the type to fall in love," Kitty said. "Especially the type to fall in love with a woman who clearly isn't in love with you."

> An advisor has got to be a man with good horse-sense, well-balanced, good judgment; got to be a man of decision, instinctively just; got to be a man of sympathy. Clean, cold, vanadium justice will not always get the best results.

Andrew's death had hardened Kitty somehow, as had Carl's departure. Though she usually had kindly motives, her help sometimes felt more like the dagger than the scalpel.

"I'm not in love with Sofia Ragnelli," I said.

"*Tony.*"

"If you mean Thia, I'm not the one spending my afternoons with her paving the way for feminine democracy one cucumber sandwich at a time," I pointed out. "I only asked after her just now to make conversation."

"And because you're in love with her and crazy to hear if she mentioned you."

"It's funny how so many Yes meetings are in the afternoon, isn't it? When no working woman could possibly attend, I mean. Alessandra would've—"

"I do see why you love her, Tony, really I do. I quite admire her myself. She's wonderful with the Yeses. But, setting aside the religious obstacle, you need to see that she simply doesn't—"

"I know."

She let out an explosive sigh. "Then act like—"

"If you want to help me, go explain to the Ragnellis that you can't park a car in a space if there's already another car in it. Especially if you're not driving in the first place."

"I only—"

"Or take a train to Chicago and lecture Angela about choosing wisely in love. Or just pour me some more tea."

In a sort of Tiny Tim ballet, Kitty and I tiptoed politely around one another for several weeks. Then a boy from Daszkowski's rang the bell at home. Kitty had called the store to say there had been trouble during a Yes meeting and she needed me to retrieve her from the Gluecks' home.

When I arrived, a half-dozen suffragettes were scurrying down the darkened front walk. They flinched when I raised my hat. Daniel showed me through to the kitchen, where I found Kitty sitting at the kitchen table with a few other young ladies. There was a young colored woman there as well, sitting straight and silent. She exuded such impeccable gentility that I took her for a relation of Daniel's.

"Oh, it's really too awful, Tony," Kitty said as she rose to greet me. "People can be so stupid."

She said her good-byes and steered me toward the front hallway.

She tried to herd me right out the front door, but I spotted Sigi Glueck standing almost stock still in his front parlor. Without thinking, I turned into the room.

Sometimes it's impossible to draw distinctions among mirth, fury, fear, and simple chill—sometimes it's all quiet trembling. Sigi stood trembling in his shirtsleeves, staring into the darkness outside as the bare branches of his sycamore tree waved in and out of perceptibility. The late October chill blowing through his window hinted at another glacial winter.

There were arrowheads of glass all over the floor, I noticed when Daniel returned with cleaning tools. He began sweeping the mess into a dustpan, which he then emptied into an ash can.

"What has happened to the brick?" Sigi asked calmly.

"Miss Thia took it," Daniel replied.

"Ah." Sigi stared into the night a while longer.

Kitty muttered that we ought to leave.

"Was there a note?" Sigi asked Daniel.

"'Boche,'" Thia called from the top of the stairway. "Written on the brick in boot-blacking. In a poor hand."

Her voice, like her body, was tight with anger. She descended the stairs with fast, fierce strides.

"But not by a poor hand, I think," Sigi said. "Our neighbors are comfortable folk."

Thia snorted as she joined our little group. She was holding the brick tightly in both hands. "I've put Mother to bed."

"Well, Tony," Kitty began, "we should really leave—"

"'Boche,'" Sigi said flatly. "If this is better than '*Juden, geh weg*,' I can't say."

We stood there in the breeze. My arms had goose bumps, and my hands had begun to stiffen with cold. I couldn't have said why, but I was ignoring Kitty's homeward tugging.

"Thou shalt love thy neighbor as thyself," Sigi said contemplatively. "Civilization, so-called, demands this. A demand older than the Israelites in the desert. Yet it still chafes at us like new trousers."

The glass made small sounds in Daniel's bucket.

"Possibly my neighbor deserves my love because he is a part of creation, like the squirrel, the fly, the blade of grass. But can a man be said to love a squirrel? I think not."

Thia was passing the brick back and forth between her hands, nodding absently. Daniel replaced the broom with a smaller one for more precise work.

"I'm sure it was only one person," I said.

For some reason I expected Kitty to help me, but she stayed silent, and her face was blank save for the frown between her eyes.

"I'm sure," I began, "that most of your neighbors..." But I'd read the APL reports.

"Love your neighbor and hate your enemy," Sigi said. "But it is not one's enemy who says, 'We have some questions about your loyalties to this great nation, Dr Glueck.' For that matter, it is not one's enemy who says, 'Come to this ditch and die for it.' Then again, perhaps the man who says such things *is* one's enemy."

Sigi padded tobacco into the bowl of his unadorned meerschaum pipe. He lit a match with a dexterous gesture, and soon the smoke was spiraling out the empty window. Daniel finished his sweeping and left the room as Sigi puffed silently, to all appearances mesmerized by the smoke swirling into the cold.

"Well, we really must be going, Dr Glueck. Thia," Kitty said. She sounded polite, but I could feel her hand quivering on my forearm. "I'm sorry about this awful thing."

Sigi and Thia offered distracted good-byes as I let Kitty pull me out the front door. At the runabout, however, we quarrelled because I decided that I needed to go back inside.

"That woman invites risks," Kitty said. "I want to go home."

"Fine. I'll take the tram."

"You want me to drive home on my own?"

"On your ownest own." I let her open her own door.

"*Treyf, treyf,*" Thia said again. For twenty minutes, stopping only to swig her monkey swill, she had been blending together the kosher riots, her father's internment, and the brick thrown through her window.

We were at the Wiana Club, just the two of us. I was feeling more and more like a fool for being there. Thia was angry, afraid, and drunk, and I was tipsy and hoping for nakedness. I could hope for it only because it obviously wouldn't happen.

"They might as well have been chanting *treyf.* That great crashing sound, like a shell going off. Girls with glass in their hair. And Mother. Bleeding from the same scars."

"I bet it was a fourteen-year-old this time too," I said.

"*And* who threw the paint?"

"Probably."

"And who whisked Father and then Professor Kahn off to Oscoda? I understand that Father is a dangerous subversive, given his wicked desire to help people be sane. But Egon Kahn? The man teaches Goethe and flinches at the sound of trolleys, for God's sake."

I shrugged.

"And, do you know, they're lucky. Father and Professor Kahn. If the police had pressed proper charges, Father and the Professor might have been lynched. Honestly, I'm surprised we haven't had more jerry hangings than just Robert Prager. They could hang a Kraut weekly in Campus Martius, sell postcards of them dangling from the gibbet, like these new Ku Kluxers with the Negroes. They could donate the profits to the YMCA Patriotic Fund."

I looked around nervously.

Which was a mistake. "What?" she asked.

What was the room full of Ford executives—and others—intent on proving their patriotism. *What* was I didn't want to lose my job or to spend twenty years in prison for sitting across the table from a noisy violation of the Sedition Act. And she knew it. Kitty had been right—Thia invited risks.

"I'm sure I know who threw that brick," she said. "One of the little Smythe hoodlums. Beastly children. They all pick their brains out through their noses, and the eldest spends his nights trying to peep at women undressing. Their father works for your people, you know."

"*My* people? Who are—Wait, do you mean Caleb Smythe?"

She nodded.

"Smythe lives in your neighborhood?"

"Cater-corner in the back. He moved in perhaps a month ago. Nasty little man."

That didn't make sense. I'd snuck a look at Smythe's file. He received a higher salary than I, but not enough higher to live in any of the houses near Thia. And the rest of his family was far from prosperous.

"And then there's the other, two doors down from Smythe. Noonan. He works at your River Rouge plant. Some sort of executive job, I suppose, since he wears a suit. Looks like an ourang-atang in a four-in-hand. They've both been shocking to Gladys."

"Who?"

"Mrs Sucre. You may have seen her in the kitchen with the others.

Her husband is a Negro physician, and she's attended a few Yes meetings. Whenever Noonan sees her at the front door, he bellows that laundresses should go around back."

Thia hadn't gotten any quieter. So now everybody in the speakeasy knew I was a nigger-lover as well as a Kraut-lover.

"You know," she said, growing even louder, "Fighting Bob has it right. He backs women's suffrage, and when the vote came up for the war, he stood up in that Senate, stood up and told the goddamn truth. How it was a bad idea. How people in Wisconsin opposed entering the war ten to one. *Ten.*"

She counted emphatically on her fingers before adding, "Fighting Bob told how the *Lusitania* was pregnant with shells and guns for the Brits. A miscarriage, that trip was. Like the whole goddamn war."

We were getting looks. Postures shifted. Conversations quieted.

"My parents left Austria because a Jew could never feel safe there. My husband was killed by the Germans. Now my moon-calf neighbors want me to feel unsafe because I'm an Austrian? Only they actually think I'm German. Well, I'm not a goddamn German!"

The last sentiment came out at full volume, which seemed to soothe the surly parties nearby. A couple gentlemen even raised their glasses and slurred, "Hear, hear!"

She smiled winningly and raised her glass in reply.

"For God's sake, Thia. You're beery, and you're going to—"

"Don't say 'embarrass yourself,'" she snapped.

You're going to get us lynched. Spare me the fucking agonies of the rich and beautiful. Maybe it wasn't a fair thought. Probably it wasn't. But every word out of her mouth felt like a brick through *my* parlor window. I snarled, truly snarled. Before I could stop, I was standing. Without a word or a backward glance, I stalked out.

The next evening I went to Kitty's for a conciliatory tea. The leaves were still in the strainer when she said, "She doesn't, you know."

"Yes, thanks."

"It's certainly not a reflection on you. She knows fine people, but she has no breeding. For heaven's sake, she invites nigs to meetings where they're not wanted—"

"And it gets worse. I heard that she recently dined in public with some society people and brought a pair of *wops* along. Honestly, can you imagine?"

"It wouldn't surprise me," Kitty said calmly, "if that brick didn't have something to do with the nig. And besides, my darling brother, look at who she chose, despite all her talk of social equality. An Anglo-Saxon college football hero."

"And I'm just a hunchbacked wop who couldn't finish college?"

"Tony."

For all I knew, Kitty was right. Maybe the anti-Boche fuss or the inescapable sanctimony about Jesus had made Thia uncertain whether she truly was American. Maybe unthinking and unthinkingly American Peter Everett was for her as a sort of one-man Ford English School.

"I'm not seeking her love," I said. "I just—"

"Well, you're seeking something. I know you. But you don't need it, whatever it is."

Of course not, I told myself. *What a ridiculous notion that I'd need something from Thia.*

In the end, I never apologized to Thia for abandoning her at the Wiana. At first, pride prevented me, and then bigger events crowded the episode from my attention. As Mr Ford was narrowly losing his Senate campaign, rumors of a cease-fire grew stronger until finally the Armistice came on November 11. Across America, families celebrated, and in Europe America's sons and sweethearts poked their noses out of the trenches and no longer smelled mustard gas.

Within a week or two of the Armistice, the APL started dying. The more enthusiastic operatives continued to file reports, mostly about routine union meetings or farfetched Bolshevistic plots. Suddenly, the wartime reach of the APL—the eavesdropping, the letter-opening, the reports to the Bureau of Investigation—all seemed chimerical. The Terrible Threateners went back to sounding like a bandit gang from a Tom Mix picture.

Even with the APL withering, I had plenty of work to do for Educational. Ford was deluged by demobbed men. Many were able-bodied and posed no particular challenges, but there were hundreds, thousands, of gouged and perforated men. At that time, there were about eight thousand "cards" at the Highland Park plant, each corresponding to a single task. We quickly learned that about one-third of the cards could be performed by one-legged men, seven hundred by one-armed men, and two by armless men. Blind men could sort cylinder head gaskets by touch (removing the asbestos and then separating the brass or tin from the copper).

Through some fluke, I was assigned both of Ford's armless employes.

In addition to the many men who had left bits of their bodies in Europe were those who, like Frankie Farelli (ultimately dispatched to Ann Arbor alienists), had left bits of their minds behind. They were passengers on an irregular and involuntary phantom ride through old perils on continuous projection, and there were no cards set aside for them.

Despite dealing with the whittled, shattered, and vacated, and despite having heard nothing from Carl since he'd left Newcastle for Russia, at first I felt no anxiety about my brother's fate. The war was over. Carl and the other "Polar Bears" (as the Americans in the Allied excursion to Archangel had come to be known) must soon come home. From the Armistice until St John's Day, each day Kitty spent a few hours preparing her home for Carl's return. Mother did the same with our home and also began reminding certain of her friends what an eligible match Carl would make their daughters. I frequently reminded Lisa that she should be especially kind to Uncle Carl when he first returned.

But in early December, still without further news from Carl or the Army functionaries we constantly asked for information, it became clear that the Polar Bears wouldn't be returning with the rest of the army because the White Sea had frozen too deeply for even icebreaker ships. Carl would spend the winter surrounded by ice, snow, and well-armed Bolsheviks. Kitty began going less often to the Church St house, and Mother reduced her cleaning and planning. They went to Mass instead.

After New Years, Ross started coming by some evenings. He'd often returned to the cathouse in Ferndale since we'd gone together, and he'd gotten a few doses as souvenirs. The doctors had cussed him, and he'd cussed himself. He swore that he was done with it, all of it, that he needed higher-toned ways to spend his evenings. He must have meant it, because our home was hardly a merry place to spend two or three evenings each week.

Our entertainment generally consisted of studying maps of the Archangel Oblast. We learned the placement of the White Sea, of Onega Bay and the Bay of Archangel. We traced the courses of the Onega, the Emtsa, the Tioga, the Pinega, the Dvina and its tribute the Vaga, the courses of the Volodga and the Murmansk railroads. We discovered how little daylight northern Russia received in winter, how temperatures could easily reach forty degrees below zero. We memorized the locations of villages—Kotlas, Toulgas, Chekuevo, Shenkhurst, Smolny, and all the rest. After that, we read treatises upon the tsarists, the Mensheviks, the Bolsheviks, and the downtrodden *moujiks* and their peasant philosophy of *nitchevo* (which none of us ever managed to understand). We did all this without knowing whether Carl had even survived the journey to Archangel. We diligently mastered every detail because we didn't know which one might turn out to matter.

Two weeks after Christmas, the postman at last delivered what the Army censors had left of this letter:

American North Russian Expeditionary Force

Russia
September 15, 1918

Dear Grams Family,

Please permit me to introduce myself. My name is Nathaniel Adams, in times of peace also a resident of Detroit. I am a of the Battalion, which is assigned to the city of Archangel in the Archangel Oblast, and I have recently become acquainted with your son and brother Carl Grams.

"And uncle," Carl adds. And uncle, then.

Carl sends his love and good wishes. I regret to say, that he cannot send them himself as he fell rather ill with a case of Spanish influenza en route from England aboard There was an outbreak of the illness on that Carl is a fine, brave doughboy and seems certain to make a speedy recovery.

Any errors about your family in the remainder of this letter will be entirely my own fault, as Carl has just fallen asleep.

I know that Carl very much wishes to hear from you, but I must warn you that in the winter months, with the White Sea frozen, all communications must come via the Murmansk railroad and the vagaries of drosky cart.

So please do not be alarmed should Carl not reply as promptly as you might hope. If necessary, I will write again with further news, but Carl should soon be able to write on his own behalf.

I am glad to have made Carl's acquaintance, and I shall hope to make yours in better times. Until then, I remain,

Sincerely yours,

N.T. Adams

Op. 3011 rptg.
——3378. 10/17/18.
Op. reports that "some sneaky son of a b____ is still distributing Wobbly propaganda in Y Bldg."
Copy enclosed of IWW leaflet in question ("With Drops of Blood...") Wobblies went deluxe for this one--note the realistic blood droplets.

We charge that members of the Industrial Workers of the World have been beaten, imprisoned, and deported and cite the cases of Bisbee, Arizona, where 1,164 miners, many of them members of the I.W.W. and their friends, were dragged out of their homes, loaded upon box cars and sent out of the camps. This was done by the mine operators, including Phelps Dodge, who cut the telegraph and telephone wires to that town to conceal what was happening. Those same operators financed the Sheriff's office as well as the so-called Citizens Protective League and the Workman's Loyalty league, and all of these "deputies" effected the deportation of the miners by violence and threat of violence. They went so far as to mount a machine gun atop one of the box cars on which the deportees were imprisoned. The miners were confined for months at Hermanas and Columbus, New Mexico...

We urge members to remember the case of an I.W.W. member under arrest at Birmingham, Alabama, taken from prison and placed on exhibition at a fair given in that city where admission of twenty-five cents was charged to see the I.W.W. ...

Chapter 19

LIKE THEIR CLOTHES, GULSA AND MERRY LOOKED WORN BUT DEEPLY respectable. The young gentlemen were spotless and unsubdued.

The Torassians' house was already bare, their belongings packed into trunks. They had sold the emptied furniture. Removal men would collect it later.

> *In scant moments, the whole pile was ablaze, and not too much later, it was a sullen mess of ash and ember*

There had been no farewell party, only a series of leave-takings.

"A party seemed strange," Merry said, as we stood alone upstairs, looking through the second-story dormer onto the mostly frozen river. "In Kirkuk, when I decided to leave, many of my family were angry. My father was a carpenter, as you know, and I was no good as a carpenter. But I was the son, and I was supposed to stay home. Still, even though they were angry, when I left we all gathered together, my family and also some of the neighbors, for food and farewell. But here..."

I felt even smaller than usual.

Merry chuckled and patted my shoulder. "Ah well, but then I didn't like many of those people, did I? I see now that my father was not all bad, but I would have stabbed him with a chisel if I stayed. Here, I love the ones coming with me."

He lifted his glass of *arak* in toast, and I touched mine to it.

Merry looked at his glass. "I hope I'm not contributing to your degradation," he said with a smile.

"*You're* not," I said.

He caught my emphasis and smiled. "I will miss you, my friend."

The 928 said that my next interviewee was Mrs Stanley Johnson. There was a woman waiting for me outside the door to the Johnsons' apartment. She was of medium height and sturdily built, with a few touches of gray in her hair and more than a few signs of anger in her eye.

"Tony Grams?" she asked.

The intonation, the implied glob of phlegm to the eyes, it was all very familiar. This wasn't Mrs Johnson. I knew her even before she said, "I'm Mona Ragnelli. Adamo Ragnelli is my husband."

I cursed myself—I already knew Ragnelli's employe number. I should have learned his address too. I tried to knock on the door behind her, but she blocked me. There was a movement in the hallway behind her, someone listening from an open door.

"I've said all I have to say about Sofia," I told her.

"Oh, you're done talking. How nice for you, Prince Charming. But maybe I'm not done."

"Maybe that's the problem with your family. All talking, no listening."

"I'm listening now. I'm listening to hear how Prince Charming is proud of how he takes advantage of an innocent—"

"Shut up if you're going to listen. You know it was a baby of normal size and born at a normal time. And you know I met Sofia seven months before the baby was born. And I'm the father? *I'm* the father?" I demanded. Startled by my fury, I tried to sound amused. "Sister, pull the other one."

"Took advantage of—"

"Bunk and buttercups. You want Prince Charming, find the guy who shoved his pea into her mattress."

I brushed past her and to knock at the door. A tall, dark young woman with hair down to the small of her back opened the door before I'd finished. "Mrs Johnson?" I asked.

She smiled carefully and nodded.

Mrs Johnson was clearly visiting relatives in the country. I caught Mona Ragnelli's eye and gestured at Mrs Johnson's belly. *You plan to blame this one on me too?*

Mona Ragnelli flushed with anger.

"What do you want, Mona?" Mrs Johnson asked.

"My business is with him," Ragnelli said.

"Yeah, well, his business is with me," she said sharply. "Please come in, Mr Grams."

After closing the door firmly on her neighbor, Mrs Johnson led me into the parlor and then into a comfortable armchair. Within seconds, a short, plump woman with corn-silk hair brought me tea. Mrs Johnson introduced the woman as her friend, Sarah Matterazi.

I had hoped for a friendly interview, one of the old-fashioned ones. That had been foolish. Sitting beside one another on a tilted sofa, their solid arms crossed beneath their worn, frizzy shawls, Mrs Johnson and Mrs Matterazi were stone-faced with ill-suppressed resentment.

About Mrs Johnson's husband, I had only a few memories supplemented by the 928. (He'd returned home a few months before the Armistice, I noted, which was a relief given his wife's five-month belly.) He'd definitely struck me as an example of the *new* new men, those who had only half returned from the wars. They weren't crazy like Frankie Farelli. They were just detached—transitory and suspicious of the walls around them. Every week, like a great smoky bellows, the factory inhaled and exhaled such men. Gone were the days of 15% or even 25% turnover. Turnover in 1918 had been 50%, and in 1919 it would reach 75%. That was, of course, nowhere near so dreadful as the 600% in the rest of the city. Still, it showed the restlessness and ill ease of the times. The new new men had seen a world beyond Detroit for the first time, seen bullets, blood, organized lunacy, and astonishing heroism. Being without a pay envelope didn't scare them as much as it had before the war, not even in the face of Detroit's increasingly wretched housing and its rising cost of living.

I paused my scrutiny of the scant records that Mrs Johnson had dropped in front of me.

"So?" Mrs Johnson asked. *Does my husband keep his job? Do we eat this week, have shelter next week? Will my baby be healthy at birth?*

The lines of the bank book seemed to flicker slightly, as if in their own private firelight. I withdrew from my pocket the spectacles which I had grudgingly begun to wear for reading, but they didn't stop the flickering. "Are these all your records?" I asked.

"I got a dozen Victor records, if you want 'em," Mrs Matterazi interjected. "I bought 'em second-hand, so they ain't an extravagance." She drawled every syllable of "extravagance."

I glared at her. After all, my job was at stake too. Every few weeks, another brushfire of panic about dismissals would sweep through Educational. So far we all still had jobs, but in truth we were baffled by that. Admittedly, the increased turnover meant plenty of new men, so perhaps we were needed. Still, it was hard to figure what purpose our interviews served. When the new year began, the men would be raised to six dollars a day, but that amount went half as far as five dollars had five years before. High Cost of Living. Since the war had ended, "HCL" was all anybody needed to say. Frozen pipes? Dead rats in the pantry? Holes in the roof? A forty-cent loaf of bread? HCL. It was especially difficult to find lodging that in our optimistic heyday would have been merely "Fair," and "Good" wasn't to be hoped for. The Johnsons' apartment, though painfully scrubbed, was only somewhat better than the hovel which Merry and I years earlier had declared unfit for the Abramoffs' habitation. In such circumstances, it was hard to see what purpose an advisor served. No lesson on hygiene or thrift could lower inflated prices.

"Your husband gets his profits," I said, setting the bank book on the table beside my tea.

They smiled for the first time. Mrs Johnson looked to be debating whether or not to thank me. I waved a preemptive hand. "If you can save anything, do it. Not for Ford, but for emergencies."

The hallway was free from Ragnellis, but someone had deflated the tires of my runabout.

Was there something about the unhealthy convolutions of my guts which whispered, "Here is a man who can keep any mess quietly inside"? Why did people think that I should read their secrets? Sardinian deserters, Turinese Socialists, and Detroit patriots all pegged me as a man who needed to know the ugly and the hidden.

Russia

Dec. 12, 1918

Dear Tony,

I'm sending this to you at Ford because I want to say some stuff, but I don't want Ma and the others to know.

I'm in Archangel (the city) again. The good news is that I get a break from the front. The bad news is that I'm in the hospital. This time it's not the 'flu. Just a bullet. Went in my back and stopped somewhere near the ribs. Lt. Cudahy wrote from ██████ that he just might kill me for letting the Bolos put a hole in my O.D., but he don't mean it.

Everybody around here tells me I'm a hero but then they laugh like ~~hienas~~ hyenas. We're most of us just guys too clumsy or dumb to duck when a 75 hits. The fellah next to me has been hit by shrapnel four times. He says he's a shell collector. Even Lt. Adams admits that's funny.

I guess the papers back home have a whole bunch of crank talk about us just generally dying all the time of frostbite and starving. Don't believe them. Sure, doughboys and the Tommies ██████████ but we've got all the cold weather clothing a man needs and then some. ██████████ I wish they hadn't given us these Shakleton boots, though. I don't know how that man made it to the South Pole slipping and falling every five feet. Anyways, except for the falling down and the stink that those little moojik houses get with nobody opening a window or a door if they can help it on account of the cold, it isn't too bad here.

And the getting shot. I guess that's a problem too.

I'll try to send a telegram around Christmas to let everybody know I'm jake, even if I am far away. You might know this because you paid attention in Latin and all that, but Lt. Adams just told me that 'tele' means distant. So I'll be a tele Grams sending a telegram.

I don't know if you heard about it, but the Reds celebrated Armistice Day by invading ██████████

where I was stationed with Co. They hit us pretty good, and the Canucks almost didn't have time to turn around the big guns. I came through that fine—not like some—only I got shot by a sniper while I was on patrol a week later. I just fell over and couldn't figure out why. Didn't even hear the report, so I guess the sniper was pretty tele himself. Did I tell you already the Bolos leave propaganda lying out on our patrol routes? To show us that they know everything about us, I guess. And also to tell us how we're only here because the Bolos won't pay back the Tsar's war debts and how we're scabbing against the moojiks. We always pick up the propaganda. Some of the fellahs read it, and most of us figure you can never have enough fuel for the fire (or paper for the latrine). I was reaching down for a stack of leaflets when I got hit. The felchers say if I'd been hit a half inch in most directions I probably would of croaked. So guess I owe the gentlemen at The Call a thank-you letter for saving my life with their I Won't Work prosing. I should probably apologise for bleeding all over it too.

Don't tell the others about me getting shot. Ma gets like she does about Gennaro, and Kitty has Andrew to think about. Angela would only pray for me a little harder, and praying hasn't done any great shakes for her, has it? You can tell Ilaria. She'd laugh how Red propaganda saved my life from a Red bullet.

Well, Doc Adams says it's time to hit the hay, and I guess he's right. Give my love to everyone.

Your brother,
Carl

Just before my birthday, Smythe handed me Carl's letter. I pointed out that somebody had worked open the censor's tape on the envelope.

"How odd." His tone was bland, but his rat mustache quivered at some hidden scent. I'd grown accustomed to his snooping about my files and my conversations, but I'd assumed somehow that the end of the APL would have decreased his zeal. But clearly it hadn't. I was going to have to do something about Smythe eventually. I simply had no idea what.

Although my visits to other men's homes felt less advisory and more condolatory, at least my own home regained some of its comforts once the APL reports disappeared. I no longer spent nights at my desk, straining my eyesight and my optimism beneath a banker's light.

Still, neither my eyes nor my hopes were treated more easily in the parlor, where Ross and my shrunken family sat peering at maps and fretting about the Polar Bears. We also wrote a great many letters. Kitty and Mother each sent two or three each week. They enlisted Ross' help sometimes, asking him for funny stories about politicians and other crooks. I sent a brief weekly letter, and even Lisa managed to write twice a month or so. Once Carl rejoined his company at the front, he wrote back every few weeks. His letters were cheerful and usually empty of information, but Mother and Kitty would spend whole evenings spinning inferences.

Almost every evening, Lisa wheedled to go to the cinema with her friends. I would've been an easy mark, but Kitty and Mother refused to let her leave home on a school night. She despised us, of course, but no more than most pubescents despise their kin. Occasionally she retreated bitterly to her room, cold though it was. Wherever she was, she disappeared into *Photoplay* or Gothic novels. I itched with the knowledge that Gennaro and Alessandra wouldn't have approved of their daughter's new interests or expectations.

But I didn't know what else to do about Lisa. I was fighting on the one hand Mother's longing for Elisabetta and on the other post-Armistice America, that chiaroscuro of brightly lit, dim-witted Coney Island hedonism and dark, unspoken bitterness. Against Mother, I counted it a triumph to spare Lisa from attending more than one Mass per week. Against the new America I had even less success. One weeknight, I took pity on Lisa and escorted her to *The Little White Savage.* She sat a few inches and several infinities away from me, frozen inside the light-and-dark geometries of Carmel Myers and her love interests. A heaven of lipstick, hair cream, and passionate gestures, of wealth and vamping. Lisa's upturned, immobile face was the face of everyone in the theater, the face of all the congregants at Mass who would not be denied their worship.

Most nights, while Mother and Kitty speculated on Archangel, inventing a thousand improbable torments and blessings for Carl, praying to the statue of St Michael on the hearth beside Gennaro and the icon of the Blessed Virgin above them. While Ross played along with them, I sat with them in the parlor, reading in an armchair beside the hiss and clank of our radiator.

I too was thinking of Carl, thinking what I couldn't say aloud in that parlor, in that nation. I was thinking that the Allied excursion to Russia was a case of fools making other men rush in where angels feared to tread. I was thinking that most of the fools had never so much as thought about *why* they'd sent Carl and the rest. To be sure, they had reasons. But those reasons changed with the breeze. First the Allies were in Archangel to recover the mountains of armaments which our government had sold to the Tsar before the revolutions. But long before the Allies landed, the Bolos had moved those weapons hundreds of miles south. (Though they *were* generously returning the shells and bullets just as fast as they could fire them.) Next our boys were there to keep Archangel free of Germans. Only, no German soldier had ever set foot in Archangel, and clearly none would do so after the Armistice. Then Carl and the rest were there to spread democracy by backing the Russians determined to overthrow the Bolos. Which, naturally, was why the Allies had sent 10,000 troops to fight the 50,000 Bolos in an area the size of Texas. In all Russia, Trotsky had fully a million men under arms. And they were truly under arms, unlike earlier in the war when the Tsar's corrupt generals had sold their own men's rifles so often that only one Russian soldier in ten had a gun.

Yet the American government and its English overlords seemed not to notice the problem. I found it obnoxious enough to listen to my family spin fairy tales of joy and despair while I rested my elbows on the fraying upholstery of my armchair. It was maddening to know that, in the oiled leather chairs of some London club, red-nosed gentlemen were reassuring one another that the Bolos must inevitably give way before the superior vigor of Anglo-Saxon blood.

Carl and the others could only hope for an outpouring of patriotic support from the *moujiks* determined to fight the Bolos. But although I never managed to understand the *moujiks'* beliefs, I understood them well enough to know there would be no such outpouring. Carl's letters, even after the censors cut them apart, made that obvious: those *moujiks* who joined the Allies did so for food and shelter, and the Bolos were offering those too. The *moujiks* had no patriotism for Russia. Russia meant no more to them than "Italy" had meant to starving little Scimmia caked in Ghilarzan dust. Patriotism was the province of shiny-buttoned aristocrats who, Carl reported, generally treated the *moujiks* like dogs.

I could only hope that General Ironside and the Allied officers under him in Archangel understood all this and were explaining it to their superiors in pungent language. If the Allies didn't retreat when the ice broke, the Bolos would attack them in earnest. And, whatever the leather-chair lords believed, Anglo-Saxon blood—Italian blood—wouldn't flow from wounds any less than would other blood.

Sometimes, instead of reading news about Archangel, I would search the 'papers for mention of Thia while pretending to myself that I wasn't doing so. Her name appeared often, in large part because she was connected to Emmeline Ward, who had indeed become Detroit's first lady policeman. The 'papers adored a beautiful lady policeman from a socially prominent family. (Ross' editor repeatedly threatened to dismiss him for trying to smuggle in phrases like "a comely lass who delights in surrounding herself with hardened police dicks.") Moreover, Thia's name frequently appeared in the society pages, which made note every time the Yeses poured tea in the name of the implacable Nineteenth Amendment. To her delight, Kitty occasionally made the 'papers as an "also present."

Then there was this item:

EVERETT, MUELLER TO WED

DETROIT, April 1—Peter Everett, scion of prominent Grosse Pointe, etc. has announced that this July he will take as his bride Cynthia Mueller, daughter of eminent Detroit physician, usw.

You're a stubby, grubby monkey, Grams. Surely you didn't expect some other outcome?

Given the date, I initially hoped that the actual announcement was a hoax. After its reality sank in, I spent a while being thoroughly not at all in any way upset by the engagement and feeling very happy for goddamn Thia and her goddamn Bakelite beau.

Thia's engagement was just the spy of sorrow. The battalion arrived not much later, delivered by a Western Union bicycle boy. He wasn't far from soldiering age, and his uniform wasn't so different from the uniforms we'd seen march to and from war. Some surprises you see coming ten thousand miles away.

It was Carl, of course. He'd been killed. A telegram for a tele Grams.

Days after we learned of Carl's death, reports of a mutiny in "I" Company reached us. Detroit men in Archangel were demanding an explanation for their purpose in Russia before they returned to the front lines. Those rumors were confirmed, denied, redefined, and ultimately "I" Company returned to battle long enough for a few more deaths on all sides. Five weeks later, the skin of the White Sea shattered and the Polar Bears came home. Mayor Couzens met them at New York Harbor and escorted them back to Detroit. Men who had ridden an armored train bristling with machine guns along the Vologda line now found themselves chugging toward Detroit's Grand Depot under the protection of their fat-faced, white-haired mayor.

When they reached Detroit, there was a large parade from Campus Martius to Belle Isle. Mother dragged Lisa, Kitty, and me to watch it. As we had four years earlier for Americanization Day, we stood at the edge of the square, not far from where the Opera House met the Wonderland building. My back spasmed, and Kitty's faithless leg left her leaning hard on me. Mother, too, leaned on me, quivering with the contest between fury and resignation. She was too drained to cry, though rims of near-tears shimmered on her lower eyelids. Lisa stood in front of us, her face turned away.

Fifteen hundred living soldiers and two hundred fifty dead and missing marched past in crisp field uniforms. Proud men marched. Joyful men marched. Tired men marched. Limbless men, arms and pant legs answering to the winds, marched. Strong men invisibly cut marched, their smiles fixed like bayonets, frozen like brown leaves in winter ice.

It was about that time I became a spy, again and more fully a spy. A spy of and on sorrow, stupidity, and all man's birthrights.

PART THREE

Bravely and Instantly

Chapter 20

For a long while, I'd been mulling over Merry's tip that Smythe was visiting Cast-Iron Charlie Sorensen over at the Rouge. A month or so after Carl's wake, I finished some sleuthing and worked out to my satisfaction at least some of what Smythe was doing. I began to take counter-measures by requesting a few moments alone with The Boss.

"I hope this doesn't strike you as impertinent, sir, or as overly suspicious," I began, as I took a seat at the edge of the cushioned leather chair across the desk from The Boss. "But you mentioned once that you found my work for the APL to be satisfactory—"

"'Judicious' was the word I used, I believe. If you've a concern, Tony, I naturally wish to hear it."

"Well, sir, it's Mr Smythe." I paused.

He raised his eyebrows slightly but said nothing.

"Of course you know, sir, that Mr Sorensen has taken control of the Rouge and that he's largely relying on Harry Bennett to monitor the men there. And that Bennett's methods are, ah, somewhat different than ours here in Educational."

Harry Bennett was an ex-prizefighter, and by all reports, he wasn't much for scrupulous 928s and the spirit of fraternalism. He preferred to get his information from finks and to change his laborers' behavior via blunt men wielding blunt instruments. Both Sorensen and Bennett mattered increasingly because, with all the expansion and the improvements, it was clear that within a few years the Rouge could be larger and more powerful than Highland Park.

The Boss nodded slowly. "Yes, I've told Henry many times of my dismay over how Charlie Sorensen conducts his business. I firmly believe that it undermines the moral progress of the men, as well as the authority of this department. But Henry puts great store in Sorensen's judgment."

"Yes, sir, and that's why I was, let us say concerned, to discover that Mr Smythe—"

"And you know," The Boss interrupted with a peevish edge, "it doesn't help one whit that Henry and Sorensen are both so taken with the Reverend Bradby. Not only is the Rouge plant pitted against this one, even this one is divided against itself. We have practically two Educationals."

I controlled my irritation and nodded. The Rev. R. L. Bradby had nothing to do with Smythe, but The Boss was wise to worry about him nonetheless. Although all Ford men in theory were the concern of Educational, once colored workers had started replacing the men gone to war, Ford muck-a-mucks had started using the Rev. Bradby (himself a Negro) to select suitable Negro laborers and to maintain discipline among them. This was no minor matter. Detroit was burgeoning (its population had doubled to a million in the preceding decade), and its Negro population was growing especially fast—increasing sixfold in the same decade. The end of the war hadn't stopped that growth in the slightest. Certainly Negroes were an ever-growing presence at Ford. In 1916, the company had employed about two hundred Negroes, but a mere three years later there were seven or eight times that number on the pay rolls.

This made the Rev. Bradby a cause for concern for us in Educational. To be sure, I had consulted with Bradby many times and found him likeable enough. An imposing six-footer with a strong build and a booming voice, he had worked his way out of a childhood nearly as hungry as my own to become the pastor of Second Baptist Church. Despite his likeability, however, I often found myself regarding him the way Smythe regarded everyone—as a sneak thief bent on filching my job while I slept.

Yes, Smythe. I returned to my original purpose. "Well, sir, as I was saying, I recently chanced to hear that Mr Smythe is in the habit of visiting Mr Sorensen and perhaps Mr Bennett at the Rouge, weekly or even more often. I've since had the chance to confirm those reports."

The Boss raised his eyebrows and stared into my face. "I see."

"Again, I don't wish to be impertinent, and naturally I can't speak with certainty..."

"Go ahead."

"Well, sir, it seems to me that Mr Smythe may well be serving as an operative of Mr Bennett. And, unless I miss the mark, I can't think that will help us here at Educational. Quite the reverse, I'd wager."

The Boss closed his eyes and leaned his head back with a frown on his face. Eventually he tilted his head back down and looked at me. "I confess too that recently I have begun to develop some ... misgivings about Mr Smythe's commitment to the Educational spirit. Still, I'm surprised—Or perhaps I'm not. I shouldn't be. Seen clearly, a beautiful plan such as the one Educational serves has all the grace and majesty of an ocean liner. But it has the same susceptibility to attack from those who would lurk beneath the surface and torpedo it without ever showing themselves."

He pressed his fingers together and rested them at the bridge of his nose. "What I am about to say must remain between us," he said.

"Of course, Dr Marquis."

"The problem is not only at the Rouge with Sorensen and that Bennett person. This recent strike at the Wadsworth foundry and the way in which the Ford men sent over to replace the strikers refused to 'turn scab'—and of course the favorable settlement for the strikers—has some important men worried and angry. Very worried and very angry."

I nodded cautiously. So far this intelligence hardly merited my promise of confidentiality. In recent months, the Auto Workers Union and the Wobblies had been loudly denouncing Ford, and the Ford bigwigs had been loudly denouncing the unions. Indeed, much of Detroit's manufacturing royalty had been fulminating to the 'papers about "crime unions" and their "unpatriotic" strikes.

"I've learned," The Boss continued, "that employers throughout the city are hiring on fantastic numbers of men to spy upon their employes. O'Neill's Detective Agency, Bob Williamson's men, Corporations Auxiliary, the Detroit Employers' Agency, the Pinkertons." He shook his head. "And it's happening here, too. In this very plant. Bill Klann, Alex Spark in Employment, and many others are seeing 'Reds' where once they saw 'Krauts,' and they're sending in operatives to spy on the men. *My* men." He paused. "Alex Spark is already running something called, though only unofficially, the Service Department or the Watchman Department."

He handed me a report dated only a few days earlier. It was a short note on plain paper from "19" to "A.S." The former was reporting that an employe had called Mr Ford and Bill Klann "dirty scabs" for sending men to replace the striking Wadsworth workers.

"Here in Highland Park, such reports go daily to Spark's office," The Boss said. "As many as ever went to the APL. More, perhaps. At the Rouge they go to Bennett and then to Mr Sorensen. The organizations at the two plants, I believe, are separate from one another. Bennett and Spark seem even to be rivals. But they do the same work—spy on all the men, not just saboteurs."

I blew out slowly. That was indeed a worry. For Educational's power, for its existence, and certainly for its ability to do anything beneficial for Ford employes. My feud with Smythe was turning out to be part of a much nastier and more important battle.

"What do you want me to do, sir?"

He chuckled mirthlessly and drummed his fingers on his desk. "To go to work for Mr Spark."

That same day, The Boss promoted me to the position of senior advisor. I received only slightly more in the way of wages, but I was granted my own little office, a distinction conferred upon few men in the department. My new responsibilities officially made me Smythe's equal, which ensured his undying hostility. At first, he had hated me only for having The Boss' favor. Then he had hated me for refusing to be caught by Sofia Ragnelli and the countless other little snares he'd set for me. Smythe worked against any man at Educational who showed any sign of ever getting ahead, though, so much of his animosity had been impersonal. The promotion changed that. Perhaps he saw me as a greater threat, perhaps as a greater affront. Whatever the reason, he watched me more than ever, more angrily than ever.

But I didn't have much leisure to worry about whatever schemes Smythe was hatching against me, as I was too busy hatching schemes against Alex Spark. The Boss insisted the promotion was simply reward for my exemplary work, but I suspected that he also thought it would make Spark consider me a more attractive recruit for Service. In any event, Service particularly needed recruits at that moment because Spark had recently been obliged to send many of his operatives to Mount Clemens, where Mr Ford was suing the *Chicago Daily Tribune* for calling him a pig-ignorant anarchist. Mr Ford had established a news bureau in Mount Clemens to help him spread his version of the trial. (Which was necessary because the other versions of the trial were making him sound like a pig-ignorant anarchist who was unable to define "anarchist" and who believed that Benedict Arnold had been a writer of some kind.)

Though he was too tactful to say so, I suspected that The Boss also thought that Carl's death would establish me as a man with no love for Bolos in particular and Reds in general, making me all the more desirable to Spark. Perhaps he was right. In any case, Service approached me. It was O'Hara again.

> *You maybe aren't entirely a true American gentleman, but you submit your reports on time and know which side your bread is buttered on... You are washed in the blood of your brother, and your birth and your pigment are forgiven... Be sides, you want to stop the bastards who killed your brother, don't you?*

Yes, I said. Yes, I wanted to stop them. Yes, I would obey; yes, I would join.

And then I was standing outside O'Hara's office, desperate to steady my shivers, to slow my heart, to calm my gut. I hadn't lied when I'd said I wanted to stop the bastards who'd killed Carl. I'd even meant the Bolsheviks. But not only them.

> *It is not one's enemy who says, "Come to this ditch and die for it."*

Alex Spark's office was in Employment where the Ford building came to a corner at John R and Manchester. His secretary was a hard-eyed man about my age named Slyker. Each morning I picked up the anonymous raw reports from Slyker and returned the processed ones. No matter how early I arrived, Spark was already in his office, and sometimes he summoned me inside.

Spark made me nervous. He had a solid build and light, thinning hair which he kept closely cropped. He'd come to America from England as a child, some said as an orphan. He certainly had the wariness and the half-suppressed truculence one associated with men accustomed to fighting their own corner.

Responding to his summons that morning, I found him sitting as usual at his maniacally tidy desk. Sometimes he would watch through his window while men in the alley below unloaded produce for the grocer. This time he was poring over reports.

At his gesture, I gave him my report. "Was there anything else, Mr Spark?"

He grunted vaguely and shoved some silence at me. Spark was a ferocious listener who knew that a suspicious silence made others talkative. I smiled but tried not to speak.

"Anything I should know?" he eventually asked, with his customary faint stutter and traces of some lower-class English accent.

"Some useful stuff, but nothing different."

He gave another vague grunt and continued reading. I felt as if he were using my report as a mirror to watch my face. "Nothing about Sorensen or his Irish midget?" he asked.

The Irish midget (a couple inches taller than I, mind you) was Harry Bennett. Though Spark generally revealed little about his concerns, it had quickly become obvious that he hated, feared, and admired Bennett in equal measure. He was always hungry for information about Bennett's maneuvers to establish control over Employment at the Rouge. I suspect he was convinced that Bennett would come for Highland Park once he had the Rouge, and he was probably right. Characters like that don't stop voluntarily.

"Nothing on Bennett or Sorensen, sir. But Councilman Stanley joined the Klan last week. Bill Klann almost did too."

Spark snorted, perhaps amused by Klann's joining the Klan.

At least I was fighting the Klan. Service fought any organization that threatened to organize the men differently than the demands of the line did. I still thought of Alessandra's murder every time I helped an operative snitch on a Ford man for posting union handbills outside Michigan Malleable, but fighting the Klan let me feel less guilty. It's important not to feel guilty, especially when you are.

Here's another half-truth I told myself about working for Service: It was no different than simply living in Detroit, or in America for that matter. True, Service was seeing Bolos in the cupboard, but so was everyone else. Really, when it came to Reds, Service was far *less* hysterical than the 'papers, than the men in the blind pigs and the housewives in the shops. Service tracked and marked men who went too often to the bathroom, who stole naps behind piles of material, who diddled their piece counts, but they—we—didn't consider such men Bolsheviks. We reserved that label for the Socialists, the Communists, and union men. Outside of Service, however, the Red scare made people promiscuous in their definitions of Bolshevism. Bolsheviks were anarchists, and many, many Americans had as much trouble defining "anarchism" as Mr Ford. In general, a Bolshevik was somebody whom somebody else disliked. The crape-hanging and the party-going, the boorish and the broad-minded, the soda-jerk who underpoured an egg cream and the telephone operator who lingered a few extra seconds on the line—Bolsheviks each and every one.

It seemed sometimes that paranoia and hatred were monstrous energies which could be created but not destroyed. During the war we had summoned them with incantations of *krautkrautkraut,* and afterward the monsters lingered on, swimming the rivers and lakes, skulking the alleyways, only now nourishing themselves on chants of *redredred.*

It seemed that way, but I knew better. Paranoia and hatred and all the rest came out of how men related to each other, and how they related to each other depended upon how they earned their daily bread. At Ford the roar of the monster was as much as anything the roar of the blast furnace and the boiler, the clacking of its teeth the clatter of the line.

Chapter 21

IN THE MIDDLE OF JULY, SIGI AND MARTHA GLUECK INVITED ME "AND companion" to a small dinner in honor of Dr Henry Sucre's return to Detroit. On the invitation, Sigi had written, "I remembered our earlier interesting conversation and thought you might wish to know Dr Sucre and to see the Rev. Bradby again. I suppose I need not warn you that there will be Negroes present."

My first response was to wonder whether Thia had persuaded her father to invite me. Or had she tried to *stop* him? Then I reminded myself that I didn't care what Thia thought.

Ross laughed dutifully at Kitty's comments about nose bones and cannibalism, but I wouldn't have asked either of them to be my companion in any case. So I would have no companion—unless I invited Sofia Ragnelli. Of course, I didn't care what Thia might think of my inability to find a companion. Her companion—her *betrothed*—had a chest stuffed with moral fiber and a skull packed with bran. Her judgment meant nothing to me.

I bought a new suit at Godfrey's and paid additional to have it altered in time.

The night of the party, Sigi himself answered the door. "Daniel," he explained as he showed me into the parlor, "is in the kitchen helping Martha."

The drapes were drawn against prying eyes and flying bricks, and electric bulbs spread soft light through tasteful shades. Thia was there, naturally, several labor riots crowded gorgeously into a blue dress. She was conversing with the Rev. Bradby (tall and discreetly resonant as always) and with the demure colored woman I'd seen in Sigi's kitchen the night of the broken window. Dr Sucre's wife. A few feet from them, an elegant blonde of early middle age ran her fingertips over her forearm as she talked with a nattily dressed Negro. It looked like the wedding scene from *Birth of a Nation*, and I paused uncomfortably at the threshold. Mercifully, there was no sign of Peter Everett.

"Come meet Dr Sucre," Sigi said, gesturing toward the natty Negro.

One expects successful Negroes to be light-complected, but Dr Sucre was every bit as black as Thia's hair. His teeth flashed white as he smiled engagingly.

"A pleasure, sir," he said in an Eastern accent of some sort. Bostonian possibly.

"Likewise," I said, wishing that it were. But, really, confronted with a Negro doctor, most men can only feel resentful. Or wasteful.

"Tony, how lovely to see you," Thia said, resuming her conversation before I could reply.

"Likewise," I told myself.

Sucre smiled at me with delicate ambiguity. I smiled back.

"Henry," Sigi told me, "is just returned from Paris. He was in France for the war and then remained to study at the Sorbonne."

"Sigi makes it sound impressive," Sucre said, "but the Sorbonne turned out to be unhelpful, medically speaking. Especially compared to the war, sad to say. During the war I had the honor of being a nurse in Dr Cushing's base hospital," (again that ambiguous smile) "and he's an absolutely brilliant man for head injuries of all sorts."

"Henry makes me think," Sigi said, "that perhaps I should not have given up so easily on the physical brain. It appears as if it might be possible to understand one day something about it. Still, the war has taught us a great deal about the mind as well, especially how men handle psychic trauma."

"Honestly, Father," Thia interjected, "you make it sound as if the soldiers should have brought school desks and inkwells to the trenches."

I remembered Frankie Farelli, inky and dismayed.

Sigi looked at his daughter, then at me, and blushed faintly. "That's not at all what I meant, *liebchen*. And I meant no disrespect toward your brother, of course, Tony."

My hand waved with a magnanimity which the rest of me didn't entirely share.

Sigi and Sucre chatted a while longer about shell shock and cerebellopontile angles (at first I thought Sigi was saying "angels," which would have been more interesting). I made sure to look attentive to them, rather than to Thia, who was laughing uproariously at something Mrs Sucre had said.

A little while later, Sigi went to the door again to receive a mulatto built according to the same general blueprint as Peter Everett but with heavy Negro features. The mulatto had a sleek-haired 'high yella' beauty on his arm. Dr Sucre left me to greet the man and woman warmly.

I stood awkwardly alone, trying to look as though I weren't avoiding Thia's eye. Soon Sigi rejoined me. "Captain Allan," he told me, inclining his head toward the newcomers. "And his wife, Bethany. Friends of the Sucres."

"You're a brave man," I whispered to Sigi, "to open your house to so many Negroes. With popular sentiment what it is."

"Our neighbors," Sigi said with a tight smile. "Yes. Smythe and Noonan behind us especially." He added quietly, "I confess that I hesitated, but Martha made me feel like a terrible coward. Ah, speak of the angel."

I followed his gaze to see Martha Glueck stepping into the parlor. Her dress was a simple, sleeved black gown with touches of silver.

"I was just now telling Tony that you and Thia have given me the courage to defy our neighbors," Sigi murmured to his wife as she drew close enough to hear.

She waved her hand. "It is nothing to do with courage. Many times I have told Sigi that I need a new garden shed. And we have learned that the cheapest way to get bricks is to anger our neighbors."

Soon enough, Daniel summoned us to the dining room. As the guest of honor, Dr Sucre sat at the head of the table, and Martha kept her place at the foot. I was seated immediately to her left, with Bradby to my left and Mrs Sucre directly across from me. Fortunately for my increasingly unreliable digestion, Thia was at the far end of the table.

Martha and Sigi were resolutely cheerful hosts, and the conversation was interesting and remarkably good-humored, especially for a dry party. I had to remind myself to remain guarded. I couldn't allow myself to forget that the Rev. Bradby reported to Cast-Iron Charlie Sorensen.

Capt. Allan turned out to have been an officer in a Negro infantry regiment during the war. "The Black Rattlers, we called ourselves," he was telling the table. "Also 'Pershing's Bastards' because General Pershing put us in a bassinet and left us at the Frenchies' doorstep. Did us a favor, I'd say. I can't say as the *poilus* loved us much, but they were better than the doughboys."

His tone was lighthearted until the last few words. He seemed to be looking at the Rev. Bradby, who was concentrating on his roast beef.

"Still," Allan continued, "we never gave the Boche an inch of those trenches, never had a man captured. Whenever Pershing or the Froggies wanted fighting done, we did it and did it right."

"The Negro's courage and fortitude are beyond question," the elegant blonde said.

Mrs Sucre looked at her expressionlessly.

"Oh, we're a useful people," Allan said. "Though too often a foolish one."

"Bill," said his wife in a calming tone.

"Well, we are," the Captain insisted, though less bitterly. "Easiest way to get a man to work like the devil is to assume that he's incapable of the work. He'll spend the rest of his days proving you wrong."

He and Sucre chuckled resignedly.

"Gladys accuses me of doing just that with the children," Sucre said. Mrs Sucre smiled. "Henry shook his head in such disappointment at Henry David simply because the poor boy learned the alphabet a fraction slower than Regina."

"I hardly—" Sucre began.

"*And* he did the same with Regina when she didn't learn her multiplication tables fast enough to suit him. And again with her violin lessons."

"Well, *if* I am guilty as charged," Sucre said, "I should point out that Henry David and Regina are able little scholars, quite precocious for six and eight."

"Very true," his wife conceded with a proud smile.

"Naturally, you are both impartial," Martha remarked with a small grin which the Sucres returned.

"But I think that is not what Captain Allan meant," Sigi said slowly. "Expressing disappointment is simply another way of showing that one expects success. Captain Allan meant to expect failure, I think. And expecting failure generally encourages failure."

"Which does Ford do, Tony?" Thia asked. "Expect its men to fail, or to succeed?"

There was a trap in the question that I didn't understand. "What would you say, Reverend Bradby?" I asked.

"Yes, Reverend," Allan asked, half teasing and half taunting, "what does Ford expect of its Negroes?"

"Mr Ford," Bradby said with stiff dignity, "gives his Negroes better pay and greater hope than many."

"And Negroes give their Mr Ford greater effort and less trouble than would union men," Allan replied.

Bradby frowned. "That's not—"

"Oh, don't mistake me, Rev.," Allan said. "Believe me, I appreciate the difficulties of your situation."

I was beginning to appreciate them as well. Bradby's every report to Sorensen must have been at least as complicated and nerve-wracking as my conversations with Alex Spark. He too must always have felt like a traitor and a target.

"Tony still hasn't answered," Thia pointed out. "Tony, how do you see it?"

"I suppose I'm like Peter," I said. "I don't give such things much thought. And why *isn't* your beloved with us tonight?"

"He's ill," Thia said shortly.

After an awkward silence, the conversation fractured into smaller groups, and Bradby turned to me to begin an earnest discussion about his hope that Educational might take a greater interest improving the treatment of Ford's Negroes. I listened carefully, aware that I would have to report back to The Boss. I wondered whether it might even have been Bradby who had suggested that Sigi invite me to dinner simply so that we might have that very conversation.

For three days, the Thompson & Black auditors had been in the Educational measuring desks, counting paper-clips, and pondering how many of us could be replaced with adding machines. I was surprised that all of Smythe's toadying hadn't given them warts.

"I don't think they're related to Service," I told The Boss. "Service doesn't care about accountants."

"But what *does* it care about?" The Boss asked, plaintively. "What does Spark want?"

"What Cast-Iron Charlie Sorensen wants over at the Rouge," I said patiently. "To keep the men from organizing."

"Yes, naturally." The Boss pursed his lips. "But this man you mention, this Lipowicz, he wasn't conducting union business on company time. Or on company property. And yet Spark has dismissed him without so much as consulting this department."

Could he really not understand? I had become paranoid enough to wonder whether The Boss' lack of paranoia might be some manner of ruse.

Once a week or so, The Boss had been calling me in "to discuss one of my men." With scrupulous honesty, he would then actually ask me a few questions about some Farelli, Sullivan, or Lipowicz. (I usually spent this time wondering if Spark yet had spotted my treachery and whether, if so, he'd merely have me fired or would instead send some dead-eyed thug to drag me to the sand pile and tattoo me with a lug wrench.) Only after that would The Boss ask me what Spark wanted.

These conversations inevitably and increasingly frustrated me. At first, The Boss had seemed up to the task of battling Spark and Sorensen. He had the intellect, certainly, and the dedication. But it was increasingly clear that The Boss was too worried about morality to attend fully to the question of power. Although he was more attuned to the world than many priests, and although I admired him for avoiding the priestly snare of seeing moral progress as a pilgrim's progress in which a man somehow becomes better by stripping away all ties to this life, at bottom he seemed to think his struggle with Spark and Bennett was a matter of hymnals and homilies, and I was starting to believe that this would be the end of Educational.

Then again, the end of Educational was beginning to look inevitable regardless of who was at its helm. Many, perhaps most, powerful Ford men resented us because we interfered with their dominion over their laborers. The sort of man who could have successfully defended Educational's power against such enemies almost surely would have wanted to preserve *only* its power. He wouldn't have cared one whit about the new man. Most of the big bosses had only ever suffered Educational to exist because Henry Ford had supported it, and he had supported it largely because it helped to keep turnover down and productivity up. But by then it was unclear that Educational was still necessary to achieve those ends. Turnover was up, yes, but not enough to justify the expense of keeping it any further down. And productivity was unparalleled.

For the big bosses, the real threat was no longer the risk of workers' moral disorganization. It was the risk of union organization. But even that could be controlled, especially, as Capt. Allan had noted, if the unions kept posting "No Niggers After Sundown" signs around their headquarters. All-white unions ensured a reserve of Negro laborers who would gratefully work cheap in order to escape scratching a sharecropper's mouthful from soil which sprouted lynch mobs as easily as cotton.

"—worrisome, of course," The Boss was saying. "I really do think I should make Henry aware of this."

My face must have said something. "You disagree?" he asked.

I disagreed. There was no point telling Ford anything. He already knew. He knew that struggle among the laborers discouraged unionization. For that matter, he clearly believed that struggle among the big men led to success and innovation. This was a man who, a few months earlier, had made his son Edsel the titular President of the company and had then continued to run the company himself, constantly backing Sorensen against Edsel.

Brief though they were, those meetings with The Boss left me bone-weary and feeling as if one of Spark's men had already clubbed me and left me in the sand pile.

"I'll be honest with you, Landucci," I said. "Mr Jackson thinks you're a malingerer." I stared at him grimly.

Landucci and I were seated across the desk in my tiny office. The door was open, so Smythe was eavesdropping. I was fairly certain that Smythe was reporting to Spark as well as to Bennett, but I wasn't sure which master he was serving and which he was betraying. Unless they were both in league against The Boss.

I'd often seen Landucci, but this was our first genuine conversation. He was a plump man of about forty with virile, swirling hair everywhere but the crown of his head. During that particular conversation, he slouched into his chair, his chinless face set in an expression blending grievance with long-suffering. But usually he hummed burlesque tunes and wore a winning grin which seemed in constant peril of sliding off his chinless face. If I hadn't known what he was, he would have reminded me of Merry.

"I put in an honest day's work," he said. "Ain't my fault Jackson thinks I'm a Wobbly."

Landucci *was* a Wobbly. In fact, he was a paid-up member of every labor group that issued cards and collected dues. But that's because he was Service Operative 19, Spark's prize fink, and it was his job to spy on Ford workers. If the apostles had used membership cards, Landucci would have bought one and passed the bill to Pilate's secretary.

Landucci was one of the few Service operatives who could report directly to Spark, so I saw only his lesser reports, which he wrote in a cramped, ungrammatical scrawl despite attaching to each report a reimbursement request for typewriter ribbon and carbon paper. He was a hero in the face of his rheumatism (triggered by physical labor and cured by unbaptized liquor and six-bit blowjobs). Above all else, he excelled at his job. Other Service operatives came and went. They would fall under suspicion by the men. They would fail to be suitably suspicious of the men. They would get ground down by constantly winning and betraying confidences. But not Op. 19. Op. 19 endured. Op. 19 thrived.

Landucci was still acting his rôle. "Even if I was a Wobbly, that ain't Jackson's affair. I mill a hundred and eighty gears a day. Honest count, not like some coots as do one-sixty but put two hundred on the board."

"Mr Jackson isn't the sort to tell tales," I said.

"Comes to me, he's a regular Grimm brother."

"Well, *do* you have a medical excuse for Wednesday?"

It was all a little bit more fun than it should have been. He handed over an envelope, and I skimmed its contents: a set of reports on potential troublemakers among the laborers. "Very well," I said grudgingly. "But don't think you've a free pass around here, Landucci."

Landucci grinned ironically and ambled outward.

"A bit flinty with that one, weren't you, Tony?" asked Smythe, who'd materialized at my threshold.

If he was being sincere, then he didn't know who Landucci was, which suggested that Spark didn't much trust Smythe. Smart man, Spark.

I slowly moved Landucci's report back and forth on the desk, but Smythe's eyes didn't follow it.

"Flinty, hell," I told Smythe. "It would be just deserts if somebody started a fire on that piker's hindquarters."

Chapter 22

> We lay great stress upon family condition. We make every effort to re-unite a man and wife who are living apart. We bring together every sort of physical force in bringing about the reunion of families. We have made a discovery. You have all heard that the family is the foundation of the Church and State. We have found that it is the foundation of right industrial conditions as well. Nothing tends to lower a man's efficiency more than wrong family relations.
>
> – The Rev. Samuel S. Marquis

IN LATE JULY, ANGELA AND ILARIA APPEARED AT MY DOORSTEP. ILARIA HAD left her children at home with Martin, but Angela was lugging all the little Baggios: Gasparo, Brunella, Gianluca, Gisella, and Crocifissa. Many of them I had encountered only in their pupal forms, but at that point Gasparo was the eldest (twelve), Crocifissa the youngest (five). Each was presentably dressed and scrupulously clean, yet somehow off-putting. Askew. Gianluca was sickly and pampered, Crocifissa seldom made a sound, and the other three had the wariness of street-corner grifters. Though all wrist bone and gristle, Gasparo was already taller than I and squeezed hard when we shook hands.

The Gramazios would have scoffed at the idea, but the Gramses (even Mother) decided that our home was too small for everyone. Poor Kitty found herself hosting Angela and her brood. Ilaria settled into Carl's former room. Though Angela and her children slept at Kitty's home, they crowded my parlor for most of the day. They didn't disturb me with noisy play. Just the reverse. They disturbed me with their uncanny quiet.

Angela had arrived wearing heavy cosmetics that did little to conceal her black eye and bruised cheek.

"She wants me to tell people she was in the hospital for appendicitis," Ilaria said on the second evening after their arrival as we walked north on Woodward.

I wanted to misunderstand Ilaria's meaning. Even in shirtsleeves, I was syrupy with sweat from the summer heat, and I had just finished another futile discussion with The Boss. I was so grubby and tired and everything else that I desperately wanted to believe that Stefano, for all his flaws, was no wife-beating coward and that Angela, for all her flaws, was no aspiring martyr.

Ilaria read my expression and shook her head slightly. I was ashamed, but I laughed too. It was a relief to have someone who understood me. I hadn't seen Ilaria since the summer after Lisa had arrived in Detroit, and I hadn't realized how much I'd missed her. When we were apart I still tended to think of her as the girl who had helped to hold the family together while Father was in prison. But she was becoming motherly. In fact, she looked like Mother had back in Ghilarza, or least like Mother would have looked had she been able to wear pristinely white cotton dresses and fine straw hats teetering between the elegant and the ludicrous.

"You looked like Angela just now," Ilaria said. "When I try to talk to her about that swine."

"Probably felt like her too. 'It's even harder to ignore this if the rest of you won't play along.'"

She laughed faintly and then started to speak once or twice.

"That bad?" I asked.

She nodded. "I think Stefano has started to beat Gasparo. In earnest."

I cursed. Gennaro, Andrew, Carl, all dead. And this Stefano, by all accounts, obnoxiously hale for a forty-year-old drunk. Once again, I wanted to get on a train and pound the son of a bitch like a railroad spike. Once again, I wanted to be physically capable of pounding the son of a bitch like a railroad spike.

"Not until she leaves him for good," Ilaria said with calm clairvoyance. "When that happens" (sign of the cross) "Martin and I will go to the police."

"She won't testify against him. They never do."

"No, but he never repays the money we loan him, and we always make him sign for it. He has even stolen from us. And once he's in prison, perhaps... Well, horse, then cart, I suppose."

A flash of realization must have crossed my face. Ilaria laughed. "Yes, she might be here a while. But it's easier for you than for Kitty. Angela doesn't criticize men."

"Then she doesn't consider me a man."

She smiled. "Can you afford it? Martin and I will help, of course. Are you paying Kitty's mortgage?" she asked. "And for her food?"

"Just her food, for now. Andrew left her some money, and she's entitled to his death benefit if it ever comes. Carl's hasn't. And there's been some hold-up with his—Carl's—Michigan service bonus as well. So far all we've gotten is his Manship ring."

She raised her eyebrows.

"Some fellah named Manship designed some silver rings for the Polar Bears," I explained. "They all got them. And Carl got medals, too. It turns out he was a hero, at least to foreigners. The French gave him the Croix de Guerre, and the Brits gave him a Military Medal."

Lt Adams, from the hospital in Archangel, had sent the medals from New York via an expensive courier. He'd enclosed only a brief, faintly bitter note hinting that Carl and other doughboys had been criminally slighted by Colonel Stewart, the Americans' commander in Archangel.

"I'm not sure what the medals are for," I told her. "But the French one has a little silver star on it, and the British one has a laurelled silver bar. I asked around about those. Whatever Carl did, he did it more than once."

"Carl never was very original," she said.

But her eyes were wet. Mine had been too.

The next week Smythe tried to discredit me by altering one of my 928s to make it look as though I had approved for profits a man who clearly deserved dismissal. The Boss had dismissed the matter with unusual curtness toward Smythe, but I was still furious with the filthy schemer and frustrated beyond measure to be unable to beat him with a brickbat. So, after the third time that evening Angela said that Carl's death had been "part of God's plan," I angrily clapped shut my volume of Ricardo.

"Can God," I demanded, "truly be such an imbecile as to send good Catholics thousands of miles to die at the hands of atheist Bolsheviks?"

Ross, who was by then coming by often enough that I started to suspect that he had feelings for Kitty, kept his eyes on the atlas. But the women all looked up, and the children all drew back. Even Lisa. I felt like a melodrama villain with a cape and a mustache. Well, why else had the Divine Planner given me a hunch?

"Either God is a fool or he needs better boosters," I said.

I'd expected Angela to denounce me angrily. Instead, her face sagged, and I fancied for a moment that I could see the shadow of a lingering black eye. I felt liked I'd just kicked a cripple's crutches. I stomped out of the room, furious at my family for making me abuse them.

I realize now that Angela had been kicking my crutches too. In those days I needed to believe, above all else, despite all evidence, that wisdom and personal effort could save us.

A few days later, The Boss called me into his office to say that Assistant Superintendent Klann wanted a man from Educational for a walk-through of the factory. There apparently would be more bigwigs along than usual.

"I hoped you might 'keep an ear to the ground' for me," The Boss said.

When the walk-through began a half-hour later, there were indeed a lot of bigwigs, including Ford himself. He was upright, whippet-thin, and dressed in a conservative suit that gave him the look of a prosperous undertaker. That day at least, he didn't speak much, and when he did he very much sounded like a rural Midwesterner (he actually used the word "poppycock," for example). Broad-shouldered Charlie Sorensen had come over from the Rouge with his enforcer and spy-chief, Harry Bennett. Highland Park's superintendent and Sorensen's chief rival Pete Martin was joined by Clarence Avery (his deputy) and Bill Klann (Avery's deputy). Even the Rev. Bradby was there, though he remained as anonymous as I.

As the walk-through began, I watched Bennett with particular interest, knowing that Spark would have questions about him. Walking or waiting, Bennett stayed a step behind Sorensen's shoulder. In turn, a beefy, broad-faced Irishman with a long scar over one eye stayed a step behind Bennett. Between the two big men, Bennett looked small but still dangerous. A former welterweight who hadn't added flab, he could stand girder-straight when he chose. It was easy to believe the rumors that he'd put a pistol range in the basement of the Rouge administration building and aspired one day to build himself a castle complete with guard tigers.

As we walked, the bigwigs talked among themselves, and Bennett and his goon kept alertly quiet. With nobody interested in our presence, Bradby and I discussed a couple of his men (nominally my men).

Eventually we halted in final assembly, where all the different lines from the plant merged into finished Model Ts.

"This all the faster the line goes?" Sorensen asked. "What is that, thirteen feet?"

"Fifteen," Klann said.

When I'd started at Ford, the Highland Park line had moved at seven or eight feet per minute. But every time the men got a raise, every time Henry Ford intuited that the market could absorb more Model Ts, the line sped up. When the men could no longer keep up, the bosses would slow it a half-notch. The Rouge worked the same way.

"Fine work, Bill," Ford said, heartily slapping Klann on the back.

Klann's yelp was audible over the factory din.

"Right, right, sorry, Bill," Ford said.

Klann had an open wound over his scapula where a surgery of some sort had gone wrong. Twenty minutes earlier, he'd removed his jacket to show Ford a bloody handprint where Ford had slapped him the first time.

Sorensen sniggered, and Klann paused a moment to glare him. But Klann didn't make a fuss about it. Ford's executives were expected to suffer a bit at the hands of their chief and even of their peers, and Sorensen had certainly endured his share of torment. It was well known that when Ford and Sorensen had recently been traveling by train away from Detroit, Ford had arranged for Sorensen to receive a prank telegram telling him that the Rouge plant was burning to the ground. It was also rumored that on a fishing trip for Ford big men, somebody had once spotted Sorensen dozing alone in rowboat and tossed a bundle of rags soaked in motor oils into the boat—a bundle which, for good measure, the jokester had first set ablaze. Sorensen supposedly had capsized the boat trying to put out the flames.

Once Klann had finished glaring and Sorensen had finished sniggering, we started moving again, continuing along final assembly. Ten-gallon galvanized steel gas tanks, having dropped off a belt on the fourth floor, issued from a chute onto a bridge over the assembly line. From the bridge a man with a gas pump injected a gallon of gas into each tank before its installation.

By that point, our party had slowed to fifteen feet per minute, pacing the same growing car, but as we drew near the bridge Sorensen broke from the pack, moving swiftly toward a man on a stool. I winced. Sorensen hated to see men sitting on the job and was famous for kicking chairs from beneath them. But then he noticed that the man was one-legged. Sorensen stood there for a moment, shoulders taut. Then he turned grudgingly and stomped back to the group, which continued onward as Martin and Klann explained the improvements they'd made.

I half listened to that conversation as I watched each laborer do his single task. The hand brake lever went in, then the gas feed pipes and the fender irons. After that, a heavy hoist settled the motor into the still-moving chassis while men bolted it in place. Once the motor was in, the dash unit came down from the second floor. Then came the steering gear, the coil, the horn, and all the motor wiring. I watched in fascination as the inflated tires dropped through vertical chutes in the ceiling. Surprisingly soon, the fully attached rear tires dropped with a springy thump onto a set of grooved, motorized wheels sunk into the concrete floor, which sent motion through the car's differential and drive shaft. We'd reached the end of the line.

"New drive wheels limber 'em up ten percent faster, starts 'em just as good," Klann said. "Then we drive the chassis out to the yard same as always, put the bodies on, load 'em into box cars."

"Fine work, Bill, mighty fine," Ford said.

Another slap, another yelp.

Sorensen laughed a Viking laugh. "Careful, Mr Ford, he's got his monthly bleeding."

The others laughed dutifully, but Klann made girlish squealing noises and pantomimed slapping at himself to put out a fire. Sorensen flushed and took the same first steps toward Klann as he'd taken toward the cripple.

But before anything further developed, a mass of profane hollering was rushing toward us. Adamo Ragnelli. He was yelling and gesticulating with some auto part still clutched in his upraised fist. "Pretty fancy company you keep," he bellowed at me. "Look at the big man with his big friends. But God knows. God knows and I know what you did."

At this point a straw boss corralled Ragnelli, who managed to spit something about *sciupafemmine* before the straw boss clamped a hand over his mouth. Another man arrived quickly, and the two of them muttered apologies as they dragged Ragnelli away.

My cheeks burned with anger and fear until I noticed that everyone in our party was looking around with the same mix of anger and defensiveness. I repressed a grin. Ragnelli could've been yelling at any of us. Given how cross-eyed he was, he could have been *looking* at any of us.

"You the Educator?" Martin asked me.

"Yes, sir."

"He one of yours?"

"Mr Smythe's, sir. Mr Caleb Smythe." I smiled as if simply providing helpful information.

"Well, if that man's a good worker, tell Smythe to dock him a week's pay and to keep his goddamn yap shut if he don't want me to jam a pink slip in it. If he's a piker or a Wobbly, can him."

"Yes, sir."

Bennett was giving me the eye. I had the uncomfortable sense that he had read the situation better than the rest. Still, as I trotted away to execute Martin's orders, I was smiling broadly. The confrontation could have gone better only if it had been Smythe doing the yelling.

After yet again offering my family some biting observations on the quality of God's planning, I'd locked myself in the bathroom. Ten minutes later, my hands were still shaking.

Through the flimsy bathroom door, I could hear leave-taking downstairs. Ross was escorting Kitty, Angela, and Angela's children to Kitty's house. Once they left, I risked returning to my room, where I lay in the dark and longed to dangle from something, to feel nothing but a burning in the shoulders. Instead, I lay back and thought about Theda Bara. And Thia Mueller (soon to be Thia Everett). Yes, that was it, I thought, unbuttoning my fly. How long had it been? Weeks, maybe longer. Surely that was medically unsound.

I was perhaps thirty seconds from health, freedom, and joy when there was a knock at the door.

"What?" I yelped.

"Tony?" It was Ilaria.

"I'm tired," I called.

"So am I," she said cheerfully, "but we should still talk."

I sighed and made myself decent before stomping to unlatch the door. She closed the door and stepped past me.

"How far is it to Canada?" she asked.

I realized my fists were clenching and unclenching. "Seven miles to

Windsor. I could be in Toronto in a day. I really am tired, Ilaria."

"Try having Mother and Angela lecture you all day about God's love for fruitful wombs."

I managed a chuckle and gestured to the chair at my desk and sat on the edge of the bed.

"She can't go back to him," she said. "Angela. I meant it earlier that he'd kill her. Maybe on purpose, probably by accident. But he will."

"Does *she* know that? Because I see this at Educational. If they can't—won't—see the danger, they won't leave."

I always advised such wives to leave and take any children with them. Either they did or they didn't, and it seldom had anything to do with me. Sometimes they didn't speak English and had nowhere to flee and no money with which to flee. Sometimes they had some pestilent priest telling them that the fate of their immortal souls depended upon their turning the other fractured cheekbone. Sometimes they simply wouldn't accept that life had dealt them a busted flush.

There was a peremptory knock at the door. "Uncle Tony?"

"Come in, Lisa," I said.

Lisa paused when she saw Ilaria but then set her shoulders resolutely and stepped forward. It was a womanly gesture, and I realized with something between gratitude and panic that Lisa wasn't too far from womanhood. (Already there had been a discreet excitement about her first menses, which I wasn't supposed to have understood.) Oddly, the more she detached herself from us, the more she looked like a pale version of Kitty.

Lisa carefully closed the door behind her. "Uncle Tony, how much longer is Aunt Angela going to be here?"

"Ilaria and I were just wondering that," I said.

"Tony," Ilaria reproved.

"She won't speak English," Lisa said. "I've asked."

"I know, dear," I said. I admired that.

"And I don't want to play with my cousins anymore. They're vulgar, except Gianluca, and he's mopey. Gisella is tolerable, only she spends hours hiding under the kitchen table."

"She does?" I asked Ilaria, who nodded.

Our Chicago branch had an Educational Department. Maybe it had a Service Department too, and maybe they could send some anti-union goons to Stefano's blind pig, where they'd actually do some good.

Chapter 23

ILARIA AND I WERE SITTING IN THE GLOAMING, PARLOR WINDOWS OPENED IN supplication of a breeze. We had the house to ourselves. Mother had, at last, mercifully stopped baking and gone to call on Mrs Daszkowski, and I'd given Lisa a dime to go to the pictures with a smug little girl she knew from school. (Ilaria suspected that there was a boy involved.) Out of habit, Angela had already exited in a medium-height dudgeon, and her children had dutifully followed her to Kitty's.

"Angela calls me Scimmia when we're alone," I said.

"She told Mother today that Martin and I must be using French safes to have only three children. Honestly."

I laughed. Then I wondered.

"None of your concern," she said. "Two weeks we've been here, and every day brings me closer to taking a rolling pin to her."

I tried to smile, but I'd had the same impulse, and few things will make a man feel dirtier than the urge to beat his sister until she stops letting her husband beat her. I thought again of Gennaro at sixteen, eyes flashing and shoulders broad in the uniform of the Carabinieri. I thought of the photographs which Alessandra had sent. In those photographs, I'd seen my brother grow into full manhood, each day looking more like the hero he had learned better than to become. Andrew in his uniform, Carl in his. Somewhere, those uniforms, those heroes, had gotten holes in them and then been dropped into holes in the ground. Square shoulders into square boxes into square holes, cemented with stories, the foundation stones of a world filled with failed men who beat their wives and small men who couldn't stop them.

"What?" Ilaria asked.

I shook my head. The more the house filled with the living, the more it filled with ghosts. Ghosts in dreams, ghosts in rustles, ghosts in the words of the loved and resented. They filled the house like the humidity, like the heat of Mother's desperate cooking.

"And of course," I asked, "you have offered to let Angela and the children live with you?"

She nodded. "Yet again this morning, in fact. She said she doesn't wish to expose her children to a household with such different notions of *virtù morale*."

Her smile was unconvincing. We sat silently for a while.

"At least she's not in Chicago," I said. "And Mother enjoys having her. They cook. They condemn. They make Ghilarza sound like the Garden of Eden."

"They do, don't they?" She thought for a moment. "She cannot go back to him, Tony."

"Definitely not."

M. Torassian
1177 Citrus Ave.
Los Angeles, California
August the 10th, 1919

Dear Tony,

We have not talked for a long time, so I hope you are well, my friend.

We at last settled in our own home here. We are among Polish Jews here in Boyle Heights, which is on the east side of town. Gulsa says we should have waited to convert to our new religion until we knew our new neighbors. Probably the preachers shouldn't hear such things but I know it is only joking. Gulsa is not a person who changes her mind or lives in~~side~~ regret. Neither am I of course and this is what I teach the little gentlemen, optimism.

I am proud to say the little gentlemen (I am considering to call them "intermediate gentlemen" but it is unfriendly to the tongue) they do not need any longer much tuition in optimism. Gulsa tells me that every day they walk the neighbor girls to school and back. Every afternoon they stand on the girls' front stoop and try for kisses. The little gentlemen have had no luck so far, Gulsa says, but the girls are delightfull laughing blondehaired things so I think my optimistic gentlemen will persevere and I remind them it took our boys in the trenches a while to bring down Haji Wilhelm and the sultans.

I am glad to have good neighbors like Lech next door and his choosy daughters. God willing I will have them and others like them always. And I think it is Gods will because we did not choose exactly to live here. There are "covenants" in this city saying where a man may live. In some places we are not the right kind of people. Gulsa and I get angry sometimes because in Turkey we were Kurds and that was bad enough, but it is worse being treated like Kurds by men too ignorant to know what ~~to~~ a Kurd is. Still, God has placed us among good people, and that is reason for optimism. Gulsa reminds me, "The only important covenant comes with the rainbow." God willing, every man should have such a wife.

And this is a great city full of hope and wonders of strangeness. The rich Americans here live in Pasadena, north of Los Angeles itself. Perhaps you have heard of their parade, when they fill the streets with roses? It is not just roses, either. It is many flowers, grown as I told you with water carried across the desert. And they built the Port of Los Angeles out of a mudflat, and then they sent the city south in a little ribbon like a kite string twenty miles long to bring the port into the city. The city is now a very strange shape. I have raised my little gentlemen to be engineers because I learned from Mr. Ford that the men who build things shape the world. But maybe also they will need to study painting because only the sort of mad artist who cuts off his ears and paints everything with inside out cubes could draw all the lines in this city.

But the flowers, Tony! They alone are worth it.

Yours in friendship,

Merry

Another letter from a port of angels.

By this point, my night alarms came more often. Since I could return to sleep only slowly, if at all, I began to keep my books of political economy at my bedside. The grim numbers of Malthus, the brutally optimistic numbers of Smith and Ricardo, became my nighttime companions.

When I had finished with my shabby second-hand copy of *Principles of Political Economy and Taxation,* I breathed deeply and moved on to Marx. As an adolescent, I'd concealed tawdry dime novels by stripping off their lurid covers and tucking the pages inside more acceptable covers (usually Horatio Alger's *Ragged Dick* or *Bound to Rise.*) With Marx, I returned to the tricks of my childhood by gluing a cheap Italian edition of the *Grundrisse* (courtesy of Maria Tomaselli) inside the sturdy cover of a Zane Grey novel. To my surprise, I found Marx exhilarating. It's something important when, even in darkness' odd noises and dozy menace, a book can make the world *more* real. I don't know if I've ever read a book both so quickly and so carefully. I could fly through some pages, nodding in agreement, and then find myself devoting twenty sceptical minutes to a single sentence. Sometimes I would stop entirely and think of Alessandra, of Gennaro.

One night I had another thought altogether, and it lingered during work the next day, which is why I rang Dot at the Girls' Protective League and arranged to meet with her that evening.

Dot's office was every bit as impressive as The Boss'. When I arrived, she was wearing a conservative dress and talking to a small, slightly dowdy gray-haired woman in an expensive black dress and matching hat. They both stood when I entered. The older woman turned toward me. It was Clara Ford.

"Tony. Oh, rattle-headed old me!" Dot exclaimed. "I'd forgotten our little meeting. Clara, I don't suppose you know Mr Grams? He's in your husband's employ, though I suppose that hardly narrows it down."

Clara smiled cautiously and permitted me to take her hand.

"It's a pleasure to meet you, ma'am. And I'm sure that Dr Marquis would send his compliments to you and your husband."

Her smile grew more open. "Do you work under Mark, then, Mr Grams?"

"Nearly four years now, ma'am." What a very long time.

"How wonderful," she said. "Dot, dear, I do suppose we've finished here, haven't we? I really ought to be on my way."

"Quite finished, Clara."

"I don't suppose, Dot," Mrs Ford began hesitantly as she pulled her pristine black gloves on, "that you like cocoanuts? Or some of the girls around the office? A man in Fort Myers has been sending us crates of the things, and I'm trying to find homes for them. Like kittens, really. And very nearly as furry."

"Well, many of the girls here are devoted to nuts in general," Dot said, "but as to the cocoanut I couldn't speculate. I dislike them, I must confess. Nasty, hairy things, and it's altogether too much bother to get the milk out."

Dot's expression was innocent, and Mrs Ford didn't react, so I couldn't tell if I was simply being filthy-minded.

Mrs Ford waved away Dot's efforts to escort her to the elevator. As

I closed the door behind Mrs Ford, Dot settled back in her chair, her feet on the desk, her ankles pressing at sheer stockings. What I could see of her calves looked quite nice.

"She still won't pick you, you know," she said.

"Mrs Ford?"

"Thia."

"That's been clear for a long time," I said. "For one thing, I never played football."

"And you're too bourgeois. Thia is a champion of the workingman now. I keep saying she should champion the working woman. Far less competition for that job."

"Look, if you didn't want to talk to me, you could have said so on the 'phone."

She eyed me speculatively. "You haven't heard?" She re-crossed her ankles and pulled herself slightly more erect in the chair. "You haven't. The engagement's off. Seems Peter bedded some shameless tramp. A mere month before the wedding, too."

"Was he as bland as he looks?"

She laughed uproariously, swinging her legs beneath her as she did. "Well done, Mr Grams. And, yes, dishwater dull. So what does bring you by, then?"

"Foolishness, clearly." I could understand cheating on one's spouse. I saw it all the time. But to fuck in cold blood one's best friend's fiancé, well, that required an unusual heedlessness or cruelty. And Dot wasn't heedless.

"Think what you will," she said, "but they owe me a debt of thanks. Especially Thia. She's chasing something, our Thia, and I don't fault her for that. All women are, and mostly we don't even know how to explain it. But to marry a man simply to take vengeance on the finest parts of her spirit because they're inconvenient, that's—" She paused. "Besides, if she'd married that fool, she would have killed him, which would been a sticky pickle for her *and* poor Officer Emmeline."

She smiled cynically, probably hoping that I hadn't noted her lapse into honesty. "So what does bring you by, Mr Grams?"

"I wanted your professional help."

She chuckled mordantly. "Any fiancés in the picture?"

"A husband. My sister Angela's."

Her expression turned sober. "A cruelty case?"

I nodded, and an unironic anger transformed her face. Strangely, she looked less dangerous than usual. She listened intently as I explained Angela's situation.

"And what do you want from me?" she asked.

"A way to keep her away from Stefano. No, a way to convince her to keep herself away from Stefano."

"I suppose there'd be no point my talking to her," she mused.

I snorted with laughter.

"Well, give me your address," she said, "and I'll think of something. In the meantime, don't let her get anywhere near the cocksucker."

"I won't," I said as I wrote out the address.

As I turned to leave, she asked, "Shall I give your love to Thia?"

I waved good-bye over my shoulder.

The doorbell rang later that evening. Although by then we were fresh out of young men's bodies to receive from Western Union, we inevitably clenched our jaws when the doorbell rang unexpectedly. But on opening the door, I found only a man of about my age standing on the porch. He was fair-haired and slight, of medium height. Even in the dim light, I could tell that his suit was expensive, as was his straw Panama.

"Mr Anthony Grams?" he asked. "I'm Nate Adams. I—"

"Carl's lieutenant from Archangel," I said. After a slightly shocked moment, I extended my hand, which he shook firmly. "We got the medals you sent. Carl's. Thank you."

"It was nothing. I've come to pay my respects. But if this is an inconvenient time..."

Realizing that he was still standing on the front porch, I invited him inside. In the light, he briefly regarded me with something like surprise or pain, probably noticing my resemblance to Carl.

I ushered him into the crowded parlor and introduced him to everyone. Angela dispatched her children to Kitty's house with instructions to remain there and to send Kitty to us. At Mother's urging, Lt Adams settled easily into the large chair by the fireplace. Mother and Angela made disbelieving noises about his claims to be neither hungry nor thirsty and disappeared into the kitchen.

Ilaria watched them go and seemed to decide that there would be enough ovaries near the stove. "Don't say anything about Carl, Lieutenant," she warned him. "You'll only have to repeat it when the others arrive."

After insisting that we call him Nate, he told us that he'd stayed with friends in New York during the intervening months rather than return directly to Detroit with the Polar Bears. When Ilaria asked whether he had found securing a position in New York as difficult as returning soldiers had in the rest of the country, he looked faintly embarrassed.

"Oh," Ilaria said. "Well, after combat, I suppose one would want a respite."

Nate smiled wryly. "I'm afraid you overvalue my endeavor, Mrs Spinelli. I will resume employment in due course, but my position is much more difficult to escape than to secure."

"Those Adamses?" I blurted. The Adamses were an old Detroit banking family, only slightly less wealthy and influential than Henry Ford.

The wry smile returned. "I'm afraid so."

"A prominent family, I take it? You'll pardon me as a Chicagoan, I hope," Ilaria said. "And if I'm to call you Nate, you'll have to call me Ilaria."

"There's no call for pardon, Ilaria," Nate replied. "It's a pleasant thing to have position, but I don't expect praise for an accident of birth. My time among the Russian and British officers cured me of that."

He said it jauntily enough, but a deep bitterness flickered across his face.

"Were they really so unpleasant?" Ilaria asked.

"Oh, there were fine men among them. And brave. But—" He stopped himself as Kitty arrived.

After Mother and Angela returned from the kitchen, Nate spent the better part of an hour charming us with anecdotes about his time in the city of Archangel, which he described as a wartime assignment for those who found violence distasteful.

Kitty was sitting beside him on the sofa but talking to her lap. While Nate politely chewed some *redentore* cheese which Angela had unearthed somewhere, Kitty looked at her lap as she asked him, "Carl's commanding officer, the one who wrote us the letter about Carl..."

bravely and instantly

"Lieutenant Cudahy," I said.

"He came calling after the Polar Bears returned," Kitty resumed hesitantly, "and he said that some of the Archangel widows have started to hold meetings?"

That same bitter expression flashed across Nate's face. "I believe so, yes."

"You don't suppose that they might allow me to join them? My own husband, you see, died in France, and though at the time I didn't..."

Nate clasped Kitty's hand. "I'll ask some widows of my acquaintance. I can't imagine that they'd refuse you."

Angela forced a disapproving look from her face (the closest she came to generosity in those days).

For another half-hour or so, Nate found ways to say "bravely and instantly." Eventually, I managed to prise him from my family's grasp. At the front door, he handed me his calling card. "I've written my 'phone number on the back. I'd very much like to talk to you again. When it suits, naturally." His smile was politely affable, but something in his tone suggested urgency. I wasn't sure that I could cope with further urgency.

The next day was a Saturday, so I was home in the afternoon when Angela and some of her children returned from the corner store. After depositing Mother's share of the shopping in the kitchen, Angela asked the crowded parlor whether we knew a Nita Paldi.

Lisa exclaimed that she'd just read an article about Nita Naldi, an Italian starlet from New York. "John Barrymore is en*am*ored with her," she said.

"*P*aldi," Gianluca said in his know-it-all tone. "Mother and I met her at the store. And she wasn't beautiful. Her eye is deformed."

"Gianluca," reproved Angela.

"You can keep your ugly old Appaldi," Lisa told her cousin.

"*P*aldi," Gianluca corrected.

Lisa smirked at him and announced that she had to ready herself to go to the pictures with Miss Veronica, her venomous little friend from two blocks over. For all her film-crazy giddiness, Lisa was neither smug nor unusually cruel, so I wasn't sure why she spent so much time with Veronica. My best guess was that Veronica's family was Turinese, which annoyed Mother. As Lisa clattered up the stairs, Mother muttered about the value of money and the sinfulness of motion pictures.

With Lisa gone and the children playing their own games on the floor, the conversation drifted into Italian.

"What's interesting about Signora Paldi?" Ilaria asked Angela.

Angela frowned faintly as if she couldn't remember the source of her interest. "She simply seemed very pleasant."

"What's wrong with her eye?" Mother asked, as though the Gramses could scarcely be expected to consort with people who couldn't properly tend to their eyes.

"Mother," Ilaria reproved.

"She was kicked by a horse," Angela said.

"You asked her?" Ilaria exclaimed.

"Crocifissa did," said Angela, smiling wryly.

Her first smile since she'd arrived. Three weeks and three hundred miles for such a small smile. I wondered again about Service goons in Chicago. One letter on Educational letterhead...

Life's little surprises. Though she talked for weeks about doing so, Kitty never met with the Archangel widows. But during those same weeks Angela did meet—several times—with the mysterious Mrs Paldi. She didn't tell us this, however. Not at first. Which left Ilaria and Kitty minding the children and wondering aloud where Angela was.

Mrs Paldi, it turned out, had once been Mrs Tonti, and Mr Tonti had been two-fisted both as a drinker and as a debater.

(Ah. "Kicked" by a "horse.")

Angela was telling us this in late August, six weeks after arriving in Detroit. She had sent the children to Kitty's house, and the rest of us were seated in the parlor. I was the man, so she faced me. But in fact she was addressing Mother, or perhaps Our Omnipresent Lady.

Signora Paldi, Angela emphasized, was of course a good Catholic woman. A great Catholic woman. Compared to Signora Paldi, Joan of Arc had stopped her ears to the word of God. Naturally, Signora Paldi had excelled in all her wifely duties, never once objecting to her husband's sins until one day in praying to her icon of St Monica, she had realized that deep within her the Devil was whispering that she should kill her husband. And she realized that, in her womanly weakness, the only way to avoid the Devil's snares was to flee temptation. She had moved with her three children from Cleveland to Detroit, where her cousins could help her resist Satan's lures. Divorce, of course, she would never have contemplated. So she prayed for her husband's repentance and for God's forgiveness of her frailty.

"Did her husband repent?" Ilaria asked.

"I don't know," Angela said. "He died a few months after she left him. From drink." And then she added softly but without a quaver, "I hope that Stefano will. Now that I've left him."

Ilaria and Kitty were obviously trying not to grin, same as I was.

Mother and Angela wore the same nervous frowns, and they studiously avoided one another's gaze. I feared that Mother would say something destructive of Angela's resolution, that Angela herself would say something.

But neither did, and the next day Mother returned home from Gratiot with an icon of St Monica. She moved Michael to her nightstand and placed Monica over the hearth beneath Gennaro and Our Lady. Ilaria, Kitty, and I were giddy with relief for days. I was even willing that, at least in the near term, Angela should continue to stay with us. Until her resolve strengthened or (I beseech you, St Monica) Stefano picked a fight with a moving locomotive, she shouldn't return to Chicago.

It wasn't until days later, during an insomniac expedition into *Capital*, that I realized what had happened. The next evening I took hothouse orchids to the Girls' Protective League to thank Dot for sending Signora Paldi. Dot was very gracious. I still wasn't sure why she'd climbed Mt Everett, but I was sure that she wouldn't have been caught if she hadn't wanted to be. From then on, when I thought of Dot behind her tiger maple desk, I imagined her as Irene Adler with her own detective agency.

Chapter 24

THIA, CHAMPION OF THE WORKING MAN, SPENT LABOR DAY EATING POTATO salad at the Socialists' annual picnic in Gardner's Grove. I spent it clenching my teeth against a spasm that made the muscle between my shoulder blades hard and angry as jagged steel. When I could walk without wincing, I took my back to Dr Blodgett at Ford Hospital, hoping against reason that there might be some surgical remedy.

It had been ten years since Dr Blodgett had operated on my spine and I'd stared afterward at the ceiling, drifting in and out of Mother's scrupulous conjugation. He still had bushy eyebrows and a kindly expression.

"Beyond salvation?" I asked after the examination.

"Beyond scalpel, at any rate," he said. "Relaxation and hearty exercise might help. A bit of the old Bull Moose. Might you take some time away from work?"

I thought of Ford's hand thwacking meatily on Klann's back and shook my head.

After leaving his office, I wandered along the corridors without a plan. Beyond scalpel—suddenly that idea seemed heavy and general. I felt lost. I'd known all along that surgery was a tremendous long-shot at best. If I'd thought even half seriously that it offered any prospects, I would have asked about it years earlier. I couldn't understand how my hopes could feel so bruised. But still they did.

My despair and disorder matched my settings. Ford Hospital was overcrowded, still not entirely finished (it was supposed to have been the Detroit City Hospital, but it had run out of money until Henry Ford stepped in). I took a seat in a cramped, makeshift waiting room on the second floor of the laboratories building, where only slap-dash beaverboard partitions separated the doctors' offices.

A deep, resonant voice was coming through the beaverboard: "You're welcome to return to your quack at the clap shack, but it won't do you a bit of good. You're already in need of neosalvarsan. Had you let it go untreated for another month, I would probably have been obliged to infect you with malaria."

The patient replied in an unintelligible mumble. I wondered briefly if it was Ross, if he'd fallen off the chastity wagon. But, no. Ross had become a regular altar boy. Even so, what *was* I supposed to do about him? He and Kitty seemed sincerely interested in one another, and I wasn't sure precisely when I was supposed to tell my kid sister, "By the way, Sis, he's a swell galoot, but he's had more V.D. than some platoons."

"—utterly serious," the doctor was saying. "High fever kills the syphilis spirochete, and a good dose of quinine often will cure the malarial infection once the fever has done its work."

Mumble, mumble.

The doctor laughed. "The fever must be general and burn internally. The remedy you propose would simply result in localized third-degree burns and severe difficulties with micturition."

"Brother, he ain't kidding, neither."

I looked up to see the mild, smiling face of Carl's lieutenant. Nate Adams. I flushed faintly. I'd ignored at least two polite letters from him.

"Pleasure to see you again, Tony. You're not ill, I hope?"

I stood to take his proffered hand. "Visiting. A man of mine, from Ford." I tried to radiate the fine democratic spirit of helping the other fellow. "You?"

"I work here now. Well, volunteer. As an orderly. I enjoy tending to the patients. You'd think I wouldn't, after the war," he said. "Walk with me, if you will."

He led me to a broader corridor bustling with doctors and nurses. For a moment, everyone was forced against the walls by the regal progress of a dandypants in a formal morning coat, ascot, spats, and silk hat. I recognized him as Ernst Liebold, Henry Ford's chief secretary.

"Fancies himself Kaiser of the hospital," Nate explained. "The doctors despise him because he's even more puffed up than they are."

I nodded. When Henry Ford is your friend, you can withstand a lot of enemies. Which was just as well for Liebold, who had enemies aplenty. Most of America's Jews, to start with. He and Bill Cameron, the editor of Ford's *Dearborn Independent*, had been Jew-baiting in earnest for several months by then, and their attitude was inexorably obliging most of Ford's Jews to find employment elsewhere.

"Worse," Nate added, "he meddles. The docs almost strung him up when he told them to do hernias on Mondays, appendectomies on Tuesday, that sort of thing. I'm surprised he doesn't try to put the patients on a conveyor belt."

"Lieutenant Plute!" called a voice from an intersecting corridor.

Nate turned around and waved to a brown-haired, pallid man wearing a shabby dressing gown and leaning on a cane. He was haggard, bag-eyed and stoop-shouldered. He was much younger than he'd first seemed, I noticed. My age, give or take.

Nate crossed to the man and shook his hand warmly. I followed at a distance.

"I was hoping to parley-vous with you," the man said. "I'm worrying about—" He paused as I drew closer.

"This is Tony Grams, Jeff," Nate said in an exaggeratedly casual tone. "He works at Ford. In the Sociological Department, isn't it, Tony?"

"Educational," I corrected automatically.

"Same department," Jeff said. There was nothing casual in his tone.

"Tony's visiting a Ford man," Nate told Jeff. "Tony's brother served in Archangel. A corporal in Company 'B.'" He turned to me and added, "Jeff was with Company 'I' in Archangel."

"Your brother walking okay back in brogans?" Jeff asked me.

"Buried in them," I said.

"Sorry," he said. "Archangel?"

I nodded. "Two weeks from withdrawal."

"Exactly," Jeff said.

After an awkward silence, Nate said, "Well, Tony, I was actually hoping to speak with you, but..." He removed a calling card from its case. "Do ring when you have a chance."

"In the meantime," Jeff said, "leave the poor bastard you're visiting in peace."

> ...At last Socialist meeting Branch 1 secratary Al Renner told Miss Mueller that Socialists are'nt getting the Negro in with them because Negroes are too spookie, too believing in God and ghosts to think about this life, Miss Mueller got hot and told Renner the Negro was drafted in the army same as the white man, and that they have their Doctors and Lawyers and laborers and there

was no point talking about spookie and hopeless when there was organizing Negroes to be done...

"By the way," I said into Alex Spark's frightening attentiveness, "I know a woman slightly. Young widow who adopts causes like stray kittens. Suffragism, Girls' Protective League, something with lady policemen. Anyhow, she ended up at a Socialist meeting and said she found it 'entertaining.'"

Spark's lips twitched, possibly toward a smile.

"She wasn't going to go back because 'some of the people there weren't quite respectable,'" I said in my snootiest tones. "But I said maybe it was the kind of situation where she could learn something about the Bolos worth telling her lady policeman about. And of course that I'd always want to hear about it myself, taking a keen interest in politics as I do. Figured it was better if I didn't say, 'Go snoop around for me.' Anyhow, I gave Mr Slyker her name and address so that, if we do any police business, her name won't go to the wrong people."

Spark grunted in faint assent, and I escaped. I smiled at Slyker on my way out and restrained my shivering until the hallway. I was lying, of course. I hadn't spoken with Thia since the dinner party for Dr Sucre. But I'd seen her name in Landucci's reports enough to make me nervous. I didn't know whether my lies would help Thia at all, whether she even needed my help. But I found myself telling them anyway. To Spark, of all people. For a woman who no longer deigned to see me.

Does everybody yearn for those who make them angriest? Was it even anger, or just envy? Was Thia so much better than I was, or was she simply wealthier and differently furious?

I was reconciled to backaches. To ulcers. To all of it, really. Night sweats and sleepless dark hours. But, especially once Ilaria returned to Chicago, less and less could I endure the literal teeth-grinding and headaches brought on by never being able to tell anyone what I actually believed.

Mother and Angela prayed thrice daily to St Monica. But I said nothing, as they had found a way within their labyrinth of lunatic obligations to do the sensible thing.

Lisa went often to the motion pictures and never wholly left them. If she ever spared a thought for the proletariat any more, it was only that "Prola Tariot" might be a good screen name after she ran away from home to seek stardom in Los Angeles.

Kitty wept now and then over Andrew, but spent most days smiling and saying that she'd begun to feel as optimistic as ragtime. Sometimes we sat together in the front parlor and listened to actual ragtime records, speaking only on safe topics. To my relief, Ross often sat with us there, or in Kitty's parlor, and entertained us with stories about corruption among the new so-called reformers at City Hall, about daily violence and the tawdry doings of Detroit's citizens, big and small alike. Of course, he told his readers much less frightening, much less amusing versions of those stories. Or, often, nothing at all.

O'Hara sat with his feet on his desk, explaining to me that the difference between Reds and real Americans was that Americans didn't go around forcing a fellow to live his life a certain way.

Mr Spark said almost nothing.

The Boss said, again and again, that it didn't make sense what Sorensen, and Bennett, and Spark were up to, neither human sense nor business sense. And because I was a good American who thought about the new men and the new dispensation, of course I *didn't* think—and therefore couldn't possibly tell The Boss—that the problem with his outlook was a problem he shared with Maria Tomaselli's vulgar Communists: a mystic and mistaken faith in the righteous power of ordinary men; even though it was obvious everywhere from Red Russia to the Rouge River that ordinary men long above all else to wield unrighteous power over other ordinary men.

With a sternness I found intimidating, Kitty had recently forbidden Lisa to go to another motion picture, even at the week-end. Lisa had taken to moving through the house with languid, boneless motions like a fish swimming against a heavy current of tears. She conversed in fragments or grunts, not even strong enough to glare at Angela's children for mocking her.

"No more love scenes for you," Gasparo was telling her.

She said nothing. He kissed the back of his hand noisily, then raised it up and showily slapped it. As he shook the index finger of his triumphant hand at her, she turned and trod upstairs.

"Gasparo," Angela said sharply.

"But, Mom—"

"No 'but Mom.' Polite."

"Not my fault she's a *puttanella*," he muttered.

"You want to eat tomorrow?" Angela asked. "You want to eat, you shut your mouth."

I left this tender scene of Madonna and child to go to Kitty's, where I found my sister in the back parlor with Ross. They were under the chaperonage of Brunella and Gisella, who were shoving floppy dolls through a tale abounding in marrying and dying.

Ross greeted me with a cheerful wave. "I was just telling Kitty about the bootleggers' war brewing between the Bernsteins and the Licavolis."

"Brewing," I reproved.

"Tony and I are backing the Licavolis, naturally," Kitty told Ross. "We Italians stand together."

"Unified to the end like family," I said. "Gasparo's being a spectacular brat to Lisa."

"Is he?" Kitty asked carelessly. "Perhaps he's just cross from lack of sleep. Speaking of which—girls, time for bed."

The girls protested quietly as Ross rose to his feet. "I suppose that goes for me too. Early to bed, early to rise, and all that."

"I bet you don't even know what the 'all that' is," I said.

He laughed and clapped my shoulder on the way out. *And the clap is only* one *of the V.D.s he's had, Sis.*

When Kitty and I were alone, she said quietly, "I'm going to tell you something, but you need to promise me not to be angry."

Were all my little V.D. jokes clairvoyant? I would kill Ross–

"It's about Lisa," she said.

I calmed myself. "Oh. What is it?"

She sighed.

"Kitty?"

"Well," she said. "The good news, I suppose, is that she hasn't been spending as much time at the movies with that nasty little Veronica creature as we thought."

"And the bad news?"

She looked down the hall to make sure that the girls were still brushing their teeth. "She's been with a boy. They've been... driving out to Janek Sedlacek's meadow, the one where we used to..."

"And they...?"

"Yes," Kitty said evenly.

"Jesus, Mary, and Joseph." My thirteen-year-old niece. "Is she...?"

Kitty shook her head. "Thank God."

"How did you...?"

"Gasparo. The little shit—Lisa's beau, I mean—is spreading it all over Highland Park, and Gasparo fought him. I had to fetch him from the principal's office a few days ago."

I remembered the bruises. I'd just been glad they weren't from his father. "Did he win?"

"He still has his teeth, and the other boy is sixteen. I'd call it a victory."

"Who is the little shit?"

"Does it really mat—"

"Who?"

"His name, I think, is Joseph." She sighed again. "Joseph Ragnelli."

"You ungrateful little slut!"

"I'm *sorry*, Zio Tony. I'm sorry. I'm so sorry!"

Lisa was crying. She'd started as soon as I'd stormed into her room, Kitty following close behind me. By now her face was a mess of tears, snot, and splotching, and I was glad of it.

Angela had taken one look at me as I'd entered and sent the remaining children to Kitty's.

"Sorry?" What a stupid word. What a stupid *concept*. Being sorry was the moral cripple's way of having a conscience after he'd already done whatever he wanted. "Did you charge him at least? If you're going to be a whore, you should at least earn a wage."

"*Tony!*" Kitty said. "He doesn't mean that, sweetie."

"And a Ragnelli? You know they're trash. Trash! But you went right to them like a cockroach, didn't you? Antennas up and legs squirming."

Lisa was crying too hard to speak.

"Your father and mother dead for a purpose, for love, for you, and you're out in a cornfield like a goddamn cockroach—"

That was more or less when Angela and Kitty dragged me from Lisa's room and closed the door behind me.

"*Shut up* right now, Tony Grams," Kitty hissed in my ear. "Or I will never forgive you, and neither will she."

"Forgive?" There was another stupid concept. Forgiveness was a crutch that moral cripples loaned one another depending whose turn it was to go begging.

"You're lucky Mother is out," Kitty said. "Or you'd have ruined everything."

"*I'd* have ruined everything?"

When Angela nodded, I knew the answer was *yes*, always *yes*.

The next day, The Boss sent me on another bigwigs' walk-through. I trod at the back of the pack, carrying a wrench up my sleeve and looking for Adamo Ragnelli.

The walk-through was a gathering of Highland Park locals this time. No Sorensen, no Bennett. Bradby had come along, though. I wasn't sure why I was there. It was hard to believe that any of these men had really asked for someone from Educational.

Klann's back seemed healed, but he was still keeping well away from Ford.

We'd toured W Building from sixth to first floor and were stepping out into sunshine and something more like clean air when the shouting started.

"Fight, fight!"

The noise was coming from the nearby lumber piles, and the bigwigs beetled toward it. We found two men, each about twenty, one blond, one Negro, standing in light crouches, shifting their weight gingerly. Both held razors before them, and both were bleeding slightly from their hands and forearms.

"Nigger."

"Cracker."

They spoke almost gently, like sweet-talking rapists.

Martin and Bradby independently stepped forward. "What the hell's going on here?" Martin asked.

"You'd best step back and take your pet shine with you," the white one warned.

"You'd best think who the fuck I am," Martin said. "And who the fuck you are, and who that is standing behind me."

The white one, then the black one, looked over, really recognizing Martin and Ford for the first time. Their razors wavered but didn't drop.

"Either of you," Martin said deliberately, "cuts the other one again, even if you're just trimming his neckline, you'll still be bruised and bleeding when the judge locks your backward ass in Jackson."

"I got my pride," the white one said.

"And I got mine," the black one said.

"And I got a plant to run," Martin snapped. "Put 'em away right now and maybe you'll still have jobs tomorrow. Maybe your momma and your brothers will eat tomorrow night."

They looked at each other and at Martin. But it was Mr Ford's presence, in the end, that decided them. In wary synchrony, they lowered and stashed their blades.

"Send 'em home," Martin told the foreman who now stepped forward. "They go to Henkel tomorrow morning." He turned around and rejoined the group. "I'm sorry about that, Mr Ford."

"No, Pete, you did a fine job," Ford said.

"I'd like to speak with that man," Bradby said, meaning the Negro knife-fighter. "If no one objects."

"I'll accompany you," I told him.

Bradby looked at me in faint surprise but only shrugged. I discreetly set aside my wrench and trotted after him.

"Barney," Bradby called. "Barney MacIntosh!"

The Negro turned, as did the one escorting him. They both stopped at the front fender of Ford chassis. When we drew closer, it was clear that MacIntosh had a shamed expression on his face. His escort looked fretful.

"I'll look after him, Andy," Bradby told the escort. "You go on back to work."

The escort looked briefly at me and carefully at Bradby.

"It's all right, Andy," Bradby assured him.

"If you say so, Reverend." With one last worried flicker of the eyes, he walked away, moving more briskly the farther he went.

MacIntosh stood there, shifting his weight uncomfortably, looking every bit as naked as the car behind him.

"I'm sorry, Reverend."

"You ought to be."

"But he called my sister a slut."

"Which one?" Bradby asked.

"The cracker with the knife."

"Which *sister*?"

MacIntosh looked shamefaced. Bradby sighed. "Barney. Did that man know for a fact that you *have* sisters?"

MacIntosh stared at the ground.

Bradby turned to me. "Mr Grams, I wonder if you'd permit us a moment alone? But I would like to speak with you afterward, if I might."

"Of course."

I walked toward the nearly complete Model Ts, watching the drive wheels in the ground spin the cars' tires. The sound of their engines gurgling to life cloaked Bradby's words to MacIntosh. The autos had no body panelling yet, so they were chrome-colored and their innards revved visibly. *You can have them in any color you want.*

"Mr Grams?"

I looked up to see Bradby's face.

"Not the first knife fight in the plant, Reverend," I said. "Involving a Negro and a white man, I mean. Will it get worse?"

He *hmmphed* uncertainly. "The races *can* work side by side, Mr Grams. But not everyone thinks so, and the... doubters among our white brethren can be persistent."

I looked around, but MacIntosh had already disappeared from sight.

"To be frank," he continued, "I wanted to ask you to put in a good word with Mr Henkel about Barney. He's a good man and hard worker. And he served under Captain Allan in the war, and, well..."

I nodded, and he thanked me. Wary but friendly, he shook my hand and headed back inside.

After dutifully putting in that good word, I trudged home. Mother and Angela were in the kitchen, and Gianluca and Gasparo were doing or ignoring their schoolwork in the parlor. I found Lisa upstairs in her room, seated at her little table, staring blankly at a schoolbook. She looked up at me and then turned aside, screening her face with her hair. I didn't know what to say. "Sorry" would have been about right, I suppose, but that was too complicated. I nodded and closed the door.

Every night I came home and looked at Angela's unbeaten children. I looked at Mother cooking cheerfully, at Kitty and Lisa unstarved by Gramazio poverty, and Angela praying unbowed to mortal man, and I couldn't tell myself that, more than anything, I needed to leave Ford.

That night, as Gianluca and Gasparo gathered their school books to go back to Kitty's, Gasparo told me with great casualness that he'd heard how *someone* had slashed Adamo Ragnelli's car tires and cut a hole in his car's canvas top.

"*Someone,*" I said, "must feel much better now."

We winked at one another, and I tousled his hair as he walked by. Someone had done well, I thought. But it wasn't enough. Not nearly.

Chapter 25

I was eating an excellent steak with Nate Adams at the Ponchartrain. He'd rung me that afternoon, and I hadn't invented an excuse fast enough.

We were in the same dining room that the Sociological Department banquet had occupied so many years before. I wondered with crawling guilt how Merry was. He had written a dozen more letters about flowers in the desert, and I had replied to perhaps three.

"I'm a little surprised," I told Nate, "that you're not dining with the Prince."

The 'papers had been breathless about the arrival in Detroit of His Royal Highness, Edward Prince of Wales, who at that very moment was dining in splendor at the Essex Country Club in the company of Henry Ford and the rest of Detroit's high society.

"I haven't much use for kings," Nate said. He turned the discussion to Archangel city—the Dvina running through it, the blue dome and golden stars of its great cathedral, the spires of its lesser minarets, the two-story log homes with their high fences, the clattering trolley line running along the rough cobbles of Troitsky Prospect and between that street's narrow, occasionally rotten plank sidewalks, its open sewers. He told with relish a dozen stories about Carl—his concern for his bank balance, his getting drunk as a lord in the hospital on Christmas Eve, the day he spent acting out bits from a Harold Lloyd one-reeler they'd watched at the Red Cross.

I savored the stories. Once Carl had moved to the boarding house—longer than that, now that I think about it, much longer—he'd been distant from the family, so distant that after his death I'd started to forget him as an adult, started to remember him instead as a hungry waif in

Ghilarza, New York, Chicago.

Amidst all the stories, Nate clearly was searching for a way to tell me something else. So I wasn't surprised when after dinner he suggested going to a blind pig near Connor's Creek. It was a refined pig—oak tables, solid chairs, plush booths, and tasteful fabric wallpaper, even over the steel door. The player piano was pinging out popular tunes of decades past. Soon after we took our table, "Mr Dooley" began to roll through, and I thought again of Merry. Of my previous, optimistic self. Even those who hadn't died had become ghosts. *There are spectres haunting Tony Grams...*

By the time "Mr Dooley" finished, Nate was already reaching for second gin drizzled with tonic. We toasted Carl again, and I found myself holding the glass in the air, suddenly struck by everything which had put it there. Not just the accidents of fate which had created Nate and me, the horseshoe nails lost and found, the ova hit and missed. More deeply, I was struck by the sweat, genius, and strategic numbness which had mass-produced such intricate fragility, had safely transported it miles or thousands of miles, had conceived and constructed Edison Illuminating generators to wrench electricity from coal and send it along the city-girdling wires to burst from fragile filaments and through the tumbler's facets.

"—idiotic prohibition," Nate was saying. "Booze is a drug, and you can't stand between dopes and their drugs. Two weeks ago, at the hospital, I was sitting in the break room with some of the nurses when we heard a god-awful racket. Two of the nurses had been in the war with the YWCA, and we thought we were being shelled. But it turned out to have been a bulk metal milk can rolled down the stairway by some dopes on the ward. It was a diversion. While we were investigating the noise, the dopes were pillaging the narcotics safe. They all apologized and promised never to do it again, but they will."

"Maybe they're doing it right now," I said, raising my glass in ironic toast.

He sighed and fell silent for a while. Eventually, he said, "You really do look like him, you know."

Then he told me the other, less amusing stories. How Carl had earned those foreign medals in Toulgas and elsewhere. How he'd been killed in Siskoe during "B" Company's last engagement in Archangel—a brief, inconclusive exchange of rifle fire between his patrol and some Bolo scouts who'd stumbled across one another as "B" Company had been making its final retreat from Russia.

"Bravely and instantly," I said bitterly.

"Bravely," Nate said, "but not instantly. Still, he didn't suffer, I shouldn't think. That's the virtue of shock, really. He said a few words before he went, they told me. But in Italian, so nobody understood." After a pause, he added, "I was very fond of your brother. We were fond of each other."

On some other night I probably wouldn't have noticed. But that night the ghosts had formed a North Atlantic fog, and I'd already been remembering the night that Andrew had sat nervously in the parlor and asked for Kitty's hand in marriage. *I am very fond of your sister.* I made the mistake of looking at Nate. If I hadn't looked, I could have ignored everything and misremembered it later.

If you can credit it, my first thought was: "Well, *of course* Dot wants to destroy Thia."

My second thought wasn't so much a thought as a reflex. I stood and stalked away. I was aware even as I did it that this time it was probably even worse than when I'd done it to Thia. But such awareness had long since stopped preventing me from doing anything. I still had my glass in my hand when I reached the street. I hurled it down an alley, and it shattered satisfactorily on an ash can.

A broken glass respects the past and stays broken. But memory is resilient and adhesive, both starfish and hermit crab, and it will make itself anew, make itself whole from whatever is to hand. That night, I'd learned a great deal about Carl's life in Archangel from Nate, which knowledge I added to what I already knew. So around that time I started knitting the scraps together and seeking out new scraps, finding myself especially fascinated with Bolos' attack on Toulgas. Possibly the more my own life became alien and frayed, the more I wanted a clear sense of how Carl had felt and thought in that far off and improbable place, during that far off and deranged invasion...

In Toulgas, the Bolos attack on Armistice Day. Maybe they think doing it today will make us wonder what the hell Archangel is all about. Maybe they just sniffed the first snows and decided that if they're gonna charge machine guns, they don't want to do it in waist-deep snow.

Anyway, they come, yelling, "Hourra, hourra," like the crowd at The Corner after a home run.

Toulgas is actually two villages, Upper and Lower. They're about two miles apart, and they're both little clumps of low log houses like all the moujik villages around here. Upper Toulgas clings to a hill above a large plain. There's a stream running between Upper and Lower. There's about five hundred of us here, mostly from "B" Company, and, brother, we know there are plenty more Bolos than that.

The first sign of them comes upriver of Upper Toulgas. Lt Dennis' men take a few shots at them and then pull back to the lines. Meanwhile, up on the hill the Saskatchewanians are swinging their big eighteen-pounders toward Bolos. But then, the Bolos are gone, just as quick as they were there. A few minutes later a lot more of them pop up downriver from the hospital. The first stuff was just a diversion.

I'm in Lower Toulgas, near the hospital with seven other guys. We're manning two Lewis guns hidden in a cottage, and we open fire soon as we see Bolos. We hit a mess of them, dozens, and that slows them down long enough for the Saskatchewanians to range the eighteen-pounders. Those Canucks have killed and been killed for four years on every front in the war, and when they fight, they roar, and their guns roar. I can't hear the Canucks, but I can sure hear their guns, and the shrapnel is going through the Bolos like a Fordson tractor through wheat. And our Lewises aren't doing so bad either, at least until we run out of ammo. Then we have to use the damn Russki rifles the limeys stuck us with in Newcastle.

The Bolos beat a retreat, and when I'm sure they aren't kidding about it, I take a couple doughboys back to the compound with me, and we swap Joe Nelson and his spurting thigh wound for fresh ammo and some more doughboys. Then we beat it back to our Lewises and keep an eye out while "B" Company and the Royal Scots send men to see to the Bolo snipers in the upper village and the ones still hiding in the woods. All this time, the eighteen-pounders are spreading death and confusion through the Bolos and the houses they just took.

Maybe the Bolo officers talk like Reds, but they lead like tsarists—from the rear while we grind their men into mince. And that's what we spend the afternoon doing. They kill a hundred of us, including in the end Joe Nelson. But we bring down five hundred of them, not counting the ones who are gonna bleed to death in the woods or just freeze to death overnight.

So we win, but shit. It makes you sick going around afterward. Six hundred dead soldiers. And then the civilians. We all figure it's a bad omen that Toulgas' priest got killed when the shell broke his home. Especially how he died, shrapnel taking a clean slice off the top of his skull like somebody ran it through a top-notch bandsaw. Looking at the glistening gray mess, I think of

Angela and how she feels about priests. After a while, I run outside and sick up in the street.

The other fellahs are finding the same kind of thing everywhere—body parts and gallons of black blood splattered around a dirty little room, parts of the same bodies found inside and outside. The funny thing is, the shells can also kill you without cutting. The concussion just pulps your guts. Some corpses look like they're asleep but a little confused, like they have to do long division in their dreams. Sgt. Macgregor found a baby girl in her crib but didn't know she was dead until he picked her up and her stomach sagged like a bag of water. He cried when he told me. Got kids of his own.

And now we're getting prisoners. Half of them are lucky we don't shoot them, how they play possum until you're twenty yards away and then pop up to surrender. Then, some of them aren't nearly so keen to surrender. Those are the ones that heard how the Amerikanskis will execute them for their crimes against Andrew Carnegie. I hate these prisoners. More mouths to feed, more prison details. But their clothes are the worst of it. They don't have uniforms. They just wear moujik clothes—heavy coats, knee-high leather valenkas, high gray and black hats made out of curled fur. They look like every other damn Russki, and there's no way to tell our Russkis from the Bolos. Hell, the Bolos know so much about every goddamn thing we do, sometimes I wonder if we really have any Russkis of our own, or if they're all just finks.

That's maybe why our officers tell us to burn Upper Toulgas. But we probably need to burn it anyway. Too many cottages to patrol, so they end up prairie dog colonies of Bolo snipers.

The moujiks from Upper Toulgas get three hours to drag out what they can, and then we circle the village to keep the Bolos out. Maybe also to put a scare in the villagers. And then we take up the torches and start setting fire to the roof thatching.

It starts to snow, then, because Mother Russia just has to snow if she sees peasants without a roof. The villagers are just standing there with what they can hold, standing there or sitting on the handmade crates that the richer ones put their stuff in. They don't understand, and they won't forgive. But they're not complaining. Not yet, not to us. The women weep at the stars, and the men stare stony-faced at the forest.

Looking at the moujiks, I feel awful. But thinking of Wes Burns and Dave Bukowski and all the other guys who got killed by Bolo snipers hiding in those burning houses, I feel like I'm back home on Pilgrim Street, sitting in front of the fireplace. And I sure haven't been this warm for a month.

Chapter 26

Surely, I soon decided, if Good Home Conditions could cause Right Industrial Conditions, then if one had Bad Home Conditions, the fault must come from Wrong Industrial Conditions. And I had Bad Home Conditions. My thirteen-year-old niece had been seduced by a family enemy. My dead brother had turned into a punk. My *inamorata* had never been enamored of me.

Clearly, it was all Caleb Smythe's fault.

Clearly, the only logical course of action was to burgle his car.

And so, on a warm autumn evening, I was standing visible to God and passers-by as I nonchalantly opened the passenger door to his car, which was parked not too far from his usual blind pig. My fingers hadn't trembled so hard since I'd sat inches from Thia, that first night in Dot's house.

The Boss was already inclined to distrust Smythe. However, with typical self-defeating nobility, The Boss didn't want to dismiss a man based on mere suspicion. Had I perused company records diligently, I probably could have found enough evidence of Smythe's malfeasance to justify The Boss' firing him, but I'd already been doing that as a hobby for a few months, and Smythe's caution made it slow going. Fortunately, Alex Spark was far less hampered by nobility. If I could make him suspicious enough that Smythe was double-crossing him to Harry Bennett (triple-crossing him to Harry Bennett?), he would dismiss Smythe out of hand. And maybe have somebody break a few of his fingers. No doubt I would've felt deep remorse had someone broken Smythe's fingers, but I resolved that, if doing so proved necessary for the interests of justice, I would have to bear that psychic burden.

And so there I was, taking Smythe's attaché case from his car.

Careless, Mr Smythe, to leave it exposed like this. Very careless.

I closed the car door gently and forced myself to walk calmly around the nearest corner. All day I had devised scheme upon complicated scheme to get at Smythe's attaché case, which he guarded zealously while at Ford. But in the end I'd settled on simply waiting for him to go inside the pig and then snatching it.

My hands and legs shaking violently, I managed to make it to the nearest soda fountain and settle in for a Coca-Cola and some sleuthing. It only took me five minutes to find something useful—a simple list, no title or signature. But it was clearly in Smythe's hand, and it clearly named Service operatives and gave their employe numbers. I say "clearly" because my time with Service had given me enough clues to recognize several of the names. But most of the names were unfamiliar and there were several dozen of them, making for a far longer list than any I could've produced. Far longer than any list Smythe should've been able to produce. In fact, only Spark and perhaps Slyker knew those names, and I couldn't for the life of me imagine a circumstance in which they would have told them to Smythe.

Unless, of course, Smythe was actually spying on Bennett for Spark. In that case, Spark might have told Smythe to make such a list for Bennett. It was possible. Back in the APL days, before Smythe had started sneaking off to the Rouge plant to meet with Bennett, he'd been hovering near Spark. So if I took the list to Spark, would I simply be marking myself as a meddler, a liability? I couldn't afford to weaken my hand or to strengthen Smythe's. But I also couldn't afford to lose the opportunity presented by the list.

After finding nothing else of interest in Smythe's attaché case, I decided that returning the case to his car posed too many risks. So I simply dropped it in a pile of reeking refuse in a nearby alley. It was the most gratifying thing I'd done for a long time.

I was still plotting how best to use the list of operatives against Smythe when another complication arose. In a routine Service report dedicated mostly to the Socialists' recent bickering over whether and how much to support women's suffrage and how to deal with the loss of members to the newly formed American Communist party, I found the following remark: "Miss Goldberg and Miss Mueller (known to us) swung knuckledusters, because Miss G accused Miss M of running around having butter crumpits with plutes and niggers and it being people like her who ruined the Canton strikes."

"Known to us." That was ominous. There was nothing in the report itself about Thia that couldn't be construed as mere slumming and dilettantism, but nonetheless she was putting herself at risk. And, truth to tell, she was putting me at risk also. I'd already lied to Spark about using her as an unofficial operative, so it was best if she kept out of trouble and never had to test that alibi. Especially because she didn't know *she* had that alibi. I'd been too ashamed of working at Service to mention it to anyone, especially Thia.

Possibly that would have to change. I 'phoned her from the drugstore that night and asked if she wanted to meet some place discreet. She made a witty remark.

"Not that kind of discreet," I said.

She suggested her parlor, and we set a time.

Then I went to see Dot, ostensibly about Angela, and mentioned Thia's name in passing. And there it was, love outraged but unrenounced. I'd seen it on my face in the mirror after Thia had refused me. It suddenly seemed clear that whatever Dot had sought since Wisconsin, whatever degree she hoped would annul her MRS, Thia had never wanted it. Naturally, that insight produced in me an upswelling of fatuous optimism which I had to vent carefully before permitting myself to ring Thia's bell.

Daniel showed me, surprisingly, into the kitchen, where Sigi was standing at the counter, popping the cork out of a bottle of beer. He wore a shabby purplish crimson dressing gown and pyjamas, the frayed cuffs of which flopped comically over his house slippers. He resembled a slender, bearded beetroot. He smiled slyly and swept over his attire with his pipe hand. "Martha is visiting relations in Cleveland." He raised a beer and added with false piety, "This, of course, is ginger beer. Would you like one?"

I said no, then yes.

He extracted a beer from the flour jar and tapped off most of the flour before handing it to me. "Some of the most feared bootleggers in Michigan are Jews, you know," he said with a note of pride.

He gestured that I should sit. I did, and he did the same in a chair across from me.

"The kitchen is an interesting place," he said. "No polish or show, unlike the rooms we create for others. Humble things tell us of the important things. *Are* the important things, really."

I nodded politely.

"My daughter, I think, takes an interest in humble things. Humble people. Maiden prisoners, poor Negroes. But sometimes I wonder whether she appreciates the... difficulty of the relationship between humble and the privileged."

Sigi took a large bite off a roast beef sandwich and chewed contemplatively. I waited silently. Dealing with Spark had taught me that.

"Although," Sigi said at last, "I think there will be fewer maiden prisoners and lady policemen now. Thia has resigned her post at Girls' Protective. She doesn't tell me why, of course, but I gather it has something to do with the Socialist meetings which she secretly attends."

And there we were. I sipped my beer defensively, wondering what I owed Thia in this situation. I hated to think that I probably owed her nothing.

"Tony," Sigi said, entreatingly.

"Sigi, what do you want from me?"

"I spent several nights in a barn, guarded by a boy with a rifle, though I had done nothing wrong." he said. "There are rumors of Red arrests, and I do not wish my daughter to be guarded by a rifle."

"One does hear rumors." Rumors, threats, the voices of the dead demanding justice and loyalty—one heard them at all times.

He stared at me. "One hears that you hear things. I can't imagine Thia has given you reason to come here. Romantic reason, I mean. I'm sorry if this is unkind to say. Yet you've come here even so."

"I'd rather tell Thia directly."

"Yes." He sighed, and his fingertips nudged his sandwich about the plate. "Only, she rang earlier it was to say she is not coming. She asked me to apologize."

"I see." I started to rise.

"*Tony*. I thought, yes, he would not come if it were unimportant. And Thia would not sound so falsely carefree if she considered it unimportant. And so..."

I remained in the chair. For want of a better activity, I finished my beer as I searched for the right words. "I ask that you tell no one what I'm going to say now," I said.

"Agreed."

"Given the nature of my duties, I hear things. Read things—reports by men who check the mood and the habits of the laborers. These men who write the reports, they obviously take an interest in the labor question, which means they take an interest in the Socialists. Among others. Those reports eventually make it to powerful men at Ford, ruthless men. Men on good terms with the sort of men who had you interned. Those men know Thia's name, and Thia must suspect it. Every self-respecting Socialist suspects that at least one fink is spying on him."

Sigi stared at me alertly. "Is she in danger? You must be worried to come here."

I shrugged. "Not terribly worried. But I did want her to *know* what she merely suspects. To *believe.* I think deep down she doesn't believe in the danger. My father spent years in prison," I said, surprised to hear myself say it, "possibly for embezzlement, though more likely for political reasons." I was also surprised to hear myself say that. I wondered if Gennaro too had come to suspect Father's innocence. "Several years teach a child to believe in danger. Several days, perhaps not. Perhaps it even teaches the opposite."

Sigi merely nodded. I sighed and swigged my beer before continuing. "Honestly, Sigi, I can't even say why I came. What good I thought it would do. Please tell Thia that I have tried to intervene on her behalf by telling the powerful men that she has been attending these Socialist meetings partly on a lark, partly so that she can tell me if she hears of anything... untoward, I suppose."

Sigi stared at me for a while. "That was a risk to you, yes? To do that. And again to tell me? Thank you. I will tell Thia when the time is right."

I said good-bye soon afterward. As Daniel showed me out, I felt bemused and deeply tired. Obviously, I doubted that Thia could be fully devoted in her Socialism, but I knew that she was as sincere as any of us are about justice, about reason. So I could understand what she was chasing. But I'd lost track entirely of what I was chasing. Maybe I'd been reduced to chasing my tail, or simply to twirling around before sleep, a weary mutt able to chase sticks only in dreams.

A week later I was still going in circles on how best to make use of the list I'd stolen from Smythe. But then Smythe himself greatly simplified my choices. I returned to the office after a home visit to be called into The Boss' office. It was only the two of us, and almost apologetically The Boss informed me that Smythe had just now brought in Adamo Ragnelli so that Ragnelli could complain that I'd defaced his auto.

"Is there any truth to this, Tony?"

"I never touched the man's car, sir," I said with utmost sincerity. "Though his son does have some talent defacing autos. He once let the air out of my tires. So maybe the culprit is closer to home. To be blunt, sir, this is the same Ragnelli whose sister falsely accused me of seduction, and Mr Smythe led that parade too. I guess Ragnelli still believes the girl. Or maybe he's angry with me because nobody else believes her. In any case, I never touched his sister. I never touched his car. And the only time I touched him is when my face got in the way of his fist back on the line, if you'll remember."

"I do." The Boss pressed his fingers to the bridge of his nose and sat still for a while with his eyes closed. At long last, he looked up and said, "Though I have my doubts, I am willing to treat both Ragnelli and Caleb as simply… mistaken in this matter. Perhaps prejudiced by their dislike for you. I will have to beg your patience, for the moment."

"Of course, sir," I said, silently resolving that my patience wouldn't be required.

The next day, Op. 19 sat across from me in my office. His foreman had sent him there at my discreet request.

Op. 19 looked sincerely offended. I looked sincerely disapproving.

"I'm fed up seeing you in here, Landucci," I said sincerely.

"I'm fed up with lying foremen," he said. "Show me where I don't do good work, and I'll apologize to Henry Ford himself."

His face was straight as the path of virtue. I sighed and handed him a folded "reprimand" on which I'd written this: "Adamo Ragnelli. E-7741. Piker, certainly. Wobbly too?"

And then, a few hours later, I was in Alex Spark's office, trying to look calm. I passed him Smythe's list of Service operatives. To keep my life simple, I'd simply told the truth about how and (more or less) why I'd found the list.

"And so this is your vengeance?" Spark asked.

"That's your choice, sir. But if that is what I think it is, I knew you'd want to see it, regardless."

And then it was done. Either I'd made myself look like a meddling ass, or I'd ended Smythe's career with Ford and, possibly, gotten a few of his fingers broken. I tried to practice feeling remorse as I walked back to Educational.

As Christmas of 1919 drew near, The Boss informed us that the Ford

Profit-Sharing Plan would end on New Year's Eve. After that, the men would simply receive an annual bonus based on length of service and degree of skill. *Merry Christmas,* we thought, knowing that come January there would be even fewer advisors in Educational, probably no more than two dozen.

The Boss privately assured me that I would remain with the department. We both knew that my real job with Service had saved my apparent job with Educational.

A week later came the news of another unsurprising ending: Adamo Ragnelli received his last pay envelope and was sent out the John R gate. His suffering wasn't enough, not nearly. I didn't even get to see it happen. I wanted to go his apartment and eavesdrop while he told his son what had happened. I wanted to stand on the walk in front of their building, Lisa's hand in mine, to watch him and his scheming son and his blinkered wife pile up their belongings in homemade crates while snow fell on their burning building.

I had better luck with Smythe, who came to work one morning to find that Service goons had ransacked his office. They'd been especially enthusiastic about dumping the contents of his desk onto the floor.

I and the dozen other early-arriving advisors had a chance to watch Smythe's shoulders pull back as he blustered angrily at the world in general. Beneath his thinning hair, his scalp turned the same delightful tomato red as his face, and he'd used up most of the obscenities in the English language when Edwin Mulock, The Boss' secretary, opened the door and told Smythe that he was wanted within.

Ten minutes later, Smythe stepped out, his face still flaming like a light bulb wrapped in flesh. I stood at the doorway to my office. He stopped when he reached me. "You had something to do with this," he said, waving his arms wildly to illustrate the scope of "this." "I know it. I know that's the truth."

"Well, the truth is always best, Caleb," I said cheerfully, patting him on his shoulder.

He trembled, glaring wordlessly. I thought for a moment he might start bleeding through his pores. And then he slowly turned and stomped away.

By asking around, I learned that Smythe spent the week of Christmas like a latter-day rodent version of the Holy Family, wandering from department to department, only to be told that there was no room at any Ford inn. Between them, Spark and The Boss had closed every door to him at Highland Park, and Bennett apparently saw no benefit to hiring a spy known to be a spy.

I wanted to have watched Smythe beg for a job. I wanted to want something higher and better, of course. But I didn't.

Thia wanted something higher and better. Although she had indeed broken with both Girls' Protective and Emmeline Ward, she continued with the Young Suffragettes. Moreover, Landucci reported that she had left the Socialists for the Communists. I presumed that Sigi had told her about my efforts to protect her because when she encountered me in Sigi's kitchen she treated me as befitted a contemptible bourgeois stool. The few scraps of conversation she granted me were either coldly polite or fervidly condemnatory of capitalism and its bootlicking lackeys.

Thia styled herself a forward-looking foot soldier in the triumphant march of the proletariat, and maybe she was. But she looked like a hobbyist—while her clothing grew far more subdued, it became no less expensive—and I hoped that appearance of harmless slumming would keep her safe from the dozens of operatives targeting the Communists. Still, I worried for her. And for everyone else too. As the unions grew stronger, the employers became more ruthless in their suppression, and the important men on both sides of the struggle were anything but hobbyists.

By February, Service spies were reporting (only in passing, of course) that Thia seemed to have taken up with a strapping English Communist called Union Jack Anderson, whom Party headquarters in New York had dispatched to help Detroit's Communists connect to the unions. Even beyond my jealousy—which I ignored unsuccessfully—that news made me worry further. Anderson was bent as my back and almost surely working as an agent of the Employers Association. Of course, the very fact that Thia had taken up with him suggested that in some way she suspected him of unworthiness, and from this I took a perverse comfort.

There was plenty in which to take comfort at home as well. Angela and the *nipotes* had settled more permanently into the Pilgrim and Church St houses. During the daytime, Gianluca, Brunella, and Gisella joined their mother at my house when not at school. Gasparo and Crocifissa spent most of their free time sledding in the park or sipping hot cocoa in front of Kitty's fire. Gasparo was surprisingly tender with his little sister.

By then, Kitty was no longer praying to Our Lady that Angela would return to Chicago. She even went out of her way to be kind to Angela's children, especially Gasparo and Crocifissa. She also tended to Lisa as I no longer could (and perhaps never had). Lisa spent most of her time with Kitty and had begun to shrink from me in the same the way which I imagined Angela's children shrank from their father. I deserved it, I suppose.

Ross and Kitty were courting more openly, and Kitty was pointedly ignoring Mother's recurring discovery that Ross was neither Italian nor Catholic. (To my ongoing astonishment, Angela treated Ross cordially.) For Kitty's sake, I was pleased at this development, but on my own account I found him dismayingly changed. He'd gotten a bit thin at the crown and thicker around the middle and made shy jokes about that now and then, but I don't mean he was physically changed. I mean he'd become wholesome. His charm had always lain in combining amused cynicism with joyous dissipation. Some cynicism lingered, but Kitty's new steel-girded optimism had made it more a matter of words than temperament. And his dissipation, of course, had given way to new ambition and higher and better ideals. I told myself this was all to the good. I hardly wanted a degenerate courting my sister. Still, with Ross' reformation I had effectively lost a friend, and I had few friends those days. None, really, except perhaps Sigi, which was its own species of mess.

Ultimately, though, I had to be grateful to Ross. Though many things were going well at home, money was becoming tight. We never received Andrew's or Carl's service bonuses, and Andrew's death benefit had ended without explanation a few months earlier. My salary was being stretched to cover ten mouths and two mortgages, and Carl's savings were dwindling fast. If Ilaria and Martin hadn't been sending Angela money, and Ross hadn't been quietly helping Kitty, Mother would have been back to pinching pennies.

Those cold nights I thought of poverty and slept even less. My back spasm throbbed between my shoulder blades like another nervous heart. I wondered sometimes whether I should have been kinder to Nate Adams. There are worse things than perversion.

Chapter 27

> Any employe born in the United States, with the exception of the Negro and Jew, is to be considered an American. If an employe is of the black race, he is considered a Negro. If Jewish, the name of the country he was born in should immediately precede the word "Jew" as "American-Jew," "Russian-Jew," etc.
>
> – Ford Educational Department policy

MORE AND MORE, KITTY HAD BEEN PRACTICALLY SHOVING ME OUT THE door so that I wouldn't interfere with Ross' visits. She and Ross were never alone, of course, but I think my particular presence interfered with his repertoire of adoring gazes. Without anywhere else to go, I passed more and more evenings with Sigi, whose company I enjoyed immensely, enough to endure Thia's distant contempt. Martha was also quite interesting, but I saw little of her because she seemed to believe that men generally should be left to their own devices. (Or possibly that *she* should be left to her own devices.)

A cynic would have said that I kept returning to the Gluecks' because some buried part of me was longing for Thia to fall repentantly into my arms, but I knew better than to take that prospect seriously. Besides, since returning Peter Everett's ring, Thia's falls into and out of other men's arms seemed simply exhausting for all involved. She certainly broke spectacularly with Union Jack Anderson. For weeks after that, she was so dangerous that Sigi and I became furtive in arranging our kitchen conclaves.

Eventually, Thia resumed carrying on conversations that didn't end with stormy departures. At first she had little to say beyond invective against the men in charge of the Communist Party. "The women of the Battalion of Death," she declared once, "sharpened bayonets, not goddamn pencils. If Lenin tries to send my Russian sisters for coffee, may they wear his guts for garters."

But eventually she became able to converse normally, even with a capitalist lackey such as myself. And, as spring came, she even began to speak admiringly of people again, particularly of Alice Paul and her National Woman's Party. Women's suffrage had already passed in Michigan, but it still required ratification in seven states, so Thia threw her energies back to the Yeses and to the NWP. Soon, her dresses and her moods brightened noticeably.

"If American Communists ever learn to smile and dance," I told Sigi one day after Thia had left us, "they'll sweep the country coast to coast."

"Not if they are Negroes," Sigi said with a sigh.

"Dr Sucre still can't find a home?" I asked.

Sucre, Sigi had mentioned more than once, was trying to move out of the Negro Holbrook-Clay district into a more genteel setting, but Detroit's genteel neighborhoods were white—and intended to remain so.

Sigi shook his head and took a thoughtful swig of beer. "I think, my friend, that those Communists will have trouble sweeping. Already the capitalists let the Negroes sweep the country from coast to coast."

I've never been sure if he knew how right he was.

Stefano had long since served his three months in prison for stealing from Ilaria and Martin. After his release, he'd left Chicago without telling anyone where he was going. I hadn't expected him to send any money to Angela and his children, of course, but I wouldn't have objected.

Fortunately, the Grams women knew how to economize. Ghilarza had taught Mother and Angela, and they had taught Kitty. Nobody complained, not even Lisa. In truth, I'd hoped for some foot-stomping or icy silence from my niece. But she'd been wan and silent since the seduction. *Since your tantrum,* said the voice at the back of my head. I wanted to win her back. I even apologized on three separate occasions. But still she answered my questions with limp politeness and never volunteered a word. Kitty said she was only slightly better with the others, except for Gasparo, who had made himself her defender at school.

Gasparo had also made himself a breadwinner for the family, first by getting hired on as a stock-boy for four hours a day at the Daszkowskis' store, and then securing a similar position for the summer at a store on Woodward across from the plant. He did this without our urging or knowledge. We'd thought he'd been playing stickball until he stepped proudly into the parlor to make his announcement. Looking at him then, with his drive and compact sturdiness, I couldn't help but think of Carl at age thirteen. I wondered how to forbid him from becoming *too* friendly with the neighbor boys.

Sometimes, although I hated myself for it, I hated all the little Baggios, even Gasparo. Like tapeworms, they crowded my dinner table and slurped my salary. Mostly, though, I loved them. Tough, enterprising Gasparo. Quiet little Crocifissa with the unmistakable spark of thought in her eyes. Dreamy, self-effacing Gisella who loved nothing more than to pass her evenings in a kitchen chair while Mother and Angela gossiped in Italian and rattled pots at their fears. Morbid Brunella and scholarly Gianluca, who brandished his fragile sense of superiority like a melodramatist with a prop sword.

I wondered often if I'd been like Gianluca at age eight. Probably, though I'd been dirtier and hungrier. All of us had been dirtier and hungrier than these children, and we would do anything to keep it that way. I would even go back to Ford day after day.

Is an hour of a strange woman's touch worth three dollars when money is tight? Probably not. But the more one fears being poor, the more one spends money one doesn't have on things one doesn't need. Or on things one does need, whatever others say, whatever one wants to need.

At least by then I no longer needed to fuck imaginary scars.

I tried to keep alive outside of work. Saturday evenings, when the day's heat relented slightly, I went strolling with Lisa and Brunella. Walking helped my back spasms, and I hoped that our spending time together might eventually endear me at least a little to Lisa, who was at last starting to talk more freely with the others. On our walks, she and Brunella generally spoke of fancy gowns and dead birds.

One Sunday afternoon, when Lisa and Brunella were needed to chaperone Kitty and Ross, I took my usual drive to see Sigi. Usually, I went around back, the easiest way to the kitchen, but that day I stopped at the front porch to chase off a rosy-cheeked kid selling subscriptions to the *Dearborn Independent.* I told the kid that Bill Cameron and his whole Jew-baiting rag were full of lies. He told me I was full of bug guts.

Sigi opened the door after I rang. "Daniel has gone to help Henry," he explained, as he led me toward the kitchen.

Dr Sucre had finally found someone in a respectable neighborhood to sell him a house—in fact, he now shared a back wall with the Gluecks. "The Sucres are still arranging the home?" I asked.

Sigi grimaced and shook his head. "They're cleaning. Someone has burnt a cross on their lawn."

"The Klan?" I answered myself: "No. Imitators, probably. Neighbors."

Sigi caught the tone in which I said "neighbors" and chuckled faintly. "Yes, probably. Thia suspects the Smythe boy, and perhaps his father. Probably she is right. Though I have no high estimation of Noonan on the other side or *his* children."

By asking around, I'd learned that Smythe had managed to find work at the Detroit Employers Association. I was surprised that he could still afford to pay his mortgage after losing out on the extra money Bennett must have been paying him. But the Employers Association certainly had the money and motivation to pay a few employes well to keep from having to pay all their employes fairly. In any event, I knew from Sigi that Smythe had been particularly hateful when the Sucres had purchased their home. He'd very nearly managed to block the sale, and he'd certainly helped to turn many, if not most, of the Sucres' neighbors against it. If Dr Sucre hadn't been a proud and even stubborn man, he might well have sold the house before the removal men had brought in the first stick of furniture. I certainly would have.

"But, of course," I said, "the police don't know or care who burnt the cross."

Sigi said that the police actually had investigated the matter and that they would even be patrolling the Sucres' street at night. That morning, the Sucres had hung a large, gold-painted cross on their front door, but they'd taken it down at noon, when a policeman knocked on the door to point out that his job was hard enough already.

Since the start of summer, Sigi had been keeping his beer in the icebox rather than the flour canister. He took two out and handed one to me. I pulled back my collar and pressed the bottom of the bottle to the nape of my sweaty neck. It was late evening but still unbearable.

As Harry Bennett solidified his position as Cast-Iron Charlie Sorensen's chief spymaster and enforcer of obedience, more and more rumors about him circulated. Of course, the notion that he had converted part of the basement of the Rouge's administration building into a pistol range so that he could hone his skills with a .22 turned out to be utter malarkey.

He used a .32.

The range was large enough to accommodate four or five shooters, and Henry Ford was known to drop in from time to time. On the day I was first brought there, however, Bennett was the only one with a weapon, which he dangled lazily against his thigh, as if he'd forgotten it. The bruiser with the scar over his eye who accompanied Bennett during the bigwigs' walk-throughs was slouched against a wall. There was no way to keep them both him and Bennett in sight at once.

Bradby was there as well. Earlier, he'd knocked gently on The Boss' door during one of our meetings to say that Mr Sorensen had requested my presence at the Rouge to consult with Mr Sorensen on an important matter. But once I got there, Sorensen hadn't been available. (He'd never planned to be, I assumed.) So Bradby had led me down to Bennett's pistol range instead.

"I need a favor," Bennett told me. "You see a lot of information. About unions and the like."

"Educational lets me learn a lot about my men, sir."

"Educational." Bennett chuckled shortly and mirthlessly. His gorilla followed suit. "We got a lot of sonsabitches up to no good 'round here, and they talk to each other better across the plants than we do sometimes. Way I see it, I know a fellah's a Red or an I Won't Work, I should let Spark know. He knows, I should know."

"Well, I work for Dr Marquis, of course," I said. "But I've had dealings from time to time with Mr Spark, and I could certainly mention it to him."

Another mirthless chuckle. "I mentioned it to him. Now I'm mentioning it to you."

"You want me to report directly to you, then?"

"Through the Rev. is fine," he said, tilting his head at Bradby.

"I see." I paused. "May I ask something, sir?"

"Asking don't hurt."

"Why me?"

"The Rev. there took a shine to you," Bennett said, smirking at his own joke.

Asking doesn't hurt, but getting answered can. So I just nodded and followed Bradby out of the range.

I didn't sleep much that night. This new problem could, of course, be as simple in its origins as Bennett had claimed. Possibly he'd merely asked Bradby for a useful name, and Bradby had supplied mine without any notion of endangering me. But it was also possible that Bennett had somehow gotten wind of how I'd freed myself from Smythe, and he therefore was setting up my punishment for interfering with one of his finks. Or maybe Bennett simply figured that I owed him a replacement for Smythe. Maybe I was caught up in some unknown chess match that I would never understand. None of the options was appealing.

Early the next morning, I stopped at Spark's office to warn him that Bennett was trying to recruit me. Spark nodded as if he'd already known (I realized uncomfortably that he might have). He told me to pass Bennett just enough information to appease him. I had to pause for a moment in the corridor to remind myself whom I was betraying to whom. It was far too late try to remember *why*.

When I told The Boss about the latest wrinkle, his voice shook slightly when he thanked me. His hands were shaking too. I felt awful for him. He'd finally noticed the writing on the wall. *Thus falleth virtue's empire.*

Soaked in summer sweat as I walked to the Gluecks', I very nearly bumped into Smythe.

I raised my hat fractionally and muttered his name, hoping to pass easily. It was too hot to gloat, too hot to fight.

Smythe stepped sideways to block my path. "Off to see your nigger-loving Jew friends?" he asked.

"They're Austrian too, Caleb. Don't forget that. For a proper slur, you have to fill in *all* the blanks of the 928."

"They're ruining this neighborhood. They—you—shouldn't be allowed to walk down my sidewalks."

"Cheer up, Caleb. If they lower the worth of your home enough, then you might be able to afford to stay in it. Though I imagine you've found some way to graft in your new position. Unless you've already gotten caught again."

His face twitched. I'd simply been goading him, but apparently I'd stumbled upon the truth. I laughed. "You've been given the sack at the Employers Agency too, haven't you, Caleb? You learned nothing at Educational, and then you got fired from Employers." I laughed even harder.

He cursed me thoroughly then, which distracted him from blocking my progress, so I stepped around him, walking backward for several paces to make sure that he didn't attack me unseen.

In Sigi's kitchen, I pressed the cold bottle to my neck, sighed gratefully, and tried not to wonder how much of my mockery of Smythe had been simple self-hatred.

"I calculate," Sigi said, "that I have been sticky" ("schticky") "for seven weeks."

"And a stick in the mud for several decades," Thia said. She had skipped into the kitchen in a yellow frock as gay and light as her tone. "Gentlemen," she declared, "raise your ginger beers to toast Harry Burn."

"Who is this Burn?" Sigi asked.

"A state senator from Tennessee."

"It has passed?" Sigi asked.

Thia grinned. "Leen just rang. Fifty to forty-seven. Soon I will be a voter."

Her father stood to embrace her. I rose enough to shake her hand.

"You have told your mother?" Sigi asked.

"Of course," she said. "She was so overjoyed that she very nearly stopped tending to her tomatoes."

"In Martha's case," Sigi told me, "that is in fact overjoyed. Martha is a great one for gardening."

"And now that I can walk the street as your equal," Thia proclaimed, "I will escort you gentlemen on an evening constitutional."

Sigi and I followed the still-skipping Thia outside. After stopping at a florist so that Thia could buy each of us a yellow suffrage rose to match her own, we walked to the water works. Despite the heat, there were quite a few people in the park. The children had the vigor to run about the grass and chase toy sailboats along the riverbanks, but we older folk promenaded gently or kept to the shaded benches. The women carried parasols and looked unchanged, though the younger ones had much shorter hair and perhaps slightly shorter hemlines than one would have seen before the war.

"The world does not look so different, does it?" Sigi asked, reading my mind.

"Oh, give it a day or two, Father," Thia said breezily. "Indeed, in some places, it might take as long as a week for women's suffrage to mend all ills. Isn't the river looking especially blue today?"

It actually looked brownish. Clever boys refused to swim immediately downriver of the Rouge plant.

"And the sky as well?" Thia asked.

Even beyond the late sun glowing off her yellow dress, she was radiant. As she led us on laps of the park like an Olympic athlete, I realized that I had never before seen her truly happy. On our second or third circuit, we bumped into Ross and Kitty. Kitty was nearly as giddy as Thia.

"Citizen Kitty," Thia said gravely.

"Citizen Thia," Kitty replied.

They stayed solemn for a heartbeat before hugging one another at high pitch. Ross grinned at me over Kitty's head. It looked like his old cynical grin, but he was probably thinking about cherubim and flowers.

The ladies led us on another lap. Kitty leaned on my arm, and Ross escorted Thia. At first, Ross was full of chatter and jaunty gallantry, but soon he was short of breath and notably favoring his bum knee. A sad look flitted across my sister's face, and I knew that she was thinking about Andrew running through Janek Sedlacek's meadow.

Once all of us but Thia were panting or limping, Sigi invited us for a light supper, and everyone was too cheerful to decline. As we turned along Bewick toward the Gluecks' home, twilight was just beginning and the trees and bricks glowed in its forgiveness.

"Should we pop in at the Sucres?" Thia asked. "I'd like to thank Gladys for all her work among her people, but I shouldn't like to disturb them at the table."

"I think Henry would not object to some friendly faces," Sigi said, "and we need not stay if they are eating."

Kitty made vague, ladylike noises. Ross and I kept quiet.

Not long after we crossed Waterloo, Sigi was proven profoundly right about the need for friendly faces—the Sucres' house was already surrounded by angry faces. There were a few dozen, mostly male, all paler than mine. Eyes glinted from the front porches and parlor windows of the nearby houses.

A half-dozen yards from the forward edge of the crowd, three cops stood athwart the Sucres' walk, watchful and stony-faced. The oldest one, I realized, was Sergeant Regan, from my anti-fraud days. He was somewhat grayer and possibly a bit portlier, but he was still broad-shouldered and upright.

He halted Thia with an upraised palm. "Far as you go, Mrs Mueller."

"Sergeant Regan," she said warmly. She looked closely at his uniform. "Lieutenant Regan. Congratulations."

"Thank you, ma'am."

"Have you arrested Dr Sucre, Lieutenant?" she asked.

"*Doctor*," hissed a scornful voice not far from my ear.

"Or his wife?" Thia continued. "Or his small children?"

"Arrest, hell," someone said from the back. "Arresting's too good. Monkeys come down from trees, you hang 'em back up."

The muttering agreed.

"And that's far as *you* go," Regan said louder, addressing the crowd, which was creeping toward the house.

"Well, if nobody's under arrest," Thia said firmly, "I've come to call on the Sucres."

More than one person whispered "nigger lover." Sigi and I elbowed our way forward to stand beside Thia.

Keeping a protective arm over Kitty's shoulder until it was safe to pull out his notebook and pencil, Ross did likewise. "Ross Robertson, *Free Press*," he said loudly, with a wink at Regan. He asked the police, "Any you boys wanna get your picture in the 'paper?"

"Get along with you," Regan said. "Ain't no story here."

"Then the police aren't guarding a Negro's house against an angry white mob? And they aren't preventing this lady"—Ross pointed to Thia—"from visiting friends?"

The mob protested being called a mob. Regan said he wasn't preventing nobody from visiting nobody.

"I'm delighted to hear it, Lieutenant," Thia told him before sweeping past him.

Nobody breathed as she walked to the front door and pressed the bell.

Several curtains on the first and second stories flapped open and closed. After a long pause, the front door opened a crack. None of us could see who had opened it. Thia talked for a little while, and then the door opened wide enough for her to enter. It closed as soon as she'd stepped through.

"Maybe I'm the nigger's friend," said deep voice from the rear of the crowd. "Maybe I'd like to go inside and shake my nigger friend's paw. Maybe I'd like to go give my nigger friend and his little tar babies a great big hug."

I could see enough of the speaker to know that he was a tall man with a scar over one eyebrow—Harry Bennett's favorite goon. He was looking straight at me.

"That's enough out of you, Declan Noonan," said the skinny, ill-shaven cop. "This ain't the time for your stirring up."

Noonan glowered but stayed mum.

"It's time for something, though, isn't it?" said a familiar voice from somewhere beside Noonan. "While our homes are still safe. And decent."

"That goes for you too, Caleb Smythe," Regan told him. "You want your homes safe? Go back to 'em and stick. All of you."

Nobody budged, and nobody spoke. As the seconds dragged silently, nothing happened save twilight's dimming. Then, as if it had blown through on a breeze, there was a general muttering of *nigger* and *rape.*

"Enough of that," Regan barked.

But the muttering grew. I noticed Noonan and Smythe whispering intently to one another. After a moment or two, Smythe melted away, heading home. Cowardice, perhaps, but one seldom saw cowardice so a-tremble with rage.

Just as a long spell of angry rumbling started to die down and the imminent danger seemed to pass, a kid of fourteen or so burst from the crowd. The skinny policeman lunged toward him, but not in time to stop him from throwing a rock. It shattered one of the upstairs windows at about the same time that the cop hit the kid like a defensive end tackling a quarter-back. As the two went to ground in a tangle, the crowd pushed forward. Chaos seemed inevitable.

Then an explosion froze everyone in place.

"That was me, shooting at the moon," a voice called from the second story of the Sucres' house. The barrel of a rifle appeared through the drawn curtains and knocked away the remaining glass of the shattered pane. Then the curtains drew back, and the lights came on, revealing Capt. Allan standing at the window, rifle in one hand, beribboned Negro girl in the other.

"This," he said, "is Regina. She is eight years old. She excels at reading and knows some pretty songs on the violin. When I was in the war, I shot three Boche soldiers at sixty yards to protect a house full of Frenchmen and their children, and I didn't love those *parlez-vous* kids half as much as I love Regina and her little brother. Next time it won't be the moon, is what I mean to say."

He pulled the curtains closed again and the lights went off. It was impossible to tell whether he was still at the window.

Most of the crowd suddenly strove to look menacing in retreat. But Bennett's goon Noonan wasn't budging. "That buck just admitted he shot white men," he said. "Are we going to leave a white woman in a house with him? Are we going to let our neighborhood fill up with murdering, raping animals?"

Most of the crowd kept inching away, but a few, all of them men, began to shoulder forward, moving past me with eager expressions.

There was another detonation, this time from Regan's service revolver, which he held above his head, barrel pointed straight up.

"Moon's ending up Swiss cheese tonight," he said. "We told you to stop working your jaw, Noonan. Now take it home while it's still on its hinges. Same goes for all of you."

The third policeman unholstered his revolver also. He pointed it uncertainly toward the ground. His hand was trembling, and he looked painfully young.

Noonan continued to protest. "A nigger shoots at white men—"

"White moon," Regan said.

"Shoots at white men, and that goon tackles my boy?" Noonan pointed to the young rock-thrower, now standing sullenly with an arm wrenched behind his back by the cop who'd brought him down. "You're gonna take that nigger's side?"

"I take the law's side, Noonan," Regan said. "And the law says go back to your homes before I start shoving people into the paddy wagon."

Most of the crowd was stepping quietly away, and even the men who had pushed forward were wavering.

"*Now,*" Regan said. "Go home right now. All of you." Even the waverers began to move.

"You've still got my boy," Noonan said.

"You'll get him back soon enough. Now go."

After a nasty hesitation, Noonan went. A moment later, the street was empty except for our party, the police, and Noonan's surly boy.

"You can move along, too," Regan told us, more hopefully than commandingly.

"I will await my daughter," Sigi declared quietly.

"So there's definitely no story here, then?" Ross asked Regan. "That was just a neighborhood quilting bee, I'm assuming."

Regan sighed loudly.

It was nearly dark by the time Thia came out.

"Thank the lord," the third cop said.

Before Thia reached the rest of us, there was another crash of broken glass from the back of the house. The skinny cop went running toward the crash, freeing Noonan's brat to leg it down the street. The young cop started to chase him but pulled up after only a few steps.

The next part is much clearer than it needs to be. Smythe, his now-familiar angry expression clearly lit by the burning rag stuffed into the bottle cocked near his shoulder, lunged from the shadow of a tree at the edge of the Sucres' front yard. He took several steps toward the house before pulling his arm back to throw the bottle. Then he collapsed to the ground in an unnatural jumble. He'd fallen at the same time a gunshot had cracked from the second story of the Sucres' home.

Within seconds, the burning rag reached the gasoline in the bottle, and the flames rose. For an instant, it was possible to see in some detail how the bullet had removed much of Smythe's angry expression. Then the flames spread to his clothes, which blazed like kindling. He must have spilled gasoline on himself in his haste. Sigi rushed a few paces toward Smythe before realizing he was beyond help.

The street was deeply silent. The only sound was the disgusting sizzling from Smythe's corpse.

I'd just stood there the whole time, I realized. There had been a gunshot, and I'd just stood there. Sigi had moved to help Smythe, Thia had moved to restrain her father, and Ross had leapt in front of Kitty, who had ducked. But I'd just stood there. Was this why we all died, the Grams men—because we stood by bemusedly when the shooting started? I should've been shot, I thought. It had been my night to die, but somehow Smythe and his burning bottle had stumbled in front of my bullet, and now I was living somebody else's life.

I was still caught up in that conviction when a boy not much older than Gasparo burst out of the same patch of shadow from where the dead man had emerged just an instant earlier. *Why* he did so only then I have never understood. The boy had a half brick cocked and ready, and I thought he also would be shot. And maybe he did too, or maybe he only then truly understood what was smoldering on the ground not ten feet from him. Whatever happened, he didn't throw the brick at the house. But even so, as if unable to stop himself, he threw it.

It thudded into Sigi's temple, and Sigi crumpled to the ground.

"Father!" Thia cried.

The boy stared dumfounded at what he'd done. The skinny policeman, who'd just returned from the back yard, collared him roughly.

Regan was swearing under his breath. "Gotta do it," he said. "Gotta do it," he said louder. He was talking to himself. Eventually, he sent the young policeman to ring for an ambulance and a paddy wagon.

I went to Sigi, who was lying limply in the grass with Thia kneeling beside him. Blood was flowing from his temple. He moaned slightly for a while, then fell silent. Thia told me to get Sucre.

It was a lot of blood. I thought of Dr Collins and his blood for the blacksmith.

"Henry Sucre," Thia told me. "He knows about head wounds. Go!"

I went, but nobody answered my knock. The paddy wagon arrived then, and soon Regan was shoving Captain Allan out of the house, toward the paddy wagon. Sucre was following along behind. He tried to go to Sigi, but a cop restrained him. Along with a third man I didn't recognize, Sucre and Allan were bundled into the back of the paddy wagon while Thia screamed incoherently at the cops.

Kitty, Ross, and I waited with the kneeling and weeping Thia. Smythe's corpse had burnt itself out, and the evil light had disappeared. But there was still a lunch counter smell in the air.

The ambulance was too slow in coming, we decided. The nearest car was Sigi's. I told Ross the address, and he hurried around the block. Long moments later, Daniel was parking Sigi's beautiful Pierce Arrow at the curb and I was helping Ross to lift Sigi into the rear seat. We decided that Ross would drive Kitty home in his car, and I would ride to the Ford Hospital with Thia and Sigi.

As I was going round to the front passenger seat, I heard more glass shatter at the Sucres' house. I braced myself for another gunshot, another corpse. But the house stayed silent. Declan Noonan waved at me, and then rubbed his hands at a job well done before stepping back into the shadows.

I rode in the front seat, and Thia sat in the back, her father's bloodied head in her lap. I turned again to look at her, and through the rear windshield I could see the darkened corpse akimbo on the lawn and what might have been black faces peering at it from the house beyond.

Chapter 28

Sigi was no longer making noise when Daniel and I carried him into the Ford Hospital. His chest hardly moved, and one of his eyelids was twitching erratically.

Thia sat stunned for a half-hour in the corridor outside the examining room. Then she began to pace. "Why?" she asked the air occasionally.

While that was going on, I plunked a dollar's worth of nickels into the 'phone, trying to convince the police to let Sucre out of jail to treat Sigi. Nobody would admit to knowing where Lt Regan was, and nobody would admit to having Sucre in custody. I got Emmeline Ward's number from Thia, and Ward called the Police Commissioner himself. He told her that Sucre—along with Capt. Allan and another man—was under arrest for murder and conspiracy to commit murder, and that the police wouldn't even finish processing him for several hours. "Processing," I suspected based on Ross' stories, would involve bars of soap wrapped in towels. There was no hope of Sucre's tending to Sigi.

While I was thanking Emmeline, Daniel returned with Martha Glueck. Thia and her mother withdrew into dread and soft weeping. Martha's arrival made me feel even more irrelevant. Angry, too, and frightened. I went outside to compose my thoughts. I walked up and down North Grand several times, as far as Northwestern High. I realized that I knew of a workingman's pig not too far away. Countless Service reports had etched the address on my eyes, and I even knew the current password.

The password got me in, and in the pig's dim light the bloodstains on my suit could have been any stains, which made the suit less suspicious. Still, the conversations around grew quiet as I passed, so I settled with my monkey swill in a spot conspicuous enough that I wouldn't be considered a lurker. My nearest drinking companions were two men exchanging noisy, comical insults. Occasionally, they would pause to recite along with the battered Victrola on the bar. Eventually I realized that they were listening to a record of Harding's return to normalcy stump speech.

isn't anything the matter with world civilization
fever has rendered men irrational
wandered far from safe paths

I listened to the insults, to the recitation. I looked at the unstable table in front of me. I drank slowly, my throat burning each time I swallowed.

"You don't belong here," a rough, drunken voice told me.

I kept my head down. "I don't want trouble."

"The world was that easy, hell, wouldn't hardly be enough trouble to go 'round," the voice said. "Only the swells could afford it." A full glass of beer and a crossed pair of threadbare forearms settled on the table in front of me. Maybe it wouldn't be a fight, after all.

not nostrums, but normalcy, not revolution, but restoration

I risked looking up at the man's face. After a moment's confusion, I recognized the pallid, unkempt man who'd greeted Nate Adams in the hospital. He said, "You're the galoot with the dead brother, right?"

Brothers.

"Sorry how I was prickly then," he continued. "Nate told me you were jake by him, and Nate's okay for a plute. Jeff."

"Tony."

We shook. His palm was sandpapered with calluses.

"So what the hell you doing here, Mr Jake By Nake? Nate."

"See, bo, thing is," I said, "not so long ago, I'm over at Royal Oak Country Club chowin' on some *fwah grass* and pullin' a Daniel Boone when this duffer with a holey coat and a big bushy beard comes up to me and sits down."

Jeff sat there, maybe amused, maybe confused.

the infinite God never intended such a program

"The duffer, name of Fred, tells me he knew how it is for guys like me, young guys with more greenbacks than challenges. Then he sorta surprises me by saying he used to be like that too.

revise human nature and suspend the fundamental laws of life

"Turns out Fred's the son of some Fritz bigwig as owns a lot of factories, and he grew up wasting his time and his dad's money just like me. Only his dad put him in a crate and shipped him to England to set him straight. He says that's where he met a bright boy, name of Karl Marx, who played him some swell chin music and showed him this book he wrote, a real lulu called *Capital.*

false economics
utter chaos

"It takes stuff from a whole bunch of good books and it puts 'em together in a way that really comes across, even to a thickhead like him, the guy says. This guy, he tells me, 'You can bet I gave up jib-jabbin' at swareys and joined up with Karl to get the worker a square deal, and things was goin' great till Karl got sick and I promised him on his deathbed I'd sell those copies of *Capital* for him. Only after Karl died, this snooty mug of a publisher who ain't never liked him one bit says I can't have the books until I pay for 'em. Only I can't pay for 'em till I sell 'em, so—"

Jeff bellowed with laughter. "Shit, I lost two bucks on that one right before I shipped over. Used to bother me like all get-out, losing that money. But then I got to Archangel, and two bucks didn't bother me none." He did some damage to his beer. "Archangel. Shit. Fifty degrees below in winter. Moujiks who hated you, Bolos looking to kill you, and half the time no way of knowing which was which until somebody pulled a trigger."

Inspired by his theme, Jeff rose swaying to his feet, wobbling upon a wobbly chair. He held a rafter with one hand, his glass with the other.

"I hated the Bolos then," he said, declaiming to the half populated pig. "And I don't trust 'em now, even if half you coots would marry 'em and squirt out little Red babies."

Heads began to turn. A few men hissed.

Jeff raised his hand. "But it was their country, the Bolos, so okay. But those British officers"—he spat a mouthful of beer which landed silently in sawdust—"well, they wouldn't even tell us what it was about, not one solitary word of *why.* The Armistice signed, everybody else back home front of their fireplaces, but there we were under the ice sword. So we said *no. No,* we weren't going to freeze and die again, not till we had some answers. And they called it mutiny, and the men broke, and there we were back in the snow and the blood."

The hissing had stopped. There was some thumping of tables and cheering.

"We left good men in Russia. Bad men too, but what the hell. *Men.* And I came home, who fought in tundra, fingers too cold to pull a trigger with Bolos sighting me across the wasteland, and I took a job over there at His Majesty's Crystal Palace. And I was still proud, if you can believe it, still wearing my Manship ring."

He pointed to an empty finger on his right hand.

"But back here there's these fat-bottomed men as never saw shooting, 'less it was the Buffalo Bill show, and whenever I try to talk about the way of things, they give me nothing but their sharper patriotism and their *That's all right, Jeff*s and *That's as may be, Jeff*s. I bet I'm in their fink files for saying maybe the Wobblies have it closer to right than anybody wants to think. Well, I say to hell with 'em, to hell with all of 'em. Write me up, finks. Jeffrey Parks, E-5106. 470 McKinstry."

At this, Jeff pumped his fist, which cost him his beer, which cost him his balance. He fell with a drunkard's pliancy to the floor. Hilarious with laughter, the men who'd been singsonging along with Harding helped him to his feet.

After we sat back down, somebody brought Jeff a beer. He looked at it critically, as if wondering whether it met his approval. We talked for a while, drinking slowly. I kept thinking I should go back to the hospital, but I couldn't imagine why.

The rafters were calling to me, and eventually I grabbed one and swung there, trying to keep my memories from turning painful. After a while, I looked down and saw Nate Adams putting a friendly hand on Jeff's shoulder.

He turned his eyes toward me. "Hello, Tony," he said cheerfully.

I saw red. I swung my legs up and thrust both feet at his head. They hit his shoulder instead, so I swung back and then forward again, propelling myself at him. I landed on him, knocking us both into the filthy sawdust. I got in a couple good punches before he freed himself and scrambled to his feet. I was on one knee and getting ready to grapple him again, I think, when he punched me in the face. He did that some more, and I had the fading impression of the earth shifting around me.

I regained my senses in the night air. "There's money enough in his wallet to take him where he's going," Nate was telling a cabby. "Don't worry. He's out of puke."

The next morning I learned from the mirror that Nate had bruised me in several spots and from Ross' front-page story that Sigi had died of cerebral hæmorrhage less than three hours after arriving at the hospital. More than a week later, I rang the Gluecks' bell—Sigi's bell—and was surprised when Dot answered it.

She smiled wanly. "Thia probably won't be leaving her room again this afternoon. Do you want to come in and have some tea? Daniel seems to need things to do. He's polished the service twice today."

I shook my head. But I also didn't want to leave.

"How badly is she?" I asked. I hadn't seen her since Sigi's funeral a few days earlier.

"Very. It doesn't help how stupid the whole thing was. Stupider than Benjy, even."

"Sigi would laugh and laugh," I said. "Killed by a neighbor who'd meant to attack a different neighbor."

"That's what Thia said last night," Dot said.

She gestured to a pair of chairs and settled in without waiting for my help. I sat beside her.

"Poor thing," Dot said. "She and Martha both. They loved him terribly."

"We all love terribly," I said, risking a sideways glance. "If we ever loved well, the world would come to an end."

She surprised me by taking my hand. We sat there quietly for a while. I closed my eyes. The evening sun turned my eyelids orange, and the heat crept reassuringly into my bones.

Chapter 29

Mother knew it was coming and had gone to Mrs Daszkowski to mutter, but I'd started to suspect that her opposition was merely a matter of keeping up appearances. Angela and the children, including Lisa, were at Kitty's. Kitty herself was in Mother's kitchen, boiling water on every inch of stove top.

Ross was in the parlor with me, his face redder than his hair. "Tony, you know I didn't start coming here— But the way it worked out— Thing is, well, I think I can make her happy, you understand, and..."

"Just look both ways crossing the goddamn street, will you?"

You don't often see Scotsmen hugging other men, I don't think. They store it up, I guess, for when they need to yank a guy off the floorboards.

The clean-shaven, pomaded matinee idol of a police lieutenant wanted to yank me off the floorboards and to keep on yanking till we reached Police Headquarters. For the moment, he was contenting himself with sitting twitchily on my sofa and glaring at me while a peach-cheeked patrolman scribbled our words into a note-book. Amusingly, I resented them for coming into my home and asking me questions.

"And you're sticking to your story that it was Smythe who had the bottle in his hand? The burning one?" Lt Pomade asked me.

"It's not a story," I said. "It's the truth, same as it was ten minutes ago. Same as it was ten days ago, if anybody had asked then."

"It couldn't have been thrown *from* the house?"

"Don't you have any questions for me about Harold Smythe?" The boy who had killed Sigi with a brick was Smythe's eldest, Harold. "He killed a man too, I believe."

The lieutenant ignored my question as thoroughly as I'd ignored his. The patrolman went through half a pencil before the lieutenant called a ceasefire.

Back at the shooting range, the tableau was nearly identical to that of my previous visit—Noonan standing athwart the exit, Bennett slouched against the wall, pistol dangling in his hand. The only difference was that the Rev. Bradby was absent, Noonan having come for me himself.

Bennett was pretending to be hurt. "Gee, Tony, I wish you'da told me how you and dear, departed Caleb never got along."

I was working hard to keep my voice level and my hands steady. I don't think I was deceiving either of them, but I felt it important to keep a little dignity. "Truth to tell, Mr Bennett, I didn't know you knew Caleb."

It was worth at least trying to lie on that point. Doubtless, Smythe had spent the months when he and Noonan were neighbors complaining to Noonan that I'd helped get him sacked from Educational, but it was entirely possible that Smythe hadn't known I was the one who'd filched the list. And it was possible that neither Noonan nor Bennett was aware that I'd known that Smythe had been working for Bennett.

"Deck says," Bennett said, "you talked to the police about that jigaboo riot, and he's curious if his name came up."

Noonan smirked at me. He didn't say much, but his smirks were eloquent enough to have swayed the Senate.

I shook my head. I'd known that it was bad enough seeing Noonan do what I'd seen him do, bad enough taking the side I'd taken. I knew I'd pay some sort of price for that. But I knew I couldn't afford to pay the price for openly attacking one of Bennett's lieutenants. "They didn't ask much, and I didn't offer anything. I figured that's how you'd want it."

"Smart fellah, this one, ain't he, Deck?" He turned back to me and added, "Make sure you don't say nothing, yeah?" Bennett shooed me from the room with a hand gesture.

As I left, Noonan nodded and smirked. It was nice somebody had something to be cheerful about.

My punishment for siding with the Sucres began soon after that trip to the shooting range. Ironically, it came at the hands of Bennett's sworn rival, Spark. I wasn't sure whether Bennett arranged it by subterfuge or simple request, but in any event Spark began sending me ever fewer and fewer Service reports. And those I did receive were from operatives who either saw a Bolo hiding in every cylinder bore or who couldn't have found a Bolo in downtown Moscow.

My punishment coincided with and paled beside Detroit's punishment for some great, unknown offense. Slowly, inexorably, you could feel the economic depression take hold in the city. Housing became even more abysmal or unaffordable, usually both. Families were living in canvas tents on the outskirts of town, some on lots they had bought in the hopes of building a house, some as squatters. In 1915, Education had joined Detroit's reformers in seeking to tear down all unfit housing, but five years later we were routinely begging the Board of Health to permit families to live in condemned buildings so that their squalor would at least have something like a roof over it.

As fall set in, most of the other auto concerns shut their gates, hibernating until better times, and even at Ford you could feel the fear as the men and the machines cursed and banged at one another with ever greater urgency. The men knew they were one accountant's dispassionate decision from the plant's shutting down, one straw boss' angry decision from losing their positions. And the straw bosses were forever at the edge of anger, forever squeezing because they were being squeezed by the foremen, and so on up. There was always a larger hand squeezing, and one twitch was all it would take, and then the nights would keep getting colder but there wouldn't be any coal in the coal bin. Then the shivering and the coughing would begin, then parents would wonder which of their children a merciful God would gather to Himself first.

Some men chafed, fought back against their bosses, their company, whatever they could find to fight. A fink who, like me, couldn't keep busy amidst the fear and the unrest could definitely feel the squeezing.

As Service lost interest in me, The Boss seemed to lose interest in Service, in Educational, and Ford altogether. Though he still met with me, he mostly talked about his happy times as Dean of St Paul's Cathedral or his theories on how best to raise boys from a young age and truly mold them into decent men.

Given my fragile position and given Marquis' growing indifference, I spent most of my time fearing the sound of that second shoe. Incessant spasms hunched my back, and my intestinal problems often made having enough food on my plate a mixed blessing. But it was still a blessing, and I knew it. And when Angela went to work at Bagnasco's, preparing corpses for funerals in order to make money for the family, I saw how easily that blessing could disappear, how easily I could be buried alive again. Michigan's soot-soaked ice could easily cover me over, cover us all over, just as heavily and as finally as Ghilarza's sun-baked dirt.

Chapter 30

I WAS IN FRED O'HARA'S OFFICE. EDUCATIONAL HAD CEDED FURTHER GROUND to the accountants, and I'd lost my office in our retreat.

"The point is, Tony, we've got to do more with less, just like everybody else. So no pikers, no malingerers. You got your start here stopping fraud. So go stop fraud."

I'd kept my head down. I hadn't protested, but somehow O'Hara sensed that I was horrified by the fact that Educational now taught men how to save money only by example, only by denying them wages and benefits that they were justly owed.

"Yes, sir," I said.

He stared at me hard for a while. "Good man." He picked a folder off a stack in front of him and glanced over the 928 on top. "So. A familiar face for you."

I took the folder from him and waited until I'd left his office to open it. Tatyana Abramoff. Her 928 had been edited and retyped several times since Merry and I had visited her five years before. The new material read like the tale of Job. Nearly all her husband's family in Russia had died in the war, as had much of hers. Then his sister had died in New York of "immoderate drink," and soon after that he'd irreparably mangled his right hand on the line. He'd accidentally (!) drowned in the river not a month afterward. Tatyana Abramoff had gotten a wife's job with Ford and done it well for nearly two years, till her dropsy had made it impossible to work.

Before Sorensen had laid off most of the Ford doctors, they'd said that "improvement was not to be expected" in her case, and her former advisor had recommended that she continue receiving her sick benefits. But O'Hara wanted her benefits nixed, and he wanted me to do the nixing. Giving me Tatyana Abramoff's case was his way of saying that I could save Ford the expense either of her sick benefits or of my salary.

I drove out to see her the Friday after Thanksgiving. Gone were the days of the new gas stove. Even the days of well-scrubbed poverty were over. She lived in a filthy rat-trap on Oakland, unappealing even by the standards of Detroit's lower east side at that time. The dirt was part of the woodwork, and under my feet the floorboards buckled and skittered. Three of the four pieces of furniture were unacknowledged kindling. Indeed, the whole building should have been burned, if only to keep the neighbors' sickly children warm for a few hours.

Who is the guy that asks you why your money is all spent,
And quiz-es you and wif-ey too about e-nor-mous rent?

I found her lying supine on a narrow bed without a headboard. A rope ran across the bed from one nearby wall to the other, from which hung two small pieces of rubber hose whose purpose I couldn't identify until my approach woke her. She carefully raised a tremulous hand to take hold of a piece of hose and then repeated the process with her other hand, tugging herself into a sitting position. She looked even more birdlike than when I'd last seen her, though the swelling around her eyes gave her face an initial illusion of plumpness. She blinked at me quizzically.

Who counts the kids and lifts the lids, to see that things are clean?
And sure he'll say most an-y day, your bank book must be seen.
In-ves-ti-gator, In-ves-ti-gator

"I know you," she said hoarsely.

"I'm sorry." I put the few dollars in my pocket on the rickety nightstand and strode out as fast as the floorboards permitted.

In the car, the shaking slowly subsided into mere shivering with cold. I sat there, thinking of Merry and his determined optimism, his scrupulous reports. A scruple, I had learned, is a unit of weight equivalent to twenty grains. One gram is therefore three-quarters of a scruple. It's queer, now, to think how long I sat calculating moral fractions. And then I updated Tatyana Abramoff's 928, recommending that her sick benefits be continued. Some people, I wrote, could not be expected to improve.

That afternoon I went back to work only long enough to give Tatyana Abramoff's file to O'Hara. At home, I found the girls were in the parlor, doing their lessons. I stood and watched them. This was an hour of the day foreign to me, and I felt privileged to glimpse my home at that time.

It was only the girls because Gasparo and Gianluca were at their after-school jobs and their mother was at the mortuary, applying cosmetics to the dead. I wondered how many corpses came in with wounds like Sigi's that needed disguising. With wounds like our brothers'. Like she herself had needed when she'd come to Detroit with a black eye still visible. Awful and comical both, how we learn our trades.

Mother was surprised to see me home so early. Worried. I wondered if I looked then as Father had decades earlier when he'd come home to tell her that he was to be tried for peculation.

"Antonio?" she asked. "Is something the matter?"

"Uncle Tony?" Lisa asked. "Are you okay?"

I realized that I'd settled into my familiar chair by the radiator. That a few tears had started to slide down my face. I brushed them aside and forced a smile. "I'm going to have to be a good man for a little while," I told everyone. "I'm sorry."

I only sat in my parlor for a few moments before forcing myself to stand and go to the downtown offices that had been hired by Daniel Huxley, the famous Chicago lawyer conducting Henry Sucre's defense. His secretary eventually ushered me to the great man, six feet of smooth suit and leonine white hair.

"Tony Grams, sir," I said. "Somehow my name has not been included on your witness list."

I continued to go to Educational as usual, to discharge my increasingly scanty and unpleasant duties there, because every day's salary helped. Soon enough it was time for the trial.

The prosecutor, Conyers, looked like a cousin to Lt Pomade—a sharp mouth and a sharp neckline in a sharp suit. In his opening statement, Conyers told the jury that they'd see "what's what" pretty quickly. "A white man dead, and a nigger pulled the trigger," he said several times, savoring the rhyme. He pointed accusingly at Heaven and Earth, at blind Justice and nearsighted jurors. He clutched punishment in one hand and made of the other an angry fist. He told the gentlemen of the jury that a whole herd of nigger bucks led by Henry Sucre had descended upon a white neighborhood to stir up trouble. That they drunkenly had devised and executed an un-American conspiracy to shoot respectable white Americans in their respectable white sleep. Only by the grace of God and good offices of the Detroit Police, said the punitive fist of justice, had the bloodshed stopped with the death of but one respectable white man.

And, he allowed in passing, one arguably respectable Jew.

But, he said. *But.* The slaughter could have rivalled Belgium and the assembly-line rape could have stretched all the way back to the dick-dense jungles of darkest Congo.

By the time Conyers had finished, several jurors looked baffled that we were going to bother with a trial when rope was cheap and tree branches provided by outraged Nature.

But Huxley, and his elegant suit and his elegant hair, restored at least a few scruples of doubt and some faint interest in fairness. He pointed out that, of the eight conspiratorial rapists and murderers in that house, three were women and two were children aged six and eight. He pointed out that there had been no drunken plot because there was no drunkenness and, indeed, that the conspiratorial doctor's conspiratorial wife was a well-known dry who allowed no liquor in her conspiratorial home. He pointed out that the arguably respectable Jew had been killed by a white boy. He noted that it was peculiar that respectable white Smythe in his respectable white sleep should somehow have ended up in his neighbor's yard, burnt by his own disreputable petard.

When my turn to testify came at last, I tried not to look too closely into any one person's eyes. As he had throughout, Sucre sat in upright silence, occasionally making a note on the pad in front of him. Sucre's brother, himself a lawyer, was doing much the same. Capt. Allan sat stiff and blank-faced, the wise man's defiance. Three men captured, no inch given.

"But you didn't see who fired the actual shot?" Conyers asked me.

"No, sir. But I can't see why Capt. Allan would lie about that. And he definitely had the rifle earlier. He was a war hero, I think."

Conyers made a face at "hero" for the jury's benefit. "So you weren't watching events that night very closely?"

"I was very closely watching Caleb Smythe trying to set the Sucres' house on fire," I said.

"You didn't like Caleb Smythe very much, did you?"

"No, sir. But I managed to not fire-bomb his house all the same."

"So," Conyers said for the jury, "you *say* you were watching. Mr

Noonan says you weren't."

"Mr Noonan was too busy to watch me carefully," I said with a calm that absolutely astonished me. "First he spent all that time whispering to Mr Smythe just before Mr Smythe went to fill a bottle with fire. Then he—Mr Noonan—was looking around for rocks to throw at the Sucres' house."

There were a few more questions, possibly including whether I'd let my sister marry a nigger, and then I was dismissed. The trial would last another several days, but I was finished in the courtroom and in so many other places.

I had testified in the afternoon. The following morning in one of Bennett's heavyweights came to Educational to say that his boss would cherish the honor of my company at the Rouge.

Throughout the silent, ominous ride, I tried to keep calm, to remind myself that this wasn't surprising. That we all knew that Noonan would never be brought to trial, so my sins didn't merit worse than harsh words and perhaps a lost job.

I tried very hard to believe this as the goon shoved me through the door to Bennett's shooting range, where Bennett and Noonan were waiting for me, Bennett with his empty face, Noonan with his eloquent smirk.

"Gentlemen," I said, trying to sound casual.

Noonan dismissed my escort with a small shrug and latched the door. Bennett stayed leaning idly against the wall, enjoying the light glinting off his gun's barrel. The muzzle never pointed more than a few degrees from my heart.

I realized suddenly that this was serious, that there was a man ten feet from me with a loaded pistol and that another man with a chest like a stripped chassis, all metal and horsepower, stood between me and the only exit. The intensity of my body crowded out thought. There was only the rushing and pounding of my blood, the sudden profusion of fragile parts—knuckles and teeth, ribs and arches, Adam's apple and eyes.

Bennett tossed me a fountain pen and pointed with his chin to the firing range. I tried to pretend that I didn't understand.

"Go," he said.

Facing him the whole time, I walked slowly backward until I was eight or ten yards away from him, partway to the targets.

"Hold it up," he said.

I understood then that I could die in that little room—or anywhere else—and that whoever killed me would face no punishment, no condemnation. I pissed myself a little, and Noonan grinned wolfishly.

"Hold it up," Bennett repeated.

I tried at first to slot the pen into my left hand between my pinkie and ring fingers, but it kept slipping out. Noonan laughed, but Bennett just gestured to raise the pen. Between my left thumb and pinkie, I did. Up and as far as possible away from my body. The pen was slick in my sweaty fingers, and I was afraid of what would happen if I let it fall.

"Don't move," he said.

He stared at me for a long while, enjoying the tremor that was trying to take over my hand and arm. Then he took careful aim. I'll give him that. He put both hands on the pistol and concentrated.

The report came just as I looked away. At first, my ears hurt more than my hand and arm, but soon the hand and arm took over. My hand was entirely red, and my first thought was that Bennett had shot it off. But it was just red ink from the fountain pen, which covered not only my hand but also the entire left side of my face and body. I could have printed hundreds of Wobbly fliers with all the ink. Red ink—as though black would've been too subtle.

All my fingers were there, and they all moved. The pain seemed to be from the bits of pen which had lodged in my hand and forearm. It felt like there might also have been shrapnel in the back of my head.

It took me a while to sort this out.

"I hit what I aim for," Bennett said. "Case you wondered."

He and Noonan sauntered out, leaving me alone in the shooting range.

Once the skull-echoes of the gunshot had faded to a tinny ringing of false church bells, I took the long tram rides back to Highland Park, back to Educational. I would have thought myself beyond surprise, but in truth I was surprised to learn that a desk is merely wood, screws, glue, and, above all, habit. And one can change a desk's habits easier than a man's. Give a goon a red fire axe, and suddenly a desk will be a shambles. And a cheerful shambles at that—the axe was jutting jauntily from the remains of my desk like a cherry on a sundae.

After that, I sat for hours in a cheap working-man's restaurant with weak coffee and runny slices of pecan pie that hurt my guts. The setting made me dwell upon that long-ago *truffatore* and his invented encounter in a lunch counter with the noble Mr B, the man who had put him on the straight and narrow. Until the restaurant closed, I longed for my own Mr B. Then I took my queasy feeling home and spoke to no one for two days. I spent working hours wandering the city so that my family wouldn't know I'd been dismissed.

On the second night after my firing, shame or vengeance or something else drove me to gather all the Ford papers in my possession, all the papers showing that I had been a witness to, an accomplice of, the making of new men. I took them into the back yard and burned them in an ash can. There was an early snowfall as I did, and I was glad for the warmth. There was surprisingly little, perhaps two attaché cases' worth, so the papers burned only briefly, and then I was cold again and teary from the smoke. They seemed so paltry, the ashes of my noble intentions.

Miraculously, Henry Sucre's jury ended up hung, so Sucre and his co-defendants didn't.

I went by a few days after the verdict to congratulate the Sucres. Before I could do so, however, I'd had to explain myself to the unfamiliar policemen standing in the front yard and then dodge past the Negro workingmen beginning the family's removal to Philadelphia. Sucre had been obliged to sell the house at a considerable loss.

"I came by to congratulate you," I said. "But..."

"I should be grateful, I suppose," Henry Sucre told me. "In many cities, they would have lynched us. And yet..."

"And yet," I agreed.

Sucre and I were sitting in the front parlor's two remaining chairs. Mrs Sucre had insisted upon bringing us tea in delicate china. My cup and saucer were resting atop the large packing crate between us.

"I am grateful, actually," he said. "Immensely. For so long, I insisted to Gladys and the children and, well, to everyone, that *of course* we would be found innocent, that the facts of the case were so obvious and overwhelming that we must be acquitted."

"And yet," I said.

He smiled slightly. "I was the happiest man alive that first night home. But then I woke before sunrise, and I was angry. Furious, really. I should feel *grateful* to be permitted to defend myself against a man who tried to burn my home to the ground? Against a mob that would have cheered the deed? No." He shook his head.

I nodded in agreement.

"I've never felt such a fury. I had to spend that entire day in the basement so that the children wouldn't see me." He sighed and stared at the bare wall. "They say the boy who killed Sigi won't so much as appear before a magistrate."

I nodded.

"Won't even appear," he said. "Of course, he is just a boy. But he did kill a man, a good and decent man I was honored to call 'friend.'" He paused. "Still, the boy is hardly the guilty party in all this."

"No," I said.

"Nor would it do anyone any good to force a mere child to rot in prison. Not Sigi, not Martha, not Thia. It would help no one."

And yet, we thought.

Winter came early, but Mother kept the house warm. Over the next week, I did my shivering, my worrying, outside. I took long, aimless walks through a city—a life—that seemed suddenly alien. I felt as if I had forgotten the names for its objects, the procedure for assembling fragments into a whole.

There are colder and more brutal places than Detroit in winter, of course. Carl died in one. But Detroit is brutal enough. Implacable frozen winds come off the lake, off the river, off the flat, unresisting spaces all around the city. Walk only as far as the nearest open space, say, the State Fair Grounds or Forest Lawn Cemetery. Go there and stand with your back to the city, and you'll feel connected still to the trees shivering under wind and snow for a thousand miles and more north to Hudson Bay. You'll feel like an interloper in an unceasing war between the arctic air and the sullen, hunkering earth, either one of which might destroy you if it could spare you a thought. But of course the earth doesn't think. The air doesn't care. Such things have no enemies, nor even prey. I find that reassuring. Some find it otherwise. Some would rather be hated than ignored. This, I think, explains religion.

In truth, winter's true brutality is urban. It's on every street corner, down every alley. Any morning, when the sun is still only a dim gray suggestion to the east, you can find the same scene repeating itself. Walk along Grand past the Central Michigan railroad track and turn onto one of the evocatively named streets near the old city limits—Metropolitan, Goodson, Playfair. Walk them as I did and you'll find a streetful of men, each with a pickaxe in his hand and obscenities on his tongue as he tries to hack his car free from the ice frozen over the rims of his tires. And it's not just the drivers, of course. Each day, thousands of men and women of every profession tramp in place at the streetcar stops as they wait to board boxes so cold it's a wonder the conductor doesn't hang the riders from hooks and sell them to butchers. There are tens of thousands more trudging through the snow to whatever time clock calls them.

It's *how* they drive, or ride, or slog. They do it, we do it, without once ever leaving a landscape shaped by human hands. All around us are the streetlamps, the sidewalks, the freshly paved streets, the wires for electricity, telegraph, and telephone. All around us great smokestacks spiral dark proofs of power into the muted silver skies. At every step along our journeys, the world has been transformed by our labor, by our fathers', our brothers', even our sisters' labor and our ingenuity as it feeds into a system as great and girding as that web of forests and freezes reaching to the Hudson Bay. All around us a new world is becoming ever larger, ever more complicated, ever more potent.

And the new world doesn't care about us either. That's the real brutality. We invent gods because we can no longer really believe that nature cares about us. And when gods grow distant we invent industry. Every invention demands more and offers less, and this is how we measure progress.

Chapter 31

Giuseppe, ees strutta about lik' da keeng,
An' laugh at da hard-worka man
Who grinda da org' a few neekles to bring
Or sella da ripa banan'.

After a week of wandering the freezing Detroit streets, I went to Kitty and Ross' wedding and kept an admirable smile in place throughout. I danced with the bride, and I told the groom I'd cut his balls off if he ever gave Kitty V.D.

As Ross' cousins sang highland laments, I decided that Bennett would allow me to live. I decided that I'd been extraordinarily brave to testify at Sucre's trial. I decided that Ross and Kitty would be happy together. I decided that a brave man who sought his own happiness could do only one thing.

So the next day I went to the Gluecks' and worked the bell until Daniel showed me into the front parlor. Thia appeared atop the stair seconds later. She'd been crying, I could see. But she smiled as she came down to greet me. I rushed to her at the foot of the stair and told her that I'd never stopped loving her. She raised an aloof eyebrow but couldn't sustain it—she smiled and trembled and admitted it was the same for her. We kissed, and when I regained my senses, I saw Daniel and Martha smiling at us from separate corners of the room. I proposed marriage then and there, and she kissed me again to say *yes.*

Well.

I rang the front doorbell, and Daniel showed me to the parlor. After a while, Thia came down the stairs, slowly but without pause.

"I came by..." I started. "Just to see you, I guess."

She settled heavily into the chair in which she'd sat that first time I'd seen her home. "Thank you, Tony."

"Your mother...?"

She shook her head faintly. "Angry. Heartbroken. But in time she'll recover." After a pause, she added, "Would you care for supper?"

I shook my head.

"Just as well. Mother and I don't have much appetite these days, I'm afraid. When we do eat, we stay in the kitchen, mostly. Father is still there, a little, I think."

We chatted vaguely of kitchens and the surprising kindness of neighbors. "Quite a few people came by," she said. "Especially at first. Some were just hoping for gossip, and others felt guilty that their husbands were there that night. But, really, people were quite thoughtful. Even Gladys Sucre sent a casserole and a note, and her husband was somehow on trial for murder for defending himself against..."

I murmured something stupid about the basic decency of man.

She smiled slightly at that. "And you have been kind too. All along. I owe you more apologies than I can count."

"No," I began, "you don't owe—"

"Oh, but I do," she said. "All of us can be stupid about love, but I think I'm particularly... capable." Again, a faint smile. "More than I deserve, you have offered me love. Ever since I've known you. I won't apologize for my feelings then, but I do want to apologize for my behavior."

She stressed "then" just a little, and her eyes held mine as she did so. A whole future hummed in that word, an offer of reconsideration, a prospect of change. I accepted that, indeed, I *had* offered her love. Whatever else there had been, whatever foolishness and greed, whatever frenzy of an undersized mutt scrabbling toward heat musk in the park, there also had been love, which I had learned to mock without learning to let go.

We stared at each other, her expression earnest, contemplative. I could see that this wasn't the same woman who five years before had floated in an ocean of gin, rage, and grief after losing her husband, her children, her womb. She had learned that she could suffer and survive, that she could find solace in what remained. Whatever fear of love, whatever self-contempt had led her from one fool to another was muted, tamed. She was now able to face her own vulnerability without revulsion. I could see a path to her acceptance, to our bond.

We continued staring, scarcely blinking.

But though I could see so much new in her then, I couldn't see or imagine that she would ever look at me as Kitty looked at Ross, much less as Kitty had looked at Andrew. And so I couldn't imagine myself sitting in Sigi's kitchen and approving of myself for seizing this chance. Love has many guises, but none of them is resignation. I smiled and stood. "Thank you," I said.

Knowing that I was taking my leave and perhaps sensing that I was saying farewell, she ignored my proffered hand and embraced me tightly. We were both trembling, separate aftershocks along a common fault.

After Ross and Kitty returned from their honeymoon in New York City, I went by their house for lunch. They looked happy. Decently and justly happy. I got a little teary when I asked them to take care of Lisa.

"Take care of her?" Kitty asked.

"You're leaving?" Ross asked.

I was leaving. I'd probably never again be permitted to work at a desk in Detroit, and working on a line would have broken what was left of my back. At home everyone was kind enough to cry a little over my departure. Even Lisa. But, in truth, Lisa didn't need me. Ross and Kitty would gladly look after her, and even Angela could help. They would stand between Lisa and the ghost of Elisabetta at least as well as I had. Still, I had hopes of rejoining Lisa at some point, if she'd have me. But in the meantime, I would be nothing to my family except another wound to bandage, another mouth to feed.

I gave most of my savings to Mother and spent some of the remainder on a cheap suitcase and a train ticket to Los Angeles. When I had secured a new position there, I would send more money home. In the meantime, the others would manage without my help, just as they had when Father had disappeared to sinner's prison. In some odd, perhaps foolish way, I felt as if I were at long last being permitted to go to war.

A day later, I was watching lonely farmhouses flash by. At a distance, the lights of a receding town looked sometimes like a dead man in the grass, burning lower.

"They've beaten me," I say.

"Yes?" Sigi asks through his pipe as he looks at the moving landscape. "Yet still you feel more sinner than sinned against?"

I nod.

"And still you want absolution, yes? To be cleansed and ground shiny before you reach Los Angeles?"

I nodded vigorously.

"I'm a head-shrinker," Sigi says. "Not a rabbi. Or toolmaker."

"Were a head shrinker."

"Even so."

Somewhere in the American night, I begin to shiver. Something has finally sunk in.

Chapter 32

IT'S VERY SUNNY IN THIS PORT OF ANGELS. THE LIGHT IS SANDPAPER ON MY eyes but gentle fingertips on my cheekbones.

I take one of Merry's letters from my pocket and read his address to the cabby. When I ring the doorbell, one of the intermediate gentlemen answers. By the time he remembers me, his father's voice is charging down the hallway. "Tony Grams? Is that Tony? Gulsa, it is Tony Grams. From Educational!"

Merry reaches me soon after his voice, embracing me vigorously. It hurts, but I don't mind.

"But, Tony— What brings— Why…?"

"I've come to see about the flowers," I say, which is true enough for now.

Merry's home in Los Angeles isn't so large or nice as the one he had in Detroit. But Gulsa keeps it clean and cheerful, and the whole family keeps faith with the future.

Meanwhile, I breathe the past. Elisabetta. Gennaro. Alessandra. Andrew. Carl. Sigi. I am surrounded by the dead and the greater legions of the lost. They find me more easily here in this ruthless sunshine, and I think I frighten Merry and the rest because I weep often, sometimes without noticing. I know that I too must find a way to keep faith with the future, a future. I can't simply long for things to return to some small pocket of past joy. At its best, longing for the past is longing to become a ghost. At its worst, it's longing to make everyone else a ghost. It's standing, burning bottles in hand, yearning for the Rapture, aching to be lifted to Heaven simply in order to have the best view of creation being consumed by pestilence, gutted by scythe, and burnt forevermore from existence, from memory itself.

The trick, I now believe, is to hope for a future—for a good world—without expecting to live in it. We will none of us skip whole and happy down a road of yellow brick to a good world. And, in a horrible way, that's for the best. We're too much the products of this poisoned world to survive a good one. We could no more live in a world without evil than on an Earth without oxygen. It simply isn't in us—or if it is, it's so far within us that we must be destroyed for it to escape. And very thoroughly destroyed. The heat of the melting pot isn't enough, not nearly, nor the flames that consumed Smythe. No, the good world is like Dr Collins' iron dots in our blood, and to forge that world, we would each have to burn from within, each have to burn away not just our sickness and cruelty but also our hopes, our personalities, our very bodies so that history could sift the deep drifts of our ashes with a magnet powerful enough to extract the useful flecks. And those flecks would then have to go into a further furnace, to be melted and alloyed so that a wiser blacksmith might shape it all into parts to be assembled along the long, slow line producing the new men, those vanadium steel creatures which we cannot truly imagine and which, much to their credit, couldn't imagine us either.

Historical Note

The New Men began when I was researching how changing economic and technological conditions of the late nineteenth and early twentieth century altered the ways in which people understood—down in the bones—what it mean to be a person and how that understanding played itself out in the fiction written during that period. I was poking into the explosion of neurasthenia diagnoses at the end of the nineteenth century when I stumbled across Ford's Five Dollar Day and the Sociological Department tasked to enforce it. I knew then that the subject was rich and important, but I also knew that I was getting a Ph.D. in American literature and had a lot essays to write. So I put the Five Dollar Day on a back burner.

Still, as I continued researching the period, the Five Dollar Day kept intruding on my thoughts and demanding that I look into it further. So eventually I made a pilgrimage to Dearborn, Michigan, slept on an air mattress in a rented room, and made a nuisance of myself in archives for a month, particularly the Benson Ford Archives. At the time I justified the project to myself as a practical undertaking that would lead to academic articles—possibly on the very question that had appealed to me at the time—how does becoming the right kind of worker for an assembly line both require and demand that someone become a new kind of person altogether? What was Ford Motor Company teaching its workers? What was the assembly line teaching them? What did they learn from streets transformed first by trolley cars, then by automobiles? What did all of that mean while European streets and meadows alike were becoming assembly lines of death, dismemberment, and madness?

I pored over blueprints of the various Ford plants, descriptions of its increasingly international business empire, over schematics of the line, Model T drivers' manuals and advertising, over the surviving records of

Sociological/Educational, of Service, of Espionage, and of the American Protective League. I read operatives' reports, employees' memos, letters, and telegrams, newspaper articles about Ford Motor Company or Henry Ford that Ford employees found interesting or worrisome. I lingered over lengthy transcripts of oral histories from Ford employees from the period.

And I eventually realized that it was too big for an article. That, in fact, it was too big and powerful and complex for me to do justice to as anything but a novel. So I spent some more months researching it, and then sat down to write. And rewrite. And rewrite some more until the era and the characters started to take on the vibrancy that they deserved.

In addition to the profoundly helpful archival materials made available to me by the patient and knowledgeable staffs at the Cranbrook Archives and the Benson Ford Archives, I am indebted to dozens of writers whose works helped me to do justice to the period. There are too many to list here, but I would like to mention some of the most important.

In terms of Ford and his company, Steven Watts' *The People's Tycoon: Henry Ford and the American Century* (2006) was an invaluable resource. Samuel S. Marquis' *Henry Ford: An Interpretation* (1923) was crucial to understanding Marquis' ambitions for and frustrations about what he renamed the Educational Department. Charles Sorensen's *My Forty Years with Ford* (1956) also gave vital first-hand insight into those formative years of the Ford plant and Ford's Detroit. Ford R. Bryan's *Henry's Lieutenants* (1993), Stephen Meyer III's *The Five Dollar Day: Labor Management and Social Control in the Ford Motor Company, 1908-1921* (1981), and Neil Baldwin's *Henry Ford and the Jews: The Mass Production of Hate* (2002) all provided further useful information about the Ford plant during the relevant period.

In understanding the people and cultures of 1910s Detroit, I learned a great deal from August Meier and Elliot Rudwick's *Black Detroit and the Rise of the UAW* (1979), Henry Pratt's *Churches and Urban Government in Detroit and New York, 1895-1994* (2004), Russell Magnaghi's *Italians in Michigan* (2001), Robert Rockaway's *The Jews of Detroit: From the Beginning 1762-1914* (1986), and Arthur Woodford's *This is Detroit, 1700-2001: An Illustrated History* (2001). For a more general understanding of the period, I also consulted Helen Sumner's *History of Women in Industry in the United States* (1910) and Philip Mason's *Rum-Running and the Roaring Twenties: Prohibition on the Michigan-Ontario Waterway* (1995).

Two books written by Detroit soldiers who served with the Polar Bears taught me a great deal about the United States' inexplicable and depressing incursion into Russia's Archangel Oblast: John Cudahy's *Archangel: The American War With Russia* (1924) and Joel Moore, Harry Mead, and Lewis Jahns' *The History of the American Expedition Fighting the Bolsheviki Campaigning in North Russia 1918-1919* (1920).

My editor insists that at least some readers would enjoy having at least some sense of how much of this historical fiction is history and how much is fiction. She's probably right. Even so, I flinch at trying to clarify that. As I write this, it has been almost exactly a hundred years since Ford Motor Company launched the Five Dollar Day. I believe that all those who had anything to do with it are dead, many of them for generations. At such a remove, even proper "I've got a research grant, a sabbatical, and six thousand footnotes" history is partly fictional—inferences drawn, causality ascribed, events pruned, teased free, and arranged to make a point. And *The New Men* isn't that kind of history. I was driven by a powerful sense that this was a fascinating and important chapter in American history, and I felt an ethical and—more importantly—a literary duty to get it *right.* But "getting it right" with historical fiction is a complicated and somewhat self-contradictory goal. My first drafts were, well, boring because they were all archive and no life. So I had to inject life by rethinking my characters and their stories, by getting how it *felt* to live the history when it was the present. So although a great deal of *The New Men* is factually accurate (often painstakingly so) and intended to reflect accurately how people at the time thought and were able to think—and although I'm proud of that accuracy—I still didn't hesitate to tweak, omit, or imagine details, events, and characters where doing so made the novel come to life. I did my best to avoid anachronisms and impossibilities, so there aren't fighter jets or knights errant anywhere in the manuscript. But if the novel demanded that an event happen Tuesday at two o'clock in the afternoon, I didn't lose sleep if historically it happened Wednesday at two-thirty.

Because this is a work of fiction, even the characters based on historical figures are ultimately works of fiction. Certainly, there were historical figures with the same names as many of the novel's characters—Henry Ford, Clara Ford, Charlie Sorensen, Samuel S. Marquis, Robert L. Bradby, James Couzens, Harry Bennett, and John Gillespie, to name a few. And when the character has the same name as his or her historical source, I tried to be faithful to what I'd managed to learn about that person's biography and personality. Even so, in many cases I had to draw inferences about or simply imagine how that person would react to fictional characters in fictional circumstances.

Other characters have some connection to actual historical figures but are so far removed from those figures that I changed their names to prevent any confusion. Merry Torassian, for example, owes his existence to an anecdote told by a Sociological investigator named "M.G. Torossian" and recorded in a Sociological Department collection of success stories. And Emmeline Ward was inspired by Josephine Sears Davis, a Girls' Protective League member who appears to have been Detroit's first female police officer. There are many more along these lines, including crucial characters in the novel. But I don't want to distract readers who don't care about these details—or to ruin the sleuthing for those who do.

And, of course, some of the characters I simply made up. History is generally more creative than I am and has at least as cruel a sense of irony, but sometimes it simply refuses to provide a decent love interest or a wryly amusing supporting character.

—Jon Enfield
Somerville, MA
May 2014

CPSIA information can be obtained
at www.ICGtesting.com
Printed in the USA
LVHW112223231218
601559LV00001B/160/P

9 781938 757129